Highland Magic

The Macleans

The Third Book in The Medieval Highlanders Series

K.E. SAXON

Copyright © 2009 K.E. Saxon

All rights reserved. No part of this book may be used or reproduced by any means, graphic, electronic, or mechanical including photocopying, recording, taping, or by any information storage retrieval system without the written permission of the author K.E. Saxon, the copyright owner and publisher of this book, except in the case of brief quotations embodied in critical articles or reviews.

This is a work of fiction. Names, characters, places, brands, media, and incidents either are the product of the author's imagination or are used fictitiously. Any resemblance to actual events, locales, organizations, or persons, living or dead, is entirely coincidental and beyond the intent of the publisher. The author acknowledges the trademarked status and trademark owners of various products referenced in its work of fiction, which have been used without permission. The publication/use of these trademarks is not authorized, associated with, or sponsored by the trademark owners.

Cover Photo obtained from Period Images
Cover Design created by Angela Waters Graphic Art & Design

* * * *

ISBN: 1499706480
ISBN-13: 978-1499706482

CONTEMPORARY BOOKS BY K.E. SAXON

Sensual Contemporary Romance
Love Is The Drug
A Stranger's Kiss (novella)
A Heart Is A Home: Christmas in Texas (novella)

Sensual Romantic Comedy/Fantasy Romance
Diamonds and Toads: A Modern Fairy Tale

AUTHOR'S NOTE

The twelfth and thirteenth century Scottish Highlands is a fascinating time in history. Although much is known, there is still much that remains in shadow and supposition. The old laws of succession, and the old Celtic systems were mixing with the new feudal systems brought in by the Norman-influenced kings of Scots (the first key figure in this being David I, who became king of Scots in 1124).

Although, by the time of William the Lion (William I), who ruled Scotland from 1165 to 1214, the feudal systems were more firmly established in the southern region of Scotland, the king had managed to exert his influence and sway in the wilder northern and western regions as well. Mostly through alliances with foreigners to whom he chartered land, or to natives who sought a royal charter for their land in order to secure it for their own offspring.

My vision, therefore, was of a kind of "melting pot." The old ways, not completely abandoned, yet the new coming to be embraced.

Although I did many, many (many) months of research into this time in the Scottish Highlands history, I still found it necessary to take some creative license on certain aspects in order to fulfill my vision for the romance, and allow for less confusion to the romance reader. I won't list the licenses I took, but hope that the history purists will close an eye to these instances and simply enjoy the tale.

K.E. Saxon

* * *

GLOSSARY

Anail iasg: Fish Breath, or as close a translation as I could find (thank you so much *fiairefeadha* from the *www.irishgaelictranslator.com* forum, who gave me the Irish Gaelic so I could look up the Scottish Gaelic spelling)

Bealltainn: The Celtic May Day Festival (May 1 or 2)

Boabhan Sith or Baoban Sith \baa'-van shee\ Scottish Highland fairies that look like beautiful women but are really vampires thirsty for the blood of young men. They appear first as ravens, then as girls in white or green dresses with hoofed feet. Iron is said to repel them

Canonical Hours: Lauds, dawn; Prime, 6 a.m.; Terce, 9 a.m.; Sext, 12 p.m.; Nones, 3 p.m.; Vespers, sunset; Compline, after sunset, usu. after the evening meal

Daoine sìth: fairy-folk

Hogmanay: December 31

Ingeniator: latin word meaning 'to devise in the sense of construct, or craftsmanship'. Root of *engineer*

Northvegia: Medieval latin name for Norway

Seed wool: cotton wool not yet cleansed of its seeds

Uisge beatha: Lit: 'Water of Life', a.k.a. whiskey

Samhainn: the first day of November, marking the beginning of winter and a new year for ancient Celts; a.k.a. 'All Souls' Day'

Sìdh Chailleann: Schiehallion is a prominent mountain in Perth and Kinross. The name Schiehallion is an anglicised form of the Gaelic name *Sìdh Chailleann*, which is usually translated as 'Fairy Hill of the Caledonians'

Oidhche Shamhna: the eve of *Samhainn*; a.k.a. 'All Hallow's Eve' or 'Halloween'

Kipper: To claim the armor and weapons the knight employed a vassal or squire as his 'Kipper'. A Kipper was expected to collect the 'Spoils of Combat' as the tournament proceeded. The word 'Kipper' originated from the Scandinavian word 'Kippa' which means to snatch or to seize. The weapons and armor of a knight were very expensive and a fallen knight would not give them up easily. The Kipper was therefore armed with blunt, but heavy clubs, with which they could knock the unfortunate Knight into an unconscious state and collect the spoils of combat. See: ***http://www.middle-ages.org.uk/knights-tournaments.htm***

<u>Tryamour</u>: Lit. 'Test of Love'. A fairy that fell in love with a Welsh knight. She promises to give him everything he desires, but in exchange, he must never reveal her to anyone. *This is from a 12th century French lai by Marie de France titled, 'Lanfal', which was later adapted to Middle English as 'Landavall', but the fairy lady does not get named until the 14th century english version titled 'Sir Launfal' by Thomas Chestre

*****

Historical source for joust:

Jager, Eric. *The Last Duel: The True Story of Crime, Scandal and Trial by Combat in Medieval France.* London: Random, 2006.

PROLOGUE
Cilgerran Castle, Southern March Region, Cambria
The Betrothal Feast, July 1205

GAIALLARD DE MONTFORT settled back in his chair and studied the chaos all around him. This betrothal would bring him the demesne he'd been craving, but at a price for which he was growing more resentful as each day passed. He was expected to wed an awkward rustic, a mere girl! He, whom the ladies of the court had given the title 'golden wolf', both in and out of the bedchamber. Oh, she was pleasing to look upon. Her dark hair framed her face in a becoming enough manner and accented her most attractive asset: her large eyes bore the color of kings in their amethyst depths. But even his young sister had more curves than this boyish girl. And she was as green as his page—and just as unschooled in the ways of the court, mayhap even more so. How many times now had he been humiliated in front of his comrades by her graceless overtures and simple dress? If he had not given her, as a betrothal gift, the lovely purple velvet dress she now wore with the gold embroidery edging the square neck and sleeves, or the gold silk chemise beneath it, he had no doubt she'd now be wearing that godawful saffron woolen thing she'd worn to at least five of the seven previous evening meals this past sennight. Had she no understanding of the place she would be taking, had already been expected to take by his side? She was no good representative of his position in the hierarchy. In fact, she had made him a laughing-stock at court. And last eve, when she'd stumbled upon him with his sister—well, she would simply have to grow accustomed to such encounters as they were a well-established part of life amongst those of noble birth. He clenched his jaw to keep from groaning aloud in frustration. Why, oh, why had fate not been kinder to him? If all had gone as he'd planned, he'd even now be presiding over the demesne of *Castell Crychydd* with his chosen mate, Caroline de Montrochet. Now, there was a beauty, a perfect example of nobility, virtue, and womanliness. Gaiallard's eyes were drawn once more to the trestle table below where the lady in question now sat nibbling a portion of sea fowl.

* * *

Branwenn watched her betrothed from the corner of her eye. He'd made it plain these past days that he was not as pleased with this match, with her, as he'd first pretended. And last eve—*last eve*! She'd stumbled upon him in his sister's chamber. The poor lass had been in a distressing state, her gown torn and hanging from her shoulder, exposing red marks on her tender arm and chest where the drunken knave had abused and beaten her. Would he have gone further still—done the thing Branwenn feared had been his true purpose, if she had not interrupted his savage attack? And 'twas clearly not the first time the lass had been the outlet for his violent lust either, for there had been older bruises in plain view as well. She turned her sight on the lass, Alyson, who even now sat much too quietly with her silver-blond head bowed and her hands demurely folded in her lap. The poor dear had barely touched the food on her trencher, nor the wine in her goblet. She was far too young to have been exposed to such lechery, for she surely was not more than twelve summers. Aye, 'twas truth that according to tradition, she was a woman full-grown, capable of becoming a wife, should her father contract such an arrangement, but in Branwenn's view, 'twas much too young an age to be expected to perform such duties.

Reys ap Gryffyd dipped his head and whispered in her ear, "Have you second thoughts so late in the game, then, Branwenn? If so, you've dallied too long, my little dove, for your vows will be heard before the bishop and all this fine assembly in but a few hours' time at the morrow's morning mass."

Branwenn bit her lip and turned her troubled gaze to the dark-haired, blue-eyed man she'd only discovered to be her kin a mere seven moons past when he'd been the first to cross the threshold of her heart-family's keep, the Macleans, after the feast of *Hogmanay*. He'd come there to find her and bring her back to Cambria to wed this flaxen-haired Norman nephew thrice removed to the Earl of Pembroke that sat at her other side. For the marriage would make a blood alliance between her Cambrian cousin, twice removed, Prince Llywelyn, and the Norman usurper, Guillaume le Maréchal, the Earl of Pembroke. And tho' she liked Reys well, even from their first meeting, she still did not feel the same strong bond with him that she felt for Bao Xiong Maclean, the man who'd raised her, the man who, in her heart, was her brother in truth. Should she tell Reys of her discovery? She'd been debating that very question these past hours since finding her betrothed with his sister. And tho' the hour was late, she needed some guidance, some words to soothe her worry. "Brother, I have something I must speak with you about in all haste, but it must be in privy, for I have no wish for any here to learn of what I must tell you."

Reys had been jesting with her, believing that she was merely uneasy, as any new bride would be, at the prospect of her wedding. He sat forward and truly studied her worried countenance for the first time that eve. With a brief nod, he said, "Meet me in the chapel after supper. 'Twill be empty, as all here will be enjoying the pipers and players afterward. Say that you wish a few moments alone to pray and light some candles. No one will say you nay, even this eve before you wed, for your desire to pray will be seen as an act of true piety, a great virtue for a new bride."

Branwenn's shoulders relaxed for the first time that eve. With a sigh and a nod, she said, "My thanks."

* * *

An hour later, Branwenn, on her knees in the chapel with her head bowed and her eyes closed, felt someone settle beside her.

"We are alone now—all are in the great hall enjoying the players. Tell me what troubles you, Branwenn," Reys whispered.

Branwenn slowly opened her eyes and, settling back to rest upon her calves, she dropped her clenched hands to her lap and turned her gaze upon this almost-stranger who just might give her the heart's-ease she so desperately craved. "I know not how to begin...."

Reys placed his hand over hers. "Begin by telling me the thing that is giving you the most dread."

Branwenn dropped her gaze to her lap and nodded. She took in a deep breath and released it on a sigh. "Aye, 'twould seem to be the best place, I trow." She cleared her throat. "Last eve..."

When she didn't immediately continue, Reys dipped his head in an effort to see her countenance. "Aye, last eve—what happened?" he prompted.

"I came upon my betrothed in his sister's bedchamber,"—she lifted her gaze to her brother's once more and said in a rush—"he had *beaten* her, Reys! There were purple and red marks on her chest, her shoulders—even her arms! And her gown was torn, it looked as if he'd ripped it away to expose her breasts. And what is more, I could see other, older bruises on her flesh as well. Godamercy, Reys, I do believe he intended to...to...bed her!" There, she'd said it.

Reys's eyes widened even further in shock and disgust. *Why, the lass was barely out of swaddling clothes!*

He'd known Gaiallard to be a man who enjoyed the sexual privileges bestowed upon him due to his noble birth, but he'd had no true understanding of how dissolute, how morally corrupt, the man had become until just now.

Branwenn's eyes misted with unshed tears. "I knew not what to do—I fled the chamber and have said naught about it to anyone, not even Gaiallard."

"You cannot wed him, then. You must away this very night." Reys pressed the base of his palm into his eye.

Branwenn grabbed hold of his wrist and held tight. "But how can I not? 'Twould mean war—war with not only the Earl of Pembroke, but with the King of England himself, for he has decreed that this match must take place!"

Reys nodded and turned his gaze upon his sister once more. "Aye, and forget not that our cousin will surely skin me alive before hanging me on a gibbet to rot—and he'll lock you in the tower gaol for all eternity, I doubt it not." He turned and faced Branwenn fully. Taking both her hands in his own, he said, "But we must at least try to release you from this contract. I will speak with our cousin forthwith. There must be a way to delay this wedding, at least until I can procure our cousin's agreement to free you from this bad bargain."

Branwenn dipped her head and gazed down at their clasped hands. 'Twas no use. Her fate was set, and there would be naught to stop it. For, she knew her cousin would never agree to such a thing; his empire was much more important than she in the scheme of things. "My thanks, brother, tho' I know not how you shall manage such a feat." All at once struck with an idea, she lifted her head once more and gazed, wide-eyed with hope, into the midnight-blue depths of Reys's eyes. "I beg you, do not be angered—or hurt—by the proposal I am about to make, for I mean you no injury—"

"Aye?" Reys said anxiously, "have you a plan then? Tell me quickly, I swear I shall listen without prejudice."

Branwenn tightened her grasp on her brother's hands and leaned forward a bit as she said, "Would it not fulfill the spirit, if not the letter, of the contract were *you* to wed *Alyson* instead?"

"Wha—?"

"Nay, hear me out before you balk. Do you not see? This is the best solution for all. The lass clearly needs a protector and you—well, I know you do not like speaking of the recent tragedy that befell your poor wife and bairns,"—Reys looked away, his mouth set in a grim line, and Branwenn brought her hand up to his cheek and gently forced him to look at her once more—"but you know that you are now free to wed. And you told me yourself, when first you found me in the Highlands, that the contract would have been fulfilled whether you'd found a brother *or* a sister, for the brother would have been contracted to wed the niece. You were not free to wed then, and I, for my own reasons, agreed to return to Cambria with you."

Silence reigned for many long seconds as Reys struggled to breathe past the heavy pain of guilt and longing that now gripped his chest.

Branwenn remained still, fearing that any movement on her part would send her brother fleeing from this sanctuary, from her, leaving her honor-bound to fulfill the terms of the contract.

At last, Reys gave his answer. "Gather only the most precious of your belongings, only what you can easily carry, and meet me in the stables in half an hour's time."

"You will arrange this thing, then?"

"Aye." He rose to his feet and brought her up with him. "As you said, 'twill fulfill the intent of the contract, if not the actual terms set down in writing."

"How will I get past the gates—to what destination will I travel?"

"Dress in those same lad's clothes you wore as a disguise when you traveled to our cousin's war camp on the edge of the Maclean holding last spring. I know you kept them, so pretend not otherwise. The disguise will aid in your escape."

"But to where?"

"I shall tell you more when we meet later. For now, suffice to say, you shall be safely out of Gaiallard's influence by the time the ceremony is to begin. Now, make haste to your chamber."

Branwenn nodded and, without forethought, flung herself into her brother's embrace and held tight. "I do believe I shall miss you," she said, wonder in her voice.

Reys smiled and gave her a bit of a squeeze. "And I you as well, you little midge."

"However will I repay you for such a sacrifice?" she

whispered brokenly. She kissed him on his cheek and fled without waiting for a reply.

* * *

Reys watched her leave before collapsing onto the bench directly behind him and covering his face with his hands. Branwenn was right, this was the best solution. For, he no longer cared who he wed, as his heart had died with his love, his wife, and his sweet little girls, in the fire at the convent where they were staying two moons past. And he must wed—he must have offspring, a son, to inherit his position, his property. 'Twas the way of things, and he was honor-bound to fulfill his duties. At least he liked the young lady. And by wedding her, he would not only free her from her brother's wicked clutches, but give both himself and her a few years' time to heal before embarking on the more amorous aspect of the wedded state. Surely the lass would appreciate a bit of a reprieve from such duties—at least until she was older.

And he would not subject his sister to the same type of evil that their dear mother had been forced to endure the last moons of her life, the same evil even Branwenn in some indirect way had endured as well during that exact time—for his mother's kidnapping and enslavement at the hands of the murderous Highlander, Jamison Maclean, had occurred while she'd carried Branwenn in her womb. 'Twas for the sake of his mother's sweet memory that he had at last settled on the decision to, in effect, embark on this act of treason by securing his sister's safe passage away from her betrothed and her signed contract to wed. He must somehow find the words to convince his cousin and the Earl of Pembroke the propitiousness of this change in plan.

Reys rose to his feet and hurried towards the front entrance of the chapel. But first, he must get his sister as far from Gaiallard's clutches as possible—and to a place no one would ever think to search for her. For 'twas no feat of reason to imagine the tirade that would ensue when Gaiallard realized he would lose his chance at the demesne he so coveted.

* * *

The bar across the door lifted with less effort than Branwenn had been expecting, but with more sound. Anxiously looking over her shoulder at the still-slumbering maid settled on a pallet only a few feet from where Branwenn now stood, she breathed a sigh of relief and opened the door to her bedchamber. 'Twas just past midnight and the corridors were dark. Tho' it chafed her to do so, she took a valuable moment to stand with her back against the wall as she allowed her eyes to become adjusted to the much darker outer perimeter of her chamber. Oh, how she'd love a candle at this moment, but she dared not risk it. Nay, 'twas much better that she remain quiet and hidden as she descended to the lower level of the keep. The way down to the courtyard of the castle would be manned with servants and, mayhap, even soldiers, but she would not quell her intent to escape this place this very night.

Twenty minutes later, she'd made it to the stables. "Reys?" she whispered into the darkness.

"Aye, over here." he whispered back.

Highland Magic

Branwenn moved in the direction of the voice. "Where are you? 'Tis as dark as pitch in here. Will you not light a taper?"

"Nay, 'tis too dangerous. The stableman that was left to guard the horses slumbers in the corner, but we must be careful not to wake him. The sleeping herb I put in his ale will not last long, I fear."

"I see—Oh!" Branwenn stumbled over a rise in the straw-covered earthen floor.

Reys swept his arm around her middle to catch her before she fell. "Watch your step," he cautioned. He led her to her mount then and took her hastily-packed satchel from her nerveless hands. "I shall travel with you as far as the coast and then I shall return here, for I must be back by sunrise."

"The *coast*?" Branwenn asked dazedly.

"Aye, the coast. There are trade ships there. One of which will take you to my wife's cousin in Ulster on the northeast coast of Ireland. None will think to look for you there, for no one knows of my friendship with the man."

"But I thought...I believed you'd be sending me back to *Aber Garth Celyn*, to our cousin's estate."

"Nay, 'tis the first place Gaiallard will look for you, youngling."

Branwenn's brows drew together in confusion. "Why would Gaiallard look for me—he shall surely be relieved that he will not be forced to wed a ceorl such as he clearly believes me to be."

"Because he shall lose the demesne he was to gain with this alliance, tho' I do not believe he is aware of such now. I think he is under the belief that he is to be given sovereignty over the demesne, no matter what lady he weds, that he was just to receive it sooner, if he agreed to this alliance."

"I see." Branwenn felt dizzy, her thoughts spinning madly about inside her skull like one of the Persian dervishes her brother, Bao, had told her of. "You will not be traveling with me?" she said weakly after a moment.

"Nay, I cannot, for the meeting with our cousin and the Earl cannot wait. Surely you ken, 'twould not be good for them to discover you gone before I explain the new scheme to them. And the bishop has traveled many miles to be here—as have most of the guests." He shook his head and sighed. "Nay, the wedding must take place, and at the time originally planned. The only difference will be that 'twill be I and the Earl's niece who wed for the sake of the alliance instead of you and that devil *Gaiallard de Montfort*." He'd said the name as if it were the bitterest of tinctures upon his tongue. Reys placed his hands on her waist and lifted her onto her mount. "We must away in all haste; there is no more time for discussion, else I'll not be back in time to stand before the bishop and exchange vows with the lady Alyson," he said as he walked the animal out into the courtyard.

Branwenn was surprised to find his mount already saddled and ready to go. How had she missed seeing the animal earlier? She shrugged. No doubt, her mind had been much more occupied with not getting caught at the time.

After Reys mounted his steed, 'twas not as difficult as Branwenn had anticipated for them to depart the holding. The journey to the coast took two hours.

The wharf was dark and dank. More abandoned than Branwenn had been expecting, even at this dim hour of the morn.

"Stay upon your horse," Reys cautioned as he handed her the reigns of his own mount, "and do not move more than a pace or two from this spot until I return, for I shall not be long. I must negotiate your safe passage with the captain of this vessel."

"Aye," Branwenn replied with a nod of her head. After her brother had been gone a few minutes and she was convinced that she'd not be accosted by any wayward, drunken seamen, she relaxed a bit and took stock of her surroundings. The wharf had the smell of the sea—no surprise. But there was the smell of something else as well. 'Twas as if the sea creatures had crawled to the shore to die, for the smell was caustic, harshly bitter, the air filled with the smell of rot.

In another moment, Reys came into view once more. His expression was somber as he briskly walked up beside her mount. "I've secured passage for you on the Irish ship, the *Maighdean mhara mhear*." He took hold of Branwenn's hand. "I wish there were another way, but there is none."

"I care not—"

"Branwenn, heed me well. These are men of the cloth—monks from Strangford Lough on the coast of Ulster. They are just returning from Cumberland with more stone and iron ore for the abbey they are building.

If all goes as planned, you shall arrive there in a matter of days. I have claimed corody for you as a kinsman of Prince Llywelyn, so you may stay with them until all is settled. I will come for you then, so do not stray from that place until that time. 'Twill not be long, I vow it."

Branwenn's heart pounded in her chest. Tho' her hand trembled with fear, she managed to slip it from her brother's embrace. Taking a deep breath, she straightened her spine, and showing more courage than she felt, she said, "Worry not, I shall do as you say. For, where else could I go without fear of discovery? I do not dare go back to the Maclean holding, as I wish no harm to come to any there—nor do I wish for them to ever discover that I was almost wed to such a man as Gaiallard de Montfort."

"We must make haste, then, for the barge will sail in but a quarter-hour's time. These mariner monks use naught but the sun's bright beam during the day and the star's light that twinkles in the northern sky at night to guide them. But fear not, they've assured me they've made this same journey many times since their patroness, the wife of John de Courcy of Ulster, founded their abbey but a few years past."

Reys took the reigns of his and Branwenn's mounts and led them to the ship's loading plank. After helping her to dismount, he placed the scroll in her hand and settled his own long-fingered hand over hers. "Use this document as your introduction to the abbot. The letter explains that you are my brother and that you are also the cousin of Prince Llywelyn.

"But—"

Reys lightly covered her mouth with his fingertips. "Nay, my little dove, it cannot be helped. You must continue in your disguise until I come for you, else you will not be allowed to remain at the abbey—corody, or nay. And do not take those clothes from your frame at any time during the voyage, not even to bathe, for 'twould not do for these men of the cloth to discover that a member of the fairer sex is on board their vessel."

With a stiff nod of the head, Branwenn turned and gazed at the huge sailing vessel she was about to embark upon. The ship was long, with at least 25 to 30 oars on each side and a long mast that hung suspended over the entire length of the deck.

"There is more I would give you before you are gone," Reys said, turning and rummaging inside the leather satchel he had attached to his saddle. A moment later, he was lifting her hand, palm up, and placing a small leather purse upon it.

Branwenn's brows drew together. "What is this?"

"There are silver coins inside—enough to purchase several more moons of shelter and food for you than what I have arranged already with the monks."

"But, you said you would return for me soon...."

"Be at ease, little one. I shall take not one moment longer than I must, but I cannot allow you to travel so far—and with strangers, tho' men of the cloth they be—without *some* bit of coin, just in case. Do you see?"

With a long, forlorn sigh and a shrug of her shoulders, she sadly nodded her head. "Aye. I do see. My debt to you is growing greater and greater."

"Nay, you owe me naught. I beg you, trouble yourself no more on that score." Reys took hold of the hand she held the purse in. "Look inside," he coaxed, loosening the string that held the neck of the pouch closed. "For you will find something of our mother's which I wish for you to keep. I planned to give this to you on the morrow, as a gift to celebrate your wedding, but, I confess, I am much more pleased to give it to you now as a token of my great affection for you as my sister."

Still holding the scroll, Branwenn managed—rather awkwardly—to place two fingers inside to find the object he spoke of. She discovered it immediately and drew the cold, circular band of gold metal and amethyst gemstone out of the pouch.

"'Twas our mother's betrothal ring. The same ring, in fact, that Bao gave the priest at the kirk he had our mother buried in. The ring was left with the priest as a means to prove that 'twas truly her grave, should her family come searching for her there."

Branwenn's hand began to shake with more violence and her eyes filled with tears. "This was my mother's?" she asked brokenly. 'Twas lovely. The small, polished, oval stone was set high on the narrow gold band.

Reys took the ring and settled it on her finger before Branwenn's next thought had time to form. "There now, I knew you were a near twin to her, but now I have proof. See how nicely it fits you?"

"Aye," she replied wonderingly, "I thought it surely too small for my hand." She looked up, into her brother's eyes and said, "I thank you for this memento of my mother."

Reys gave her a brief nod. "We have tarried long enough, I trow," he said abruptly. "Come," he continued in a softer tone, "we must find the captain and get you settled in the space he's allowed you in the hold before the ship sails." And with a bit of gentle pressure to the base of Branwenn's spine, he prodded her to begin ascending the rough, wooden plank of the ship.

* * *

The vessel had been at sea for no more than three days and three nights when brigands, pirates of the sea, rammed into the side of their ship sometime around the chimes at midnight, bombarding it with large stones flung from a mangonel, and sending missile upon missile of fire-tipped spears and arrows onto the deck, killing many of the men who were unfortunate enough to be on duty at the time.

"GET YOU DOWN BELOW, LAD!" The grey-robed captain pushed Branwenn toward the stair leading into the hold. "'Tis the safest place for you. Fear not, we will rout these robbers in little time."

Branwenn did as she was told, fearing she'd be more cumbrance than aid were she to stay above and attempt to fight.

Despite the captain's assurance, she was still not free of doubt that all might be lost. And if it were not for the tempest of severe proportions that howled down upon them with a deafening force mere moments after she'd settled in her snug nook below deck, making the pirates' fiery offense upon them moot, Branwenn was certain that she and all who were still alive aboard the vessel would have been doomed to a watery grave at the hands of the greedy robbers.

The sounds of attack now silenced, Branwenn went directly against the captain's orders and, after slinging the long strap of her satchel, which held her dearest possessions, around her neck and over her shoulder, went topside.

The brigands' much smaller vessel slipped away into the darkness on thievish feet and in moments, the monks' galley was once more alone on the sea. Unfortunately, it had sustained quite a bit of damage in its hull and the vessel began to take on water. In minutes, it lurched to its side, sending anything that was not nailed down slamming against the railing. Branwenn had barely stepped two paces away from the stair leading below deck when she was sent flying against the railing herself. She only had time to grab hold of a stray plank of wood before she was swept off the ship and into the dark, cold, unforgiving depths of the frigid, briny water.

Tho' the wood acted as a buoy in the violently tossing sea, she was still buried beneath the crashing waves, forced down, down, down, into the unrelenting dark chasm. She held tight to her anchor in the storm, and, after long, terrifying seconds, she was finally thrust back up, like some volcanic spew from an island mound, until she at last broke free of the surface of the abyss and was once more able to draw breath into her burning lungs. When her mind and vision cleared, she realized the tide had propelled her much too far from the vessel to be seen or heard.

Holding tight to her plank of wood, she allowed herself to drift, fearing that if she fought the tide, she'd only end up at the bottom of the sea. For the next few hours, she could do no more than wait. Wait for the light of dawn and keep her mind occupied with any thoughts other than the terrifying ones that niggled at the edge of her mind. Nay, she refused to think upon what sea monsters might even now be skimming under her and around her dangling feet. Nor would she think upon what she would do if she did not find land soon. Instead, she filled her mind with happy thoughts, dear remembrances of the merrier times. Like dancing— dancing for the very first time—around the *Hogmanay* fire this past winter. How gleeful she had been then. Until, of course, that pompous man, Callum MacGregor had spoiled it for her. Nay, she would not think of him. Instead, she forced her thoughts back to more pleasant aspects of that night. Aye, had not the hall been lovely, with the mistletoe, holly, and hazel adorning the trestle tables, and rowan branches above every door? And the scents! Of roasted swan and berries, of juniper, of ale. Aye, that was a happy time.

At long last, dawn arrived in a mist-shrouded glimmer of mauves, pinks, and blue-greys. As the sun came up over the horizon and lit the world around her, Branwenn studied her surroundings. Her heart pounded with joy in her chest, for there, in her sights, was land! And she was near enough to the shoreline— of whose sovereign soil, she knew not—to paddle the rest of the way inland.

* * *

CHAPTER 1
*A Sea Cave on the West Coast of the Highlands
Scotland, Late Summer 1205*

BRANWENN ROSE THROUGH the foaming waves of the emerald-green sea for the last time and absently scraped her newly-shorn raven hair out of her eyes and off of her brow. The dingy, white finely-woven chemise she wore clung to her slender form, revealing more than it concealed. As had been her habit these past days, she swiftly lifted the outer covering away from her body as she moved toward the boulder upon which rested her green woolen tunic with the wide sleeves, her seashell-and-sandstone girdle, and her filet made of the same material. After clothing herself in the items, she slowly trudged up the rocky shore along the water's edge, gathering pretty seashells and small stones as she went. This last hunt would give her enough to complete the bracelet she'd begun making to match the filet and girdle she now wore.

'Twas early yet; the sun was just rising over the craggy cliff of the sea cave inside of which all her earthly possessions now resided. A seafowl shrieked overhead and she tipped her head back to watch its circling flight as it followed the path of the breaking surf before surveying the banks of the strand for its meal in the swell's wake. 'Twas time and past, she thought wryly, for her to break her fast as well, tho' hers would be even sparser fare.

Another wave crashed onto the shoreline just then, its frothing edges soaking and tickling her calves and feet as it sent its salty mist into the air around her. She breathed it in, exalting in the feeling of freedom it manifested inside of her. Tho' 'twas still quite dim all around her, the sun had begun to bathe everything in its pinkish-golden glow, making even the most mundane scenery appear mystical. After another moment of quiet communion with her surroundings, Branwenn turned once more toward her secret hideaway.

She'd been living along this seashore for nigh on a sennight and had yet to see another soul in the area, for which she was deeply thankful. After being swept overboard into the northern reaches of the Irish Sea that horrid midnight and then continuing to be pushed further along with the unrelenting movement of the water and driving wind current, she at last came close enough to land the next morn to make her way to shore by her own propulsion before being aided by a fisherman. It had not taken her long to realize that she was once more in the land of William, King of Scots, for 'twas a western shore she'd landed upon, not an eastern one, as had been her intent upon setting out on her journey the night of her betrothal feast. Her conclusion was negated, however, and most resoundingly in fact, by her fish-procuring savior. Nay, 'twas not the shore of William's land she tread upon, he'd told her, but the isle of Arren, ruled by Ragnald, King of the Isles, who refused to be subject to the Scottish crown. The fisherman then set about filling her belly with a portion of his morning catch before allowing her to take her rest on his cot. When she'd awakened a few hours later and found his hut deserted, she'd left one of the precious few coins she possessed on his table and quietly slipped out.

Afterward, she'd bought passage on a fish merchant's coracle that traversed the Dunbreton Fyrth between the isle and the mainland each day. Once on the mainland, it had not taken her long to attach herself to a band of pilgrims who were traveling by land further north to a holy site along the coast. When they'd reached their destination a fortnight later, Branwenn had said her farewells to her traveling companions and purchased a few of the more essential tools for survival and a bit of bread, cheese, and bannocks in the village attached to the abbey before continuing her journey northward on foot. She'd kept to the coast, finding it the easiest means to travel, as there were many caves for shelter and plenty of food sources that were left behind with the tide each morn and eve. 'Twas a blessing she daily gave thanks for that she'd been trained so thoroughly to survive such harsh conditions by her brother Bao this year past when they'd lived undetected in one of the caves in the Maclean wood for so long. By the time she'd come upon this idyllic, seemingly deserted place, she'd been relieved to at last take a long, and much needed, respite from her journey and quickly settled in one of the more habitable of the caves this Highland shore offered.

'Twas a craggy climb to the cave's opening, but her tender feet were slowly becoming accustomed to the rugged terrain. The jagged gray sandstone rock-and-pebble coast abutted a natural seawall of tumbled boulders above which lay the green grass and shrub-covered red sandstone cliff that housed her cave. There were several such caves, she'd discovered, along this rocky path. But hers, she believed, was the least easily seen from shore, making it the best candidate for her permanent abode. The opening was low but wide and the ground sloped down sharply just inside it, making it impossible to see its interior without actually entering the cave.

The box holding the flint and striker was under a small shrub to the left of the mouth of the cave. She was just lighting the taper that she'd placed next to them when she heard a loud commotion, as if something quite heavy had fallen several feet, followed by a hoarse groan coming from deep within the dark interior of her seaside home. After a moment of anxious inner debate, she at last decided to face the intruder. She could not afford to lose the few possessions she still owned, nor the meager amount of foodstuffs she'd managed to cobble together on her journey. Nervously reaching for the dirk that she kept strapped to her upper thigh, she pulled it out of its leather sheath before entering the ebon cavity. After sliding forward feet-first onto the flat, stone-strewn sandy floor, she lifted the taper high above her head, but the small flame could not illume further than a few feet in front of her. Her eye was instantly drawn to the cave's craggy ceiling. There was now a bit of natural light shining down from up above. A hole, she surmised, tho' how she'd not discovered it before was a puzzle she would need to solve after she'd ousted the trespasser.

"*Who goes there?*" she thundered boldly, tho' her heart thrummed in her ears and her palms sweated so profusely that she had difficulty maintaining the death-grip on her weapon.

Silence.

After a moment, Branwenn forced her feet forward, determined to face down her fear and find the origin of the noise.

'Twas not until she'd reached the furthest end of the cave's front chamber that she found a dark mass on the floor next to the north wall. With some trepidation, she moved toward it, not stopping until she stood over what she quickly ascertained was a slumbering male form. He lay curled on his side in a ball, the edge of his cloak masking his visage.

She stepped back and nudged him with her foot. The man grumbled low in his throat, but remained unawakened. She tried again, and then once more, each time using a bit more force than the time previous. Was he sotted? She bent forward and sniffed. Nay, he smelled not of spirits. More curious than afraid, now that she realized the man was of little threat to her, she crouched down and cautiously edged the cloak away from his face.

Callum MacGregor! "Blood of Christ," she whispered. Was she on the MacGregor holding, then? What strange force was at work that would bring her to her foster brothers' kin when her deepest wish was to stay as far from those she loved and might endanger with her presence, should her Norman betrothed decide to search her out? And this man had been a particular thorn in her side from the moment of their first meeting. He'd surely cause her naught but more grief and misery, should he discover that she'd sailed away from her nuptials and somehow landed on his holding. And he'd no doubt immediately run to the Maclean holding and tell both her foster brothers that she'd broken the contract they'd each signed with Prince Llywelyn.

* * *

Callum slowly regained consciousness. His head was pounding and his eyelids felt as heavy as a castle's cornerstone. Where was he? There was a distinct smell of the sea in the air—was he on the shore, then? Nay, 'twas too quiet. Mayhap, he was in one of the sea caves. He tried to open his eyes once again, but to no avail. Why was he in such a state? He truly could not ken it. The last event he could recall with any certitude was taking a swallow of that abominable wine his father-in-law, Laird Gordon, had encouraged him to try. The two had come to an agreement about the validity of the contract the MacGregors and Gordons had in regard to the tract of land both clans claimed belonged to them. Had the man poisoned him, then? Aye, that would attest to his sore head and persistent stupor.

Callum tried once more to open his eyes, this time with greater success. Peering through the narrow slit in his eyelids, he saw what seemed to be a mystical creature standing before him holding a lighted taper in its hand.

Dressed in a jagged-hemmed tunic of dark woolen, the waist of which was cinched and draped with seashells, the sea creature studied him as well. The brightness of the taper the being held kept its features in darkness, but illuminated its form enough for Callum to see what looked to be winged arms attached to its hands. 'Twas just as the tales had described. "Be you water goddess...or selkie?" he croaked.

The cogs in Branwenn's mind turned swiftly. The arrogant man had just given her the perfect solution to her dilemma. "I be selkie, sir. And you have invaded my dwelling, for which my father, the king, will not be pleased. You've strayed too close to our realm and must leave here forthwith, else you may be carried away by my kinsmen, the *daoine sìth*, never to see your home or family again."

"I fear that my wound is too great for me to rise from this place, fey creature. Tell me, how did I arrive at this place? I've no recollection of it."

"Know you not?" she asked in disbelief. She pointed up and behind her a bit. "You fell, good sir, from yon hole in the cave's ceiling. Now, truly, you must leave in all haste."

Callum attempted to sit up, but his head began to spin and he fell back into a fetal position once more. "'Struth, fey one," he said groggily, "I am in no condition to rise at this time. Will you not afford me a few more moments of rest?"

For the first time, Branwenn began to worry for Callum's condition. Kneeling down by his side, she rested one palm on his lower calf for support as she placed the other on his forehead to check for fever.

"*Ow!*" Callum groaned, "my ankle...'tis sore...do not press so heavily upon it, I beg you."

"Pray, pardon me." 'Twas now clear to Branwenn that Callum's befuddled manner was not due to some manly overindulgence in ardent spirits, as was her original belief. But what ailed the man? His skin was hot, his usually vivid green eyes were dull and void of spirit, and his face was drenched in sweat. "Your skin is as hot as a blacksmith's forge!"

"I fear I've been poisoned," Callum said weakly.

Poison! A cold tremor of alarm shook her to her core. "Callum," Branwenn said his name without thinking, "you must purge your stomach of its contents forthwith!" Not waiting for a reply, she quickly pinched his nostrils closed with one hand and forced two fingers down his throat with the other. Tho' he attempted to fight her off, he was so weakened by the effects of whatever he'd ingested, that she was easily able to overpower him, and in the next instant, he was gagging, heaving, and expulsing his earlier meal.

"By the blood of Christ, fey one...leave me be," Callum pleaded afterward, his voice now thread-like, as he rolled onto his back and turned his face away from her. His thick auburn hair, that had come loose of its leather thong, fell across his cheek and she brushed it away from his face.

"'Twas your wife who did this to you?" she was impelled to ask, no matter the imprudence of the query.

"Nay, my wife is dead," he rasped. "'Twas my faithless father-in-law who did the deed."

Dead! Lara was dead? What of her babe? She dared not question him further, however, lest her true identity be revealed.

He said naught more, and after another moment, Branwenn realized he'd fallen into a slumber once more. Leaning down, she rested her cheek against his chest and, feeling the even rise-and-fall of his chest and hearing the tempered, strong beat of his heart, expelled a sigh of relief.

She rose to her feet and retrieved a cloth and a bucket of water. With slow, gentle strokes, she cooled his brow and cheeks with the damp cloth. Afterward, she silently cleaned up the results of his purging before positioning the rolled blanket she'd been using for a pillow under his head. Leaving the taper in its holder next to her reclining patient, she walked a bit away and settled against the wall on the opposite side of the cave to continue watching him. Over the next hour or so, she monitored his recovery from a distance, but 'twas not long before questions began to spin madly about in her mind: Why would his father-in-law have done this to him? What had Callum gotten himself into this time? And, oh, God, what if he did not recover? With effort, she forced her worries down deep, for she had no way of aiding him, and, Lord knew, she had worries enough of her own without taking on his burdens as well.

A strange *smack*ing sound came from the area where Callum now rested, followed by a muffled groan. Branwenn leapt to her feet and hurried over to him.

"Water," Callum said, his voice a dry whisper.

"Aye," Branwenn answered anxiously as she lifted the candle and turned first one way and then the other looking for her leather flask. Spying it at last, she hurried to retrieve it and, after removing the stopper, settled the opening to his parched lips. "Drink slowly—and only a bit—else 'twill no doubt rise back up just as quickly," she warned softly.

Callum, his eyes barely open, surprisingly did as she bade, taking only two small swigs before rolling to his back and resting his head on the make-shift pillow once more.

Branwenn ran the palm of her hand over his forehead and cheek. His skin was still a bit too hot and much too damp for her liking. She began to worry her lip as her conscience did battle with her intellect. In the next moment, her decision made, she said, "Your fever is not lessening, sir. We must get you to your dwelling in all haste, for, 'tis clear to me that you are in need of more proper tending, else surely you will grow worse."

Callum opened his eyes and looked at her. "What is your name?"

Branwenn thought quickly. "Mai," she said with a shrug. Why not? She'd always liked that name.

"Mai? So plain a name for one so magical?"

Bristling, Branwenn replied, "I think it a lovely name. And do not change the subject. Where is your home?"

Callum, tho' still a bit groggy, was revived enough for the moment to get his bearings. He tried to sit up.

"Be careful!" Branwenn said.

He fell back with a groan. Well, mayhap he wasn't as recovered as he'd believed. "Aye." His head throbbed and his muscles were stiff and sore, but he was determined to rise. So, with a loud grunt, he lifted up again and forced his body to hold his weight this time. Dizzy from the exertion, he held his aching skull in his hands for a moment.

"Have you a sore head?" Branwenn asked.

"Aye, a bit," he said before looking around the cave once more. The fey one was right, he must get home—and quickly—for he must inform his stepfather of this latest outrage against their clan. "Stand back, I must rise."

Branwenn nodded and did as he bade, staying close enough to catch him if he began to fall.

Using the damp wall of the cave as leverage, Callum struggled to his feet.

Fighting the mental lethargy the poison and headache were causing, he strained to focus on his surroundings.

"Are you feeling dizzy?" Branwenn asked, her concern mounting.

Highland Magic

"Sshhh! I'm trying to think," he snapped.

Branwenn stiffened her spine. "Pray, pardon me, Your Highness."

Callum ignored her. Somewhere in the back of his mind, he knew that he should apologize for his rudeness, but 'twas all he could do to stay on his feet and shake the shroud of fog in his mind to think more clearly. After another moment, he breathed a sigh of relief. Aye, he knew this cave. 'Twas the one his cuckolding wife had used to make her secret departure from their fortress two moons past. If he traveled the meandering passage that began at the back of this chamber, 'twould eventually lead him to a hidden entrance inside the west tower of the fortress. He pushed himself away from the dank wall he'd propped himself up against, picked up the taper, and set out in that direction.

"Where are you going?" Branwenn asked as she stumbled into step behind him, stretching her arms out in front of her so she could catch him when he fell—for his gate was stiff and uneven as he tried to keep the weight off of his injured ankle.

"I'm going to my family's fortress."

"But...this passage leads only to my father's realm."

Callum was growing short of breath now. "Nay, it leads to a"—he stopped walking and bent forward, resting his palms on his knees as he took a couple of deep breaths—"secret entrance to the castle." He would *not* swoon, he vowed to himself.

This was news to Branwenn. She'd thoroughly explored this cave when she'd first arrived and had found no such entrance.

A drop of sweat trailed into the outer corner of Callum's eye and he blinked the sting away. After a minute more, he resumed his trek. 'Twas not long before he came to the place where the passage forked. Recessed in the entrance to the adjacent tunnel was a large portion of planked wood which had been fitted to block the opening and then curtained in a painted black and gray fabric, the design resembling the stone walls around it. The darkness of the cave, the skill with which the painter had copied the look of the stone, along with the little light even a torch could provide in the black chasm, helped to conceal the second route.

"Take hold of these a moment," he said, placing the fistful of pulled-back curtain in the fey one's hand and the taper in her other. Taking two deep breaths and releasing them, he filled his lungs once more and thrust his shoulder against the wooden barrier. Unfortunately, it gave much easier than he was expecting and the force sent it, and him, flying forward. He landed with a loud *thud* directly on top of it. "Aargh!" he yelled as he felt his shoulder bone thrust from its joint.

"Blood of Christ!" Branwenn cried out. She flew to Callum's side and dropped down to her knees. "You've hurt yourself, you simple-minded fool! And now I know not how I will ever get you up again!"

A fleeting memory of someone else speaking to him in much the same manner flitted through his mind, but 'twas much too nebulous an image for him to catch and keep hold of. So, swallowing another groan, he simply ignored the vexing creature. As this was not an unfamiliar injury for him, he did as he'd been taught should this happen on the battlefield. Slowly, he brought his arm up and placed his hand behind his head and rotated the appendage. With very careful, slow movements he began to reach toward his other shoulder. He felt the bone slide back in place. Aahhh! Perfect. But now he was beginning to see pinpricks of colored lights. Afraid he'd swoon when he was so close to his destination, he took a few slow, deep breaths and manfully shook the false visions clear before staggering to his feet once more.

"Praise be, you are still able to walk," Branwenn said with a sigh of relief.

"Why are you still here? Have you no other mortal to hound with your endless yammering?" His head ached so badly now, his stomach was threatening to spew its bile.

"Oh, and I suppose you would rather have no one here to aid you should you swoon and fall to the ground again?" *...you unthankful cur!*, she finished in her head.

The fey one had a point, but Callum would rather eat a live toad than tell her so. "The door leading to the tower is just ahead," he said instead.

They'd just come to it when, all at once, Callum's head began to reel and the cave walls began to billow in front of him. Confused, he stumbled forward, hitting his head on the frame and sliding to the ground. The taper fell with him, coming loose from its base, and rolled several feet away. The flame went out.

"Callum!" Branwenn cried out in the sudden

darkness. Moving in the direction of her patient with her arms out in front of her, she felt her way toward him. "You can*not* die yet, I won't allow it!"

Later, much later, Callum would recall this moment—and the time previous—and question how the fey one could possibly know his name, but for now, his befuddled mind could do naught more than direct its thoughts to the problem at hand. He managed to force his eyelids open and was met with complete darkness. But he felt the now-familiar hands of the fey one as she examined his head for new bumps. "I've no new wounds, but I fear my head is spinning too much and my hand shakes too badly to unlock the door." Though his limbs were now lethargic, he managed, with his good arm, to bring the leather thong that held the key out from under his tunic and over his head. "Here, take this and I will tell you the way to open the locks."

Branwenn nodded, tho' he could not possibly see the action, and felt for the key he held out to her. Grasping it tightly in her fist, she stood and explored the door with her other hand until she at last found the metal devices he'd spoken of. They were cold to the touch, and shaped like—she took a moment to become familiar with their contours—hearts? How strange. Now, to find the keyholes. "These are unusual," she said absently as she slid her fingers lightly over the face of each lock. "It feels as if they are all connected, but each also joined to its own latch—and.... *Are* they interlocking hearts?"

To fortify his waning strength, Callum took in a deep breath before answering. "Aye, they are, and they require a specific combination of turns of the key and slides of certain brass plates in order to get them all open." Luckily, even with his fading mental acuity, he could still remember what that combination was, for he'd practiced it many times with his mother after it had been installed. She was the only other person who held a key to this secret exit, as 'twould be her means of escape during a siege, should the need arise. There was a small, hand-sized door to the left of the locks that only opened from the other side and which used the same key. When open, 'twas large enough to put one's arm through and unlock the door.

Over the next quarter hour, Branwenn diligently tried to follow Callum's instructions, but because she was doing so without benefit of light, the process took several attempts before she at last found success. And, to her thinking, with little time to spare—for their nerves were frayed to their limits by this time and she could tell by Callum's groggy voice that whatever reserve of strength he'd been relying on thus far was fading quickly.

With a hard jerk of the handle, Branwenn opened the arched oaken door and found the other barrier Callum had told her of. Doing as he'd instructed, she felt for the recessed stone and pressed. The barrier opened with little effort and she peered into the chamber before her.

Praise be, 'twas lit by a torch that hung from a sconce to the left of her, but was free of human habitation. "Come, we must get you inside at once," she said, turning to Callum.

"Bmm...mmm," Callum replied.

With a sigh and a shake of her head, she placed her arm around the waist of her near-unconscious patient and, with no small amount of effort, managed to get him to his feet and into the tower chamber. His eyes remained closed and his head canted to the left the entire time she walked him to the pallet in the far corner. "Will the guard return soon so he can get you to the keep? For I dare not go further inside these walls. I want no other mortal to see me—and, I beg you, tell no one of our meeting, else my father will surely have you vexed with mischief the remainder of your days."

"Nay...sext," Callum answered, tho' 'twas all he could do to get the words past his dry throat.

"Sext! But that is not for at least two more hours!" Branwenn felt his forehead. Godamercy, 'twas still so hot—but his brow was dry as a bone now. Not good. She could not leave him here with no one to help him. She just couldn't.

An idea came to her. Grabbing a stool and an unlit candle holder from atop a small table, she hurried to stand near the opening of the secret entrance and threw them with maniacal force onto the ground. Satisfied with the loud clatter she'd made, she then began to cry out in as low and manly a timbre as she could manage. In the next instant, the sound of pounding feet on the stone stairs outside the doorway to the tower, as well as the sound of men's raised voices, filled the room. With one last quick look at Callum, she fled through the opening and hastily closed it behind her. When she was safely on the other side of the oaken door, she breathed a sigh of relief. Surprisingly, she could still hear what was going on inside, so she stood and listened as the men hustled to get Callum to the keep and made plans to find a physician in all haste. When all became quiet once more, she turned to make her way back to her own dwelling but stopped short. Hellfire and damnation! She had no lit taper. Blood of Christ and Mary and God, too! She was going to have to go back inside that chamber and get the torch. She giggled then. Well—wasn't that just the type of mischief mortals expected of the wee folk? And 'twas awfully still and quiet inside that chamber now—no doubt, the guard on duty would not return until his scheduled time. With a shrug, she turned back to the door and opened it wide. Hmmm, mayhap she would find a few other items she could use while she was about it. And she did have the key—as well as the combination—to the secret entry...hmmm.

* * *

CHAPTER 2

"*T*WAS MY IMPETUOUS young nephew who did the deed, I tell you! I knew naught of it until well past the time your stepson left my holding last eve!" Laird Gordon avowed heatedly, his brow damp with sweat and his cheeks the color of new-picked berries. "I and my men immediately went in search of Callum as soon as we learned of my nephew's son's treachery."

Laird MacGregor's eyes narrowed into angry slits. "That well may be—"

A knock came on the door just then and directly behind the sound, the door swung wide and the keep's steward propelled himself forward. "Laird,"—his eyes flitted nervously to Laird Gordon and then settled back on his liege—"your stepson lives—"

"Praise be!" Both laird's exclaimed at once.

"Where is he?" Laird MacGregor asked.

"We've taken him to his bedchamber, Laird." A

short pause followed. "He is not well. He's a fever and is barely conscious. 'Tis clear as well that he took a tumble from his steed, for his ankle and shoulder are mightily swollen and bruised."

"I must go to him immediately—have my wife and her mother been informed of the blessed tidings?"

"Nay, not as yet, Laird. But the solar is my next destination."

Laird MacGregor turned to his unwelcome guest and said, "Do not leave. I will return in an hour's time, for we must come to terms regarding recompense—as well as punishment—for this crime."

With a curt nod of the head, Laird Gordon solemnly agreed. "Aye."

* * *

Branwenn went through the remainder of the day worrying over Callum's health. No matter how hard she tried to turn her thoughts to her own problem—and how she was going to resolve it—her mind refused to cooperate. Finally, late that night, she gave in to her nagging thoughts and returned through the passage to the secret door of the tower chamber. 'Twas now nearing the chimes of midnight, and she worried that the guard would be in the chamber, but after a quarter-hour of intent listening, she heard no sound emanating from the other side of the wall, and stealthily unlatched and opened the door.

She had no idea which bedchamber was Callum's, but she decided there would surely be guards, or maids, or some-such lurking about the correct door. She was dressed in a plain brown tunic, underneath which she'd carefully bound her breasts in a strip of fine linen, and with her hood-covered, short-cropped hair, she was sure to look like one of the lads that worked with the gong farmer. If she encountered anyone on her journey, she decided to simply explain that she had been told to retrieve the chamber pot from the laird's stepson's chamber.

Thankfully, the tower stair was deserted and it didn't take her long to make her way down to the outer bailey. In another moment, she was through the arched portal to the inner bailey of the keep. Surely, one could gain entrance to the family quarters through the chapel, she thought as she set out in that direction.

All was silent as she scurried across the moonlit courtyard toward the chapel. Her feet crushed the dew-bathed turf as she went and it perfumed the air with its clean, fresh fragrance. The dark beauty of the walled enclosure at this time of night, all velvet purples and watery greens, blended well with the scent of sod and it lifted her lagging spirits.

Fortune was with her, for she encountered no one as she made her way through the passage between the stone oratory and the family quarters and then climbed the stairs leading to the upper chambers. There were few about above stairs either, and she was growing worried that she'd not learn which was Callum's chamber, when a door at the end of the hall opened and a servant carrying a ewer emerged. Praise be! She slipped into the shadows and waited for the man to pass before taking the last few steps to Callum's door.

She silently edged it open and looked around. The

fire from the hearth illuminated the room enough for Branwenn to see an aged man—the physician?—resting on his side on top of two long benches that had been shoved together and covered in a fur. Her nose crinkled as the smell of stale bile and the gong bucket wafted toward her. The physician must have given him an herb to induce more purging—or, mayhap 'twas just a symptom of the poisoning. The sound of muted snores emanated from the direction of the benches, telling her that the physician was a sound sleeper, so she silently walked further into the room. The curtain to the large bed was drawn, making it impossible for her to see how Callum faired without moving across the room to stand at the bedside.

As lightly and silently as she could, she crept across the wood floor, praying all the while that one of the boards wouldn't creak. There was a small vial next to a cup on the table next to the bed. She picked the cup up and sniffed. 'Twas the remainder of a sleeping draught. The physician must have given it to Callum to help him sleep through the pain. She placed the cup back in its place on the table. Then, lifting the taper that rested beside it, she pulled aside the curtain and gazed down at the handsome, tho' clearly fever ravaged, countenance of the man who both vexed and drew her to him at one and the same time.

Reaching out, she placed her palm first on his hot brow and then over his flushed cheek. Still dry. She looked over her shoulder at the still-slumbering physician and then toward the wash basin a few paces away. With less trepidation than she'd felt upon entering—now that she knew how hard the man slept—she made her way over to the basin and doused a cloth in the cool water. After ringing it free of excess moisture, she brought it back to the bed and lightly ran the cloth over Callum's face and neck. If, by chance, he awakened, she felt sure he'd be in too groggy a state from the draught to recognize her. And the dimness of the chamber, as well as her lad's attire would also help to keep her identity hidden.

Since the ministering seemed to soothe him, she repeated the exercise several more times. Thankfully, tho' he mumbled in his sleep, he never fully awakened or opened his eyes. After awhile, her legs and back became pained and weary, so she decided to settle next to her patient on the bed to continue the task. His face contorted and he groaned when the indention of the mattress rolled him onto his sore shoulder. She held her breath, for if anything would awaken him, this would. He resettled on his back, but his eyes never opened.

Curious to see how badly he'd injured himself when he'd burst through the barrier in the cave opening, she took a quick peek under the top edge of the woolen blanket. 'Twas wrapped tightly, so 'twas hard to tell how much damage he'd caused himself. She dared do no further investigation, however, as, from the look of things, he wore naught else. After resettling the blanket snugly over his chest, she bathed his face with the cool cloth and dribbled very small amounts of water into his mouth that, even in his stupor, he managed to swallow. She continued in this vein for the next two hours.

Highland Magic

At some point, the physician awakened and moved toward the bed, but she managed to scoot over to the other side and hide between the bed's edge and the curtain while the man checked on his patient. Afterward, he lay back down on his makeshift bed and quickly fell into what seemed to be an untroubled slumber once more.

Finally, a couple of hours before sunrise, Callum's fever broke. Unfortunately, his eyes opened then as well and there was not one tittle of confusion in them when he saw her. "Branwenn!" he croaked.

"Nay, 'tis but a dream you are having!" she whispered as she hastily descended from the bed. "And what, pray, are you doing dreaming of me, you lewd-minded devil!" she said, deciding 'twas the kind of comment he would expect from her in life—and in a dream.

"'Tis no dream," he said sleepily. Callum's eyelids drooped, then shut completely. "For, why would I dream of a laddish bairn...such as"—He yawned loudly—"yowww?"

His harsh words caused a sharp pain in her heart and Branwenn's eyes misted. In the next instant, however, fury overcame hurt and she drew her fist back and nearly punched him in the arm before reason won out and, scrubbing the tears from her eyes with the back of her hand, she took the opportunity to escape before the rest of the household rose for the day.

* * *

The next time Callum awoke, 'twas nearing sext. Pulling back the bed curtain, he peered out, squinting when the bright light coming from the window stabbed his bleary eyes. He blinked a few times and rubbed them to ease the pain. How long had he been asleep? Hours? Days?

He began to stretch, curving his back and lifting his bent elbows up in the air. "Aargh! Oww! Holy—"

The door flew open and his mother barreled forward, followed closely by his paternal grandmother, Lady Maclean. "Callum, dear! Which of your injuries pains you? I will call for new bindings forthwith."

"I am well, Mother, fear not. I only meant to stretch a bit and was instantly reminded of my sore shoulder," he said, flinging the sheet over his bare nether regions.

"That sluggard physician only just came down to tell us that your fever broke early this morn," Lady Maclean said. "Here, let me feel your forehead." Her gate was slow, and her tall frame a bit stooped, but her unusual eyes—one blue, one green—snapped with vitality as she walked over to stand at the side of the bed and proceeded to do just that. "We should not have listened to him when he told us to stay away from you while your fever raged, else we would have known of your recovery much sooner." Her gray-sprigged black brows furrowed as her eyes scanned his countenance. "A bad business, this. Your uncle...er...*stepfather*—pardon, I'm still not used to thinking of him thus—met with Laird Gordon for most of this day past to negotiate a settlement for this insult."

"Insult!" Callum yelled. "'Twas attempted *murder*!"

"Now Callum," his mother soothed, "'twas not as dark a deed as that, for 'twas—"

"How can you say such! I—"

"Hush, and I will explain," she chided gently, her voice softer, more melodious than her mother's. "'Twas the Laird's young page—his nephew—who...well...he stirred your wine with a finger he'd stuck in swine offal."

"What!?" In the next second, he was gagging and coughing as his innards roiled inside of him.

Lady Maclean placed her hand on her grandson's good shoulder. "Now, now. You didn't partake of enough to perish," —she turned to her daughter and said, "Maggie, fetch him some water, else he'll surely retch more bile,"—before turning back to Callum and continuing, "so you've no need to carry on in such a manner."

"And I suppose you would react with dignity," *cough, cough, gag*, "not even raise an eyebrow, were you to find out you'd been fed pig turd for supper?" He glared at her through blood-shot, watery green eyes.

Lady Maclean caught her daughter's eye and gave her a look that said, *'Do* not *laugh!'* "Nay, I'm sure I would react in much the same rather excessive way."

Laird MacGregor came in at that moment, for which it was clear the two ladies were very grateful. "I see you've recovered from your fever. Good, good." A middle-aged dark-haired man of great girth and height, his heavy footsteps caused the table next to the bed to jump, making the water slosh out of the ewer and onto the floor.

"Chalmers!" Callum's mother sighed and shook her head, but hurried to clean the mess with the cloth she found next to the ewer.

Her husband gave her a sheepish look. "Pardon, my beloved."

Callum rolled his eyes. Why must the man continually speak love words to her directly within her son's hearing? "What reason did my father-in-law give for his nephew's conduct?" he asked his stepfather, though his eyes never left his lithely built dark-haired mother. Would she never stop flitting about like a wee bird, lighting first here, then there? She needed more meat on her bones, and this was no way to go about it. "Mother, let the maids do that."

"The older pages dared him to do the deed," Laird MacGregor answered.

Callum's eyes swung to his stepfather and he cocked a brow at him.

"They've evidently been teasing the bairn," Laird MacGregor continued, "calling him a coward, ever since his first night sharing quarters with them when he refused to take part in their secret guild's ritual and walk the moor alone at midnight."

For the first time since realizing his drink had been tampered with, Callum's wrath lessened. He smiled before he realized he'd done it and said, "Poor lad. I remember well the insults to my own manhood I received—and gave back in turn—when I first paged." Callum shook his head, his eyes once again on his mother, following her movements as she silently tidied the bedchamber and found a stool for her aged mother to rest upon, but his mind focused inward, on memories that, until this moment, had been long forgot. "God's truth, I do believe 'twas the most difficult twelvemonth of all my years of training." He turned his eye to his stepfather again. "They've formed a secret guild?" He grinned. "I wish I'd thought of that when I was their age."

Laird MacGregor's countenance split into a big-toothed grin. Stroking his fingers over his bearded chin, he replied, "Aye, I thought the same thing when Laird Gordon told the tale to me this eve past!"

"Maggie," Lady Maclean said, half in jest, "'Tis at last clear to me what you meant when you said 'twas as if these two were cut from the same cloth. For, 'tis truth, they do seem to love mischief-making."

Callum ignored the jibe. "What recompense did you extract from my father-in-law then?" he asked his stepfather.

"I insisted he send his nephew to me to train. He agreed."

Callum chuckled. "Aye," he said with evil glee, "I look forward to meeting my wee swine-loving poisoner."

"Now, Callum, I can see the cogs in that maniacal mind of yours turning," his mother interjected, "and you mustn't do anything to upset the poor bairn any further. He's no father, he's only Laird Gordon as guardian—and you know how churlish that man can be. Why, I'm sure the lad's been punished enough."

Feigning a sigh of disappointment, Callum answered, "Aye, Mother." But, in truth, he had no intention of meting out any further punishment on the lad—especially now that he knew of his parentless state.

That thought reminded him of his daughter and he sat up straight. Worry furrowed his brow as he asked his mother, "Where is Laire? She was not exposed to my fever, was she?"

"The babe is well, fear not," Maggie hurried to reassure him. With a quick glance at her mother and then back at him, she continued, "'Tis the main reason the physician gave for keeping us as far from this sick room as possible."

"Fetch me my shirt and braies; I want to see her."

"Chalmers, help me rise," Lady Maclean said, holding out her hand toward him. "'Tis past time we allowed Callum some privacy."

As the two exited, Maggie retrieved the items of clothing her son had requested from his clothing chest. "I'll send up a servant to help you wash and dress."

"Nay, there's no time. I haven't seen my daughter in three days. I'm anxious to know for myself how she fares and I want to cradle her in my arms again.

"You'll have a bit of trouble, with the injury to your shoulder," she reminded, her voice gentle.

"I know, but 'tis worth the discomfort."

"Be careful, else you could cause more damage to it—or worse, drop the poor lass."

"Aye, I'll be careful."

She departed then as well, leaving Callum alone once more in his chamber.

Though 'twas difficult, he managed to wash and dress on his own. Within a half-hour, and with the aid of a cane, he managed to get himself to his daughter's nursery.

Highland Magic

Now, as he gazed down at his sleeping bairn, nestled snugly in her cradle, he was reminded once more of her mother. She'd gotten Lara's lovely, delicate features, as well as her wavy chestnut hair and large blue eyes. But she had a much more temperate nature. Where Lara had been extravagant in her reactions—one moment gleeful, the next in angry tears—this lass was calm, and had a sweet, cheerful disposition, for which Callum was thankful every day.

The Gordons, specifically Laird Gordon, had hounded him at first to give the babe into the care of their own clan, but Callum could not do it. For, he suspected, 'twas that very upbringing that had made his wife both spoiled with the need for luxuries and aggressive in her pursuit of male attention. And there was something more as well...some vaguely unnerving something in her manner, in her reactions to men, but especially to him the one time they'd made love, that made him wonder if she'd not been abused, mayhap even meddled with in a baser way, as a bairn. For his tenderness toward her that night had seemed to offend her, 'twas only when he'd at last done her bidding and taken her with rough force—clearly causing her pain— that she'd finally found pleasure.

But if he were right in his suspicions, he knew 'twas not Laird Gordon who'd done the deed. For everything in that old warrior's manner pointed to a moral, tho' irascible, nature. Nay, 'twas not her father, but someone else—he knew not who for sure, perhaps her stepbrother?—that may have committed such a vile crime against her. 'Twas the reason he'd remained patient with her those first few moons of their marriage when she'd driven his mother mad with her demands and incessant complaints. He knew his mother had wondered why he would not take his wife in hand and demand that she behave in a more civil manner toward the staff, but he could never bring himself to reveal his dark suspicions to her. It had seemed too...*privy* a thing to discuss with her. And, without proof, it seemed wrong somehow, as if he'd begin some terrible rumor if he gave voice to the notion.

Still asleep, his daughter took in a deep breath and made the sweetest wee sigh before *smacking* her rose-petal, slobbery lips together. He couldn't help it, he just had to see those two cherubic white teeth of hers, so he lightly pressed down on her bottom lip a moment and gazed at the small red gums with their two snowy crests pushing through. He lifted his finger to her warm-as-sunshine, soft-as-down pink cheek and lightly stroked the back of it over the soft, sleep-warmed mound.

Aye, 'twas much better that Laire remain with him.

That horrible day two moons past when he and his scouts had at last tracked his faithless wife and her contemptible lover—her grotesquely burned and still healing stepbrother, it turned out—to the cotter's hut in the Gordon wood, when he'd heard those pain-wracked moans coming from within...and when he'd, at last, leapt from his mount and rushed inside the dark hovel only to find his wife bleeding to death from the puncture wound she'd received when she'd fallen from her charging horse onto a sharp branch of a fallen tree trunk and been pierced through, he never would have imagined how deep his love would grow for this wee one not of his seed.

Tho' his wife had been weak from the massive loss of blood, and near death at the time he'd found her, she'd still been awake. 'Twas then that she at last revealed to him who'd sired her babe—her honorless stepbrother—a thing he'd been trying to learn since the night of their wedding when he'd discovered the foul trick that had been played upon him. Laird Gordon had willfully refrained from revealing to Callum that his new bride would come with more than a settlement regarding the tract of land the two clans feuded over, but she would come already bearing another man's babe. But seeing it from the old warrior's perspective, 'twas the best thing the man could have done to both make a pact with the MacGregors—and gain the advantage one last time, a thing any man of war would do—and see that his grandchild would not be raised outside of wedlock. A rather skewed, but still honorably intended deed.

Lara had pleaded with him then to keep her daughter and raise her as a MacGregor, for her stepbrother refused to acknowledge his part in the matter and, tho' she'd tried early on to lose the babe, she'd discovered within herself the past moons, while confined to her tower chamber—a punishment Callum had meted out when he'd discovered her *in flagrante delicto* with his old childhood friend, Robert MacVie—that she wanted her babe to live, to know the love of a parent who would keep her safe from harm.

And, even now, he wondered if he could possibly

love a daughter-germane more. For, 'twas truth, that from the moment he first laid eyes on her the day of her birth last spring, he'd begun to love her as his own.

His wee bairn began to fuss in her sleep, and in moments 'twas a full-throated cry. The nurse rushed over to the side of the crib, but Callum shook his head and shooed her away with his hand. Bending down, he lifted his tearful babe into his arms, gritting his teeth against the pain the movement caused to his bruised shoulder. "Hush, wee one, and I'll take you to your nurse." He turned to the lady and asked, "Is it time for her next feeding?"

"Aye, sir. And from the looks of your shirt, 'tis time to change her swaddling clothes as well."

Callum, a look of chagrin on his face, gazed at the warm, wet stain now covering the left side of his shirt. "I was so glad to hold her again, I noticed not the state of her swaddlings."

"Hand the babe to me, sir, and I'll have her cleaned and ready for her meal in no time."

Callum transferred the small, wet, still fussing bundle to the woman, but remained in the chamber for another hour as she washed, changed, and fed his most precious treasure.

* * *

'Twas not until late that night, when he was undressing for bed, that Callum at last recalled the cave, the key, the sea faery...and *Branwenn*.

"God's teeth!" Callum growled, hobbling with as quick a gait as his sore ankle would allow toward the hook that held his tunic. Not only had he—the one who'd been so adamant that the secret passage remain sealed and its two keys kept in the possession of the lady of the keep and himself—given his key away, but he'd given the combination as well! And to someone he believed at the time to be one of the fey ones!

Rushing from the room, he clumped toward the stair and took them haltingly to the level above—to his stepfather's and mother's chamber. He pounded on the door. "Mother! I must speak with you in all haste!"

The door swung wide and he was met with his stepfather's rugged—and vexed—countenance. "Aye? What need you from your poor mother at this late hour? She's worn thin and needs her rest."

Chagrined, reminded of his mother's weakened state these past moons since the chill she took over the spring that she'd only just got over in the past sennights, Callum replied softly, "My pardon, but 'tis truly of a very urgent nature—"

Maggie came up behind her husband and nudged him aside. "What has you so upset, my son? You've not got your fever back, have you?" she asked anxiously.

"Nay, Mother, fear not. But I must"—he glanced briefly at his stepfather—"speak with you privily. Just for a moment."

"Aye," Maggie replied, scooting out the door and closing it behind her. After it gave a soft *'snick'*, she folded her arms over her chest and lifted her brows in question. "Aye?" she prompted.

"I must borrow your key to the cave exit."

"Bu—"

"Please, do not ask me the reason, for 'twill all be revealed in a short time, I swear it."

With a sigh and a nod, Maggie swept the delicate silver chain holding the brass key from around her neck and handed it to him. Drilling him with a determined look, she said, "I shall expect to know the full of it come morn."

Callum placed his hand on her upper arm. "Aye, Mother," he replied. "Now, you must get your rest, for I've no wish for you to lose what strength you've gained these past sennights."

"Aye, 'tis glad I am that your grandmother arrived when she did to help with Laire, for she helped me recover as well."

Callum settled a light kiss on her cheek. "Sleep well," he said softly and then turned and strode away.

Maggie shook her head as she watched him leave. 'Twas clear by the spark in her son's eye that he was on a mission that would involve a bit of mischief—and, if she knew her son, which she did, quite well, in fact—'twould involve a person of the gentler sex.

Thank Heaven. For, since her daughter-in-law's death—nay, 'twas even before that—since that horrible debacle involving his true heart's desire, Maryn Donald, two springs past, when he lost the Maclean lairdship and all hope of ever wedding the lass, she'd seen a much too somber Callum emerge. For, all his life before that time, he'd been the charming, ever affable, and much admired by the ladies, young man. 'Twas all that had transpired these past moons that had matured him—but, to her way of thinking—had diminished him as well. And she'd begun to regret her and her husband's decision to humor Callum in his rather strange need to block, and lock, the passage to the cave in the sennights after they'd buried Lara. For, it had not, as they'd hoped, enabled him to move forward with his life, to return to some semblance of his prior delightful, carefree self. Nay, instead, he'd grown ever more quiet, ever more serious.

But this morn, when he'd nearly spewed his stomach over the outrage of the pig offal, had been the closest he'd been to his old self in much too long a time. And a romantic tryst with one of the fortress maids might just help to complete the restoration. With a lighthearted smile, she turned and entered her chamber once more.

* * *

CHAPTER 3

BRANWENN SHIVERED. The night was cooler than she'd expected it to be, else she'd have brought one of the old cloaks with her that she'd taken from the keep to cover herself in after her midnight swim.

Her mind had been full of thoughts of Callum all day—ever since her hasty departure from his chamber before dawn—so she'd decided a nice long swim might tire her enough to sleep. But no sooner had she finished the exercise than her thoughts turned once more to the annoying man. Did he remember seeing her in his bed this morn? Surely not. He couldn't. He'd been much too benumbed by the effects of the sleeping draught, and the fever as well, to recall such a brief encounter. Surely.

Though she was cold, she took her time returning to the cave. As she walked along the pebble-strewn moonlit shore, she turned her thoughts to her next destination. She'd decided to travel to Perth. She knew the town well and felt sure she could find some means of supporting herself once there. Mayhap, she could find work in one of the merchant's homes. There were plenty of them in a town that size and surely one of them would need to add another member to their staff. Or mayhap, she could apprentice as a spinster. She felt sure she could learn that trade, for she did well enough with needle and thread—and it could not be too different, could it? After all, there was thread involved in spinning as well, wasn't there?

And then, mayhap by the next *Bealltainn*, she could go home again—to the Maclean holding—to her brother Bao. Surely, by that time all would be settled to her royal cousin and the march lord's satisfaction, and she would be free once more to live near the person who raised her.

She'd leave at first light. 'Twas dangerous to stay a minute past that time, for she knew that eventually Callum would recall his time in the cave and be back to find the sea faery to whom he'd given his key. She'd left it under a rock just this side of the door leading into the tower chamber and she would find a way to send Callum word where to retrieve it when she was well on her way to Perth—tho' 'twould be a missive from the sea faery, of course. She sniggered. Wouldn't she just delight in seeing the look on his face when he read *that* letter? Mayhap, she should scrape out the inside of a shell and crush it into a fine pink dust to sprinkle over the ink. Ooh! And she should dry a bit of seaweed to tie about the rolled missive as well. 'Twould no doubt make the thing smell like the bottom of a fish barrel, but 'twould be a just repayment for the rude thing he said to her this morn. Besides, 'twould certainly add to the amusement of the scene.

A few minutes later, she entered her cave and was just lighting another candle, when the unmistakable sound of male footsteps began to reverberate inside the cavern.

Callum! Her mind reeled. He couldn't wait until the morrow to return here? Nay, that would be asking too much of the gods of fortune, she supposed. And there was no doubt in her mind 'twould be his too-handsome face she'd see in another minute.

With the fleet speed of a falcon on its prey, she retrieved her 'faery' attire and almost literally jumped into them. She blew out the candles and stood, waiting, in the darkest corner of the cave. The sound of harsh breathing filled the midnight depths of the cavern chamber, but it took a second for her to realize 'twas coming from her own throat. Closing her eyes—and her mouth—she willed herself to take in several slow, deep, *quiet*, breaths, tho' her heart actually ached as it pounded against her ribs, and the urge to fill her lungs with more haste was almost too irresistible to ignore.

* * *

Callum's steps grew quicker the nearer he got to the sea cave's front chamber. Now that he was so close to his goal, he began to wonder how exactly to go about this 'unveiling' of the lovely, tho' ever sharp-tongued, wee mite of a lass known as Branwenn. He had no desire to run her to ground—a thing he was sure to be forced to do should he boldly reveal that he knew her true identity. So he must tread lightly, give the impression that he believed her to be the fey creature she pretended to be.

But, what on earth was she doing so far from Cambria? She was supposed to be nearly wed by now to some relation of one of the Norman march lords. 'Twas evident that she had fled her coming nuptials, that she was in hiding, but why? Hell, his cousins had already endured a siege of the Maclean fortress by Prince Llywelyn in order that he might force her to acknowledge the contract he'd made with the Norman lord. And 'twas a siege that maimed, and nearly killed, her foster brother, Bao. Surely, she would not have forsaken her promise to fulfill the contract when she knew 'twould only bring more Cambrian—and mayhap this time, Norman—armies to her foster brothers' land. And, no doubt, her being here would be a bad omen for this fortress as well. So he must not dally in sending word to his cousin that Branwenn was back in the Highlands. They must begin to plan immediately for reprisal.

But first, he must get her back to the keep....

* * *

When Callum at last entered her cave chamber, Branwenn stopped breathing and stood poker-straight, hoping he'd not see her in the dark corner, as the light of his taper would not travel much further past the place he now stood.

But, 'twas not to be, for the man must have the eyesight of a cat.

"Ah, 'tis *fey Mai*, my rescuing sea faery," he said, striding with clear purpose toward her hiding place. "I hoped I'd find you here, for you've something of mine I wish mightily to retrieve."

"Oh? And what *might* that be?" she asked cheekily, lifting her chin a bit.

"Why, the key to the locks, of course."

"'Tis payment for services rendered, sir. Do not you know that?"

Callum guffawed and set the candlestick holding the lit taper on the ground beside him. "That be a good one. And—I think not. Hand it over, please."

"Nay."

"Pardon?"

Branwenn cupped the sides of her mouth with her hands. "*I said, Nay!*"

Callum, his arms akimbo now, stumped another step toward her. "Give me that..."—'twas clear he wanted to use a vulgar word, but managed to restrain himself—"*key!*"

Branwenn mimicked his stance and boldly met the big brute toe-to-toe. She had to cock her head back so far to see his countenance, her neck cracked. "*Nay!* 'Tis mine." She had no idea why she felt the need to provoke him so, but, 'tis truth, the man had provoked her first with the arrogant way he'd called her *'fey Mai'*. And she was still a bit chafed by his initial scoffing remark this day past about the lovely name she'd chosen for herself.

A calculating look came into his devil-green eyes. He relaxed his stance and crossed his arms over his chest, the cane dangling from one hand as it rested against his side. "What recompense might I give you instead of the key?"

Branwenn wasn't expecting him to give up the fight so quickly. It unbalanced her. But in the next moment, the wheels in her mind were turning once more. It didn't take but another instant to come up with something so outrageous, so thoroughly unseemly, so devilishly, deliciously *wrong*, to tease the man with. And, if he actually met the challenge, 'twould round out her sketchy knowledge and answer the questions she'd been dying to have answered ever since seeing Bao and Jesslyn together at the waterfall last year.

"You must tell me, leaving naught out, how you make love to a woman, as well as how it feels to you...and to her." Her heart was pounding so hard, she felt her throat close up.

His voice thundered in clear shock and disbelief. "Are you insane?"

* * *

Callum couldn't believe he was giving Branwenn his secret carnal fancy. Telling this virginal lass—his cousin's, make that *behemoth* cousin's, adored wee foster sister—the sexual imaginings he'd coveted lo' these many years. But he was. And he was so hard now, he ached. But, the words continued to tumble from his lips as if he were under the spell of the mystical creature the lass pretended to be.

"And then, when I feel you come—"

"*Come?*" she asked softly, a little out of breath.

"Convulse with pleasure, feel as if you're going to

burst into a thousand points of flaming joy," he explained and then repeated, "When I feel you come against my mouth, taste the honeydew that drips from your sex, that prepares you for my invasion, then, only then, will I cover you with my body and push myself into you."

"And how will that feel to me? Will I like it?"

"Aye. But not at first. Nay, at first you shall feel the pain of the slender covering of inner skin that keeps you a virgin being ripped wide by my sex. And your canal will burn, sting from being stretched wide and forced to take something larger than itself inside it, from being plowed into and forced to accommodate me as I move in and out of it.

"But it won't hurt for long, I give you my promise. Only a few moments and then, suddenly, it will feel so good, just as my tongue had felt on it, in it. And before very long...you shall experience heaven once more. But this time, it will be so much more intense."

Branwenn's breath came harshly now; she heard the sound of her ragged breath echo in the cave and it shamed her. She tried to calm herself, tried to force her breathing to a more natural meter, but could not. "And how will it feel to you? Will it hurt at first for you as well?"

Callum chuckled. "Nay, it won't hurt. 'Twill feel perfect. Hot, juicy, so narrow it tugs the skin of my manhood. I'll have trouble keeping myself from finding release before you do. But when your new-tried canal's muscles begin to milk me of my seed, I'll fuck"—he couldn't believe he was using such course language with her, but something inside him impelled him to it—"you so hard, the head of my cock will pound against your womb. And by this time, you'll be so hot, so ready for release again, it will feel quite pleasing to you."

He shook his head and repeated, "Nay, 'twill not hurt me. What hurts a man is being as ready as I am right now and not finding release."

Branwenn, now past the point of rational thought, acted purely on instinct and reached out in the darkness to find his leg.

"What do you?" he asked sharply, anxiously.

"Sshh" she admonished, moving her hand up to the junction of his thighs.

"Branwenn," Callum croaked, but 'twas too late, she'd already grasped his manhood in her hand and begun to stroke him. 'Twas bigger, harder, than she'd expected. She could see now why it would hurt her at first to take him inside of her. The fact that he'd used her name, not that of the fey creature's, didn't dawn on her until much later.

Callum lay back and rested on his elbows, his head thrown back in ecstasy, without any cognizant thought. The feel of her tiny hands on his engorged manhood was the sweetest feeling he'd had in the longest time. Too long. Since...well, since before the night of his marriage to Lara. "That feels good," he ground out. Somewhere in the back of his mind he knew this was not right, that he would regret this later. But he had neither the will, nor the strength to stop this madness before 'twas too late.

Branwenn needed to touch his skin, feel the bare weight of him without the thin cloth of his braies in the way. She rose above him and quickly loosened the ties of the garment that covered his loins. When he was laid bare to her ministrations, she continued her manipulation of him; learning him, imagining what it looked like by the feel of it in her hand. For, he'd not allowed the taper to remain lit for this frank talk.

His sex was muscular she discovered, and smooth, the skin hot to the touch. And there was a pouch beneath it, covered in wiry hair, that she held for a moment in the palm of her other hand. There were strange orbs that seemed to float inside it.

Callum moaned and ground his hips. "Stroke me, up and down, in quick motions. And hold tight," he ordered, out of his mind now with the need to find release. "*Suck me*," he thought, not realizing he'd said it aloud, until he felt her lips on him. He jerked so hard, his hips came a foot off the ground. "Arghh!"

Branwenn smiled, a sense of pure feminine satisfaction invading her psyche. Now she knew what truly pleased him. She eased onto her knees between his thighs and took him in earnest with her mouth, licking and sucking him as she continued to caress and coddle him in her hands. She was determined to make him "come," as he called it.

A slightly salty musk-flavored substance gently emerged from the rounded head as she stroked upwards and she realized it must be the "seed" of which he'd just spoken.

Curious. And extremely heady. Was he coming

now? She didn't think so, for he didn't seem to be in that final state of ultimate delight he'd spoken of so baldly before.

All at once, he yelled out as his hips surged up, jamming his manhood deeper into her mouth. In the next instant, he violently erupted, the turgid muscles under the skin of his sex rippling against her tongue. Her eyes teared and she began to choke on the hot seed he spewed as it hit the back of her throat. She swallowed convulsively. *That was unexpected.* Afterward, when he'd settled, his breathing still harsh, but his body as limp as a damp cloth, she lifted her head and studied him. Gorgeous, pompous, Callum MacGregor.

Check-mate.

* * *

Callum sighed and opened one eye. Branwenn had the smile of a very satisfied feline plastered across her countenance. As well she should. For what she'd lacked in skill, he thought dazedly, she'd more than made up for in enthusiasm.

"You want me to do it again?" she asked. Surprisingly, there was eagerness in her voice.

He actually felt his manhood stir in response. This brought him up short and his sex-fogged brain instantly cleared. He had to get out of here. In seconds he was on his feet, sore ankle and bruised shoulder bedamned—besides, after the pleasuring he'd just received from this mite of a lass, he'd not be feeling pain for some time to come. "I'll return later this morn for the key," he said, stumbling away from her and re-tying his braies at the same time. Abashed and horrified at his own lack of self-restraint, he rushed from the cave chamber, without his cane and with nary a backward glance.

He was not more than twenty paces down the passage when he realized that this was not the best course of action where Branwenn was concerned. He had little doubt that she would be gone by morn, to who knew where, should he leave her to her own devices for long, especially after their lurid, erotic interlude.

He turned and aggressively moved in the direction he'd just come from. Hell, he'd no doubt find the chamber empty even now. What a fool he was! First to allow her to talk him into such a dangerously tempting dialogue and then to allow her to...to...well, to take him in that way. God! She was such an innocent! Even with all of his experience with the gentler sex—and he'd had a lot—he'd yet to meet one with so avid a curiosity and appetite to bring delight to him. 'Twas usually the other way around—and that was fine with him, for, as his erotic imagery he'd shared with her had shown, 'twas he who liked to do the pleasuring.

He'd just stumbled back into the front chamber when a blow landed with a harsh *'thwack'* across his cheek. "Ow! What the hell...?"

"You called me 'Branwenn'!" his lively, sharp-tongued tormentor accused loudly.

Callum rubbed his abused cheek and sighed. Damn. This—*this* was why he was an idiot. "Aye, and you were in my room—nay, in my *bed*—this morn when I awakened." He hoped that tidbit of a memory would startle her enough to give him time to come up with a way of getting her back to the keep without using manly force—a thing he was sadly, and shamefully, lacking ability in at the moment. For, tho' she was a wee thing, she had strength, and she'd no doubt claw and bite, kick and wriggle, the entire time he tried to keep her in his arms, were he to do the most efficient thing by heaving her over his shoulder and trudging back through the cave passage to the keep.

Nay, with his unstable walk and his sore shoulder—he still couldn't lift his arm very far—he'd drop her for sure. Or worse, fall on top of her and kill her with his weight.

"I was bathing your unworthy brow, you thankless, pompous curdog!" Branwenn said, at last finding her voice. "And, by the way, you're *welcome* for the clearly violently pleasurable 'release' I gave you a few minutes ago! And you forced me to swallow your seed—that can't be good for me! My stomach is all *burble*-y now."

Callum felt his cheeks burn. He'd never met another lass like this one. Such a bold tongue, but still so young, so innocent of men. She could get him riled and spitting iron nails within seconds of being in her presence. How could this be? He didn't even recognize himself when he was with her. For, 'twas a well-known fact, was it not, that he was the charming one, he was the affable one, *he* was the one all the ladies wanted to share company with? "I...*ahem*...I...uhhh..." Through gritted teeth, he released a very long sigh—and growl—of frustration. "Damnit, Branwenn, enough. You're coming back to the keep with me right now."

"Nay!" That silky, short-cropped, black-haired head of hers adamantly shook a negative.

"You can either gather your belongings now or get them later, I care not which." He guessed he'd be carrying her after all. And he *would not* drop her, he told his much abused body. Christ's Bones, but the lass was a menace.

* * *

An hour and a half later, just past dawn, Branwenn sat by the hearth in the solar with her Grandmother Maclean and Aunt Maggie. Though she was of no true relation to the two ladies, they'd taken her into their hearts and under their wings last summer and winter, and had insisted upon her calling them by those familiar epithets.

"And your brother Reys knows not where you are?" Lady Maclean asked, her brow furrowed in worry.

Branwenn shrugged. "I know not—I think not. For, 'twas only by the grace of God that I managed to stay afloat long enough to find land." She dipped her head and studied her tightly clasped hands, pressed deeply into her lap. "He no doubt believes me dead—if he knows of the wreck at all."

Maggie reached over and softly patted Branwenn's knee. "There, there, lass. You mustn't fret so, for we shall send a missive forthwith to inform him that you are safe and sound and living here with us."

Branwenn's head snapped up. Her eyes as round as saucers, she quickly shook her head. "Nay, you mustn't!"

"But, why ever not? Never tell me you wish to let

your poor brother mourn you for one moment longer than is necessary!" Maggie replied.

Lady Maclean, who had been silently watching and listening these past moments, interjected, "Maggie, let the lass get settled first before you hare off and send missives hither and thither. 'Twill be no great sin to wait another day or two, surely."

"Well...I suppose that is so," Maggie replied.

Branwenn relaxed. Thank heaven for Grandmother Maclean!

Maggie cleared her throat and resettled herself more comfortably on her stool. Picking up the discarded piece of embroidery she'd been working on until a few minutes past, she put another stitch in the cloth before lifting her head and drilling Branwenn with a penetrating stare as she asked, "So...'twas you who found my son in the cave this day past? You who helped him get back to the keep?"

"Aye, tho' 'tis truth, he did most of the work himself. I only got the locks and doors open."

"And you bathed his brow, forget not." Maggie reminded.

Branwenn sat forward, sure that that handsome devil of a son of Aunt Maggie's had opened his big gob and told the lady that she, the brazen Branwenn, had invaded his manly sanctuary the night before and gotten in bed with him. She now tried valiantly to explain. "I only wanted to see how he fared, Aunt Maggie," she said in a rush. "He was quite ill when I left him in the tower chamber. 'Tis only that I got weary from leaning over him as I cooled his skin with the damp cloth, that's why I rested beside him on the bed. I swear." Branwenn didn't realize it, but she thrust her lower lip out a bit when she continued in a mumble, "And anyway, that old Physician did naught but sleep the whole time I was there."

A cold chill crept up the back of her neck, making her scalp tingle as she at last noticed the stunned expressions on the faces of the two women who sat before her. *Damnation, Callum MacGregor, I hate your lily-livered, toad-eyed, bird-beaked, simple-minded self! You are the bane—the bane of my existence!* Branwenn couldn't help it, she squirmed. "*Ahem*...umm... Well, 'tis good that he recovered so quickly, do you not agree, Grandmother Maclean?"

The two ladies flashed a quick glance at each other, but thankfully must have decided to allow the change in topic, for Lady Maclean answered lightly. "Aye, lass. And God be praised 'twas not a poisoning plot of Laird Gordon's, as Callum first thought."

Branwenn's brows arched. "Truly? But who did the deed then?"

Maggie chuckled and Lady Maclean joined in. "'Twas the doing of a wee lad—one of the new pages in Laird Gordon's household—his nephew, in fact," Maggie told her.

"Why on earth would the lad have done such a horribly vile thing?"

"No, you misunderstand, Branwenn. 'Twas naught more than a wee—very, very wee—bit of pig offal"—

Branwenn slapped her hand over her mouth and laughed so hard she snorted.

—"that got stirred in Callum's wine which laid him so low."

Feeling much better now that she knew her nemesis had had such a fine blow to his overweening pride—especially after the way he'd manhandled her, slapped her on her bottom as he carried her here earlier, and *never thanked her* for the services rendered—she settled back with a sigh and calmly began a new set of stitches in the tapestry she was helping Grandmother Maclean to make.

* * *

Callum's shoulder was hurting with a deep, burning ache now as he paced the floor of his bedchamber. He might have made it back here without re-injuring the thing, had that smart-tongued lass not provoked his temper so thoroughly with her gibes and insults to his manhood that he'd actually forgotten the state of his shoulder and given her lovely *derrière* the much needed '*whack*' it deserved.

He'd not spoken with his stepfather yet, but he knew that Bao would need to be sent word of his foster sister's arrival forthwith. Why on earth was she here? That question had continued to plague him since he'd first recalled that 'twas her lovely black-lashed, violet cat-eyes that he'd awakened to this morn past. And her gentle hands that had cooled his fevered brow. And her wide mouth, with those fleshy pink lips, that had felt like warm silk stroking and encasing him as it took him to heaven.... He forcibly turned his mind from that arousing memory, but his thoughts remained on the complicated puzzle of her.

Lord, but she was such a tangled mix of vixen, virgin, and vexation. The treble V's. He had no doubt that she should be branded thus, to warn any unsuspecting man before he attempted to woo her and got castrated by the sharp edge of her tongue. Her tongue.... Callum shook the image clear.

Blood of Christ! He'd gone for so many moons without the touch of a feminine hand, and had managed quite well to keep his mind clear of such thoughts as he slowly, diligently, rebuilt his favorable repute amongst his clansmen. But now, after that incredible interlude, he couldn't seem to stay focused on the task at hand: to get the lass to her foster brother's keep as quickly as possible. Because his mind—his body—screamed for more of her. More of her mouth on him, but also, this time, more of his mouth, his hands, on her.

God, what would she taste like? Her skin was soft, he'd noticed that already. And there was a faint smell of roses in her cropped hair. The pleasant scent had drifted to him as he'd hauled her over his shoulder back at the cave. Aye, the flower of her womanhood no doubt had the heady scent of roses and...*woman*....

"Blood. Of. Christ! No more!" Callum yelled, lifting his good arm and scrubbing his hand across his eyes and face.

* * *

Branwenn's eyelids drooped and her chin dropped to her chest. "*What?*" she cried out, instantly waking when she nearly teetered forward and fell flat on her face.

"Lass, 'tis time and past for you to take a rest. We are not such a staunch lot that we would have you sacrifice your health to keep the appearance of piety," the young priest said.

"But, Father, I must finish my prayers first."

With a gentle smile and a dip of his head, he moved away from the altar where she knelt.

"Oh, Lord, just one more thing. Please do not allow my aunt and her husband to tell any of my brothers that I am alive, Lord. 'Tis not truly such a terrible lie, Lord, is it? Not if it could save their lives?" No response. Well, she wasn't exactly expecting one, but still. It would have been nice to know for sure that He was on her side in this matter. With a long sigh, she stood up and did a quick genuflection before scurrying from the MacGregor chapel.

She took her time going back into the keep, for her thoughts had not settled, as she'd hoped they would, by doing a bit of praying for forgiveness for her less-than-ladylike behavior this day. And she wasn't speaking of her arguments with that auburn-haired, too-handsome to look upon for long, devil-man, either—'twas the other thing that happened between them that now weighed so heavily on her conscience.

For, she'd not gone to the chapel originally to request aid from the Lord Almighty with her dilemma regarding her family. Nay, she'd gone there, contrite and filled with horror that she'd been so...so...well, so *brazen* with Callum—feelings that only recently took hold of her when she'd been obliged to sit beside the man at table and he'd remained so quiet, so indifferent toward her, that she had begun to suspect he was now disgusted by her. But she was not yet ready to reveal such a thing to the priest in order to do penance for it, so she'd decided upon a heart-felt prayer of forgiveness instead.

A momentary flash of sense memory involving Callum—and the feel of his invitingly bare nether regions against her palm—invaded her thoughts just then, but she forcefully closed her mind to it. What was it about that man that—she begrudgingly admitted to herself now—appealed to her so? Her heart had actually skipped a beat when he had walked into the great hall to break his fast a bit ago. And why did she have to start feeling guilty *now* for making him so mad that he hurt his shoulder again when he spanked her bottom? Why should she care if he was now unable to hold his wee motherless daughter?

But she did care. A lot.

* * *

"She's such a lovely, wee thing, Grandmother Maclean," Branwenn said softly the next day as she turned from side to side with Laire cradled and cooing quietly in her arms. "Aren't you, my wee apple blossom?"

Laire cackled, her arms and legs flailing wildly as her bright blue eyes twinkled up at Branwenn with delight.

"Aye, she's got her mother's look, but blessed be, not her temperament."

"Hmm. Even with all I know of Lara's behavior last *Hogmanay* at the Maclean holding, still I cannot believe that she actually *ran* from Callum—ran from this precious babe—'tis unpardonable in my estimation."

Lady Maclean sighed. "Aye, she was not a good match for our Callum, and would not have been a good mother to our Laire. Even so, 'twas a tragic end to her, which I would not have wished on her in any event."

"Mmm."

A glob of slobber trailed down the side of Laire's cheek, but Branwenn managed to catch it with the edge of the swaddling cloth she held in her hand before it made its way onto the sleeve of the borrowed—and rather cavernous—gown she wore. She brushed a kiss across the babe's warm brow and rested her lips there a moment as she breathed in the sweet babe-smell of the lass's skin. After a moment, she turned her head and said to Lady Maclean, "Must we swaddle her again? Surely, her limbs are not so fragile now that we must keep them bound to prevent deformity." She turned her eye back to the babe in her arms. "Just look, Grandmother, how happy Laire is to be free of those restraints!"

"Aye, but 'tis not my decision to make—'tis her father's. And my grandson is so careful with his daughter, making sure he follows every rule regarding the proper care of a babe, that I doubt he'll allow us to unswaddle her until she's another moon or more older."

"Well, I'm not going to do it. If he wants her bound up like a shank of mutton, then 'twill be he who can do the deed."

Callum, who'd been silently watching the exchange regarding the swaddlings from the opened doorway, his arms crossed over his chest and his good shoulder leaning against the jam, straightened and took a few steps into the chamber, saying, "Hand her to me."

Branwenn nearly jumped out of her skin. Whirling, she faced him, but held the babe tightly to her chest. "Not if you're going to do what I think you are going to do."

"And, what, pray, do you believe I'm going to do to the lass?"

"Roll her in this"—she waved the swaddling cloth in the air—"like some silkworm's casing."

"And, by what right do you take this stance with me—the babe's *father*?"

Her chin tilted high, she responded dryly, "By the right of all women, for 'tis well-known that we are born with the instincts for mothering."

"You call yourself 'woman'? Why, you're merely a lass. You know naught of the ways of tending bairns." Callum had no desire to swaddle his wee one again either, but the lass didn't have to know that, did she? "As I said, hand her to me."

Hot color washed over Branwenn's cheeks. He believed her callow, 'twas clear. Callow, but too brazen by far. Traits not highly regarded when looking for potential mates. "I am not, and I do, too," she mumbled, momentarily confounded for more cutting words to throw at him. In the next instant, the decision of the swaddlings was taken from her when the babe turned her head in Callum's direction and, clearly recognizing him, gave him a gummy, wet grin and squealed, "*Da!*"

A stunned, euphoric expression moved over Callum's countenance and, in a hitch-stepped rush, he strode up and took the babe from Branwenn's numb arms.

"*Callum!* Your shoulder!" Lady Maclean exclaimed, taking a step forward with her arms out as if to catch the babe should he drop her.

"Worry not, Grandmother, the shoulder's better this day."

Lady Maclean nodded and said, a bit doubtfully, "Aye, well be careful."

Callum nodded and turned his eye back to his grinning daughter. "'Tis the first time she's called me that," he said softly, a matching wide-mouthed grin moving across his own countenance. Until this very instant, he'd only understood in the vaguest sense how deep the emotion must have gone for his cousin, Bao, to have done all that he'd done to keep Branwenn safe all those years as he'd raised her. But now as he gazed down at Laire, he fully perceived the depth of that feeling; the reason why there had truly been no other choice for his cousin but to do as he'd done.

"'Tis more likely just wee babe sounds, as she's yet too young to speak in truth," Lady Maclean advised. When Callum only continued to grin down at his daughter, she continued, "Well, 'tis call for a feast in any case!" Her own smile beaming so brightly, it could have lit the darkest chamber, she said, "We must tell your mother and stepfather; they shall be thrilled."

Branwenn could not take her eyes from Callum. He was, without any doubt, the most gorgeous man she had ever seen. And what woman could resist a man who loved his bairn so much? She was in deep, deep, deep trouble. Is this what Bao feels for Jesslyn? What Daniel, her other foster brother, feels for Maryn, his wife? She was beginning to believe it was. God's Blood! 'Twas true! She *loved* the charming, green-eyed devil! And he, it had become clear to her these past two days—at least, since the morning meal this day past—wanted naught more to do with her. Ever again.

* * *

CHAPTER 4

OVER THE NEXT sennight, Branwenn managed to keep her distance from Callum, for her bruised heart could not take the coldness, the angry silence, of him. And not one of Branwenn's brothers had arrived, a thing she was exceedingly grateful for. Evidently, Grandmother Maclean had prevailed upon Laird and Lady MacGregor to give her a bit more time before her location was revealed to any of them.

Taking a nice, juicy *chomp* out of one of the apples she carried in her arm basket, she walked toward the training field. She was on a mission; one that, if she could have avoided it, she would rather have perished than do. But, 'twas Grandmother Maclean who had asked this of her and, after all that that fine lady had done for her these past moons, she could not say her 'nay'.

So, here she was, at the mouth of the lion's den—the training field where Callum now practiced—about to beard the lion.

As she scanned the field, she took another bite. Lord, but these apples were good. Many she'd eaten were rather sour—used mostly for cider—but these had a rather sweet, tho' still tart, flavor. Her eyes at last landed on the object of her errand and a slow, lethargic, heat moved through her veins, across her skin, weakening her knees. Her mouth's cavern, which still held the partially chewed bite of fruit, became as dry as the Holy Land desert.

Had he always been this *large*? Her mind scanned back to that first day they'd ever met, the day almost exactly a year ago, when Callum had come to the Maclean keep to request aid in mitigating a feud with the Gordons. Nay, while he'd certainly not been without muscle, his chest and shoulders had not seemed this broad. And although she'd noted some physical difference in him since she'd last seen him even this past *Hogmanay*, she'd had no notion just how much breadth he'd actually gained. Until now. For, who could miss the change in him with the man standing as he was, bare-chested, with only his braies between him and her—and full nakedness.

She only allowed herself one more fleeting moment of sensual enjoyment before she quickly finished consuming the bite of now-dry apple and waved to the man who'd been the other player in all her carnal daydreams—now that she knew, in detail, what to dream about—these past days, since their last encounter in the cave.

It took a minute, but she finally got Callum's

attention. He nodded to her and then turned and spoke to the man who'd been giving him direction as he carefully exercised his shoulder, before grabbing his shirt and tunic from the squire who'd been holding it and jogging over to where she stood.

He pulled his shirt on. "Aye?" he said, but with little inflection. The tunic came next. What a shame.

"Umm, Lady Maclean would like for you to"—she ran her tongue over her lower lip—Was there still some apple there? Why was he staring at her mouth, for heaven's sake?—"meet with her and your parents in the solar in a quarter-hour's time."

His eyes lifted to hers, but she could read no emotion in them. "All right."

They both turned and headed, in awkward silence, toward the keep. After a moment, Branwenn, all too aware of the man beside her, decided to take another bite of the apple she still held in her hand. Surely, this should make her seem unmoved by his nearness.

Callum watched her eat from the corner of his eye. He truly did not know how much longer he could keep up the pretense of indifference. When the hell was Bao going to get here, for Christ's sake? They'd sent the missive the day after he'd brought the lass here, but there was still no sign of her foster brother. Granted, it would have taken the messenger two days to get there, and even if Bao had waited to depart until the next day, he should have arrived no later than this day past.

Branwenn took a really big bite out of her apple, angry now at both herself and the vexing man beside her. A drop of juice ran over her lip and onto her chin and she swiped it away.

"You seem to be enjoying that apple," Callum said the words before he even realized he had opened his mouth.

Branwenn gave him a sour look, expecting him to make some snide comment about the mess she was making. When she discovered the pleasant smile on his face—a thing she'd not seen aimed at her since way before 'the interlude'—she relaxed and pulled another one out of her basket. Holding it out to him, she asked, "Would you like to try one? They are very good." 'Twas not much of a peace offering, but 'twas a start, she thought hopefully.

He laughed. "Nay, I much prefer watching you enjoy them."

Branwenn shrugged and, since she *was* still hungry and she'd finished the other one already, took a bite of her proffered fruit. Unfortunately, this one was even juicier than the first, and the sticky substance once more left drops on her lower lip. She hurriedly consumed the bite and then ran her tongue over her mouth to clean it.

"Damn it to hell! 'Tis too much!" Callum said under his breath.

In the next instant, she was crowded against the shadowed side of a stone wall—were they already to the chapel?—and jailed between Callum's massive arms as he rested his palms on the cool stone to either side of her head. Without any further warning than that, he kissed her. And, Good Lord in Heaven, what a kiss it was! There was little gentleness in it, only hunger. He wouldn't allow her to keep her lips closed. His tongue invaded her, ran over her teeth, delved deep—like he said he'd do to her...down there? He took her bottom lip between his teeth and nibbled before soothing it with the most erotic suction she'd ever imagined.

At some point, her limbs had gone numb and she vaguely realized that the basket of apples had dropped to the ground. Tentatively, she put her arms around this so-handsome, massive man that now boldly kissed her, testing the feel of him there.

He lifted his mouth a fraction from hers and murmured, "God, I shouldn't be doing this." But he didn't step away. Nay, instead, he answered her action with one of his own. He brought his arms down and wrapped them tightly around her shoulder and waist, lifting her up until her pelvis was fused with his. Good Lord, he was as 'ready' as he had been the other day! Did that mean he wanted to mate with her now? The thought both frightened and excited her. "*Branwenn*," he whispered, his lips, his warm, moist breath, fluttering like dove's wings against her cheek. A thrill ran down her spine. He'd said her name as if it were a benediction. Her womanhood spasmed. She turned her head and brushed her lips across Callum's, not really sure what she was doing.

But he knew. And in seconds, he was ravishing her mouth again with his lips, with his teeth and his tongue.

Her thoughts became fragmented as an aching need infused the apex of her torpid lower limbs. She wanted...she wanted...her hand traveled down between them and began to caress the long, turgid, length of him.

He froze, his muscles taught, and then he let go of her as if he'd been burned, stumbling back a pace. His eyes were dilated to such a degree, they looked like black agates instead of green emeralds, and his breathing now was so harsh that his shoulders bobbed like waves with the struggle to put air in his lungs. "Stay as far away from me as you are able until your brother comes to get you," he demanded darkly.

There was anger in his voice—at her? This brought her own hackles up. "Pardon me, Your Highness, but 'twas not *I* who did the shoving-up-against-a-wall and kissing just now, if you recall! And I *have* been staying away from you, you bleating goat! I only spoke to you this day because that fine lady in there,"—she jabbed her finger in the direction of the keep—"your grandmother, asked me to do this favor for her and, after all she's done for me, I could not refuse."

* * *

"Do you think our ploy worked, Mama?" Maggie asked. The two of them were sitting in the solar, waiting for Callum to arrive.

A calculating gleam came into the older woman's eye as she nodded and said, "Aye, and mayhap a bit better than we had hoped. For you know your son well, and only one thing could keep him from arriving on time when he's in the company of a female." Her brow furrowed. "Tho' I do hope he doesn't take advantage of Branwenn's rather bold, inquisitive nature."

Maggie patted her mother's knee. "Worry not. We've raised a fine man—an honorable man. If aught unseemly takes place between them, 'twill not be long before he'll be wanting to wed the lass." She smiled slyly. "And, is that not just what we desire for them?"

Lady Maclean sighed. "Aye, it is. Tho' I cannot help worrying that she's not seen the last of that fiendish Norman she was betrothed to wed."

Maggie looked at her in surprise. "That seems unlikely. For, how ever is he to learn she is here with us? Surely, they will only think to look for her at the Maclean holding. And possibly the MacLaurin holding, since her other foster brother is living back there now."

Lady Maclean nodded. "Aye, and if they do go to Daniel's land, his fortress is so strong, the Normans are sure to not gain entrance should they attack."

With a wave of her hand, Maggie said, "Besides, surely her brother-germane will not let leak the fact that Branwenn survived the shipwreck."

"Nay, my impression of the young man when I met him last *Hogmanay* was that he cared for Branwenn even before he ever met her. Nay," she said again, "Reys will do all he must to keep those tidings from ever reaching the man's ears."

"Aye, and in the meantime, just in case, if the lass is well-wed by the time the Norman arrives..."

Lady Maclean met her daughter's eye and nodded. "Precisely."

* * *

Bao arrived with little ceremony the next morn. But he did have some surprising tidings to share: Daniel would be meeting them here as well.

"When is he to arrive?" Lady Maclean asked. She,

her daughter, Laird MacGregor, and Callum were all gathered in the great hall and seated on benches around the hearth.

Bao shrugged. "I expect he shall be here on the morrow, or the next day at the latest."

"Pardon, but I ken you not," Callum said, glancing around at all gathered. "Why must Daniel meet you here? Surely, 'twould be better for him to meet you at your own fortress once you and the lass arrive back there."

Bao looked at Laird MacGregor in confusion, saying, "Am I misinformed? I thought the missive said that you would keep Branwenn here with you, as a safety, until we know for sure what Gaiallard de Montford's plan may be."

"*What!* Nay, nay, this is not a good idea," Callum protested, rising to his feet and walking over to the buttery. A very hard lump formed in the pit of his stomach, for he now knew his doom was drawing near, and he needed a drink of something with a bit of spirit to numb the horror.

"Now, Callum, of course 'tis a good idea. Gaiallard de Montford has no knowledge of this clan's close ties to the Macleans and would not think to look for the lass here," Lady Maclean reminded him.

He took a long swallow of *uisge beatha* before replying, "Aye, you are right. I hadn't thought the thing through. Pray pardon me." He would only make himself look further the fool by giving argument to such a sound scheme. And there was also the dreaded possibility that he might let slip exactly *why* he was so loath for the lass to remain here—he wanted her desperately. But, mayhap, that might be the better plan—for, if he allowed Bao to see the danger to his sister's virtue that he presented, then Bao would kill him, and the problem would be solved. Except, he had a bairn to raise. God's teeth! What the hell was he going to do?!

The conversation had gone on without him for the past seconds as he pondered his predicament, and he was brought up short when Laird MacGregor asked, "Do you not agree, Callum?"

"Pardon? Pray pardon me, I was thinking of something else," he said. He felt his cheeks flush. Damn it to hell! He no doubt looked like some callow youth to all of them.

Lady Maclean and Maggie glanced at each other and shared a silent, delighted, communion before hastily sobering their countenances and turning their sights back on Callum. "Your stepfather thinks it best that you train with Bao and Daniel, in case another siege is in the offing," Maggie said. "We will be the last line of defense, should this happen, for we shall send our army to come in from behind to attack the aggressors. And your stepfather—and Bao—want you to lead that assault. But Bao and Daniel have had more years' warring experience than you, and they have much in the way of cunning to teach you."

Callum turned to Bao. "So, you and Daniel will be staying on here awhile?"

"Aye. But we cannot be away from our clans—or our wives and babes—for too long a time. I will no doubt stay a bit longer than Daniel, for I've a need to spend time with my sister. I've missed her." He craned his neck toward the door. "Where *is* the lass, anyway. I thought sure she'd have flown in on winged feet the moment I arrived." There was a bit of hurt in his voice, Callum noticed.

Lady Maclean patted her grandson on his knee. "She knows not that you've arrived. In fact, she knows not that we even sent word to you that she is here. The lass was so set on keeping all her brothers safe from that loathsome Norman, that she wanted us not to reveal her whereabouts—even to Reys. But we thought that more cruel than kind to allow the poor lad to grieve, in case he believes she perished in the sea, so we sent word to him as well."

"What did this Norman do to her?" Bao ground out. "If he touched one hair on her head in anger, he will die by my sword."

"Nay, 'tis naught like that. But 'tis a tale that you should hear from Branwenn's lips, not ours," Laird MacGregor intoned.

* * *

An hour later, Bao at last found his wayward sister. He jogged across the bailey toward the well where she now stood, looking down its dark, black hole, with the most familiarly sweet look of bewilderment on her countenance. What had the lass gotten herself into now? he thought with a grin. "Branwenn!"

Branwenn looked up and over her shoulder. Joy and wonder spread across her elfin face, immediately followed by dark thunder clouds of vexation. "Bao!"

she said, storming toward him "What do you here?" 'Twas an accusation, not a question.

"I missed you, too, mite!" Bao said jovially, ignoring her angry outburst, as was his usual way. "Have you no other gowns? Surely, two of you could fit in this thing!"

"'Tis Aunt Maggie's. And I like it!"

He lifted her in his arms and swung her around. "Well, we shall have to get some made for you, then."

"*Eeek!* Put me down! Else this morn's meal will be this noon's tunic dye!"

Bao dropped her to her feet so quickly, she nearly toppled onto her behind. He bent his knees and looked her straight in the eye. "Are you with child?!"

"*Nay!*" Branwenn's cheeks flamed. "Why ever would you think such?"

"You wear overlarge clothes and just said you were going to lose the contents of your stomach! Pray, what else should I think?" Bao stood straight once more.

Branwenn rolled her eyes. "Lord, but you can be so witless sometimes. How ever does Jesslyn stand it?"

Bao crossed his massive arms over his even more massive chest and gave her his most charming grin. "That, mite, is something for me to know and for you to *never* find out."

She stuck her tongue out at him. "Ha! Ha! I already know. Do you not remember? I *saw* the two of you at the waterfall!" Branwenn bit her lip. Hard. Now why had she reminded him of that? Mayhap, 'twas *she* who was the witless one.

Bao's eyes narrowed. "I thought we agreed to never speak of that again. God knows, the horror of the thought of it still has the ability to make me cringe." A calculating look came into his eye. "Unless, you are simply looking for a good pounding on your behind—which I never gave you, though 'twas richly deserved. And as vexed as I am now, 'twould no doubt be pleasant for me."

Branwenn backed away a step, her hands covering the extremity in question. "Nay," she said, shaking her head, "no need."

Bao laughed. Hard. So hard, he actually slapped his knee a few times. "You are so easy to tease!" He came up to her and wrapped his arms around her. "Lord, how I've missed you."

Branwenn melted, both physically and emotionally. Her eyes welled with tears and she threw her arms around her brother and held tight, with all her might, relaxing all her weight into him. "I...mmm...missed...you toooo! So much!"

They stood thus for several long, silent moments, until Bao at last spoke. "Tell me what happened in Cambria," he said softly. "Why are you here, and not wed to the Norman, as your princely cousin was so set for you to do?"

Branwenn sniffled. "Gaiallard de Montford is..."

"Aye?"

"Base, vile."

"Aye, as all Normans are," Bao said, still waiting to hear what had caused her to flee the man.

Branwenn looked into her brother's eyes, shaking her head. "Nay, I *truly mean* base and vile. He beat his sister—regularly, evidently—and...Bao"—The words rushed out of her—"I think he was bedding her against her will."

Bao released her suddenly and stumbled back. He turned and raised his fists in the air and bellowed, "The man will *die*!"

Branwenn hurried over to him and placed her hand on his shoulder. "Bao, there's no need. I am safe, as you see."

He was silent for long seconds. His voice was low, so low that Branwenn strained to hear the words when he spoke. "Aye, but his sister is not."

Branwenn stepped around him to face him once more. "Oh, but she is! Reys has wed her by now and gotten her far from that fiend of a brother of hers."

Bao gave her a quizzical look. "How is that?"

"Why, do you not recall that the contract, as writ, said that either the nephew or the *niece* of the Earl of Pembroke could fulfill the terms." She frowned and dipped her head. "Sadly, we learned upon our arrival that Reys's wife and bairns had been killed in a fire at the convent they'd been visiting while he was prisoned in our tower during the seige."

"That is gloomful news indeed, little one." He brought her chin up with the tips of his calloused fingers. "Tell me the rest of it, then."

She shrugged. "Well, as Reys is also cousin to Prince Llywelyn, and Alyson is the Earl's niece...Reys agreed to wed her and aid me in my escape of the Norman's clutches."

* * *

"It looks as tho' she's managed to soothe his wrath,

at least," Lady Maclean said to Callum as they looked out the solar window down into the bailey.

"Aye. I wonder what she said to him to get him so roused. I've never seen Bao lose his temper to that degree. He is always so methodical, so in control. Or, at least, that is how it has always seemed to me. Even when we've trained together, he never shows anger, never allows his feelings to hinder his fighting tactics. I've admired him for that." His eye traveled to Branwenn. "Although, 'tis truth, that lass could try the patience of the saints."

Lady Maclean smiled, but didn't look at her grandson. How long, she wondered, until they could begin planning the wedding? 'Twould be nice to have one by Michaelmas, but she was no doubt rushing things a bit. "Well, they must have finished their talk, for here Bao comes. I hope he remembers that he is to meet me here in the solar."

"What the hell does that vexing creature think she's doing now?" Callum ground out.

She did look at him then. Well, mayhap Michaelmas was not too soon, after all.

Callum turned and strode out the door.

Lady Maclean chuckled. He hadn't even said farewell. 'Twas not like her smoothly charming grandson, in the least. Aye, Michaelmas was a good time for a wedding.

* * *

Branwenn leaned over the edge of the well. If only she could reach just a wee bit more, she'd be able to grasp the edge of the bucket and get her filet untangled from the rope. 'Twas the task she'd been set to do before her brother had come upon her a bit ago. She had no idea why she cared to get the thing out, as, 'twas a fact that she felt awkward wearing it. For the ornament only helped stress the horrid state of her hair. But, retrieve the thing, she would.

She stretched her arm down as far as it would go, the tip of her toes barely touching the ground beneath them, and was able to wrap her fingers around the circular metal ring. "At last!"

"*What, by all that is holy, do you think you are doing?*" Callum thundered.

Branwenn nearly leapt out of her skin. "*Aieee!*" The filet dropped from her hand. In seconds, it landed with a dim splash in the water way down below. Scrambling up straight, and with her heart still pounding in her ears, she turned to the man behind her and growled, "Now, see what you've done? That was my only filet, you dim witted, offal-swilling—that, as a reminder of his recent misadventure—arse!"

Callum just stared at her with his arms crossed over his chest.

"Well? How am I ever to get my filet back now?"

His tone level, he asked her, "Do you have no sense?"

"I? *I* have no sense?" She sputtered. "'Tis you who has no sense. Why would you think it a good plan to *startle* a person who was so clearly near to being off balance already?"

"And why would a person think it a good plan to allow herself to get in that position in the first place, *over a very deep WELL!"*

Branwenn crossed her arms over her chest, unconsciously mirroring his stance. "You, you, *jackanapes!"*

Callum just glared at her. He felt the heat of anger wash over his cheeks. Provoked now, his smile mocking, he retorted, "I can think of a much better use for—" *that sharp tongue of yours.*

"For what?" she asked angrily.

"For...umm...the well." He said the first thing that came to mind, and instantly regretted it. *The well?* What an idiot.

Branwenn gave him the same look he would have given himself, had he been able to, and whirled around, turning her back on him. Her arms crossed, she said haughtily, "This is truly no concern of yours. Why don't you go back to whatever it was you were doing before you came upon me here."

"Pardon, but you *are* my concern."

Branwenn's heart skipped a beat as the brightest joy she'd ever felt burst from the center of her soul and rushed through her veins.

"You are the concern of every one of us here, at least until we know the danger of a siege has passed."

And evaporated into the blackest pit of despair. "Oh," she replied in a small voice. Her vision grew liquid as her eyes misted with tears. She quickly blinked them away. She'd be consigned to the hottest, fieriest, depths of hell before she'd let him see how his words had affected her.

"Oh? That's all you have to say? No bitter censure,

no foul epithets to throw at my head?"

Branwenn bowed her head. "Nay. Just go away, Callum," she said softly. "Or, have you forgot that I'm to stay as far away from you as is possible?"

Callum's short sense of victory, *plunk*ed like a lead ball into the pit of his stomach as it suddenly dawned on him that he'd hurt her feelings. He stared at her for another moment and then, striding to the well, he said gently, "Let me see if I can get the thing out of the water using the bucket."

"'Tis surely sunk by now." Branwenn took in a deep breath and released it on a sigh. "'Tis no use, the filet is gone for good now."

"How did it get in there in the first place?"

Branwenn shrugged, her cheeks heating as his eyes settled on her face. "It slipped from my head when I was hauling water up."

"Then, 'twas not a well-fitted one, anyway."

Branwenn shook her head. "Nay, 'twas the one Grandmother Maclean gave me upon my arrival at the Maclean holding last summer. But—'twas the only one I've ever owned." Except, she thought, the one she'd made of seashells, which resided now at the bottom of her clothing chest in her bedchamber.

This took Callum by surprise. Filets were standard hair ornaments for lasses nearly from the time they were first out of their swaddling clothes. "Bao didn't have any made for you, when you lived in Perth?"

"Nay. He was busy in his obligation to the King. He cared little for ladies' fashions, but made certain I was never without a warm hearth, good food, and all the other essentials in life.

"I'm sorry I startled you and made you lose your piece of jewelry."

Branwenn shrugged self-consciously. "I'm sorry I called you a dull-witted, offal-swilling arse. 'Twasn't true. Well, except for the offal-swilling part—"

"Hey!"

"Well, I know you didn't do it on purpose, for heaven's sake!" she said, getting a bit of her spirit back.

"Come on, let us return to the keep, for I'm sure your brother will want to spend a bit more time with you before I head with him to the training field."

Branwenn settled into step beside him and they walked in a surprisingly companionable silence to the keep.

* * *

An hour later, Callum knocked on the door of his mother's bedchamber.

"Enter!" Came a muffled female voice from the other side of the dark wooden portal.

Callum took in one last deep breath and let it out slowly before turning the handle and walking inside the chamber. "Good morn, Mother. How fare you? I worried when I learned that you'd come up to your room to rest that you've grown ill again—have you?"

Maggie gave her son a gentle smile and shook her head. "Nay, fear not. I'm well—only just a bit weary from not getting enough rest this night past." With a quick look to see where her maid was standing, she sat a bit forward and, giving him a conspiratorial look, whispered, "Your stepfather snores like a bear!"

Highland Magic

Callum chuckled. "Ah, I see. Well, that gives my mind ease, then." He walked up to where she sat by the hearth and took a seat beside her. After a moment, he cleared his throat. "Those are fine tapestries," he said casually, tipping his head in the direction of the wall on which they hung. "Did you sew them?"

Maggie's eyes narrowed, her gaze shrewd as she studied him. "What did you truly come here to see me about, my son?"

There was a long pause and then: "Do you recall, when Grandmother MacGregor passed, that in her trousseau—the one she bequeathed to me—there was a...um...ahem...a...um—"

"Aye? Crave you something from the trousseau, Callum?" Praise be! Maggie thought. He was going to ask her for the betrothal ring, she just knew it! Her mother was going to be thrilled that their plan was moving along more quickly than they'd ever dreamed.

Callum fought the urge to squirm. There was a distinct twinkle in his mother's eye. No doubt, she found this highly amusing. She probably thought he was going to give one of his amours (of which there were no longer any) a token of his regard. But his purpose was far different. Callum cleared his throat again. This had to be the most humiliating thing he'd ever had to do. But his mind was made up and he would complete the task at hand—and it mattered not how much a love-struck fool he would look to his mother. "Aye, I'd like the gold filet. May I have it?"

His mother slumped a bit on her stool. "The gold filet? Aye," she said, less enthusiastically than before, which surprised Callum, but he couldn't think of what else she'd been hoping he'd be asking her for, "you may have it." She rose and walked to the far corner of her bedchamber and opened a large chest. After moving the swaths of silk aside, she found the velvet pouch that held the filet and then walked back to where Callum sat and handed it to him. "Here, I believe this is the one you are wanting."

Callum untied the string and loosened the opening of the pouch before slowly sliding the golden circlet out. He held it up to the light of the hearth. Aye, this would do. 'Twasn't the most ornate of hair ornaments he'd ever seen, but 'twas certainly of higher quality than the one the lass had been given by his grandmother. "My thanks, Mother." He stood abruptly and placed a kiss on her cheek. "I shall see you at dinner, no doubt." And then he was off, giving her no chance to question him on his reasons for wanting the piece of jewelry.

He couldn't say why it bothered him so that the lass had had so little of the finer, feminine things growing up, while he'd had access to as many as he'd ever wanted to bestow upon this lady or that, but it did. It did bother him. And it helped not his sore conscience to know that he'd been the one to cause her to irrevocably lose the only one she'd ever owned—the one she'd very nearly killed herself trying to retrieve earlier that morn.

He hurried back to his room and fetched the gord he'd so diligently looked for earlier by using his hands to measure the size, holding it just as he'd done with that silken hair-covered head of hers during those long, intense minutes in the cave when she'd pleasured him. Then he quickly settled the filet around its round mass to measure the size of the band. 'Twould need to be made smaller, just as he'd suspected. Turning, he strode from the chamber and took off toward the smith's cot. Since there were no craftsmen about that could take the amethysts from his squire's ring and, using the gold from it, set them in the filet, he'd have to make do with whatever skill the smith could lend to the task.

A quarter hour later, the errand completed, he was off to the training fields to no doubt have his body broken with the strain of vigorous exercise by his cousin Bao.

* * *

When Branwenn returned to her chamber after supper many hours later the most lovely gold-filigreed filet she had ever seen, having three small, oval, amethyst stones inset in the design, lay resting on a bed of dark red rose petals atop her pillow.

After trying it on and finding that it fit her perfectly—Was this from Callum? How could he have known the size? And where had he gotten hold of it so soon after their talk?—she placed it back in its resting place on the pillow.

That night, she slept with her hand wrapped around the offering. 'Twas the first gift she'd ever been given from (she hoped) a potential swain.

* * *

CHAPTER 5

"YOU HAVE THE look of your mother," Bao said to Branwenn the next day as they walked toward the stables. They were set to take a ride to the seashore. "Tho' she was a bit rounder than you when I knew her—for she carried you in her belly at the time. And your features are quite similar to hers. Lord, those eyes..." he said.

"Aye, you've told me of my resemblance to her often. I wish I could have known her." Branwenn halted her stride and, turning to Bao, she took his hand and held it, saying, "Did she want me—love me?"

Bao lifted his other hand to her cheek and stroked it gently. "Aye, she did. She didn't want to leave you—fought hard, in fact, to stay alive for you." He sighed. "But, alas, in the end, she lost the struggle. And when I saw how sweet, how fragile, you were, I knew I would do aught that I must to keep you alive, safe from harm. And I did just that. I pray you don't hate me for what I did." Though they'd had a similar conversation the day she'd departed for Cambria, Bao still worried that his sister was repulsed by the degree to which he'd sunk into the depths of human depravity in order to raise her.

Branwenn threw her arms around her brother, holding tight. "Nay! How could I hate you? You sacrificed so much for me. I *love* you."

Bao craned his head back and looked at her more closely. "That's a fine-looking hair thing you've got perched up there, lass. Where did you get such a handsome piece? Did Reys give it to you?"

Branwenn shook her head. "Nay, actually..."—she lifted her hand to the filet and ran her fingers over it lightly—"I believe 'twas Callum that gave me this."

"*Callum!*" 'Twas an accusation.

Branwenn's head whipped up and around. "Nay, 'tis not what you think," she hoped she lied. "He only meant to replace the one he accidentally made me lose down the well this day past."

Bao's eyes narrowed as he studied the sheepish look on his wee sister's countenance. There was definitely more here than met the eye. Mayhap a very brief, very *serious*, talk with Callum would be prudent at this juncture.

"Aye," he said letting the matter drop for now.

* * *

Daniel was in the great hall, enjoying a draught of ale and a bit of cheese when Branwenn and Bao came through the door several hours later.

"Daniel!" Branwenn said excitedly, running straight

into his open arms. "'Tis so good to see you! How is Maryn, how is Nora, how are your clansmen?"

"You give *him* the greeting *I* should have received this day past?" Bao said, interrupting the loving reunion. "'Tis *I* who raised you, whelp, not he."

Branwenn gave him a slight shrug with a wink and smile attached. It didn't escape her notice, either, that Daniel's answer to that was a smug grin pointed directly in his brother's direction. His words were to Branwenn, however. "'Tis good to see you, too, my wee *sister*—this as a poke to Bao's pride—and Maryn and our babe are fine, as well as all my clansmen." He stood back, his hands on her shoulders as he put her at arms length and did a quick perusal of her from head to foot. "You're just as beautiful as ever, wee one,"—Branwenn felt her cheeks pinken with pleasure—"but 'tis truth, you need a haircut and a new gown."—Now her cheeks turned hot with the flame of mortification—"Why ever has Grandmother not seen to this yet?" 'Twas an accusation clearly directed fully upon his brother.

Bao shrugged, a bit sheepishly. "I asked her not." He turned his gaze on Branwenn. "Branwenn? Has Grandmother made arrangements for some other clothes to be made for you?"

Branwenn bowed her head and nodded, saying in a small voice, "I believe the gowns will be ready soon."

"And your hair? You cut it again, I see."

Touching the strand of bangs lying to the right of her brow, she answered defensively, "Aye, 'twas the best way to travel—I traveled as a lad these past moons."

Highland Magic

Bao shook his head. "Can you believe, my sister had hair whose tips brushed her calves the summer we hid in the Maclean cave."

"Aye, and now I've hair like a lad." No wonder Callum thought her young—why, he'd even called her 'laddish'. Mayhap, he hadn't given her the filet as a token of his regard, but truly as a salve to his guilty conscience for startling her and making her lose the thing.

Daniel, seeing her crestfallen countenance, hugged her to him, saying, "But you still look like a beautiful lass." He shot a look at Bao that said, *"We must find her a new dress. Now."*

* * *

Callum sat facing his two cousins in the solar an hour later. Tense and uncomfortable as hell, with the two men's eyes drilling into him, he forced himself not to squirm on his stool. "I tell you, I only gave the thing to her as a replacement for the one I made her drop in the well when I startled her. 'Twas naught else behind the gift, I swear." But even he knew that was a lie. There was more to that gift than simply a soothing of the conscience. Why else had he been so impelled to have the amethysts—the same shade as her eyes—set in the ornament? Why else had he gone to the gardener and paid the man for one of his rare red roses?

Daniel's eyes were shrewd as he assessed his nervous cousin. "I told you this year past that the lass is too young for you but, if you are wooing her in earnest...well,"—he briefly turned his gaze on Bao before returning it to his cousin—"'twould certainly be a better match than she and the Norman."

Callum's cheeks warmed, and clearly, Bao noticed, for he drawled, "Aye, 'twould be better to have her here—even with a callowling such as yourself,"—Callum swallowed a growl, but shot Bao a venomous look, which only made his cousin grin—"than to have her off in a foreign land, and in the Norman's bed."

The knot in Callum's belly tightened and his teeth ground together, but he managed to keep his angry retort to himself. How could her own brother speak of such? Her. In bed. With the Norman. This did not sit well, but he'd be damned if he'd take the bait—for bait it most definitely was. So, he said in as even a voice as he could manage, the truth, as he knew it. "I have a daughter now. Mayhap, this year past, I did have an idea of wooing your sister, but the events since that time have altered my course." He leveled his gaze on Daniel. "She *is* too young. I need someone capable of mothering my daughter—and Branwenn, tho' a...ahem...well—mayhap 'sweet' is not the word, but kind-hearted, certainly—lass, is as callow as you accuse me of being. I cannot take that risk." Needing to steer the conversation far from this very uncomfortable topic, he decided to take the offensive, specifically directing it to Bao. "Why the hell did you never give the poor lass a filet, for Christ's sake? Every lass above the age of five has one. How cold-hearted can you be?" He stood and began to pace, now truly riled as he recalled this bit of Branwenn's history. "Why, if you'd only seen how avid she was to retrieve that pitiful excuse for jewelry! I swear she was more in than out of that well, her toes barely still touching the ground beneath."

His ploy must have worked, because when he turned back to the two massive warriors, they were both silent and had the most perfectly amusing sets of guilty expressions on their countenances that Callum had ever seen.

Daniel and Bao looked at each other and with a shrug, they rose to their feet and spoke at once.

"—Well, if that's all there was to it..." Daniel said.

"—Aye, I should have gotten the lass a filet..." Bao said.

Relief washed over Callum. He'd just barely—just *barely*, dodged the dart.

* * *

"Oh! Grandmother Maclean! This is so lovely." Branwenn looked up from the carmine velvet gown she held lovingly in her hands into Lady Maclean's eyes. "But this is much too fine for me. I…I feel"—she shrugged self-consciously and touched her fingertips to her cropped hair—"odd wearing such fine things."

Lady Maclean stroked Branwenn's flushed cheek. "You are a lady nonetheless, and must apparel yourself as such. I'm sure, in time, you shall grow accustomed to the finery. Practice. Practice is what is needed. And this night, this gown, shall be a good start."

She dipped her head and nodded. "Aye, 'tis truth that I've admired fine things, but now…now that I have the opportunity to wear them…." She shrugged again. "'Tis only that I thought I'd have a bit more time before I had to…well, I thought the clothes would not be ready for another sennight." She lifted her gaze to

Lady Maclean's. "How were we able to get this one so soon?"

Lady Maclean did not miss the note of disappointment tinging the question and gave her foster granddaughter a gentle smile of encouragement. "Truth be told, lass, 'twas your brothers who, shall we say, 'twisted the clothier's and then the tailor's arm a bit and made them finish this one, and the chemise, for the feast we're having this afternoon."

A look of chagrin crossed Branwenn's face. "Aye, I can only imagine Daniel and Bao would not want me showing up to a feast held in their honor looking like a beggar."

Lady Maclean put her arm around the lass's slumped shoulders. "Now, you surely know that they care not for such—'tis your sweet countenance and loving nature they crave to be near. But, they understand how important it is for a young lass to have pretty things." She placed a kiss on the crown of Branwenn's head. "They did this because they love you, and I ordered the thing made for you for the same reason. We love you, lass."

Branwenn's face crumpled and she threw her arms around Lady Maclean's neck, crushing the gown between them. "My many, many thanks. Lord, how I missed you!" she said thickly.

Lady Maclean held her for a time. What a sweet, sensitive lass Bao had raised. He'd done well. "There, there, dear. Dry your tears, or 'twill surely make your brothers believe I beat you!"

Branwenn giggled and brushed her thumb under her

eyes to swipe away the moisture. Clearly feeling much better now, she drew away from Lady Maclean and said, "You should have seen how humorless, how pompous all those Norman's are, Grandmother! I *loathed* eating in the hall with them. They all looked down their noses at me—even the old, doddering goats—as if I were some poor relation or some such."

Lady Maclean patted Branwenn's hand. "Well, you are back home now where you belong." And, if she had anything to say about it, the lass would be well-wed and carrying Callem's babe under her heart long before that Norman swine ever stepped foot on Highland soil—if that turned out to be his plan. "Now, let's get this on you, lass. 'Twill be a fine foil for those lovely amethyst stones in the filet Callum gave you."

Branwenn hadn't thought of that. "Aye, 'twill!" she said, hurrying behind the screen to change into her new cream-colored chemise with the intertwining carmine rose-and-purple violet stitched border, the stems of which were the exact color of Callem's eyes. She swallowed a sigh. Would he think her pretty in the new gown? She prayed so. Mayhap, he would even ask her to dance with him after dinner, when the pipers played. A thrill of excitement ran up her spine. *Callum.*

She hurriedly drew the chemise over her head and tied the lace at the neckline into a bow. Hmmm. It certainly was a bit tighter than she was used to. And much lower than she thought proper, only just covering the rise of her breasts. *Oh, God, did it hide the ugly freckle?* Her heart raced as she frantically inspected the garment and how it covered her. She let out a sigh of relief. Aye,

aye, it did. But, mayhap, the tailor had been in a hurry and had not cut it properly. She shrugged. It certainly wasn't low enough to ruin it for use. Then came the gown. After settling it over her breasts and hips, she skillfully tied up the laces on the sides of the garment. This was when true alarm set in. She peeked around the screen at Lady Maclean. "Grandmother!" Her voice cracked with disappointment. "The gown doesn't fit properly; it's much too small in the bodice!" The material fit snugly under and around her bosom, lifting it up a bit and *smoosh*ing the two white mounds together.

Lady Maclean smiled gently, but inside she was doing mad cartwheels. "Nay, lass, it fits as 'twas designed to do. Is this your first lady's gown, then?"

Branwenn blushed. "Nay...," she said, thinking of the one Gaiallard had given her, which had been one of his sister's, and had not fit so well. Mayhap that didn't count, then? "Aye, aye...I suppose it is," she said, still unsure 'twas properly fitted. But, recalling the fine ladies at the Earl of Pembroke's castle, her mind settled. Aye, there had been much more skin displayed by them than she was used to seeing. Mayhap, 'twas truly the fashion. She shrugged again. "Well...if you think it won't make my brothers angry...."

"Why, lass, why ever should it? 'Twas they that brought it back here for you after all." She quickly crossed her fingers behind her back. 'Twasn't that much of a lie, was it? After all, 'twas all for a good purpose. A wedding. And soon.

* * *

Branwenn was the first to arrive in the great hall an hour later—or, she thought she was, until she saw Callum step from behind the screen to the buttery with a tankard of ale in his hand.

His eyes did a quick sweep of her and his brows slammed together. He strode toward her. "Where did *those* come from!" he said harshly, his eyes fastened to the bosom 'twas so hard to miss.

Branwenn's hackles immediately went up. "What do you mean '*Where did* those *come from?* They"—she was so furious, she actually *pointed* at them!—"dropped from the sky, of course, and landed directly on my chest this very afternoon." A brief pause and then: "Are you a lackwit?"

Callum's cheeks burned. "Well, they weren't there before...," he said feebly, realizing how idiotic his words had been, still were, in fact. His rudeness, his irritability, his inability to say the right thing, kept surprising him with their appearance. There was just something about the lass that lifted the social shackles from his usually glib tongue, making him say every single thought in its exact tone and wording, at the precise moment he thought it.

"I bound them, you simpleton. I couldn't exactly travel about as a lad with them hanging out for all to see! And I have been wearing your mother's larger gowns since coming here, remember?" She shrugged and gave a quick glance to her breasts before lifting her eyes once more to Callum's. "Besides, 'tis not as if they're the size of Jesslyn's."

A twinkle came into his eye and his gaze softened,

warmed, as it slid over the area in question. "Well...with your petite frame, believe me...to a man, it looks as tho' they are."

A hot thrill of excitement traveled over her skin, causing her stomach to quiver as the peaks of her breasts pebbled under the soft fabric, and that other place, where a man would someday mate with her, to tighten. "I'll go change."

Callum reached out and grabbed hold of her hand before she could take a step. "Nay, no need. The gown becomes you—and 'twas a gift from my grandmother, was it not? Surely, she would be hurt should you not wear the thing this eve, as she intended."

* * *

Callum watched Branwenn from across the hall. She was now dancing with his stepfather. She'd danced with every male member of the household, or so it seemed, at least twice. Lord, how he craved to be near her, to hold her hand as they danced to the piper's tune. But, he dared not. For he knew if he touched her while she wore that gown, he'd do something very, very, very stupid. Like kiss her in front of everyone. Or drag her off to his chamber and kiss her even more deeply before he stripped that red gown from her pale, creamy body and burrowed his face in those lush breasts he'd had *no idea* had been hiding all these moons under her clothes. Aye, he'd best keep his distance.

And then he was struck by a sudden stray thought. His eyes narrowed and he turned his gaze to his Grandmother. What, he wondered, was her game?

Highland Magic

* * *

Bao and Daniel stood with their grandmother and their aunt Maggie across the chamber, watching in amusement, the play of emotions that moved across Callum's visage as he avidly watched Branwenn swirling with Laird MacGregor in a dance. "Cupid's arrow has definitely hit its mark, would you not agree, Bao?" Maggie asked.

Daniel answered. "Aye. And not only his heart, but other parts as well," he said irritably, noting where Callum's eyes were glued.

Bao's brows slammed together, too, just now seeing the exact position of Callum's sights as well.

Lady Maclean patted Daniel's arm. "Do not be such a prig, Daniel. Why, how else should he feel? I do want to see great-grandbabes from this match, after all."

* * *

Branwenn finished the dance with Laird MacGregor and, tired of waiting for Callum to ask her, she decided to ask him for a dance. She walked with clear determination toward him, a bright smile plastered on her countenance to hide the dire fear of refusal she felt. Her heart pounding, she stopped before him and said cheekily, "Daniel told everyone you're not dancing because you got kneed in your manly parts on the training field this afternoon and their swollen. Everyone laughed of course." If this didn't get him out on the floor, he was not the man she thought him to be—proud and cocky.

Callum ground his teeth together and swallowed a growl. He was going to kill Daniel. Without saying a word, he took Branwenn's arm and led her to the area where the others were dancing. He could do this. He could. The dance would only last a few minutes and then he would leave. Because, he truly could not trust himself to keep his hands from her afterward. Mayhap, he thought, turning an evil eye on his much-too forthcoming cousin—he had been kneed, but that was decidedly not why he was not dancing; he'd been wearing a groin plate, for Christ's sake—and decided a little retribution was in order. Mayhap a wrestling match. And, if he was very thorough, he'd tire himself to the point where his dreams would not be filled with the lush body of the lass beside him. Nor, he added, his stomach quivering, that carmine mouth of hers either.

* * *

After her brothers and Callum left the great hall, Branwenn made a very big decision. Tonight, she'd give her virginity to the man she loved. For, if Gaiallard de Montfort came for her, she may for evermore be forced to mate with that horrid creature. And once, just once, she wanted to know what it felt like to make love to someone for whom she cared deeply—and someone whom she knew—nay, he did not love her, but—*desired* her. Aye, he desired her. That much had been made plain to her these past days. And, for what she had in mind, that would have to be enough.

* * *

Callum collapsed on his bed, exhausted from the wrestling matches he had had with both Daniel and Bao after the feast. He'd been so drenched with sweat when they'd finished that he'd walked to the small inlet of the sea that was near to the MacGregor fortress, and taken a bath in its cold depths. Afterward, he'd swum awhile, slicing through the water in slow strokes to work out the tension in his muscles. Then he'd taken some of the sleep tonic Daniel had made for him after Lara's death. Within moments he was deeply asleep.

* * *

Branwenn crept into Callum's room, tensing at the *snick* the door made as she closed it behind her. She waited a moment with her palms pressed on the door behind her back as she leaned against them, in case he awakened and she had to make a quick exit.

When she only heard the deep cadence of his breathing as he slumbered, she cautiously began the seemingly long journey over to his bed. Silently stepping out of her carmine gown and flower-embroidered chemise—she'd left the filet in her chamber—she carefully lifted her knee to the mattress. Fearful of waking him before she was ready, she slowly leaned down onto her hands and climbed in next to him. She let out the breath she had been holding once she was settled on her side facing him, grateful that she'd been able to get in without rocking the mattress very much.

Breathing in deeply, she took in the intoxicating smell of him. He smelled of heat and sandalwood—and man. Her mouth watered as she imagined running her tongue over his lips, the way he had done to hers that day outside the chapel.

He lay on his back, shockingly nude and obviously deep in slumber, perfect for her plan. She wished she could light a candle so she could view him fully, but worried that he'd be repulsed by the marks on her frame, should he learn of them. Thankfully, she'd seen enough of what a man looked like (though she'd never admit as much to her brother!) that day by the fall two summers past, when she'd watched Bao make love to Jesslyn, to know how things were done, and Callum's explaining the process to her the day in the sea cave had added to her understanding.

Her heart pounding with excitement and trepidation, she stroked her hand along his broad chest, her palms tingling with the contact of the crisp hairs that grew there. From there, she moved her hand to stroke the bulging muscles of his upper arm. He sighed and mumbled something she could not understand and then placed his large palm on her bent knee, absently rubbing his fingers along the crease. She tensed for a moment until she realized he remained asleep. Good. She didn't want him to awaken until she had him where she wanted him.

Deciding she must make haste to do just that, she stroked her hand down his torso, coddling his already growing manhood in her hand. Never having seen a man's sex in its aroused state before (she'd been too far away from her brother and Jesslyn to see any actual details, just some flesh colored thing jutting out from his groin, and Callum had made it vexingly impossible for her to see him that day in the cave after dousing the flame), she didn't know exactly how it worked. Callum's had already been 'ready' the two times she'd been near enough to touch it. Still amazed at the size of it, a thrill coursed through her when she felt it become even more large, more hard, more straight, as it rose up from its nesting place against the sacks below, making her fingers open wider as it grew. Wanting to feel the whole length that was barely visible in the darkness, she held him in her fist and lightly stroked up to the rounded head, using her fingers to trace the edge and press the tip, learning once more its manly attributes. A loud moan burst from Callum's throat at her exploration, and yet he still did not awaken.

* * *

Callum was having a very erotic dream. He was lying on a bed of seaweed just inside the mouth of one of the sea caves on the MacGregor land and Branwenn, dressed as the beautiful black-haired water nymph, was treating him to another of her very sensual massages. She seemed to know exactly the place on the head of his cock that would send a tremor of pleasure rocking through him if she manipulated it and she did it several times in a row drawing a moan from his lips. "Sweet nymph, I ache to feel your mouth on me."

* * *

Branwenn shot a glance at Callum's face, thinking he'd wakened and would allow this intimacy with her. But no, he still slumbered. She smiled ruefully. He was dreaming. Good. But, wanting to please him, she opened her mouth and took him in, sliding her tongue around the head and stroking it along its length. The urge to suckle came over her, and she recalled that he'd asked her to do just that the last time. So, she answered the urge, surprised and pleased when he groaned and placed his hands on her head showing her the up-and-down motion he desired from her. She tasted the musky flavor of his seed and knew from their previous encounter how close he was to completion, that she might have gone a bit too far. Not wanting this finished before she'd done what she'd come here to do, she took her mouth from him.

He groaned as if in pain but settled when she straddled him.

* * *

Lifting his hands to her straight hair, Callum tugged on it, bringing her down to meet his mouth. She tasted of raspberries and smelled of the wild pink roses that grew on the edge of the forest. So sweet. *Branwenn.* Her taste and smell intoxicated him. And her sighs sounded like the ocean breeze in the sea cave. Still believing himself dreaming, so groggy was he from the sleep tonic and exhaustion, he ran his hands down Branwenn, the sea nymph's, neck and chest to cup the soft, full mounds of her breasts, enchanted by the feel of the nubby tips teasing his palms. Moving further still, he explored her small waist and nicely rounded bottom before stroking his fingers against the wet curls of her labia as he moved his mouth to the nipple of one breast and began to suckle.

* * *

On fire from Callum's hands and mouth and afraid he'd waken, Branwenn reached down and took his engorged phallus in her hand and positioned him at her entry, pressing down, not knowing if she was doing it correctly.

But, thankfully, Callum evidently knew exactly what to do and was clearly more than ready to fully comply, for he levered his hands on her hips and pushed her down onto him, lifting his own hips up at the same time, which forced her to take him in one harsh push.

"*Owwww!?*" That hurt much more than she'd expected.

"Hhmmg?" he answered.

Too painful, in fact, Branwenn decided. She leaned forward and placed her hands on the headboard for support as she strained to disengage from him.

Callum wouldn't allow it. He rolled over on top of her, moving slightly out of her and keeping most of his weight on his elbows. He stroked the hair away from her face, clearly not fully awake. He moved into her again, this time as deep as he could go.

"*No, don't. Oh, God, it hurts!*" Branwenn pressed her palms against his chest, bowing her back.

* * *

Callum's eyes flew open. His breath harsh, he shook his head to clear the fog and gazed down at the woman he was now fully sheathed inside. "Blood of Christ! What the hell are you doing—have you done?!" Callum tried to move off of her, but, perversely, now Branwenn threw her arms around him and pressed her pelvis up as he tried to withdraw from her. "Nay! The damage is already done. Let us finish this. I *want* to finish this."

God, she was so beautiful. And lush—those tightly pebbled peaks of her breasts teased through the hair on his chest. And she smelled of woman. He'd been fighting his attraction to her for so many moons now, first because he'd been wed, and then because he knew he must wed her to bed her—and she was not old enough to take on the kind of responsibility that would require. For, with the title of wife, instantly came the title of mother as well. And there had also been the niggling doubt that she held any soft feelings for him. But, this certainly proved he'd been wrong about that. And, the deed was done; the tide had turned; fate—or Branwenn—had stepped in to change everything. And, they would wed. It had to be. A thought struck him then: She had both his mother and his grandmother to aid her in mothering Laire. All at once, those self-imposed shackles of dissent fell away, and his heart soared. He grinned in the darkness.

And then, at last allowing himself to rejoice in the feel of her tight sheath around him, and wanting desperately to taste every portion of her, the temptation proved too great and he acquiesced.

"You're not ready yet. Let me prepare you first," he said as he leaned down and kissed her mouth, rubbing his tongue along the inside of her bottom lip before stroking it against her tongue.

"Aye," Branwenn breathed into his mouth.

He remained inside her, but didn't move, determined to make her so hot for him, he wouldn't hurt her again once he began to truly take her.

He trailed kisses across her flushed cheeks and kissed away the cool, crystal-wet teardrops that clung to her lashes before making his way to her ear. Nibbling her earlobe and breathing heavily, he tensed when he felt her canal flex around his arousal. She was so good. Better than his imaginings. Moving down to her breasts, he took one of the rigid peaks into his mouth and laved it with his tongue as he softly suckled. Feeling her sheath softening with hot moisture as he pleasured her, he learned her curves with his hand and slowly rocked into her in shallow movements.

* * *

Overcome with the fulfilling sensation of sharing her naked body with the man she loved and taking his into her own, Branwenn opened her eyes to see her lover's expression. Were his feelings as acute? She gazed through the darkness and, seeing the intense look of pleasure on his countenance as he made love to her, hearing his soft murmurs of pleasure, his jagged breathing, she thought they might be. He moved his hand between them and stroked a place that sent shivers of pleasure through her. "Oh, God. Aaahhh, what are you doing to me?" she said, her voice strained with need, as he continued manipulating her with his fingers while he began to take deeper strokes into her.

Callum pressed his lips against her ear and murmured, "I'm giving you the pleasure you so generously gave me a moment ago."

The sharp pain of that first entry and the slight sting of having him motionless inside of her as he kissed her had now been replaced with a pleasurable ache, a straining need for what, she knew not. But it would come from Callum and it would come from this coupling. Moving her hips up to meet his strokes, she raised her hands over her head and arched her back, pressing her breast against his mouth.

* * *

Taking the hint, Callum opened his mouth wide over her lovely, soft-skinned breast—the same breast he'd been craving to devour those dire hours in the great hall earlier—and suckled forcefully, knowing she was close now to her very first release. As he sucked and laved her nipple, he rotated his fingers over her clitoris and began a faster rhythm of entry into her. 'Twas not long before the muscles of her body tensed. Finally, when her thighs began to tremble powerfully and she met his thrusts with those of her own, he took her over the edge with one final deep push.

* * *

Branwenn shattered, unaware that she'd called out his name. Her whole body quaked with the intense pleasure that the release caused in her, centered around the movement and manipulation by him of her womb and breasts. She felt as if she were bursting into thousands of small stars of ecstasy, each one floating off into the night sky, but reverberating along her nerve endings for long minutes afterward.

* * *

Hearing his name on her lips, and feeling the tight muscles of her canal milking him, Callum felt himself begin to come and quickly pulled out of her, using his hand to bring himself to his final completion. They would wed, but he didn't want her pregnant before they did so—he wanted no raised eyebrows regarding *this* match.

Wiping his shaking hand on the coverlet, he lay

between her spent thighs and stroked the hair from her hot, damp cheek before kissing her gently on her mouth. They didn't speak, but she ran her hand up and down the side of his rib cage as he kissed her. Incredibly moved by the gift he'd just received, he left her mouth and placed soft kisses on her cheeks, nose, chin, and brow. Rising up a bit on his elbows, which were braced beside her upper arms, he ran his fingers through her hair and grasped her head in his hands before leaning down to place a tender kiss over the lid of each of her beautiful eyes.

Her contented sigh broke the silence.

"Will you wed me, Branwenn?" he whispered softly into her ear, a grin on his face, for he was sure of the outcome.

Branwenn took in a slow deep breath, still dizzy, her eyes closed as she floated on a cloud of contentment. She answered on the exhale. "Naaaayy."

* * *

CHAPTER 6

"WHAT MEAN YOU, *Naaaayy!*" Callum leapt from atop her and stood, hands on hips, beside the bed. He turned and quickly lit the taper atop the bedside table.

Branwenn rushed to cover herself with the sheet.

Turning back to her, he said, "Well?"

She couldn't help it, she allowed them to skim down his long, muscular frame. "*That* is what was just inside me? But, it felt *much* bigger when I held it in my hand."

Callum's cheeks turned ruddy. "The thing doesn't stay that size all the time, you sharp-tongued temptress," he replied, clearly abashed. "Else, it'd be a nuisance, not a pleasure."

Shrugging, Branwenn closed her eyes and, with a big smile on her lips, said, "Ohhh. I see." Then another thought struck. Her lids flew open and her gaze settled upon him again. "Why did you not stay inside me to...finish?"

"Because, I want no scandal attached to this marriage. I won't have you with child before we exchange our vows."

That made sense, but, for some reason it hurt her feelings that he didn't want to make a babe with her now. Branwenn narrowed her eyes at him and sat up, her hands on her hips. "So, 'tis fine to make my poor stomach take it in, but not to give it into my womb—*where it belongs!*"

"You have, by far, the sharpest tongue of any lass I have ever met! And carnal bliss seems to hone it, rather than dull it—*as 'twould be the case with* most *people*, I trow!" Callum couldn't believe it, but he could actually feel himself becoming aroused again. He prayed she didn't notice, else she'd no doubt make some acutely embarrassing comment about that as well.

Branwenn shrugged again, pleased—and she couldn't say why—that she'd gotten his hackles up. She settled back on the pillow once more and closed her eyes, a smug smile on her face.

She heard him take in a few deep breaths, no doubt to calm his wrath. Then he said in a much more level voice, "Why say you 'nay' to wedding me, Branwenn?"

She opened her eyes and looked at him, the smile falling from her lips. "Because," she answered softly, "I do not want to endanger this clan as well." This much was true, but the real, true, bottom of the heart reason was much more complicated. 'Twas because he didn't love her. And she wanted that, desperately. To have what Maryn and Daniel had. And Bao and Jesslyn. She'd seen for herself how strong the bond that kind of marriage could have and, with Callum, at least, 'twas that or naught.

"But, this clan is already involved, should the Norman come for you and attempt to take you from Bao and Daniel. You know the terms to which we agreed."

She sat up and the sheet dipped before she could catch hold of it, revealing her left breast. Callum's gaze dropped. His lids widened slightly, his pupils dilated, and his nostrils flared in the brief instant it took for her to yank the sheet more snugly around herself, making sure to cover her nakedness. *Had he seen the horrid freckle?*

"Well, what be your answer?"

It took her a second to recall his last volley. *Mayhap he hadn't seen it, then?* "Aye, I know the terms," she replied at last, her eyes dropping down to study the soft wavy sworls in the draped blanket, "but, if he comes, he will come to Bao first. That holding will be the one to be laid siege to again—a thing that breaks my heart—not this one. I cannot be the cause of yet another clan's fortress being attacked, another clan's lives and livelihoods being threatened."

"Branwenn. I will protect you, fear not. My clan is strong, we'll win the day, I swear it."

Her eyes misted and she forcefully blinked it away before turning them up to him. "Aye, but at what cost? After how many lives have been lost?" She sighed and shook her head. "Nay, 'tis much better that we enjoy each other while we can and then agreeably part ways if the threat of a siege does occur." She straightened her spine, and her resolve then. "I will go back to the

Maclean holding and, if I must, I will return to Cambria with Gaiallard."

"Nay, you will not. You will wed me, and I, and your brothers, will keep you safe from Gaiallard's clutches."

She shook her head.

"Braanweennn." 'Twas a warning.

Silence.

* * *

Callum threw his hands up in the air. "Aargh! You surely test even the most saintly of saints!" He grabbed his braies and quickly tied them on, then threw his shirt on over his head. He walked over to the door and opened it before turning back to her, saying, "Stay here." 'Twas a demand.

He strode the several paces to the stairs and took them two at a time—thank heaven his ankle was no longer a problem—and then he pounded his fist against Bao's door. When the door swung wide, and a grim-faced Bao answered, Callum said, "I've just bedded your sister, but she refuses my troth. Go tell her she must wed me."

Bao roared with laughter—a reaction even he was surprised he was having—and said, "So, 'tis like that, is it?" He crossed his arms over his chest and leaned his shoulder against the doorframe. "Why won't she wed you—did you not please her well?" His words sinking in, he straightened and asked again much more seriously, "Did you not please her? You weren't a brute with her were you?"

Callum couldn't find his voice, so shocked was he at the emotional pivots Bao was taking.

Bao turned and stormed into his chamber and Callum followed, shutting the door behind him. "I should have known," Bao continued, "you'd not know the first thing about pleasing a woman. You, with your pretty face and charming ways, the ladies no doubt care little whether you work for their pleasure or not!" He whirled around, facing Callum. "But, I will tell you this now: That is not how it will be with *my sister*! You will be gentle and kind to her, and never leave her wanting. Otherwise, I will not aid you in your cause."

Callum grinned. He'd aid him in his cause? Wonderful. For, it hadn't taken but a moment or two after his initial words to Bao, for him to realize this might not be the best person to ask for assistance. "'Tis no problem, there," he said, at last finding his voice. He coughed into his fist and cleared his throat. "I assure you."

Bao actually threw his hands over his ears. "Nay! I don't want to hear it!"

'Twas Callum's turn to laugh now. "Worry not, I have no intention of telling you more than that!" He sobered. "But, you will help me to change her mind?"

Bao gave him a slow nod. A question in his eye, he asked, "What reason does she give for her refusal?"

Callum crossed his arms over his chest. "She says she will not put yet another clan—meaning my clan, the MacGregors—in danger. I've tried to explain to her that we are already involved in the plans to aid with a siege, should there be one, but this has not appeased her. She's got it in her head that we will remain lovers"—he paused for the explosion those words would engender, but, surprisingly, it never came—"until she returns to the Maclean holding and then, if the worst happens, departs with Gaiallard de Montfort for Cambria."

Bao worked that out in his own mind. He knew Branwenn very well and, though he had no doubt that this reason she gave Callum played some part in her refusal of his troth, there was something more behind it than that. Else, why would she not remain his lover *after* returning to the Maclean holding, if she was safe from harm? Suddenly, he knew. He just knew what it was. And Callum, poor man, was clearly a bit lackwitted where Branwenn was concerned. He watched Callum very carefully as he said, "So...the two of you have spoken of your feelings for each other?"

Callum's eyes nearly popped out of his head. Bao watched the man's adam's apple rise and fall in the long column of his neck as he swallowed hard before replying, "Uhh, not exactly."

That was it then. The lass wanted to know Callum loved her before she wed him. 'Twas as simple—and as complicated—as that. Well, this was something Callum and Branwenn needed to work out for themselves. He nodded. "Hmmm. Well. I'll talk to her on the morrow. Will that do?"

Callum's shoulders slumped in relief. "Aye. My thanks." He turned and opened the door, as he was stepping across the portal, Bao said, "Do not mistake my earlier amusement as approval of continued physical relation between the two of you. Branwenn sleeps in her own chamber this night. Understood?"

With a sharp nod, Callum closed the door behind him and went back to his own room.

* * *

Bao's worry was groundless, Callum discovered quickly upon entering his room. For, his bed, and his chamber, were empty of her.

He strode over and stood staring down at the rumpled blankets, at the unexpected love-alter of his most vivid contentment. He bent down and grabbed hold of the blankets and tossed them back. Several red streaks, lovely curved brush strokes of scarlet, made an abstract design on the white linen sheet. Proof of her innocence. Proof of the gift she'd so generously bestowed upon him.

He tore the sheet from the bed and reverently held it up to his face a moment. Then, slowly, methodically, he folded the material and walked over to the chest that held his most prized possessions; his knight's mail, his father's knight's ring, and his grandfather Maclean's badge. Lifting the lid, he gazed inside a moment before gently laying the linen cloth atop the other contents. 'Twould go to the grave with him, he swore then.

* * *

Branwenn closed the door to her chamber and leaned against it with a sigh. She'd been surprised, when she scurried out of Callum's bed a few moments ago, by the soreness...down there. But, Lord, hadn't the pleasure he'd given her been worth the pain? Aye. Aye, aye, aye, aye, *aye*! She wondered when they could do it again. Mayhap the morrow? After the chimes at midnight had tolled? She wandered over to the washstand and lit several candles. After undressing, she stood naked and looked down at herself. A bit of her virgin's blood still streaked her thighs. She wet a cloth and shivered a bit at the coldness of it as she cleansed herself. *"No man will want you once he sees that mark of the devil you wear, ken me well."* She forcefully ignored the oft-repeated words of the drunken nurse who took care of her while Bao was away on campaigns, but her gaze still skittered over the ugly mark on her thigh, as it usually did, refusing to pause, as she continued her ablutions. Her womanhood was quite tender, so it took a bit more time to get that portion of herself clean.

Inside, she felt so...different now. So complete. A woman, full-grown. And it had been Callum who'd led her, oh so sweetly, oh so skillfully, over that last hill in her journey from young lass to young lady. She lifted her head and straightened, dropping the water-and-blood-pinkened cloth into the washbowl. Mayhap—did she *look* different as well? Her heart did a little flip in her chest. She prayed not, for Bao and Daniel would surely spank her behind and—she didn't even want to think about what they'd do to Callum, if they found out.

* * *

Laird Gordon's nephew, David, arrived early the next morn. Callum watched the lad as he settled on the stool next to the hearth in the great hall, facing Callum's stepfather.

So, this was the page who'd given him the pig offal. He was a bit lanky for his age, his legs longer than his torso. And long arms as well. That would serve him well when he became a warrior. His hair was the color of fincly sanded oak. He didn't look familiar to Callum, which surprised him. He thought he paid more attention to the lads who served his meals. He'd have to be more careful in future.

As if the lad felt the weight of Callum's stare, he turned his head and looked at him briefly, before returning his gaze to the older man sitting across from him.

The lad's eyes were large and almond-shaped, with brows, a bit darker than the hair on his head, that slashed in a straight line over them. The shade of his eyes, Callum had noticed immediately, was a stormy blue-gray.

* * *

Laird MacGregor glared long and hard at the lad, not saying a word. Let's see just how much mettle the wee one had. For 'twas not the fact that the bairn had not wanted to go out on the glen that proved his cowardliness, 'twas his lack of courage in the face of pressure from the other pages that gave him pause. For a lad must learn early to do the right thing—even if 'twas against the common opinion—if he's to grow to be the best warrior he can be.

"I'm only seven summers! Must you lock me in the dungeon, Laird?" David said at last. He was never going to see his mother again—or any of his friends—or his hunting dog, Jasper, either. And this mean old man would no doubt put him away and give him only gruel to eat for evermore, just because he did that thing to the red-haired warrior now standing over by the buttery. He had felt bad afterward, tho', when he saw how red the man's skin got on his face. He'd just thought it wouldn't taste good and the man would make an amusing face and then all the pages would clap him on the back for making them laugh real hard. He didn't know he could make the man sick with the pig stuff. And his mama had cried all last night, saying that she'd not see her babe ever again, once the MacGregor got his hands on him. Which made him remember that Lairds liked to punish people by locking 'em away in tower dungeons.

Laird MacGregor crossed his arms over his chest and sat back a bit, peering down his nose at him. "And why should that make a difference? The outcome of your deed was the same for my stepson, whether the perpetrator was seven or seventy."

David's shoulders slumped. *Well, mayhap they'd at least let him out after he was seventy.*

* * *

Callum took mercy on the lad. "Nay, I think a better punishment would be for him to be my personal page."

David straightened on his stool and swiveled his head around, giving Callum a look that held equal parts hope and dread.

"He can sleep on the cot in the tower chamber attached to my own bedchamber," Callum continued, "and learn to take care of my clothes and armor." He pierced the lad with a sharp gaze, saying, "But you will not be allowed to serve my meals until you have proved your loyalty to me."

The lad gave him a slow nod, "Aye, sir."

His new page had a bit of the same nature as Jesslyn's lad, Alleck, Callum thought. Recalling his somewhat strained relationship with that lad, he made the decision to begin with this one in a better manner. "In the meantime, I've a hankering for a game of knucklebones. Do you play?" This time, he'd not win the games, as he'd done with Alleck. Time enough later to use the game as a tool to teach. For now, let it be a bridge to, if not friendship, then at least finding common ground.

The lad grinned then. "Aye, I play."

* * *

An hour later, Callum was hard-pressed to figure out who could teach whom the better strategy. The long-limbed mite had the lithe fingers of a true expert.

He crossed his arms over his chest and studied the lad as he made his next move. His brow was puckered in concentration and his tongue was stuck out and tipped up at the corner of his mouth.

This was the position that Branwenn found the two in when she walked through the door of the solar a second later. "*Oops!* My pardon. I knew not that anyone was in here."

Her eyes, while she'd spoken, had traveled from the lad to Callum, to the lad, and then finally settled on Callum. Her deep purple gaze warmed then, heating his blood to boiling surprisingly quickly. Ahhh. She remembered what they'd been about the last time they saw each other—that was good. He rose from his stool and strode to stand in front of her, their bodies only a whisper apart. "Good morn, *fey Mai*," he teased, giving her a crooked, smug smile, "how do you this fine day?" And then, before she could answer, he realized something critical must be learnt. "Are you very sore? Did I hurt you too badly?"

Branwenn's entire face and neck flushed a fire-red scarlet in under a second. She shook her head nervously, her head and eye darting quickly around his shoulder to look at the lad, before returning to his...chin? She wouldn't look him in the eye. How adorable. "Nay...nay," she whispered, "I'm fine, worry you not."

Lord, but she was so sweet. Without a clear plan, Callum took her by her upper arm and, turning to David, said, "Stay here, I'll be back in a while," before quickly hustling her out of the chamber.

* * *

"Where are we going?" Branwenn asked breathlessly. Would he make love to her *now*? In broad daylight? With Grandmother Maclean, his mother, her brothers and Lord knew who else wandering around the keep?

"Not far," he said cryptically, leading her down the hall and up to the next landing of the stair. He turned and placed his hands under her arms and lifted her up and settled her against the stone wall behind her before molding his own frame to hers and kissing her lips, oh so softly. "I see you are back to wearing this old rag of my mother's," he murmured against her lips before taking the lower one between his teeth and rolling it back and forth, gently tugging.

"Aye," she managed to respond, though 'twas

difficult, for her brain was now mush.

* * *

Callum's tongue darted out and did a slow glide over the lip he'd just been teasing. "Mmm. You taste so good. Like raspberries. Did you have more of them this morn, then?" 'Twas driving him mad to know what lay beneath this oversized, drab gown of hers and not be able to see, to feel, to taste, the bounty of her. But 'twas much too early to disappear with her. Bao had made it clear, and no doubt Daniel would be of the same opinion, that this affair could not continue before vows were spoken. Aye, they'd skin him alive for sure if he flaunted his affair with their sister in their faces—even with his sworn intention of wedding her. But tonight, tonight he'd have her again, no matter their opinion. Nay, he'd not enter her—'twas much too soon for that type of contact, but, there were other things he wished to do with her, to her that were just as—if not more—enjoyable.

He nuzzled her cheek and trailed kisses down her jaw to her neck, sucking and biting the soft, succulent skin as he traveled.

* * *

Branwenn's body was on fire. Her limbs were weak and her womb ached for him to fill it, take her to heaven again and again. "Callum, please," she whimpered.

"Nay, not yet," he whispered against her ear. "But tonight. Tonight. Meet me in my chamber when the midnight bell chimes." He stroked his tongue around the shell of her ear before taking the lobe into his mouth and gently suckling it.

Branwenn stiffened, her canal siezing in delight, "Ohhh, ohhh, ohhh, G-aw—awwwd!" she moaned.

* * *

Callum recognized the sound and his erection jerked in reaction. Trembling now with need, knowing that he'd just made her come with very little effort—a highly arousing occurrence—one that, in all his experience, he'd never had happen, he dragged the hem of her dress up and clamped his palm over her mons, pushing his fingers over and between her labia lips. God, she was soaking wet. So ready for him, surely 'twould not hurt her to take him.

Cognizant thought halted in that highly charged erotic moment and his body took over. He ripped at the ties of his braies and, opening her thighs a bit wider, pushed himself into her waiting womb.

* * *

"Ahhh, Oh, God!" Branwenn gasped, thrashing her head from side to side. It only hurt at the first entry this time. Now, 'twas perfect, exactly what she'd been craving.

"Aye, aye," he ground out, his face a mask of tortured pleasure as he stroked—not gently—into her. "Put your arms around my neck," he said. When she did, he slid his hands down her inner thighs to her knees and lifted them, spreading them wide. He thrust up, deep. So deep, he touched the mouth of her womb. He threw his head back. "Oh, God, oh, God, this is too good...too good."

Branwenn opened her eyes and regarded him. His

brow was beaded with sweat and his eyes were glazed. In the next instant, he was kissing her on the mouth, thrusting his tongue between her teeth and simulating the same action with it that he was doing inside her canal with his manhood. Lord, but how he could make every rational thought in her head scatter to the four winds. Suddenly she shattered, splintered into a thousand pointed shards of bliss.

* * *

Branwenn's slick inner walls pulled at Callum, begging him to give up his seed. A hot/cold chill ran straight from his manhood, to his groin, down his legs, and up his spine. But somehow, somehow, he managed to free himself from the siren's tight grip just before he crested. Unfortunately, the semen spewed all over the lower front of her ugly gown.

But neither of them was in any condition at the time to realize the blunder. 'Twas not until a few minutes later, after the two of them had stood in each other's arms as they waited for their breathing to return to a normal meter, and after Callum stepped back and resettled the gown around Branwenn's legs that it was discovered. But not by him.

"Callum! You've ruined my gown!" Branwenn chided. She fisted her hands in the material and brought it up for his inspection, making what looked like a half-collapsed tent of the thing. "How am I ever to explain this to someone, should they see me in this state before I can change? And the wash maids will surely know what the source is." Her face crinkled in humiliation. "Oh, God!" she whimpered.

Highland Magic

Callum quickly tied his braies before turning his gaze to the front of the gown. Damn! She'd made him blush like a lass. *Again*! "Well, they might not.... It looks like...I know not...cream or something. Just say you spilled cream on your dress."

Branwenn's eyes burned into him. "I? *I* spilled cream on my dress? So, I must take the blame as well as wear the pith of your loins, is that it?"

Callum shrugged, but his cheeks burned like fire. "Say *I* spilled cream on you then."

"This is only one of two gowns I have to wear until the others arrive, and now 'tis stained! Why will you not put that seed of yours where it belongs instead of everywhere it doesn't?!"

This reminded him of *why* he had not found completion inside his lovely, generous, soft-hearted, but sharp-tongued lover. "I assure you, I'm quite willing to do just that—once we are wed." He eyed her closely then. "Did your brother, Bao, speak to you this morn?"

"Aye," she said, not meeting his eye.

"And?"

"And what?"

Callum gritted his teeth and growled low in his throat. "Did he tell you to accept my troth?"

Branwenn tossed her head, her hand fluttering in the air. "Oh. Aye." She still had not met his eye.

"Aaand?"

She lifted her brows and gave a little shake of her head. With a seemingly disinterested sigh, she said, "I told him nay."

With a low rumble, Callum crowded into her,

placing his hands on her cheeks and squeezing ever so slightly, causing her lips to pucker. His eyes settled on them for long moments as carnal images leapt into his mind. Her tongue darted out and licked her lower lip. Callum lost whatever thread of thought he'd had and dived into her, devouring that lush, ruby mouth for the second time in only minutes. He was out of control. What was wrong with him? He couldn't seem to keep his hands off of her any longer. Not since he'd partaken of the delightful bounty of her twice now.

'Twas Branwenn that broke the kiss. Turning her face away, she said urgently, "Callum, we cannot do this here! Not again. We shall surely get caught."

With a nod, he rested his brow against hers. His breathing was harsh and he still held her face in his palms, though more lightly now. "Wed me, Branwenn." 'Twas a plea.

Branwenn's eyes misted. Oh, if only she could! But she would not—not, at least, until he'd given her his heart. "Nay," she whispered sadly, "I cannot."

* * *

"We shouldn't allow it, you know," Daniel said to Bao a fortnight later as they walked toward the training field to meet Callum.

Bao nodded. "Aye, I know. But, in my mind the two are already wed. 'Tis just the reciting of the vows that is lacking."

"But it cannot go on much longer in that state." He turned his gaze to Bao's. "You agree, do you not?"

With a gruff sigh, Bao nodded. "Aye, agreed. But why does Callum not tell her he loves her—is he that dense? He, who Grandmother Maclean swears always knows the exact words to give a lass to make her turn her eye to him, has even had every lass—and lady—in the shire ready to do his slightest bidding since he was old enough to tie his own braies."

Daniel shrugged, his head shaking. "I ken it not. He's either lost this much-admired ability—or simply has lost his senses, and his heart, to our sister so fully that his silver tongue has turned to lead with her."

"Aye, 'tis the latter that sounds the surest."

"So...how much longer do we allow these not-so-secret trysts before we put a halt to them?" Daniel asked.

"I cannot help but feel sorry for Callum—and I do want my sister well-wed to another, should the Norman show his ugly face. So...let us give Callum a fortnight more to either give the lass the words, or convince her to wed him without them."

"Aye—or, if fortune is with us—the decision will be taken out of our hands by the beginning of a babe growing in her belly."

"Aye, but I tell you truly, I like not that thought. 'Twould suit me better to have her wed first." Bao looked at Daniel and shook his head in wonder. "I never would have thought, a year ago, that I would be so calm in the face of my sister's loss of virtue outside the bounds of a wedded union."

Daniel slapped him on the shoulder and gave it a shake. "'Tis not so hard to understand, brother. The lass and her swain—no matter how simple-mindedly foolish we believe he's behaving—are deeply in love.

And there is no real choice for either of them—as you and I both know from experience—than to wed.

* * *

The next day, trouble arrived.

But not in the form of a Norman. 'Twas David's mother who showed up on the MacGregor doorstep, her clothing chests in tow.

"I must speak to Laird MacGregor in all haste," she said to the steward once she had gained entrance to the keep.

"Aye, my lady," the steward replied and walked out, presumably to fetch the laird of the keep.

Isobail Gordon settled on one of the stools by the hearth. She knew she should remain standing, at least until Laird MacGregor arrived and asked her to take a seat, but she was simply too weary from the journey here. Her weak heart had not grown stronger over these past days, as the physician had confidently supposed was possible, and she was almost certain now that the remainder of the time left to her in this world was short. So, she must spend these last days near her son. And try to find a permanent home for him, since his godfather—her brother—Robert MacVie, had neither the coin, nor the time, to take her son now that he was dealing with the possible loss of their clan's holding.

A sound of shuffling footsteps coming from behind brought her out of her reverie. She stood and turned, then performed a quick courtesy.

"Lady Gordon? You are David's mother?"

"Aye, Laird," she replied softly, smiling gently.

"Well, I can surely see where the lad gets his

coloring. Why, he's the same hair and eyes as you."

Isobail relaxed. Laird MacGregor was quite good-humored, naught like her vexing uncle-in-law, Laird Gordon. "Aye, 'tis truth, the lad looks the image of my father." Her smile brightened, revealing a dimple in her left cheek. "Tho' my brother, Robert, got his dark looks from my mother. You'd never know the two of us were kin, were we standing side-by-side, if you knew naught of the relation beforehand."

Laird MacGregor chuckled. With lifted brows, he asked, "Have you a need to quench your thirst, my lady? I could have some ale—or wine—poured for us."

Isobail nodded. "Ale, please. I find it quenches the thirst more than wine."

"Aye, I've found that to be true, myself. But please,"—he swept his arm in the direction of the stools—"have a seat, for you must be tired after the journey."

After the two were settled and the ale was poured, Laird MacGregor asked, "Now, my lady—"

"You must call me Isobail."

"And you must call me Chalmers. Now, Isobail, what brings you here so soon after your son's arrival? You do not think to coddle the lad, do you? For, I must be firm in this; the lad must be weaned from such in order to prepare for the knighthood."

Should she tell him the truth? Would he allow her to stay, knowing she was ill and would no doubt become a burden to them? But, to lie to this man, as she'd originally conceived doing, suddenly just seemed too wrong a thing to do. Her mind made up, she straightened on her stool and said, "I'm not long for this world, Chalmers." The man's brows shot up, then furrowed in a frown of concern. He sat forward slightly on his stool. "'Tis something with my heart. It started several sennights past with a sudden aching, and has now progressed to a point where I sometimes cannot catch my breath. I'm quite weak. Tired, most of the time."

"And you want to spend these last days with your son."

"Aye."

"Have you brought your sundries with you? If not, I shall send someone to retrieve them for you."

Isobail smiled. "Aye—"

The sound of male footsteps came from the direction of the doorway. Isobail turned and, in the next moment, Callum MacGregor came through the door. A thrill ran across her nerve endings and she smiled to herself. Lord, the man could always gain that reaction from her, even tho' there had never been anything other than friendship, however carnal it had eventually become, between them.

"*Isobail MacVie!*" Callum was beside her in three long strides. Taking her hands in his, he settled a brief kiss on her knuckles before bending and kissing her cheek as well. "'Tis been too long since last we saw each other. How is your husband—what is his name?"

Isobail swallowed past the lump in her throat. "William is dead. He died just before *Bealltainn* last."

A shadow crossed Callem's face. "I'm sorry, Isobail. I know how deeply you cared for him." He shook his head sadly. "'Twas not a good time for me, either. My own wife died near to two moons after that very celebration."

"Isobail," Laird MacGregor interjected, "Do I send for your sundries?"

She turned to him. "Nay, no need. I brought them with me."

"Are you staying here with us?" Callum asked.

Her eyes settled on Callum's face once more. "Aye, Laird MacGregor has been so kind to allow me to do so."

"For how long will you stay? I hope 'twill be for at least several sennights, as we've much to catch up on."

Laird MacGregor cleared his throat. "Would you like me to send for your son now?"

Isobail nodded.

"Son?" Callum said, his eyes following his stepfather as he gave the directive to his steward. "You've a son?" he asked in a stunned voice.

She grinned. "Aye. David Gordon? Your new page?"

Callum's eyes widened and flew to her face, then he grinned. "David is *your* son? He's talked so much of his mother these past days as we've gotten to know each other, but never once did I suspicion that I knew the lady!"

"Oh, Lord! I just realized! Was it you my lad played that horrid trick upon?"

A look of chagrin settled on Callum's countenance. "Aye." His smile returned, however, as he continued, "But the two of us have worked that out between ourselves, fear not."

"Mama!" David said gleefully, walking with a definite skip in his stride toward her. "You're here!"

"Aye." Isobail said, turning to her son and holding out her arms for an embrace. As he moved into them, she rested her cheek on his pale blond head, saying, "And I intend to stay here for a while."

* * *

CHAPTER 7

BRANWENN WANTED TO squirm on the stool she was settled upon before the hearth that night in the great hall. Her heart felt as if Callum had taken it into his large, long-fingered, warrior hands and wrung it as tight as he could, over and over again.

And he hadn't even noticed her new gown! 'Twas similar to the crimson one, but of a different color. 'Twas purple—like her eyes, Grandmother Maclean had told her. And the saffron colored chemise that rose above its neckline was lovely as well, tho' it did not have the delicate embroidery around the edges, as the other did. She'd hoped she'd gain a much more pleasing reaction from Callum with this gown, than she had with the last, even tho' she still felt awkward in such finery. But, nay, his eyes had rarely strayed from their lovely guest, *Isobail*. The two had known each other for years, she'd just learned. But how well? *Had they been lovers?* And, more importantly, now that Isobail was staying with them, *would they be so again?*

That question had been tormenting her for long minutes now as she watched the couple closely. She blinked away the sudden dew that came into her eyes—for at least the thousandth time that eve—and swallowed hard, holding her breath to keep the whimper from sounding that kept rising up in her throat every time she turned her eye in the direction where Callum and Isobail now stood.

Their heads were so close together as they shared some jest or another that Branwenn was certain Callum could brush his lips across her brow with no one noticing. For, 'twas a thing he'd done to her as they stood in just that manner only last eve.

* * *

Callum's eyes strayed once more to Branwenn. Lord, but how he wished this night would be over, so he could meet her, as they'd planned, in her bedchamber. And, by the gloom-filled look on her countenance, 'twas no doubt, she was of the same mind. But, they must stay the prescribed time with the family after the meal, else eyebrows would certainly lift. And the last thing he wanted for Branwenn—or himself, for that matter—was rumor and scandal surrounding their reasons for wedding.

She lifted her hand to her hair and brushed a bit of the cropped, shiny black mass away from her face. Those small, silky-soft hands. Lovely. And, God! What they did to him. Their time together just kept getting better and better. He'd never known that making love—for that was what 'twas for him, he was sure

Highland Magic

now, not simply a pleasurable diversion, as it had been since the first time he'd bedded a woman lo' these many years past—could affect him so deeply. Make him crave not only the physical closeness of her, but the spiritual as well. She just filled him with so much joy. More joy than he'd ever felt and, certainly, more joy than he'd felt since the utter loss of pride he'd endured after losing the Maclean lairdship almost two years past.

But...did she love him? He knew not for sure. Some days he had no doubt of it, but others...he wondered if he was mistaken. And the not knowing was killing him. But, why else would she have given him her virtue? No matter how unusually she'd been raised, he knew that Bao had instilled in her an understanding of how disappointed—even angry—he would be should she not remain innocent until she was wed—and he knew how much she craved to please her brother, do as Bao bade.

Callum scrubbed a finger over his brow. But then, if she did love him, *why* would she not wed him? Aye, there was the rub. 'Twas enough to drive him mad!

And, 'twas the reason he'd not revealed how deeply his own feelings for her went. For, what if she did not love him yet? What if, as he hoped, his carnal wooing of her was softening her heart to him, but the confession of his love frightened her away? As it had Maryn.

Branwenn resettled on her stool and his eyes traveled, for at least the thousandth time that eve, to the creamy rise of her bosom above the neckline of her gown. His mouth watered. Godamercy! That gown! It scooped down so low over her breasts, he was sure, 'twould take only the merest tug on his part to release them from their anchoring. And the color of it. Crushed violets. Just the same hue as her eyes when he was deep inside her, when she was spinning through the heavens on the shooting star of his passion. He'd wanted to rip the gown from that wee gorgeous frame of hers and take her right here, where they stood, from the moment she entered the great hall earlier.

A hand squeezed his arm, bringing him out of his impure musings. He turned to his companion. "Aye?" His voice was craggy.

"So, 'tis like that, is it?" Isobail said, a teasing smile bringing the dimple in her cheek into full prominence.

Callum grinned sheepishly. "Aye. 'Tis like that."

* * *

A shadow crossed Branwenn's vision directly before she felt someone settle beside her on the next stool. A big, beefy, calloused hand took hold of one of hers that lay in her lap and she turned to its source. Daniel.

"What ails you, sis? Feel you not well this eve?"

She forced a cheerful smile—or, at least, she prayed 'twas cheerful—and replied, "Nay, I feel quite well. Worry not."

"You've not been yourself all eve. You've said no more than a few words since you came into the hall two hours past. Something is wrong. What is it?"

'Twas hard to keep looking at Daniel, he reminded her so much of Callum. Well, Callum's face was much more beautiful. And, tho' Callum was a very muscular, tall man, Daniel and Bao stood a few inches taller than him, and their muscles would be better described as massive. But Daniel's coloring was nearly the same as Callum's. Same auburn hair, same—well *almost* the same green eyes. Daniel's were a bit bluer, more of a sea green than an emerald green. She dropped her gaze to their intertwined hands. "I fear Callum has found another lady to admire," she said in a small voice, almost a whisper.

Daniel laughed.

Branwenn stiffened, but then her face and her shoulders crumpled as tears welled in her eyes. "You find it amusing that he's bro-o-ken my heart?" She bounded to her feet and headed with as long and dignified a stride as she could manage, straight for the door. Her watery sight was set on the entrance and never wavered. She prayed Callum was too far away and too involved with his lady-love to notice.

Daniel was so stunned by what had just happened that it took him a minute to follow her. She was almost to her chamber door when he caught up to her. "Branwenn!" he called out.

She turned and looked at him. She hesitated, but only for an instant, and then she turned the handle to her door.

Daniel grabbed hold of her wrist, stopping her forward stride into the chamber. "Wait! Let me explain!" he said urgently. "I laughed not—and why you would believe I was capable of such a cruelty, I truly would like to know—because your heart was broken. I laughed because the thought of Callum wooing any lady but you is utter nonsense." His sister stood so still, her head bowed, her demeanor much too quiet, that he knew she was in a great deal of anguish.

Daniel pushed the bangs away from Branwenn's brow so that he could see her face more clearly. "He loves you," he said softly, "cannot you see that?" She shrugged and shook her head. Tears still leaked from the corners of her eyes, but she did not swipe at them. "Branwenn, the man has asked you to wed him, how many times now?"

Branwenn opened her mouth to speak, but Daniel put his fingers over her lips. "Nay, do not tell me, for that will also be the number of times I should have kept you from being seduced by that silver-tongued demon."

"If he loves me," she said thickly, "why does he not tell me so?"

"Because he is a lackwit. Truly, I do not see what is so wonderful about *Callum MacGregor*. 'Tis all I've heard lo' these many moons since first hearing his name, that he could charm the gown off of the Virgin Mary. Truly, I believe I've had my fill of such talk."

Branwenn giggled. Was Daniel jealous of Callum's ability with the ladies? Then, she remembered. Nay, 'twas that Callum had threatened a clan war, he'd wanted so badly to wed Maryn, Daniel's wife. Of course, that was before Daniel had wed her.

Daniel relaxed. *Thank God!* He grinned. "What find you so humorous, may I ask?"

She gave him a little slap on the arm. "You, silly."

* * *

Callum waited only a few more minutes after seeing Branwenn, followed by Daniel, leave the hall before bidding his good-nights as well.

Highland Magic

He would have loved to go directly to Branwenn's chamber, but another, smaller, just as precious, love called him to her first. His daughter. He must see Laire's sweet face and spend a few minutes with her at this, what had become, their special quiet time together.

* * *

Daniel hadn't been gone from Branwenn's chamber more than a half-hour when a soft rap came on the door.

She knew who it was. Callum. But he'd not gain entrance this night—nor any other, for that matter. She'd not share her body with a man whose eye could wander so quickly and disloyally to another.

Callum looked both ways down the passage. No one about. Good. "Branwenn?" he said in a low voice into the crack between the door and its jamb. "Open the door, my wee *fey Mai*, so I can finish mapping the hills and dales of your sweet form with my tongue and teeth." He scratched the wood lightly with his fingernail. "Open for me, sweet. We were just north of the delta of your desire last eve when we quit, and I'm parched. I've a craving for a long draught from it. Quench my thirst, fair one."

He'd been amused—and thrilled—when he'd seen her hurrying from the great hall earlier. Clearly, she was as avid as he to end their eve with the family and begin their eve with each other.

On the other side of the door, Branwenn bit down hard on her knuckle as she stood, not two paces from the wooden portal, to keep from giving him leave to enter.

"Braaan-wennnn," Callum said softly, pleadingly.

She threw back her shoulders and took a deep breath. He would not go away on his own, 'twas clear. So, she must do the thing she dreaded. Tell him 'nay'.

In two strides, she was at the door. Opening it a crack, she peeked out and said, "Go away."

"Have you been crying?" he asked in alarm. "Are you ill?" He tried to push the door open in order to enter but she pressed herself into it, not allowing the motion.

"Nay, I'm well. But you must leave, for 'tis clear to me now we should not continue meeting as we have been."

Callum's heart began a mad thumping in his chest. "Why? Has there been talk about us?"

"Nay, but 'tis clear you are keen for the lady Isobail, and I have no wish to be with a man whose eye can be turned so quickly to another."

"*Isobail?!* But I have no desire for that lady!" Callum knew 'twas not the time—if ever there would be—to give her the truth of his past relationship with David's mother. "We are only old acquaintances—she is the older sister of my friend Robert MacVie—remember you him? He lends his skill as knight to the Maclean clan?"

"And this is why you stood so close to her this eve? Why you spoke not more than three words to me? Why the two of you had your heads together in privy conversation, off in the corner of the hall?"

Callum's mouth set in a grim line. He could not reveal the topic of the conversation, for 'twas Isobail's to reveal, not his. Her dire sickness had taken him by surprise, and saddened him greatly. He wanted only to aid her these next sennights—or, hopefully, moons—as she struggled to get her affairs in order. "'Twas not as you believe, Branwenn. Not at all. I swear this to you."

"Oh? Then, of what did the two of you speak? Surely, if 'twasn't lover's talk, then it can be openly shared with me—your *current* lover."

Callum sighed and scrubbed his hand through his hair. "I wish I could reveal it—I do. But...'tis personal; something that she told me in confidence, and I have not the right to reveal it to anyone without her permission."

So, Branwenn thought, 'twas just as she'd suspected. He was the lowest, silver-tongued, liar of a cur dog, the vilest breaker of hearts, the last man on earth she should have ever trusted with her love—or given her maidenhead to. "Fine."

Somehow, in the last hours, the tide had turned for her, and she could not—would not—share her bed or her body with this man she loved so desperately, not again. Not, that was, unless he somehow—at last—gave to her the words she craved to hear above all others. And ignored—and mayhap, was even rude to—the lovely Isobail, as well, of course. "This has been a mistake—my mistake—and I've decided I shall not commit it any longer. Go back to your chamber, Callum, for you'll not gain entry here this night—nor ever again." With that, she shut the door and threw the bar across it to lock it.

Callum stood there stunned a moment, his hands

fisted at his sides and his breathing harsh. He could not yell, or bang on the door, or—hell—break the damn thing down, as he would have loved to do at that moment. Nay, 'twould cause the scene he'd so carefully been avoiding these past days.

After another moment, he at last turned and, not so gently, strode down the passage and down the winding stair, to the corridor that led to his own chamber door.

* * *

The next morn, a somewhat puffy-eyed Branwenn settled quietly next to Maggie at table to break her fast. Isobail was seated next to Grandmother Maclean and in an animated conversation with that lady.

Maggie placed her hand on top of Branwenn's. "Are you not feeling well, dear? Should we call for the physician?"

Branwenn took in a deep breath to relieve some of the pain of heartache in her chest before answering. She smiled as brightly as she was able and shook her head. "Nay, no need. I'm well—just a bit sleepy still."

Maggie, misinterpreting the reason for Branwenn's lack of energy as being the result of a late-night tryst with her son, smiled cheerfully and gave Branwenn's hand a little squeeze. "Well, that's fine then. Would you like some of these raspberries, dear?"

"Branwenn, Isobail was just telling me that she would enjoy a bit of fresh air after the meal. Why don't you show her the garden in the north bailey?"

This, of course, was the very last thing Branwenn wanted to do: spend private time with the object of her jealousy and dread. "Aye, I'd be pleased to do so," she answered, and, surprisingly, didn't choke on the words. Surely, she'd just earned at least one of her wings in the celestial choir.

Callum walked in with Bao just then, the two still grinning over some jest or other—who knew what warriors spoke of outside the hearing of the ladies?

Branwenn's heart leapt to vibrant life. But Callum only gave her a brief, rather irritable nod and went to sit beside Isobail. Her heart twisted painfully in her chest. Was he still angry at her for not allowing him entrance into her chamber last eve? For swearing that he'd not be allowed entrance, in fact, *ever again*? She'd had time to think on that last a bit, and had already begun to waiver on the decision. But, with his rude rebuff just now, a new worry came to mind: Was he content to have done with her and simply pressing the point that their time together was over? Oh, God. 'Twas true!

For, tho' he had, at first, seemed vexed with her when she'd said they could no longer be lovers now that his other lady-love was in residence, he'd not seemed as...well...as *persuasive* as she believed he should have been, when she'd shut the door in his face and thrown the bar, were his feelings for her as deep as hers were for him. Why, he hadn't stayed outside her door more than a few moments afterward. Surely, if he truly wanted her he would have...she knew not...pleaded with her a bit longer? Pounded on the door? Demanded entrance? Rammed the door down, as he'd done that wooden covering in the tunnel entrance? Well...mayhap not that, for she wouldn't want him to hurt his shoulder again. But, still, *some* show of force would have soothed her hurt and given her a bit of hope that 'twas truly herself he craved.

Suddenly, the filet he'd given her had the weight of a cornerstone upon her head. She would take it off directly after the meal and never put it on again, for she would not wear a gift from someone who clearly held no feeling for her any longer.

* * *

Callum felt as slithery as a slow worm, but couldn't seem to stop himself from playing this childish game with Branwenn. He wanted her. He wanted her very, very badly. But he knew not how to get her back in his bed, and eventually—he was determined—into a loving, wedded union with him.

So now, he'd decided this morn—actually, he'd only decided in the seconds just after seeing her at table a few moments past—that he would try to break down her resolve with the hammer of, hopefully, searing jealousy.

"Your lady is not well-pleased with you this morn, I think, Callum," Isobail said softly, an amused smile on her lips, as her eye scanned down the table and rested on Branwenn's red-cheeked countenance. She cleared her throat and then coughed quietly into her palm. "Pray, pardon me. This sickness is sure to get the better of me soon."

Callum's mouth turned down at the edges in a sad frown. "Isobail, are you certain you are that unwell? There's no hope for recovery?" Guilt assailed him. While he'd been stewing in his own selfish thoughts and feeling sorry for himself, his friend had been struggling with the pain of knowing she was not long for this world and must settle her affairs.

"Aye...and nay, there is no hope," she replied. But then she brightened and sat up a bit straighter. "Let us not dwell on me and my dreary prospects. Let us instead speak of you—and your obvious devotion to the lady Branwenn." She chuckled and shook her head. "I truly never thought I'd see the day when you at last tumbled from that pedestal the ladies placed you on, my dear Adonis, and humbled yourself at the feet of your Venus.

"Aye, tho' in the legend, 'tis the other way 'round—a thing, I assure you at this moment, I crave were the case. For, I'd not reject her advances, I assure you."

"So you will wed the lass, then?"

He turned and his eyes drilled into the object of his desire. "Aye," he said with certainty.

"Good. For I have a request of you. Will you meet me in the garden of the north bailey in, say, an hour's time?"

He turned and studied her face a moment. With a brief nod, he replied, "Aye. But I will have to tell Bao that I'll be late for the training field this morn."

Isobail nodded. The solution to the problem of her son's future just fell, like manna from heaven, softly and directly into her lap.

* * *

"Oh, Isobail! When I think of the terrible epithets I threw at your head in my mind last eve—and this morn as well—I want to wither up and die! Can you ever forgive me?" Branwenn sat on a stone bench in the garden next to Isobail, her hand settled on the lady's lower arm.

Isobail smiled, then chuckled softly. "Aye, I can forgive you. Am I not a woman as well? Do I not understand the pain of love seemingly not returned?"

"Seemingly? Nay, 'tis clear the man's sole interest whenever we meet is to bed me. And that desire, I fear, is a craving that, once satisfied fully, will wain and then 'twill stray to the next delectation his eyes settle upon."

Isobail studied her a moment. "I...think not. Not this time, Branwenn. There is more in his feelings for you than lust. And you should list me well, for I have known Callum for many, many years."

Branwenn's heart soared, but she tamped down on the feeling. She'd not allow her own hopes to cloud her vision where something as important as her future with Callum was concerned. She shrugged, "Mayhap."

Isobail squeezed Branwenn's hand. "Nay, not 'mayhap', but 'truly'! He loves you, Branwenn. Accept it, rejoice in it, return it, and, for heaven's sake, begin your life with him before 'tis too late!"

Branwenn broke away and stood up. "I cannot! Do you not think I crave to 'rejoice' in the knowledge of his love for me?" She turned, her arms crossed over her chest, and stood staring down at the lavender growing next to the bench. "But, he has revealed naught more than desire whenever we meet." She briefly turned her gaze to Isobail when she said, "That, and some terrible scheme to wed me—which I attribute as guilt for taking my maidenhead." She shrugged and turned back to the lavender. "Until he says the words, tells me how deeply his feelings run for me, I can only react to how he behaves when we are together."

Why, after all the times now that she'd shared her body with him, had he never felt compelled to tell her he loved her? If, in fact, he did, as Daniel, and now Isobail, were so inclined to believe. Lord, she herself had nearly screamed the words several times now when she was deep in the throes of release. But, fortunately, thus far, her heart's instinct for survival had somehow always put a lock on her tongue just as she would have said them.

Lord, what a callow lass she'd been that first night. She'd truly believed the words would tumble from his lips, like sugared berries, if not during, then certainly *after* she gave him her virginity. But, nay, all she'd received was a demand that they wed. And that, she was sure, had more to do with his jumbled-together feelings of honor, guilt and, no doubt, fear of reprisal from her older brothers. Not to mention his grandmother. And Maggie. And mayhap, even Laird MacGregor. And what about Reys, if he found out? Aye, now that she thought about it, *fear* no doubt had more to do with his desire to wed her than did guilt or honor.

* * *

Callum whistled as he strode across the north bailey toward the arched entry to the garden. The day was bright, with just the right amount of chill in the air to make training outdoors pleasant. Daniel and Bao were close to the end of what they'd set out to teach him and they would be returning to their families soon. 'Twas too bad that they'd no doubt be away from them at

Michaelmas, but at least they'd be home for *Oidhche Shamhna*, the eve of *Samhainn*. He walked through the archway and stopped dead in his tracks. Branwenn. And Isobail. Together. That could not be good. For him, at least.

* * *

Isobail looked up and, seeing Callum, motioned for him to come to her. He nodded and began striding toward them, but his visage was rather tightly drawn. He was no doubt worried she had let slip to his ladylove their youthful—rather foolish, now that she thought on it—carnal dalliance, and believed himself to be walking toward his doom. She smiled gently, but inside, to herself, she chuckled. Poor Callum. 'Twas comical, really, the depths to which he'd sunk, at least where the lady Branwenn was concerned. For, who among his many past amours would have believed it possible that he would have had to resort to the childish game of jealousy to try to win the hand of his true love? He, with the silver tongue of the devil and the beauty of a god?

"Branwenn," she said then, "look you, we have a visitor whom you will be pleased to see, I'm sure."

* * *

Branwenn turned and froze. *Callum!* Oh, Lord. She felt the heat of the flush that rapidly traveled o'er her face and neck. What a fool she'd been last eve, first accusing him of playing her false, then not believing him when he gave her his promise 'twas not the case. She'd even closed the door in his face! And now, by the look upon his countenance, 'twas clear he held only disgust for her. And with the way he'd behaved this morn, no doubt he'd decided to accept her refusal of his troth and move on with his life.

She had to get out of here. She could not, *could not*, face him now. She had to have some time to herself first to think what she could do, say, to gain his forgiveness before speaking to him again. And, then, should she gain his forgiveness and he want to resume their affair—was she willing to do such again without his vow of devotion? She just truly knew not! Her eyes darted first to the right and then to the left, but there was no other way out of the garden, except through the entrance that Callum was now in direct line of.

"G'morn, Branwenn," Callum said when he at last stood before them, but there was little modulation in his voice. And his eyes held no warmth.

Complete desolation washed over her. 'Twas too late, then. Branwenn dipped her head in greeting. "G'morn," she whispered thickly.

He turned and took hold of Isobail's hand, "G'morn Isobail" his voice held much more feeling when he said that lady's name, Branwenn noticed. When he bent down and placed a quick kiss on Isobail's cheek, Branwenn felt as if a knife had been driven deep into her heart and viciously twisted. Tears welled in her eyes, against her will. Damn it to the fiery pit of hell! Would she never be able to control this mortifying tendency to weep over him? She quickly turned her watery gaze to the lavender and then further still, to the bed of flowers just ahead. "Oh, look you!" she said as brightly as she could. "The last daisy of the summer is just there. I must cut it for Grandmother Maclean." She hustled over and bent down to the task, surreptitiously scrubbing away the moisture from her cheeks on the upper sleeve of her gown.

"Branwenn," Isobail started, but a fit of coughing overtook her.

"Isobail!" Callum yelled, falling to his knees in front of her and patting her back.

"Godamercy!" Branwenn cried, and hurried over to sit beside the lady, placing her arm around her waist for support. "Callum," she said anxiously, her eye never leaving Isobail's constricted countenance, "she must have something to drink. Go you to the keep and bring her back some mulled *uisge beatha*." She lifted her eyes only as far as his chin, saying, "Make haste."

"Aye." Callum scurried to his feet and ran quickly out the entrance to the garden and toward the keep.

In another moment, Isobail's coughing abated. "Branwenn," she said, her voice ragged, "I asked Callum to meet us here because I have a boon to request of the two of you." She took the proffered kerchief from Branwenn and delicately wiped her mouth and nose.

Branwenn felt so heartsick for Isobail at that moment that she would have given her anything she requested—even Callum—for 'twas too cruel that such a young mother should be forced to leave this world before her bairn was grown. "Aye, whatever you need from me, I shall not say you nay."

Isobail smiled wanly. "Let us first speak to Callum before you give such a vow to me, for what I will ask of you requires both of your consents."

Callum jogged back through the entry to the garden, his hand resting over the top of the silver cup to keep its contents from sloshing over the rim.

Skidding to a halt in front of Isobail, he dropped down to his knees and gently placed the cup between both of her hands. "Here, drink this down," he said before helping her to lift it to her lips.

Isobail drank deeply of the honeyed spirit. Afterward, with a sigh and a soft smile, she said to the two of them "My thanks. 'Tis clear this sickness grows worse with each passing day." With decided movements, she placed the cup next to her on the bench and, taking Callum's hand, placed it on top of the one Branwenn had resting on her knee.

Branwenn and Callum looked, for the first time that day, deeply into each other's eyes.

"I want you two to parent my son, David, after I am gone," she said baldly. No time to slowly lead the two down the path of understanding, as she'd originally planned. That had just become ever more plain to her.

Their eyes swiftly settled on Isobail's countenance, a look of surprise clear on their visages.

"But...we are not wed," Branwenn said finally. Feeling the weight of Callum's gaze settle on her face, she continued, "Is there no godparent to take the lad?"

Isobail sighed and nodded her head. "Aye, my brother Robert, was assigned that duty. But he is in no position now—nor, might he ever be—to take on that task. He is, at this very moment, speaking with his liege, William, King of Scots, to try and negotiate a way of paying my father's levy so that he—and our clan—will not lose our holding."

Callum's brows furrowed. "Robert is in danger of losing his holding? How can this be?"

Isobail turned her face away and gazed at the flowers growing in the bed to her right. "My father..."—she shook her head and sighed once again—"he spent his coin, and borrowed against future earnings, fighting the Norman earl that was bequeathed land to the south of our holding. And now, 'tis all Robert can do to keep our clan, and our holding together." She turned and gazed pleadingly at first Branwenn and then Callum. "Will you?"

"Aye, we will raise your bairn. Worry not," Callum said quickly, decisively.

Branwenn's brows lifted in surprise. And when she felt his eyes settle upon her face once more, she turned her gaze to him as well. There was warmth—and determination—shining brightly there now, again, praise be! "Aye, we shall."

* * *

A bit later, after Callum and Branwenn had settled Isobail with Grandmother Maclean and Maggie in the solar, Callum took hold of Branwenn's hand and silently led her back to the garden from which they'd just come.

When they were at last settled upon the stone bench, their knees lightly touching as they faced each other, Callum said softly, "Why do you not wear the filet I gave you?"

Branwenn nervously lifted her hand to her head and

touched the place where the ornament had been, only a few hours past, then slowly let it drift down to settle once more in her lap. She sighed. "Because...I believed you no longer wanted me; were disgusted by my behavior last eve and pleased to have done with me."

Callum reached over and took hold of Branwenn's hand and lifted it to his lips. He opened it and placed a kiss in her palm before bringing it up to his face and softly rubbing the back of her fingers against his bristle-roughened cheek. "Nay, I assure you, that is not the case. I desire you as ever, crave your touch as ever, beg your acceptance of my troth—as ever." He brought his own hand up to her cheek and tipped her chin up with his thumb so that she now looked directly into his eyes as he spoke. "And 'tis plain by your agreement to Isobail's request that you are now ready to do just that. Let me first speak to my step—Why do you shake your head?" His spine stiffened and his eyes shot emerald fire. "Braaan-wennn," he said warningly, "do not—*do not*—say 'nay' to me again. 'Tis much too late for that. We've a foster son to raise—have you forgotten so quickly?"

She twisted from his hold and turned her face away. "Nay, I've not forgotten. But, Callum, I will not wed you now. Let us first see whether the lady truly passes from this earthly realm, then"—she took in a deep breath and slowly released it—"I will wed you." 'Twas the least she could do for Isobail, wed Callum even if he'd not given his heart to her. After all, he'd not loved the lady Lara, and just look how kind and gentle—and generous as well—he'd been with her while they were wed. 'Twas clear he'd make a wonderful husband; certainly better than the Norman would have been, even had he not been a deviant.

Callum bit back a groan of frustration. So, they'd be meeting in secret again, hiding their affair from all curious eyes. He truly wanted to pull out his hair and yell like a banshee. Mayhap, even hop around like some wee brownie. "But we cannot continue meeting as we have much longer, else one of your brothers is bound to find out and skin me alive."

Branwenn turned to him. "Nay, you are right. 'Tis why I've decided we should not do so again until we wed. *If* we wed, that is."

Callum stopped breathing. *Not do so again? Until they were wed?* He'd not even think about the possibility of *not* wedding her, but to go for who knew how long without lying with her again, making love to her again? 'Twas too cruel a hell to bear.

"Are you well?" Branwenn said, alarm in her voice. She placed her hand over his. "You've gone as red as a raspberry—do you need something to drink? Callum! Say something!"

He forced air into his lungs. "I'm fine," he said in a strained voice. "Will you at least walk with me after supper each eve?" Surely, he could find some way of testing her resolve, if they could spend some time alone together.

Branwenn bit her lip. Then, at last, she nodded her head. "Aye, that should be fine." She paused only a second before continuing, "but I shall ask Maggie to accompany us as well, as chaperone. She will allow us a bit of privacy, I'm sure, but not enough to raise eyebrows." She smiled brightly. "Will that do?"

Callum ground his teeth together. "Aye, that will do," he said at last.

* * *

CHAPTER 8

*C*ALLUM FUMED SILENTLY as he stood inside the entryway to the great hall a sennight later. That blasted new guard, *Kerk*, he was called, had sidled up to Branwenn as she stood with Callum's mother next to the hearth awaiting the players' next scene. Callum had only been gone from her side no more than a quarter hour, as he had been called upon by his stepfather to aid in settling a dispute between two soldiers stationed on the curtain wall, and the man had clearly taken advantage of the opportunity his absence afforded.

Why had his mother insisted on inviting this thorn-in-his-side to supper yet again? 'Twas the third night in a row, and each night, the guard found some way or other to maneuver himself into Branwenn's company. Not only that, but 'twas clear, she enjoyed the attention he bestowed upon her, for she blushed and gave him that shy smile that should *only* be given to Callum, her lover, and soon to be husband.

A niggling worry, which he'd been forcefully pushing down these past days, reared up in his mind again, and this time, he allowed it audience. *Was Branwenn more like Lara than he at first believed?*

On the cusp of that thought, Kenrick, a childhood friend and fellow clansman, came up beside him and followed the line of Callum's vision. He elbowed Callum in the ribs and leaned close, murmuring, "She's more lovely than your last, but will she be more loyal?"

The trill of Branwenn's laughter floated over to where they stood.

Pressure built in Callum's chest. He shrugged. But then she looked toward the entry and saw him and gave him a gleeful grin, motioning for him to come to her, and the pressure evaporated. With a nod to her, he said, "Aye, she'll be loyal. She's naught like Lara."

When, in the next instant, the guard, *Kerk*, brushed his fingertips over Branwenn's and took the silver cup *much too slowly* from her hand before taking a drink from it, Callum growled and strode toward the two, leaving his guffawing friend in his wake. He tapped the new guard on the shoulder. When Kerk turned with a cocked brow and looked at him in question, Callum said, "I have something of import to speak with you about. Come with me into the antechamber." He turned and walked toward the entry, feeling the man's presence close behind.

Once there, he said to him, "You are attempting to woo a lady who is already spoken for. She is my betrothed, in case you have not heard, so keep your distance."

The guard's mouth twitched, then, as if he couldn't hold in the mirth, he bellowed with laughter, shaking his head and slapping Callum on the back, before turning away and heading back into the great hall. Callum fought the flush of heat that effused his neck and face.

For a long moment, he stood staring at the empty doorway. The guard's laugh had been one of those deep belly laughs that one has when one knows something the other doesn't and is thoroughly amused by the prospect. It set Callum's teeth on edge. He stormed back into the great hall, fully expecting to find the guard once again at Branwenn's side, but surprisingly, the man was now settled with some of the other guests at one of the trestle tables, drinking some ale.

* * *

A sennight later—it had now been fourteen long days, and nights, without Callum, for she was determined not to allow him to bed her again until she was certain of his feelings for her—Branwenn made a decision while breaking her fast. She'd go to the old woman that dwelled in the MacGregor wood—the woman she'd heard Maggie speak of in reference to Lara, though she knew not what Callum's wife had asked for—and obtain from her a remedy of sorts. For, 'twas clear from what she'd heard, that the lady had herbal concoctions and mayhap, just mayhap, there might be some that could give her heart some ease.

* * *

Callum watched Branwenn leave through the gate of

the fortress and bells of alarm went off in his head. She wasn't fleeing from him, was she? Or, worse, meeting *Kerk*, that pretty-faced new guard? He tossed his shirt and tunic on over his braies and, after giving a quick, but, he was sure, muddled explanation to Daniel as to why he was leaving so suddenly, he charged after her. Or, rather, ran to the stables, retrieved his mount, and *then* charged after her.

Where on earth was she headed? She'd been noticeably loathe these past sennights, to stray past the walls of the fortress without him, or one of her brothers, as escort. Which, he assumed was due to some remaining dread that the Norman swine, Gaiallard de Montfort, would somehow find her and sweep her off to Cambria again. So, *was* she meeting that guard?

Was Branwenn losing interest in him? God! If only he could convince her to let him into her chamber again—then, 'twas certain he could remind her of her desire for him.

Or—and this made his gut wrench at the same time it sliced through his heart—*Is* she more like Lara than he thought possible? Nay, no matter what his misgivings regarding her feelings for him, Callum could not believe she'd give her body to another so easily, so quickly, after their own carnal relations had been—and he was set on this—*temporarily* ended by her. Especially knowing how shy she still was to even allow him to look upon her naked form—a thing he had never *yet* been allowed to do. Nay, she'd not flit from one man's bed to the next so quickly.

Callum's spine straightened. Nay, but she might allow the man a kiss. And that was truly enough to send his temper rising like volcanic spew straight to the sun.

It took him a bit of time to find her tracks, but once found, an even more violent sense of alarm overtook him and his stomach twisted in his belly so tightly, it felt as if he'd taken a direct, unprotected, blow to it with a lance. *She was headed for the old woman's cot*, he just knew it. His heart began to ache. Branwenn, *Branwenn*, he thought, I beg you, do not be doing what I think you are doing. Do not. Do not follow in the same wretched steps as Lara.

* * *

The forest lined the craggy shore of the ocean and it took a bit of time for Branwenn to traverse the glen that lay between the MacGregor fortress and the ocean. But, by mid-morn she was rapping on the splintered pine door of the old woman's cot.

And, in less than a quarter-hour's time more, she was cheerfully making her way back across the glen, pouch in hand.

In the next moment, the sound of thundering horse's hooves broke into her thoughts.

She came to an abrupt standstill, her heart leaping into her throat. Was she about to be trampled then? She turned her head this way and that, but couldn't see from which direction the horse was traveling. Just as she'd decided she'd best scurry atop yon boulder, she saw him. *Callum*. And he did not look pleased.

By instinct alone, she took a step backward. Unfortunately, the side of her heel landed on the edge of a rabbit hole and her ankle twisted. "*Aieee!*" she cried out, falling backward, right on her rump.

"Whoa!" Callum yelled, pulling hard on the reins and jumping off his bay. "*Branwenn!* Are you all right?"

Branwenn rolled onto her knees and stood, rubbing her abused backside with one hand. "Aye," she said sheepishly.

Callum continued to study her a moment, but then his eye stalled on the brown pouch, it's string closure wrapped around her wrist. "Where did you get that?" he asked darkly. 'Twas an accusation.

Tipping her chin up and looking down her nose at him, she said, "'Tis none of your concern."

Callum's green eyes burned into her. "Aye, 'tis definitely my concern, if you seek to use those herbs to make my babe flush from your womb."

Branwenn's eyes grew round. "Your...your...your *babe*?!" she sputtered.

"Aye, my *babe*."

Branwenn shook her head in wonder. "But, I carry not your babe, as well you know, for you made quite certain of that each time we"—she fluttered her hand in the air—"you know." She grabbed a fist-full of the skirt of her gown. "Do you forget, this very gown I wear has more likelihood of that outcome than do I?"

His eyes narrowed. "So, you do not attempt to lose my bairn?"

"NAY!" she bellowed, and then: "Are you deaf, or only simple-minded?"

Callum's stance relaxed. A soft smile lit his countenance and his warm gaze heated her skin as it made a slow journey down her frame. "What have you in that pouch then, my wee *fey Mai*?" he said, his voice deep, smooth, sultry. He walked up to her and took hold of her wrist—the one with the pouch attached—and brought its underside up to his lips. He kissed her there, on the tender, sensitive skin that sheltered her now-leaping pulse and followed that with a deliciously evocative lick. "I've missed you. Have you missed me?" he asked softly. There was a twinkle in his eye as he looked up at her through half-closed lids.

Her heart hammered in her chest. She swallowed hard and cleared her throat. "Uhh," she croaked, "ahem...aye, I mean." She couldn't catch her breath. He did that to her. He turned her mind to mush and then the next thing she knew, they were mating like rabbits again. "Callum, stop. Please."

"But you taste so sweet, like rose petals dipped in honey." His lips lightly traveled to the string of the pouch. He began to nibble at it with his teeth. His teeth, his moist breath, tickled the thin skin there and goosebumps formed on her arms. "What's in the pouch, Branwenn?"

Oh, what was the use? He'd no doubt find it ever so amusing when she told him, but her only other option was to stand here and allow him to seduce her instead. And she had no doubt that the outcome would be the same in any case. He'd have her so dull-witted with need for him, that he'd wrangle the truth from her before the last spark was extinguished.

"'Tis a love potion," she said finally.

His head sprang up and he dropped her wrist as if

burned. "A *love* potion?" His eyes narrowed. "For whom is that potion intended? Not that new guard I saw you speaking with this eve past?"

"Nay, you dolt! The potion's for *me*!" She dropped her chin to her chest and mumbled, "and you."

"You...and *me*? He crowded into her, their bodies no farther apart than the finest of gossamer silk. He rested his hands on her waist and dipped his head so that his lips brushed her ear as he asked in a smoky whisper, "Do you love me, Branwenn?"

She shrugged.

She felt his smile against her ear and then he said, his voice low, so low, so intoxicating, the vibration of it traveled, like warm mead, down deep inside her to her womb, "Why ever would you think you needed to give *me* a love potion? Has it not been plain, as plain as...as...well, as plain as the freckle on your lovely left breast,"—her cheeks flamed at that reminder—"that I already love you? Nay, more, I *adore* you. I cannot get through one moment of the day without thinking of you?" He took her hand and placed her open palm on his cheek. "Wed me, Branwenn. Wed me, have babes with me, make love to me every day, build a life with me. Wed me."

"Aaayye," Branwenn said. 'Twas a sigh. But there was joy in her voice and joy in that word when she said it. "And I do! I do love you!"

"Praise be," he said reverently. Then he kissed her to seal the promise.

* * *

A short time later, as they walked hand-in-hand

across the glen, Callum asked softly, a bit warily, "So...you will wed me then? No more uncertainty?" He bent forward a bit and craned his neck in order to see her profile.

There was only a twinkling of a second's hesitation before a bright smile split her countenance. When she looked at him, there was no doubt. Love shown there. "Aye, I'll wed you. I already said I would, remember? Back there?"—she pointed behind her—"Five minutes ago?" she teased. "When?"

Callum let out a loud '*whoop!*' and threw his arms around her waist. He began to spin her around.

"Caaallum!" she squealed.

"Now! The morrow! Soon!" he yelled and then he tossed his head back and laughed.

Branwenn relaxed in his embrace and threw her hands up in the air, joyous laughter bubbling from her throat as she allowed herself to enjoy the revolving view. Was there ever a more beautiful, perfect day?

* * *

Later, as they lay on their backs in the tall, brown-of-winter, meadow grass and gazed up at the white clouds as they moved slowly across the pale blue sky, Branwenn's thoughts turned to the reason for Callum's anger. "Want you many bairns, then?" she asked, turning her head to watch his expression as he answered.

He smiled a bit sheepishly and turned his head also. Looking into her eyes he said, "Aye. At least five"—her eyes widened and he turned on his side and raised up on an elbow—"but, we already have one—two, if you count David," he rushed to say.

Branwenn's smile turned tender. She lifted her hand and softly moved the hair that had fallen over his brow away from his eyes. "That will be fine then."

Callum bent his head and kissed her gently. "My thanks," he whispered. Rising above her, he settled between her thighs and began brushing soft kisses over her eyes, her nose, her cheeks. "You are, by far, the loveliest, most finely fair lass I've ever met."

"Caaallummm," she said on a sigh, her eyes closed as she drifted along the sensual stream he brought her down. Her eyes flew open. "But what of Maryn?" 'Twas an accusation. "And, tell me not that you did not find the fair Jesslyn to your liking as well—the two of you were betrothed."

Callum, his fingers twined through her hair and her head cradled in his palms, lifted his head and studied her. "'Tis truth, I believe, that first day we met all those moons ago—remember?" He waited for her nod before continuing, "I believe 'twas the day my childish, selfish love for Maryn took its last breath. I shall tell you this now, for you've made it clear that you want plain talk henceforth." Branwenn gave him a vigorous nod. Callum grinned and placed a quick peck on the tip of her nose before saying, "I wanted you that day. In fact, I had every intention of returning to the Maclean holding with my cousins after the negotiations were concluded and wooing you." He chuckled, shaking his head and looking off in the distance a moment, before turning his sights back on her. "Both your brothers—especially Daniel—saw that I was attracted. But, my pride, still sore from his winning all that I'd lost, made me hide my desire with some evasion or another.

Branwenn's eyes widened, her lips tipped up in mirth—and utter happiness. "Truly? Even after I scrubbed your kiss from my hand?"

"Aye." Callum grinned. "Mayhap *mostly* because you'd done such." He sighed. "But, then, I was made the prize in the negotiations between the clans, and it became my duty to wed Laird Gordon's daughter to settle the dispute. My plan to woo you was lost to me for evermore, or so I thought."

Branwenn had barely heard the last, so intrigued was she still by the notion that Callum had actually been attracted to her all those moons ago—had intended to *woo* her. "But—my hair! I was so ugly—"

Callum stiffened. "You were *not* ugly!" he said, as if she'd given the insult to him.

She shook her head, though there was little movement, as he held it in his hands. "How could you like me then?"

His smoldering green eyes scanned her face a moment before he replied, "As I said, you are the loveliest creature I've ever seen. My heart skips a beat each time my eyes rest on you—did you know that?"

Branwenn's eyes misted. She had to swallow past the lump in her throat before she could answer. "Nay," she whispered thickly and sniffled.

"I adore you, Branwenn." Callum gave in to his craving, dipping his head and kissing her. Hard and long. His desire grew so quickly out of control that he fisted his hands in her hair and ground his hard sex against the frustratingly-still-covered flower of her femininity. With a shaking hand, he dragged the thick material up, over her hips and did the same with his tunic and shirt before quickly unlacing his braies. "Open," was all he said. 'Twas a plea—and a demand.

She did just that. "I want you inside me. Now," she ground out. She knew she wasn't yet prepared, but the need to have him fill her after so long a time outweighed the natural aversion to the sting it would cause when he at first entered her.

"Aye," Callum said, but he took a second—a small second—to prepare her a little, even using a bit of his own saliva to lessen the damp resistance before he pushed inside her as he kissed her. It abraded, but she cared not. She even helped him by clamping her hands to his hard buttocks and pushing down. She held her breath until he was fully seated. In the next moment, he was gently rocking into her, using his manhood to entice her canal to give up its juices. "God, you are so perfect. A perfect fit for me," he said, his voice strained. Suddenly he threw his head back. "Aaahhh!" He stopped moving. His entire frame shuddered violently and his breath was harsh, labored. He dipped his head, resting it on her shoulder. "God, I almost came just then."

"Good."

He turned his head and looked at her. "Nay, not good. I am still determined that you will not be with child when we wed. This marriage will have no scandal attached to it, as my previous one did."

"But this is different! We *love* each other; we *want* to

make babes together!"

He lifted up and began kissing her cheek, her neck, nuzzling her just below her ear. He brought his mouth to her lobe and nibbled it a moment, slowly beginning to move his hips once more in the ancient rhythm they'd come to know so well together in the sennights prior to the conclusion of their affair. "Aye," he said at last, the hot breath and vibration of his deep voice teasing her ear canal as he spoke into it, "but *after* we are well-wed, my love."

A desperate need for release unfurled within her womb, making her move her hips in tandem with his, making her meet him halfway, making her take him deeper with each new thrust. She tossed her head, feeling the dew from her exertion form on her hot skin.

Callum felt the first contractions of her canal and moved with more speed in and out of her, forcing the climax he knew she was on the verge of having. In seconds, she was crying out his name, yanking and clawing at the cloth of his tunic covering his back. *Beautiful.* The word flitted across his sex-fogged mind as he watched her sensual delight peak and then slowly settle into tired contentment.

He was close now himself. He gave her one last, long, deep-throated kiss as he took his pleasure of her. In the next moment, his seed began to rise. He jerked out of her. "Aargh!" he cried, his body spasming in reaction to the pleasure-pain of leaving her to complete the process outside her loving cavity. Her small, warm hand settled around him and stroked rapidly. He was lost to the pleasure then, and in seconds he was spewing his seed—on her gown.

"What a waste," she said chidingly. But there was humor in it as well, for the dimple in her cheek was in clear evidence. "At least I know now 'twill not stain."

Callum rolled over onto his back and threw his forearm over his eyes. "Lord, but you are getting quite good at that."

Branwenn grinned, rising up and resting her chin on the arm she lay over his heaving chest. "Truly?"

He cocked his head slightly and, opening one eye, peered out from under his arm at her. He grinned too. "Aye, my wee sea sprite. You've got me under your spell now. Do with me as you will—for, 'tis truth, that I have none left where you are concerned."

Branwenn giggled. A thought struck her then. A very unnerving thought that harkened back to their earlier conversation. "Did you...do"—she fluttered her hand in the air, waving it over their bodies quickly—"*this*...with Jesslyn? I mean, when you were betrothed?"

A bit more recovered from the intense release he'd just received at the hand of his faery lover, Callum's sense of humor kicked in. He rolled to his side and straddled her, tickling her ribs. "What think you?"

"*Aieee! Caaaluuummm!* Stop! That tickles!" But she was laughing uncontrollably now, trying valiantly to push his hands away and twisting from side to side.

His own laughter had a bit of evil pleasure running through it.

After another moment of this, he at last had mercy on her and stopped. Still settled astraddle her, resting on his knees, he said at last, "Nay, my love, I've had no one but you for nearly two years. Well, except for the one night of my wedding to Lara."

Branwenn's eyes grew round. Callum? Callum, the most gorgeous human male she'd ever laid eyes on? Callum, who could charm the gown off of any woman—lass or lady—with that silver tongue of his, had not been with a woman for that long?

"Truly?"

He chuckled. She was clearly amazed. Hell, *he* was amazed he'd gone so long. But gazing upon the end result of all those moons of abstention, he realized, 'twas worth every moment. And he'd do it again, if she were waiting for him at the end of it. "Aye," he finally said, "truly."

* * *

"Well, 'tis clear that we were right to inveigle that handsome guard to give his attention to Branwenn these past eves," Grandmother Maclean said to Maggie and Isobail the next day. "For, I'm sure 'tis what sparked my grandson to at last speak his heart to our lass."

Isobail grinned. "Aye, but 'tis also clear that Branwenn would get those words from him regardless—she was quite set on giving him a love potion!"

"Aye, but naught, even a love potion, I trow, could have brought forth those words from my son lest there was a good amount of feeling behind them in the first place," Maggie said.

The door to the solar swung open and Branwenn stepped inside. "Good morn, ladies," she said. Then, to

Highland Magic

Lady Maclean: "Will you give me some assistance with the priest? He is insisting that we wait until after *Samhainn* to speak our vows, as he must oversee and collect his parish's tithes to the church from this year's harvest until that time. Must we wait so long?"

"But, lass, that gives us less than a moon to put your trousseau together and plan the feast! I'll not rush the priest, for we, ourselves, need at least that long to plan the wedding."

Branwenn's shoulders slumped. "But, Grandmother..." Then, seeing the light of determination in the older woman's eyes, she said, "Oh, very well." She turned to Maggie. "Will you at least speak to your son and explain this to him? For, I cannot bear to give him these bad tidings. He was so determined that we would be wed within the sennight this day past."

"Aye, lass, fret no more about it, for I know just the thing that will turn his mind to other pursuits." She turned to Lady Maclean and said, "Mother, let us host a tournament! 'Tis been so long since we've done such and Chalmers has said his warriors are growing fractious with the onset of winter coming on. This will surely settle them."

Lady Maclean grinned. "Perfect. 'Tis the perfect solution. And I'm sure Daniel and Bao will be pleased for the diversion as well."

"But will it not take just as long to prepare for a tournament?" Branwenn asked, bemused.

"Aye, it will," Isobail chimed in, having caught the gist of the lady's reasoning. "But, the tournament will require that the men *train* quite vigorously. Long hours, in fact." She turned to Maggie, "Am I not right, my lady?"

Maggie nodded and there was a definite sparkle in her eye. "Aye, which will give my son little, if any time, to storm about muttering over the delay in the wedding."

"But what if Callum gets killed! "Nay! 'Tis a very bad plan, I trow," Branwenn said with a shake of her head.

Lady Maclean looked at her with kindness. "Branwenn, my dear, what Maggie and I speak of is a test of skill on the jousting lists, not a melee. 'Twill be no more likelihood of death than there is each day when Callum trains."

* * *

Little did Gaiallard de Montfort know, as he stepped off the sea vessel onto the craggy shore of Arren that mid-October morn, that he was setting foot at almost the exact location his wayward betrothed had stepped close to three moons prior.

He'd come on this initial search mission alone. He was not far behind Branwenn's brother Reys, whom he'd been tracking since the man departed with his new bride a fortnight past, and whom he assumed had direct knowledge of where the chit was staying. He had every intention of bringing her back with him and completing the ceremony that would make her legally his bride, giving him the demesne he'd been promised.

When he'd awakened the morn of the wedding and been hastened to meet with his uncle, he'd believed 'twas merely the formality of signing over the land that had prompted the early morning summons. But, when he'd been given the news that the girl had fled in the night—to no one knew where—and that Reys, her brother had stepped in to fulfill the contract by wedding Alyson, Gaiallard had been filled with a sense of relief. Now, he'd thought, he would at last be able to pursue the lady Caroline, as he'd wanted to do from the beginning. And that lady would surely not reject his troth now that he would be in possession of the lucrative demesne. There would also be the added benefit of getting his sister off his hands, for the thrill he'd received the past times he'd played his little game with her had palled, as she was no longer quite the untutored youngling that she'd been when he'd begun teaching her how to pleasure a man.

But his initial elation was dashed into dismal dust in the next moments when his Uncle told him that the demesne would now go to his arch rival, Guy de Burgh. Over the last year, Guy had won the day at every tournament the two had entered, bringing much praise and coin to both himself, and his liege lord, Guillaume le Maréchal.

But, he would deal with that thorny matter later. First, he must at least fulfill the original contract, as signed, then he would petition the court for rights to the land he'd been promised.

"Ho! Fisherman!" he called out to an old man just taking his boat out for the day.

The man turned and nodded a greeting.

Gaiallard jogged up to him and said, "A few moons past, was there a lass—he intentionally used the vernacular of the region—who washed up on shore? A shipwreck survivor, mayhap?"

The man's brows drew together in thought and he scratched his rather dirty, quite tangled, gray-haired pate. After a moment he shook his head. "Nay, 'twas no' a lass I sa', but a lad of mayhap thorteen summer."

Gaiallard's heart began to pound as his blood rushed. Victory was just within his grasp, he could feel it. "And, in what direction did the lad go, do you recall?"

The old fisherman shrugged. "I know no', fer the lad be gone from m' hut when I got back fro' fishin'."

Damn! A lost trail. And then: "Did a man, with hair as black as pitch, come through here a few days past?"

"Aye—he be a fine sor', too, fer he bought me whol' catch and then shared hi' spirits wi' me. And he could sing wi' the choir of heav'n, too, so sweet wa' his voice."

Reys. It had to be, for he was well known for his songs and his playing of the *crwth*, the lyre-like instrument he was rarely without. "Do you happen to know in what direction *he* went?"

"Aye, he crossed on a boat to the High Land no' two days past."

Wonderful! "My thanks, old man," Gaiallard said and strode back the way he'd come, back to where the larger sea craft were docked.

* * *

Alyson nocked her arrow, drew the bow and took aim. "Like this?" she asked Reys.

Reys, who stood behind his young wife, studied her

Highland Magic

stance from that angle and crouched down to see if her aim was true, then walked to her right side and studied her stance from that angle as well. "Aye, that's good. Now, loose the bowstring and, forget not to keep your aim and follow through until your right hand is just past your ear."

His young wife had been so timid with him the first couple of moons after their wedding, even tho' Reys had sworn there would be no pressure from him to bring forth an heir until she was older. But, one day a few sennights past, he'd decided to go grouse hunting with bow and arrow and, when she'd shown interest in the outing, he'd asked her if she would like to join him. Surprisingly, she'd said she would. That had been the first day of their newly budding friendship. For, she'd taken to the sport immediately, 'tho the bow he'd lent her was too large for her frame.

It had pleased him so greatly that she had become easier with him, that he'd done something he'd never done before: given a lady his promise that he'd not go bow hunting without her ever again! She was so avid to try her new skills after her first success—she'd brought back two grouse that first day—that she'd pleaded with him to take her out to the moors again the next day. And so had begun over these past sennights, a daily ritual in which they both roamed the moors in the small hours of the morn, hunting for grouse, geese, ducks and other wild game for their dinner.

Of course, since that first day, he'd had made for her a lovely bow, just her size. 'Twas the one she now used to expertly hit the target he'd set up for her.

"Alyson, I do believe you've outdone me in this sport," he said when he saw that she'd split the arrow down the center that still reverberated in the target with the next one she let loose.

She turned and grinned at him, the dimple in her left cheek now in full view and her grey eyes glowing. "Did you see that!"

"Yes, 'twas—"

"Oh, but I must try to do it again!" Positioning herself in the correct stance once more, she said, a bit over her shoulder, "Reys, will you please take the arrows out of the target? I want to start afresh."

Reys grinned and shook his head as he began walking that direction. "Do not dare let loose that arrow while I'm in between you and your sights, my fair young mistress!" he called over his shoulder.

Alyson giggled. "I shall not, I give you my oath!"

After several more attempts to replicate her previous feat with no success, Alyson at last relaxed her stance and began to put away her gear. "How ever did I do it? How?"

"I know not, for I confess, I was looking elsewhere when you loosed your arrow."

With a sigh of resignation, Alyson nodded her head. "Well, if I did it once, I will not rest until I do it again." Lifting her head from her task and turning her gaze to him, she asked, "When will we reach our destination?"

Reys shrugged and looked off in the direction they would be traveling come morn. "I believe we should arrive at the Maclean holding in another day—mayhap two."

"Will the lady of the keep be vexed that you've brought me with you, that she must place us in different chambers?"

"Nay, Lady Maryn is a kind woman, very generous. She shall open her home to us gladly, you shall see."

"But, will she not find it odd that you and I do not...share a bed?"

Reys, at that moment, would have given his right arm to be allowed to fold the poor girl in his arms and comfort her, but she would not allow the contact. She was still as skittish as a new colt when faced with the prospect of any physical contact with him. So, he said instead, "I truly doubt she shall give such a thought more than a second's notice, my sweet."

* * *

Late afternoon, two days later, Reys and Alyson begged entrance to the Maclean fortress.

But 'twas not Maryn and Daniel who met them in the courtyard, 'twas the lady Jesslyn.

"M'lady," Reys said warmly, bending low over her hand and lightly pressing his lips to the back of it. "I was expecting Laird Daniel and Lady Maryn to greet us; are they away from home at present?"

Jesslyn smiled. "Nay, sir, I do believe, at least Maryn is at her home—the MacLaurin holding—at this time. My husband, Bao, is the new chieftain here, you see."

"Ah, and where is Bao? Is he on the training field?"

"Nay, he's at the MacGregor holding at present." Jesslyn turned and extended her arm in the direction of the entrance. "Will you not come inside? You are in time to partake of the meal that is about to be served."

"My thanks, my lady." He turned slightly toward Alyson. "Lady Jesslyn, this is my bride, Lady Alyson."

Alyson dipped her head and did a small courtesy. "Good day, my lady. I thank you for your kind hospitality."

"Good day, Lady Alyson," Jesslyn said warmly. "And you are quite welcome." Turning back toward the keep, she said, "Now, let us go inside where we may more comfortably settle and have our repast."

Alyson walked as closely beside her husband as she was able without touching him. The lady Jesslyn was surely the most lovely creature she'd ever seen! Her flaxen brows arched prettily above eyes the color of the summer sky. She was rather tall, with a very womanly form—a thing Alyson had hoped to have one day...until...her brother. She felt her skin crawl and forced her mind back to her host. Gazing at the graceful way the lady Jesslyn moved, she tried to emulate it, but couldn't quite get the rhythm. And she was kind, as well, Alyson thought. Just as Reys had promised the other lady would be. A rather disconcerting thought struck her and she turned her eye to Reys to study his countenance. Nay, he did not look to be smitten by cupid's arrow where the lady was concerned, at least, she didn't think he did. Still. 'Twould not hurt to learn from and emulate the lady, she determined.

* * *

CHAPTER 9

*C*ALLUM ENTERED THE great hall behind Bao and Daniel. The three warriors had just come from the tilting lists and were now ready for a bit of ale to quench their thirst. Hot and sweaty, their damply crimped hair clung close to their heads—the result of wearing their metal helmets—they nonetheless were in high spirits after the exercise.

They wore only their mail, the plate armor being reserved for the practices closer to the time of the joust.

Callum, as was his usual way, since he preferred doing this particular task himself without the aid of a servant, went directly to the buttery and brought out a jug of ale and three cups.

He was halfway across the chamber when Daniel looked up from his discussion with Bao and said, "Have you any *uisge beatha*? I long for a wee draught of the stuff."

Callum grinned and whirled around. "Aye, we've

plenty," he said, striding back to the buttery and disappearing once more behind the screen.

"Think you he has any suspicion of what we mean to talk to him about?" Bao said in a low voice to Daniel.

Daniel chuckled. "Nay, I believe the poor man is completely blind to the trial by fire we're about to give him. He only thought his toughest contest this day was meeting our challenge at the lists."

Grinning behind his fist, Bao nodded. "Aye, but he has grown quite expert with the lance these past sennights. Tho' he was skilled enough when we began, he is now one of the toughest challengers I've ever met on the field."

"Aye, 'tis the same for me." Daniel clapped his brother on the shoulder. "We've taught him well."

Bao gave Daniel a baleful look. "Aye—and kept him from trailing in our sister's footsteps wherever she might go in the process."

"Aye, it hasn't been easy, for Callum is ever determined to partake of the husbandly rights he has no right to as yet, but that he's been forced to abstain from enjoying these past days."

"Truly, were it not for Branwenn having asked us to aid her in her effort to bring a bit of 'enchantment' as she called it, to their wedding night, I would have allowed the man to do as he would," Bao said, a look of surprise on his countenance. "I cannot believe, even as I hear myself say the words, that I, of all people, would allow such, but 'tis so plain that he adores the lass—and she, him—what could be the harm, for they'll be doing it soon enough in a few sennights time anyway?"

"Aye, but the lass is a lass," Daniel said. "And that means she wants their first night together as husband and wife to be memorable. If they were still meeting as they had been and doing—" He pressed the base of his palms over his eyes. "Nay, I cannot think about what they were doing! It gives me hives."

This made Bao bellow with laughter.

Daniel lifted his head and gave his brother a sheepish grin. "Well, anyway, 'twould not have the 'enchantment' of satisfying a long-felt desire."

Callum came from behind the screen of the buttery. It had taken him longer than he'd expected to find the butler's new hiding place for the amber liquor. The man was much too stingy with the stuff, a thing Callum was not used to, as it flowed rather freely at the Maclean keep. Besides, the butler should truly know better by now, as Callum had a nose for the stuff and he could sniff it out no matter how well hidden it was. "What, pray is so humorous?"

"Oh, naught of import," Bao said. "Daniel was just giving me advice about women."

Under the table, Daniel kicked Bao in the shin. "Ha! *Me?* Give *you* advice about women? 'Tis a good jest!" His eyes, narrowed slits while he looked at his brother, opened wide as he faced his cousin with an innocent mein. "Nay, 'twas Bao who was advising me on the correct stitch when sewing linen—did you know that he does all his wife's mending?" Daniel turned his sparkling grin on his brother once more. *There, get out of that one.*

Bao smiled. "Aye, and I thought it so riotously funny that Daniel asked me to show him how to sew the hole he blew in his braies from the high wind he breaks so often, as Maryn is weary of doing the task for him."

Callum guffawed. Clearly, Bao had gotten the better of Daniel with the last volley, and 'twas also clear the two were not going to give him the true subject that had caused so much mirth. "Well," he said bringing the flask and glasses to the table, "let us drink to Daniel's success with a needle and thread, for it sounds as if he needs it."

Daniel's only answer was a good-natured grumble.

The three were silent for the next few moments as they drank down some of the ardent spirits.

"Callum," Daniel said at last, "Bao and I have something we wish to speak with you about. Something to do with Branwenn."

Callum sat up straight. "Aye? She hasn't changed her mind about wedding me, has she?"

"Nay," Daniel said, shaking his head, "'tis naught like that." He looked at Bao. "We—Bao and I—well, we think it time we give you a bit of advice."

Callum's brows drew together in confusion. "Advice?"

"Aye," Bao said, "on being a husband."

Callum laughed. "Have you forgot? This will not be the first time I've been wed." He crossed his arms over his chest, his look smug when he continued, "I think I know quite a bit about the matter." He looked at Bao. "Hell, I was wed even before you were." Settling back, he looked from one to the other. "Tell me, what makes the two of you such experts, pray?"

"'Tis not that we are experts, but that we have more experience than you with, well, with this type of union."

Callum shook his head, one side of his face drawn up in disbelief. "What type of union? Male and female?" Now, he was insulted. "I assure you, I know plenty. Mayhap not more than Bao, him with his 'love for coin' credentials, but I'd wager my right testicle I know more than you, *cousin*."

Daniel's visage was filled with challenge. "I doubt tha—hey! Stop nodding your head, Judas," he said to Bao.

Bao, though still grinning at his brother, directed his words to Callum. "Nay, 'twas not the type of union we were referring to." He turned and looked at his cousin. "We are speaking more of the type of union you will have with Branwenn compared to the type you had with Lara." He paused, his eyes looking directly into Callum's. "Understand you my meaning now?"

Callum's skin actually crawled. He cleared his throat. "Tell me you do not intend for me to discuss my feelings for your sister with you. Truly. Tell me."

'Twas Daniel's turn to grin. "Aye, we do."

Callum sprung from his stool like a jack-in-the box. "Nay," he said as he took a step toward the entrance.

Bao grabbed him around his upper arm and halted his forward motion. "Aye. And you will also listen to what we, your betrothed's brothers—and co-signers on your wedding contract—have to say."

Callum, his heart pounding with dread at the

thought of opening himself wide for these two men to see, tried to pull away, saying beligerantly, "I'm going to my chamber and ordering a bath. I'll see you at supper."

"Sit down, soldier," Bao said. 'Twas his commander's voice and there was steel running through it, and steel in his eye as he continued to look at Callum.

Callum ground his teeth and growled low in his throat. "Fine." He sat back down, not too gently, on the stool he'd recently vacated.

"Good work," Daniel said, clapping his brother on the shoulder. He turned to Callum then and said, "You love our sister, Bao and I both know that."

Callum squirmed.

"But it is not enough to love the lady, you must—as Bao and I have both found out—tell your lady"—he turned to Bao—"what think you? Once a day? Or more?"

Bao opened his mouth to speak but Callum interrupted. "'Tis truth, you have no worries on that score. I have no problem telling Branwenn...umm...ahem...that." His traitor cheeks burned hot and he felt a new sheen of sweat break out under his arms. "Are we done now?"

"Nay, we are not done," Daniel said, shaking his head in vexation. "Why do you find this so hard to speak of, for Christ's sake? You act as if we are forcing you to reveal your most humiliating secret." He sat forward. "You are not embarrassed that you love my sister, are you? Because, I have to say, that does not bode well for your chances to wed her, as far as I'm concerned." He turned to Bao. "Do you not agree?" He was getting evil delight in making Callum squirm, he didn't know why. Well, mayhap he did. Maryn.

This scared the hell out Callum. "All right! I love her. I love her so desperately, she's the only thing I can think of whenever the two of you give me a quiet moment during the day between training sessions. She is the reason I breathe, the reason my heart beats, the reason I want to continue living on this earth." He put his elbows on the table and pressed the base of his palms into his eyes, unknowingly mirroring Daniel's earlier movements. "There. Is that what you wanted to hear?"

"Well, not really. But m'thanks for sharing," Daniel said, a grin as wide as the Maclean loch on his face as he gave a thumbs up to his brother.

Callum looked up, his eyes narrowed on Daniel as he mentally skewered the man with his lance. "Hatred does not begin to describe the feeling I have for you at this moment."

Daniel leaned forward and clapped his hand on Callum's shoulder. "You've passed your trial—does that make you feel better?"

"Trial? What trial?"

"Why the trial by ordeal we just put you through." Daniel sat back, crossing his arms over his chest. "Now, I trow, you should not have as much trouble speaking of such ever again." He looked at Bao, giving him a conspiratorial grin, "And that can only be good for our sister, as it took you much too long to give her the words in the first place."

"Aye," Bao said, "we were sure we'd have to curtail your secret meetings with the lass, so long was it taking you to speak frankly with her."

"You knew of our secret meetings?" Callum croaked, his green eyes as round as a trout's.

"Oh, aye—"

"But, let us not speak of that, shall we?" Daniel interjected. "Let us instead speak of the next item on our list."

Callum's heart leapt into his throat. "The next item...?" he asked weakly.

"Aye, Bao and I just want to make sure that you are prepared for all eventualities should the Norman decide to search for her; should the Norman find her."

Callum relaxed. Finally, talk of war. A right subject for fighting men such as them.

For the next hour, the two warrior brothers grilled Callum, forcing him to use every bit of cunning he had to give them his solution for any situation that they believed might arise if Gaiallard learned of Branwenn's whereabouts.

* * *

Miles away and later that day, at the Maclean holding, Reys and Alyson sat beside the hearth in the great hall with Jesslyn after supper.

"So you went first to the abbey? You did not learn of the pirates or the near shipwreck prior to that?"

Reys shrugged. "No, I can only suppose that 'twas mostly due to the fact that ship made it to its port instead of being lost at sea."

Highland Magic

"But, what made you decide to search for Branwenn here? Were the monks believing the lass had survived?"

With a short nod, Reys said, "Aye, they were. For, you see, one of them saw her holding onto a plank of wood after she'd been swept overboard, tho' they could not get to her, as every man at that time was occupied with saving his own life. And the place where the pirates attacked is where the sea becomes narrower, the land not so far away that it would have been impossible to make it to shore, assuming the tides were right."

Jesslyn bit her lip, her brows furrowed in thought. "I believe I ken you now. The monks would surely have found her, had she landed on their shore, but since they didn't, it behooved you to search for her here."

"Yes."

"And what of the Norman she was betrothed to? Has he accepted the break in the contract?"

"Yes, so it seems, for neither I nor my wife have seen or heard from him since the day of our wedding."

Alyson's heart beat a rapid tattoo in her chest. No, her husband had not heard from her brother, but she had. Gaiallard had sent several cryptic missives to her now. Threats. 'Twas not only the reason she'd pleaded with Reys to bring her with him on this quest, but 'twas also the reason that she'd been so avid to learn a means of defending herself, should he make his presence known. For, this time, she would kill him before submitting to his perversions. And, if he dared try to harm her husband—the only man, the only person, who'd ever been her champion—she would send the entire store from her quiver into him.

"And...you do not think you will, then?"

Reys gave her an appraising look. "No. I don't." Then: "Know you where my sister is staying?"

Jesslyn brightened. "Aye, I do. She is well and living at our allies', the MacGregors', holding."

Reys leapt to his feet. "That is good news!" he shouted.

Alyson sat forward, smiling at her husband's joy. She was so very pleased that he had found—or, nearly found—his sister alive. "Will we travel to the MacGregors then, Reys?" she asked softly.

"Yes," he answered and turned to Jesslyn. "I do not want to delay any longer than I must. I thank you for your generosity, but we must leave at first light on the morrow."

Jesslyn nodded, smiling. "I will have the steward give you the direction."

* * *

Jesslyn met Reys and Alyson in the courtyard the next morn and stood with them as they waited for their mounts to be readied for the journey. "Reys," she said, "I've been deliberating whether to tell you this before you leave, or allow you to find out when you reach the MacGregor holding...."

"Aye, what do you wish to tell me?"

"Your sister is betrothed to Callum MacGregor, the laird's nephew and Lady Maclean's grandson."

Reys was silent for a long minute as he digested this bit of news. If his sister wed a Highlander, she would not return with him to Cambria. And, if she did not return with him to Cambria, their princely cousin might be rather peeved. "I see," he said at last. "And when, pray, is the event to take place?"

"As soon after *Samhainn* as possible. It rests on the priest's schedule to give the blessing, I understand. Maryn and I are to be informed of the day in time to attend."

Alyson's eyes went wide with apprehension. What if her brother found out? What would he do to Branwenn? She would have to find some way to speak to her husband about those missives. She only wished now that she had shown them to him before, but she had just been too afraid that her brother would find out, and 'twas well before she'd grown so good with the bow and arrow that she'd received the last one.

Thank heavens, her brother had no idea where they were. She'd made sure of that. For, tho' Reys had misled the servants that remained at the keep, giving them a false destination, as Prince Llywelyn had decreed, she'd also lied in her letter to her father that they were bound for one of the Prince's holdings. And since neither her brother, nor her father, wanted any dealing with that man, she knew they'd do naught to verify it.

Reys nodded. "My thanks to you for telling me, I know 'twas not an easy thing to reveal."

"Aye, but now that I've done so, I know 'twas the right thing to do.

The stablemen brought their mounts to them and Reys took a moment to help Alyson get settled in the saddle before turning back to Jesslyn. "Good day to you, my lady."

"Yes," Alyson said shyly, "Good day, Lady Maclean. My thanks for the lovely chamber you provided."

Jesslyn smiled warmly at the young lass. She was such a shy wee thing. But lovely! My, how lovely she was. And she clearly felt uncomfortable using Jesslyn's first name. "You are most welcome, Lady Gryffyd," Jesslyn replied kindly, mirroring the lass's formality. The dimple that came into prominence when the lass smiled, as well as the warm blush that suffused her cheeks, told Jesslyn that she had not been called by that title yet, but was pleased to hear it.

On the third morning after their departure, they arrived at the MacGregor holding.

* * *

Gaiallard made camp in the wood not far from the village at the base of the Maclean fortress. Snow had fallen earlier, coating the ground, the trees, and blocking the entrance to a small cave he'd found. It took him several hours to dig the snow away and then find enough dry wood to start a fire. He carried his own kindling box, so starting the thing was of little moment. 'Twas keeping it going that would be the challenge. Why the hell did it have to snow today? Why could it not have waited until the morrow, after he'd had time to get enough firewood? 'Twas all his sister's fault. All his bad luck had started with her, that night that Branwenn had charged into Alyson's chamber after hearing the mewling, puling girl crying like a babe. And over what? If she'd just given him what he'd wanted of her, he'd have had done with her and then she'd not have received his fist. Tho', truth be told, he did enjoy the struggle. It made the winning much more pleasurable.

But, his fortunes had changed for the worse that night, and he'd not rest until he not only had his prize—the land, and the bride he'd been promised—but he'd had his vengeance on his sister and that Welsh troubadour she'd wed.

The trick would be to remain just far enough behind the two that they would never guess he tracked them, but close enough that he would not lose their trail.

* * *

Branwenn was just descending the stairs when she heard a familiar male voice coming from somewhere below say, *"Your wife told me I'd find my sister here. May I see her?"*

Reys! He'd found her. She bit her lip and, very stealthily, took another two steps down the stairs.

"You mean, of course, my sister, Branwenn?" she heard Bao reply.

"May I see her?"

Branwenn silently took several more steps down, her left hand skimming the cold stone of the curving wall and her neck craning forward, trying to see around the last curve into the antechamber just inside the entry of the keep.

All at once, she saw him. And Alyson, as well, surprisingly. Had he wed her then, as he'd sworn to do? "I'm here," she called out and trotted down the last four stairsteps into the antechamber. "Reys, 'tis so good to see you," she said, though her heart pounded with both pleasure and dread. She would have given him a kiss on the cheek in greeting, but had no desire to hurt Bao with such a show of affection in his presence. So, instead, she made a brief courtesy to Reys and then to his companion, who shyly returned the gesture. "Lady Alyson, 'tis so good to see you again. You are looking lovely." She darted a glance at her brother-germane, before adding, "And quite content, as well. That pleases me."

Alyson's cheeks pinkened, "My thanks, my lady. And you are looking the same."

Branwenn widened her smile. "You must surely be parched and in need of a rest. Come into the great hall and settle by the hearth. We will have some refreshment arranged for you."

Alyson's eyes settled briefly on Reys before turning once more to Branwenn. "My thanks, my lady."

Bao's eyes never left Reys's countenance. "Aye, Branwenn, settle the lass in the great hall for a time. Reys and I have much to discuss, and I believe my brother, cousin and uncle will want to meet with the man as well."

Reys, who was now in less hurry to speak with his sister, as it was plain that she was well and had survived the shipwreck with no permanent damage, met Bao's angry mien with a cocked brow and a slight smirk. "I look forward to the discussion, I assure you."

The two ladies made a hasty retreat out of the antechamber and when the room was at last left to only the two men, Reys said, "Your wife also gave me the tidings that my sister has been betrothed to your cousin, and without my consent. This, I'm sure you understand, makes the contract void, as I and Prince Llywelyn are her legal guardians."

Bao, stood with his arms crossed over his chest and his stance wide. "Aye, void the contract if you wish to have a Highlander bastard born to your ward."

Reys's spine shot ramrod straight and, with fisted hands, took a step toward Bao, "You allowed your cousin to meddle with my sweet, innocent sister so that she's now forced to wed the cur?! I'll kill the lot of you for this!"

Bao grinned at him. Relaxing his stance, he said more calmly, "Good. You do care for my sister." In a more somber tone, he said, "Calm yourself, Reys. 'Tis not like that at all. 'Tis a love match, you shall see." He turned in the direction of the entrance to the keep. "Come, let us meet in one of the guard tower chambers, 'twill have no likelihood of feminine ears o'erhearing our talk. And there's plenty of ale stashed there as well."

Reys eyed Bao suspiciously, but followed him out. Was his sister carrying the Highlander cousin's bastard, as Bao had said? And if so, what would be the retribution meted out by his princely cousin for such an offense? He'd still had plans for using her as barter in his ongoing campaign to gain power and ground in his native land. And part of that plan was to have Branwenn back safe, still chaste and unwed, with her family in Anglesea before word of her whereabouts reached Norman ears.

* * *

Several hours later, Callum, having spent much of

the morning hearing Reys's side of the tale of Branwenn's hasty flight from her betrothal to the Norman, and then convincing the man to accept Branwenn's—and his own—desire to wed and allow the match to take place, even without the Cambrian prince's knowledge, was in desperate need of some time alone with his love. And this time, he'd not be thwarted, waylaid, or distracted from that goal.

As he walked in the direction of the garden in the north bailey where a maid had told him Branwenn could be found, his thoughts turned once more to his earlier conversation with Reys. He knew that, by making the match outside the knowledge of her royal guardian, he was setting them up for war, but his stepfather had backed him, saying that they'd gather every ally they had and beat the army back, if the man wanted to fight. Even William, King of Scots, no doubt, would send soldiers to join the fray, as he owed Chalmers a favor, and Bao had been one of the king's best fighting men for years during his time at the court at Perth.

But he hoped the prince would be pleased enough with the bride price Callum would give for her to accept the union without threatening siege. For, 'twas a fortune in gold coins accumulated and inherited and would leave him only with just enough to begin building the manor he'd planned on that small tract of land between the MacGregor and Grant land that had been the subject of contention the two clans had nearly gone to war over. But, with Lara's ignoble death, Laird Grant had at last forfeited his claim on the property that horrid night of Callum's humiliating poisoning by pig gong and Callum's stepfather had signed the tract over to Callum as a gift for his labor in bringing about a negotiation and in being the means by which the two clans had settled their disagreement.

* * *

Branwenn worried her lip with her teeth as she stood with her head bowed staring blankly at the ground. "So Prince Llywelyn is wanting to use me as a pawn in his empire-building game of chess once again?" She turned to her brother-germane and gave him a pleading look. "Can you not simply return to Gwynedd and tell him that you did not find me? That you believe I perished in the wreck?"

Reys sighed and shook his head, his eyes sad. "No, I cannot. 'Twas much too easy for me to track how you came to be here in the Highlands—and that being three moons after the wreck. 'Tis no use, our princely cousin will find you out. And then I will be hanged from a gibbet for my part in the deception. No, 'tis better that you wed your Callum and we face the wrath of Llywelyn straight on, as I, your brother, do have a bit more of a say in whom you wed." He looked away from her, scrubbing the back of his neck with his hand and shaking his head. "'Tis tricky, even dangerous, but not completely traitorous." Resting his gaze upon her once more, he said, "And, with the generous bride price Callum is expecting to bestow upon him, 'twill lessen the sting considerably. 'Tis enough gold to fund many more campaigns against the Normans, as well as the other Cambrian princes he battles against in his pursuit of power and land."

Branwenn walked over to the bench and sat down, her hands clasped in her lap. "Was he *very* angry when you gave him our plan the next morn? Was there violence?"

Reys smiled and settled on the bench beside her. Taking her hand in his he lifted it and gave the back of it an affectionate kiss. "No, 'twas not as terrible as you imagine. In fact, our cousin was pleased to settle me upon the lady Alyson instead and have you far from Gaiallard's clutches, once he was informed of the man's true nature." He rested both of their hands on his knee. "Whatever you may believe of our cousin, know you this: He does not desire to have you wed to a beast, even for the sake of building his empire."

Branwenn nodded and looked away. After a moment, she straightened and turned back to Reys, saying, "And the lady Alyson? Do you think you may love her in time?" This, Branwenn now realized more than ever before, was the key to a happy life, and she wished it above all else for this brother of hers that had sacrificed so much for her.

Reys shrugged. "I can—and do—care for the girl. But love her as a man loves a woman?" It was his turn to look away as he pondered the question. He shook his head. "No, I confess, I see the girl as more of friend, almost as a younger sibling. I cannot see myself ever feeling for her the love I felt for my wife." He turned back to her then, a sheepish look upon his countenance. "Pardon, my *past* wife."

Branwenn sat forward and clasped her hand a bit

tighter around his. "But, Reys, she is so lovely, so kind! Surely, in time, after your grief is less acute, you will see her differently. At least I pray so, for, if you desire an heir, you will have to bed the lass to get one."

Reys bristled. "Branwenn! Do not speak of—"

"Nay, hear me, please. I know I should not speak of such to you—or anyone—as it isn't proper, but I have now with Callum what you had with your past wife and all I want for you is joy. I know that you believe lady Alyson is too young—and surely not ready for such with you now in any case, with the horror she was subjected to at her brother's hands—but, in time, I hope that you two can help to heal each other." She gave him a sad smile. "And, 'tis wrong for you to begin this marriage thinking of the lass as a sibling. 'Twill surely only make it harder for you to make that heir you crave with those thoughts flitting through your mind the entire time."

Reys studied Branwenn for a moment. "You are a wise one for your young age, Sister. And, you are right. I will no longer allow myself to think of the lady in that way." He straightened and took in a deep breath. "No, from now on, she will be in my thoughts only as my mate—and my dear friend. For, that, she has truly become in these past sennights."

* * *

Reys was just stepping through the arched stone entry of the garden when he saw Callum coming toward him. "Ho! Were you looking for me? Have you something else to discuss?"

Callum shook his head and grinned. "Nay, I'm on a

much different quest." He tipped his head in the direction of the garden. "Is Branwenn still in there?"

Reys's eyes narrowed. "Yes," he said slowly. "What, pray, is your intent?"

Callum shrugged. "Oh, this and that. You know."

Crossing his arms over his chest, Reys nodded, "Yes, I fear I do know. Exactly, as a matter of fact."

"Nay, 'tis naught like that," Callum replied, still set on keeping the gossip to a minimum—and his jaw in working order. "I just need to speak with Branwenn about..." He thought quickly. "...the gown she's having made for our wedding."

Reys's eyes narrowed even further. "The gown? That Branwenn will be wed in?" He laughed then. "Yes, do, go speak with my sister about her gown. May I join you?"

Callum's eyes widened. "Nay, um, Branwenn is set on keeping the design a secret from all but, um, me and, um, my mother and grandmother—oh! And Lady Isobail, also. My pardon." Callum shot around Reys and continued through the entry.

"I'll give you a quarter hour!" Reys called to him. Frowning, he shook his head. He should have given only five minutes, for, an anxious soon-to-be bridegroom could get the entire deed done in a quarter-hour. Hell, even five minutes was no doubt time enough for this particular groom, for Reys had seen an inferno in the other man's eyes as he passed him just then.

Callum didn't acknowledge the comment but continued on his course toward his betrothed. He'd have to be quick, but thorough. Could he do it? Aye, definitely. He grinned.

* * *

Branwenn looked up when she heard her brother's voice call out to someone, something about a quarter-hour.

Godamercy! *Callum!* And he was only a few paces from her. They'd be mating in minutes—a thing she was determined not to do again until their wedding night. She must escape. She leapt from her seat and dashed to her right, hoping to make a sharp curve up ahead and get around him to the entrance. "Nay! Go away, Callum! I've told you, not until we're wed!" She heard the sound of male laughter and the pounding of feet behind her and, suddenly, she was in his arms.

"You cannot get away from me this time, my sweet *fey Mai*. I won't allow it. And, why must we wait when we can enjoy each other now?" His mouth swooped down on hers and, in the next instant, she was falling swiftly into the deep abyss of her own passion for him.

Callum wrapped his arms around his love, holding her tight, one hand cradling the back of her head and the other clamped on her firmly rounded left derrière cheek. He lifted her up so that his manhood was nestled snugly into the crevassed triangle that her mons and pressed-together inner thighs made. He rocked against her, knowing the friction was teasing that hidden nub of pleasure beneath her skirts and labia lips. "It's been too long," he said raggedly against her mouth. "God! I just want to be inside you. Now. Forever."

Branwenn was beyond thought, she nodded dazedly and pressed her opened lips to his once more, thrusting her tongue into his mouth and tasting the nectar of the essence that was Callum. "Mmmm..." Her love. Her life. And soon—oh! please let it be soon!—her husband.

Somehow Callum managed to scuttle them onto the bench and lie on top of her, his hand caressing her naked inner thigh before trailing up to tease the damp curls that covered the opening of her canal. His finger had just entered her slightly when the sound of someone clearing his throat—very loudly—seeped into her consciousness.

They both turned their heads toward the noise at the same time.

"*Ohmygod!*" she squealed. 'Twas her brothers—*all three of them*—standing, like towering stairsteps, just inside the entrance to the garden, their arms crossed over their chests, their stances wide, and (she would think this much later, after the embarrassment had worn off) the most comical expressions of amusement guised as anger she'd ever seen.

Callum flew to his feet in front of Branwenn, blocking her from view, and flipping the hem of her gown down at the same time. He'd been caught. He knew he'd been caught. What could he possibly say that wouldn't dig his hole deeper still? So, he stood silent, waiting for one of them to make the first move.

Bao, thankfully, took pity on him. "See, Daniel, Reys, I told you. 'Tis clear we've worked the poor man to a frazzle to the extent that he falls over wherever he goes. This time, unfortunately, 'twas Branwenn who suffered." He turned his eye to Branwenn. "Is that not so, dear sister?"

Branwenn cleared her throat and combed her fingers through her hair to straighten it a bit before answering. She would not again wear the lovely fillet Callum had given her until her wedding day. "Aye," she said at last, "Callum fell upon me only moments before you arrived." There, that held more truth than falsehood, did it not?

"Come," Daniel said to Callum. "'Tis time for us to test your skills once more on the lists."

* * *

CHAPTER 10

OVER THE NEXT two days, the four men spent many hours on the field. Once Reys had learned that a tournament was planned, he'd immediately begun his own training for the event as well.

But a dark cloud hovered nearby, as the lady Isobail's health grew worse. After the last morn, when she could barely catch her breath and her skin grew as gray as the fog on the moors, Callum sent word to her brother Robert to make haste to his sister's side, as there was little time left.

"Isobail," Callum said softly, his hand resting gently atop her forearm, which lay, limp and cool to the touch, next to her side atop the fur blanket.

Isobail opened her eyes, though with some difficulty, as they were as heavy as iron portcullises and the need to allow her mind to drift into sleep—and dreams—was growing more and more difficult to battle against. She'd been having dreams of her husband, but this last time, she'd dreamt of another, of that long forgot time in her youth when she'd loved the wrong lad. Loved the Norman son of her father's enemy. Given him her innocence and in repayment, he'd broken her heart and humiliated her. She supposed 'twas as she'd always heard: those close to death relived their lives in the last days.

"Isobail," Callum said again. "I've sent for Robert. He should be here within the next two days; if he is at your family's holding, as you believe."

"That is good," she said weakly and took several shallow breaths. "Where is my son? I must see him again soon, before I am too weak to speak."

"He is just outside the door, waiting for me to allow him entrance." He stroked her arm to comfort her, but also as a means of comforting himself as well. "Are you ready for him now?"

Isobail shook her head slightly. "Nay. In just a moment." She tried to lift her head to look about the chamber, but she couldn't manage it and gave up in frustration. "Where is my maid?" she said. "I want her to comb my hair and wash my face before he comes in. I wish not for him to see me in this state."

Callum nodded and motioned for the maid to come to her mistress. He began to rise, but Isobail waylaid him with her hand on his arm. "You and Branwenn will not forsake your promise? You will take my lad and raise him as you promised?"

Callum sat back down. "Aye, Isobail, I swear this to you: We will not forsake our promise."

"I wish only that I could keep my breath at least

until after you are wedded, but the struggle is growing too great."

"Fair lady, can you not hold out for a while more? 'Twill be *Samhainn* in less than a fortnight, and we are set to wed the day after that."

"Aye, I will try." She began to cough. Callum quickly placed his arm behind her shoulders and, lifting her up, brought the cup to her mouth which held the tisane that Daniel had prescribed. Daniel's mother had been a healer and had taught him much of the art before her death, a knowledge that had served his family well these many years.

Isobail drank the concoction down, though she almost choked a couple of times when the urge to cough overcame her as she tried to swallow. In seconds after drinking it, however, it did calm the tickle in her chest and she relaxed back once more with her eyes closed. "My thanks," she said. A moment later, she forced her lids open once more and looked at Callum. "'Tis time to get me ready for my son. I cannot delay any longer."

"Aye." Callum rose from his stool beside the bed and waited a few moments while the maid straightened and combed Isobail's hair and washed her face with a damp cloth before opening the door and, with a quick nod, giving David permission to enter the chamber.

* * *

Two days later, Robert arrived. When Callum met him in the great hall, he was stunned. He could hardly recognize the man whom he'd known since they were youths. Where all their lives, Robert had been hail and hearty, the black-haired, grey-eyed, rugged-faced counterpoint to Callum's lighter, more evenly drawn looks, he now appeared haggard, a bit thinner—as if he'd skipped one too many meals over the last moons, and frown lines delved deep creases between his dark brows.

"Robert," Callum said in greeting with a short nod of this head. This was the first time they'd seen each other since the Roman outpost ruin on the Maclean property where he'd found his wife, Lara, and Robert together.

"Callum."

"Need you a bit of refreshment before I take you to see your sister?"

"Nay, please, just show me to her chamber. I had no idea she was ill. Why did she not tell me of this sooner?"

"You knew not of her illness?" Callum asked in surprise.

Robert shook his head. "Nay, the last missive I received from her was about five moons ago, just after her husband's death, tho' I've written her several letters giving her tidings of our clan."

"Come, let us not waste another moment, as she's very close to the end. I believe she's been holding on in hopes of speaking with you."

A few minutes later, Callum stood staring at the outside of Isobail's chamber door. Robert had just gone inside and he could hear the muffled low tones of voices on the other side.

Though he still held resentment for Robert's part in

Lara's cuckolding of him, he'd known the man for too many years—had been good friends with him, at least until Robert had found out about his own affair with Isobail when Callum and he were barely thirteen summers—to feel anything other than sadness for his coming loss, as well as for his troubles holding his clan together.

He shook his head and, crossing his arms over his chest, leaned against the wall to the side of the door and waited. He didn't care how long it took, he would be here for Robert when he at last emerged. And then, they would get drunk. Very, very drunk.

* * *

Two hours later, Robert opened the door. Callum hadn't thought it possible for the man's face to look more strained, but in these moments, it did. "Is she...?" he asked softly.

Robert nodded grimly. "Aye. The priest performed the last rights and now the servants prepare her for burial." With dazed eyes, he stared down at the floor. "You were right, she was only holding on to tell me of her plan for David."

The two men stood in silence for a time, their heads bowed.

Finally, Callum silently opened the door to the chamber and quietly asked one of the servants to inform his other family members of Isobail's death. Turning, he shut the door once more and said, "Come," before beginning to walk in the direction of the stairs. "Let us finish this discussion with the aid of a hearthfire and a bit of *uisge beatha*."

"That sounds good," Robert agreed and followed him as he descended the stairs.

* * *

The two old friends said little as Robert settled on one of the benches around the hearth and Callum retrieved the bottle of *uisge beatha* from the buttery.

"Remember you that summer—we were surely not more than ten summers—when your sister took the blame for our prank with the apple juice and *uisge beatha*?" Callum asked as he poured the first of what he expected to be many draughts of the latter into Robert's cup. "When we mixed the two and served it to the young ladies who'd traveled with Isobail and your father?"

Robert smiled and nodded. "Aye, tho' I've oft thought if 'twere not for all the puking afterward, then we'd have been thought heros rather than villains in the scheme." He chuckled and shook his head. "But, 'tis truth, we would have been given duty with the gong farmer for that one, had my sister not taken pity on us and said 'twas her own doing."

Callum nodded and took in a deep breath before releasing it slowly. "She was a very kind and gentle lady."

"Aye, that she was."

They said naught else for many long minutes, the only sound, other than the crackling of the hearthfire, being the sharp *'clink'* of the glass bottle against the rim of each man's silver cup as Callum continued to refill the vessels with the amber liquor.

"And, what think you of Isobail's plan?" he asked

Robert, at last breaking the silence.

Robert sighed and scrubbed his hand over his eyes and cheeks. "'Twas hard for me to accept at first, but she did finally convince me that, at least for now, 'tis the best thing for him." He directed his gaze on Callum. "Are you sure you want this?"

"Aye, Branwenn and I are sure. Worry not."

Robert's smile was a bit strained when he said, "Ah, the lovely Branwenn. Aye, you managed to win it all, did you not?"

Callum gave him a questioning look. "Win it all? What mean you?"

"Why, the promise of another lairdship and the most beautiful woman in the Highlands, of course."

Callum's brows slammed together. "Do you have a problem with that? Branwenn, I mean?" he asked darkly.

"Nay, I suppose not. But there was a time last *Hogmanay*, as I danced around the fire with her, that I would have battled you for her."

Callum sat up straight and eyed Robert very closely. "You danced with *my* betrothed last *Hogmanay*? I remember it not."

Robert chuckled, though even in that, a sadness and despair ran through the sound. "Aye, and I was very tempted, more so than I've ever been, to give the lass my troth, but then your grandmother took her from me and, well, by the next day, I'd sobered and thought better of it."

Callum bristled. "Aye, but you didn't manage to think better of bedding my wife that day."

Highland Magic

"Are we going to go over that again? The woman was not worthy of you, Callum. You know it, and I know it. She was determined to cuckold you, and I was in the mood to give her what she wanted, since I had an age-old score to settle with you." He sighed and crossed his arms over his chest. "If I'd believed I'd be doing any real damage to you, other than bruising your pride, which was my intent, then I'd not have done the deed."

Callum nodded. "Aye, I know." He settled back and took a long pull from his cup. Afterward he sat the silver vessel down on the table and said, "Tell me what goes on with your land, my friend."

* * *

Several hours later the two men were deep in their cups in the great hall when Branwenn walked in, Lady Maclean not far behind. "Ah, here he is Grandmother Maclean, just as I feared." She shook her head in disgust. "Getting drunk—and helping his friend to do the same." She turned and looked at Lady Maclean. "Why is this the answer to every matter, good or bad, that happens in a man's life?"

Callum, bleary-eyed and with a foolishly lopsided grin on his countenance, rose from his stool and said, "Bra'wn, my lo', c'meet Rober'." He swayed and lost his balance, but Robert swung his hand out and managed to grab Callum's arm, just barely keeping him upright.

Robert turned to Branwenn. There were three of her, first standing side-by-side, then floating together, then apart again. "G'eve. Wud'yu lik' t'dance?" He stood up and took a step toward her, but tripped over his own foot and landed, rather ignominiously, flat on his face.

"Oh, my!" Branwenn exclaimed. *That must have hurt.* "Grandmother, where is the butler? Why is he not in here with these witless creatures?"

Lady Maclean smiled indulgently at the two young men. She was much more amused by them than angered, as she had many more years experience with such antics. "I have no idea, my dear."

"How are we going to get the man up on his feet again? And listen to that!" She pointed in the direction of the still-prostrate form lying on the rush-covered stone floor. "He's snoring! If he slumbers, he will weigh a ton, and we'll need half the guard force to carry him to his chamber."

"Bao and I will do the deed, worry not, sis," Daniel said, walking through the doorway just then.

Branwenn turned. "My thanks," she said, relief in her voice.

"I'll car' hi' up th' shtair, m'luffff," Callum said, but then his eyes rolled up, his head lolled back, and he hit the ground with a loud *'thunk!'*

"Well, tomorrow's training should be rather interesting," Bao said as he looked down at the lump that was now Callum. "How many points does one get for spewing one's meal on one's opponent?" An evil light came into his eyes and he turned back to Daniel. "Mayhap, we should ask Robert to oppose Callum on the morrow. Then 'twill be an even match—both hurling the contents of their stomachs as they pass each other on the lists."

Branwenn giggled. "That is a humorous thought.

But...." She cocked her head to the side and gave Bao a questioning look. "I thought they wore helmets. Won't it just end up all inside their armor?"

Bao turned back to Daniel. "What say you? Helmets on or off? Spew on themselves or on their opponent? You decide."

Daniel shook his head at both of them. "Be kind to your betrothed, Branwenn. 'Tis clear he only meant to commiserate with his friend. And Robert has just lost a sister, have you forgot?"

Branwenn's eyes misted and she dipped her head. "Aye, I did forget for a moment," she confessed. "When I came in here, 'twas to commiserate with Robert as well, for my heart breaks for him—and David, too. But then, when I saw the two of them drunk as two priests at a brothel, I got so angry at Callum, I lost sight of my intention."

Lady Maclean patted her on the back. "There, there, dear. 'Tis understandable, I'm sure."

Bao took hold of Branwenn's hand and gave it a little squeeze of support. "Aye, I should not have made a jest under these circumstances." He walked over to Robert and, with seemingly little effort, hoisted the man up and over his shoulder. "I only hope he doesn't spew on the way up to his chamber," he mumbled under his breath, "as I'll surely not get the stench out of my tunic for many moons afterward."

Lady Maclean caught what he said and smiled, shaking her head. The events of the day were tragic but, in her long life, she'd learned that in times of loss, grief manifested itself in different ways in different people.

Some drank hard spirits, some ate, some cried, some laughed, some prayed, some baked, some sewed, some fought, some sat quietly and pondered, and some did them all. But each way aided in relieving the pressure of the sadness that underlay each one of those actions.

* * *

The next morn, with his sister's admonition to think of Alyson as a wife, and not a sibling, niggling at his conscience, and with the need to give the family a bit of privacy while they grieved and prepared for the lady Isobail's burial, Reys asked his young bride to go bow hunting with him in the MacGregor wood.

They'd only just begun the hunt when they spotted a nice-sized buck at the edge of a clearing in the trees. He was just stepping behind Alyson's right elbow to study her aim when he glanced down and saw a dark brownish-red stain on the back of the short brown tunic Branwenn had loaned her for this early morning hunting expedition. His eyes trailed down a bit further and he saw a streak of what he now knew to be blood on her lighter colored hose. He cleared his throat. "Alyson, my sweet?" he said softly.

"Sshhh! You'll frighten the buck!" she whispered.

He reached around her. She startled, but allowed the contact when it was only her hands he touched as he quickly disengaged the arrow from the bow and brought them down to his side. "Turn around," he said gently, next to her right ear. "I have something of grave import to speak with you about."

Alyson's brows lifted, but she did as he requested. "Yes?"

"Alyson...how many summers are you now?" He set the bow and arrow on the ground next to him.

Her brows drew together in confusion. "Know you not? But I thought 'twas on our contract." She shrugged. "As of this past May I am twelve summers."

Reys studied her face, so lovely, yet still so youthful. If one gazed long enough, there could still be seen the traces of a child's countenance in her features. "Have you..." *How to say this?* "Do you know..." *No, not quite right.*

"What? What have you to ask of me, Reys? Whatever it is, I shall do my best to give it, I swear. For you have been so kind to me these past moons."

Reys scrubbed his hand over his stubbled jaw and, at a loss for words, finally ended up pointing to her hose.

Alyson, thoroughly confused and a bit worried now, quickly followed the direction his hand was pointing in and let out a bloodcurdling scream. "*Oh my God, oh my God, oh my God*, I'm dying." Tears welled in her eyes and she began to tremble. Had her brother's beatings done this to her?

"No, Alyson, 'tis naught like that."

She looked up, into the gentle eyes of her savior, saying, "Are you sure? My brother—"

"*No!* Worry not on that score. 'Tis no injury from his wicked hand."

Alyson relaxed a bit, her heart beat slowing to a more natural meter. "What is wrong with me then?" she asked, unable to completely let go of the worry.

So, Reys thought, 'twas as he'd suspected. The poor girl had no idea of such things. Yet another reason to despise the brother who'd dared violate such an innocent, gentle maiden as she. Reys tried to take her in his arms, but she stiffened and pulled away. He dropped his hands to his sides and said, "'Tis your first flowering, sweet Alyson. Proof that you are now a woman grown."

Alyson bowed her head and was silent for a long moment. At last she lifted her gaze to his once more, saying, "So this is what my aunt said I'd learn of when I was older? She would never tell me what the strange, blood stained rags were that she had folded in her clothing chest."

"Aye, but now, I think we should find something for you to use until I can get you back to the keep. The ladies will be able to speak with you with more authority than I, in any case." He untied his tunic and lifted it over his head. "Here, I've an idea. Take my shirt and tie it around yourself. 'Twill help to stem the flow."

Alyson nodded and looked around to find a bush or something to go behind for a bit of privacy. "What about my hose? I cannot enter the keep looking like this! Everyone will *know!*"

"Here," he said, quickly unlacing his own. "Take these. No one will think anything of seeing a warrior a bit stripped down."

"But...they are so big...."

"Alyson," Reys said, now with just a bit of exasperation in his tone, "'tis the best I can do—and you'll only be seen in them for a few minutes while you enter the keep and ascend the stairs to your chamber. Take them." He was relieved when she did as he'd bade, but the dubious look on her face as she did so almost made him laugh out loud. Fortunately, he managed to hold back the untimely mirth.

She turned and headed toward a juniper bush.

Reys once again noticed the stain on the back of her tunic. Blood of Christ. He dared not mention it now, else 'twould surely only embarrass her further. But, how to get her inside without others seeing it? A shudder of cold shook his frame. Lord, but it was frosty in these parts. He took a moment to put his tunic back on. *Ahhh!* He just remembered. Her cloak would do nicely. Except.... He dashed over to where they had their horses tethered and quickly looked at the outside of the garment. He relaxed then. Thankfully, since it was so thickly lined with fur, the blood had not soaked through to the outer woolen material of the covering.

She was behind the shrub for several minutes when he heard her growl, "*I hate you, you witless thing! Why will you not just stay put?!*"

Reys smiled, for 'twas the first time he'd ever known her to lose her temper, and he admitted, 'twas rather a pleasing surprise. For, with enough anger, and enough skill, one could thwart almost any enemy. And he fully intended on giving her the skill. But the lack of spirit had worried him, for he knew not how to train her in that. In his experience, fear enfeebled, whereas anger stirred one to action. And that was exactly what he wanted her to do in the face of any thing or person that might do her harm in future. "Is something amiss, my sweet?" he called out to her.

"*I cannot get this...this...shirt to stay about me. Aargh! I fear 'tis no use! I will have to*—hic"—she began to cry—"*go into*—hic—*the keep with my flower blood all over me-ee-eee!*"

"Might I give you aid?" His face and shoulders scrunched in anticipation of her loud refusal.

She sniffled, but said naught. Then, more sniffles. "Yes, please," she finally said, rather thickly.

Reys straightened, his eyes widened in disbelief, but, with a shake of his head, he started toward his young wife.

She peeked her head around the shrub and said, "But you must keep your eyes closed and your head turned away!"

"All right." *All right?* Was he mad? How was he supposed to help her get the thing tied on properly without the use of his eyes, for Christ's sake?

But, his concerns were for naught, and it actually turned out to be a rather comical, pleasing diversion, with him feeling his way to getting the thing adjusted in the way he'd envisioned and her giggling uncontrollably as his fingers tickled her torso. He'd drawn the hem of the shirt through her thighs from the back and brought it up to surround her hips before using the sleeves to encircle her waist, as well as the material, and then rolling it down a few times to ensure it was snug. And she'd only tensed a few times in the process. Evidently, him on his knees, blind, and with his head turned away, gave her the courage to allow his touch. "There, will that work, do you think?" he asked her when the complicated process was finally done. He made sure to keep his eyes tightly shut as he spoke.

"Yes, I think it will. My thanks." A brief pause and

then: "Will you go stand by the horses again?"

"Yes." Reys rose from his position and walked away.

When Alyson emerged a moment later from behind the shrub, her tunic was only slightly more bulky around the waist than it had been. And though his hose drooped at her ankles, they were clean and there was no longer any trace—except, of course, the stain on the back of the tunic he had yet to tell her of—that she'd had any mishap with her clothing.

When she was next to him once more, he took her cloak from the back of the saddle and settled it around her shoulders. "Wear this until you get into your chamber, all right?"

She gave him a questioning look and he sighed. "There is a stain on the back of your tunic as well."

"Oh, no!" She immediately twisted around to see the offending mark.

"It's not very big...."

"Yes, but this belongs to Branwenn! How am I ever to tell her! Oh, God!"

"Alyson, do you not think that Branwenn has stained more than a few articles of clothing in this very same way? She will not be angered, for she will know 'twas not due to carelessness on your part."

Alyson, turned back to Reys, giving up her quest to see the offending mark, and, her head bowed, nodded slowly. After a moment she said in a small voice, "Think you she will give me instruction in this 'flowering' thing my body does? I have no wish to speak to any of the other ladies, for Branwenn is the one I know best, and she was always so kind to me during our time at my uncle's holding."

Reys's voice was gentle when he replied, "Yes, I do. She has a very warm and giving nature, as you well know."

"Good." Then, lifting her eyes to his once more, she said, "Let us return to the keep then, for I have need of a bath and fresh clothing."

Reys settled his young wife on her mount and, after picking up the bow and arrow, mounted his own horse before leading them back to the keep.

* * *

What luck! Gaiallard thought as he walked his mount out of the cover of trees. He'd found them with no need to question anyone—which, he knew, this close to his quarry, might raise suspicions and all could be lost.

But, what was all the disrobing and scurrying behind bushes? He'd thought, when he'd first come upon them and seen Reys taking off his clothes, that he'd stumbled upon a lover's tryst. But when Reys put his tunic back on, he began to wonder. And then later, when Alyson had come from behind the shrub, it had been clear the girl had somehow used the shirt Reys had given her, and his hose as well. Gaiallard shook his head. 'Twas truly a puzzle.

He waited a bit longer to begin trailing them. For now, all he intended doing was a quick study of the area before finding a place to make camp. He made note of the direction in which he was traveling, just in case he had to return to the wood for the night.

* * *

Callum gritted his teeth behind the counterfeit genial smile he'd had plastered on his countenance these past long minutes. The morning meal had proved a bit more of a trial than he'd anticipated, for not only was Branwenn not speaking to him after his drunken lark the eve before, but she'd also turned her attention instead to their guest. Robert would be here until the morrow, when he would be taking his sister's corpse back with him to their family's holding for burial.

Branwenn giggled at something Robert said to her and Callum nearly leapt from his seat and pummeled the man to a bloody, oozing, pulp. *'Leave my lady be!'* he wanted to shout, but he dared not show such emotion to the man, as that would surely only egg him further into his already improper dalliance with *someone else's* betrothed.

The same betrothed that had all morn spurned his own attentions. From the first sighting of her in the great hall earlier, he'd attempted to speak with her, share some gentle words, learn of her progress in her preparations of the wedding feast and such. Just the same easy manner of speaking they'd fallen into these past sennights as they awaited the priest's availability to give his blessing. But he'd been summarily cut to the bone with her sharp tongue then, and each time after, no matter what words he'd used to appease her anger at him for using hard drink to assuage his—and Robert's—grief the night before. Although, he did admit, parts of him—his roiling stomach and thick head, to name but two—were at this moment in direct concordance with the spirit, if not the execution, of her disgust.

But 'twas the execution she'd been using with him that had him worried. For 'twas the same mode of punishment that Lara had used upon him at every turn when she was displeased with him—which, Lord knew, had been more oft than not. Was he doomed now to a life of snubbing and cutting words whenever he displeased her in some way, instead of gracious forgiveness and calm discussion?

But even that was not the worst of it. Nay, 'twas the clear delight Branwenn was taking in the attentions she received from Robert that bothered him the most. It rankled in a way much like, but far more painfully disturbing than, Lara's enjoyment—and outright pursuit—of every man's regard. *Did* Branwenn suffer from the same need? He'd dismissed it before, but now, with this new flirtation, the old doubt resurfaced. He recalled how merry she'd been this *Hogmanay* past as she'd danced around the bonfire with first one, then another, and then another still of the young soldiers at the Maclean holding. And, again, there had also been that young guard several sennights past who'd clearly wanted her and to whom she'd freely given her kind regard. Mayhap this was not some passing interest, but a thing he'd be dealing with for their entire lives together.

Branwenn took a sip of wine from her cup and flicked her tongue across the drop on her bottom lip.

Callum stiffened, his eyes flying to Robert's face. Aye, he'd noticed as well. 'Twas a clear invitation she'd just given the man. Would he accept it?

Mayhap 'twas a good thing that he'd seen this side of her before they'd said their vows.

* * *

"Do you not think you've made poor Callum suffer enough for his indulgence in ardent spirits last eve?" Robert said to Branwenn as he spied his friend eyeing them for at least the thousandth time that morn. "Go speak to him, I beg you, else I'll surely be without my scalp in just a moment more."

Branwenn glanced at Callum before settling her eye once more on her companion. "Aye, I've made him suffer enough, I trow. But I've had some direct, and loathsome, experience with...well...someone who drank heavily of the hard spirits. And so, I am not pleased to be wed to a man who uses the stuff to the extent Callum tends to do, you see."

Robert's gaze turned keen. "Your brother Bao? The one who raised you?"

Branwenn shook her head. "Nay! Never. Bao drinks not—or at least not very much."

Robert tipped his head in Callum's direction. "He's not a drunkard, if that is your worry, lass," he said. "But, Callum's spent his life on the Maclean holding; and that lot do enjoy their *uisge beatha*, 'tis a well-known fact."

"Aye, but 'tis a habit I'd like to break him of—at least by a wee bit."

"Well, I do believe, that after this morn, he will think twice before crossing you on that score."

Branwenn smiled. "I do hope 'tis so." She turned, saying, "I will give him another chance to make amends, I think. But this time, I shall accept his confession of sorrow."

* * *

When Lady Maclean and Maggie saw Branwenn headed in Callum's direction, they rose from their seats by the hearth and moved to stand with Chalmers and Daniel a bit further away. They—all the family—had got in the habit these past sennights of giving the two lovers a bit of chaperoned privacy whenever they were all together in the hall.

"Good morn, my love," Branwenn said brightly as she settled next to Callum on his bench by the hearth. Silence. She tipped her head and studied her betrothed's tightly controlled mien. His eyes were the color of the storm-tossed Irish sea she'd nearly drowned in last summer. "Do you not wish to confess your sorrow to me once more for your bairn-like behavior this night past? For, I am now ready to accept it."

"Truly? Well, it seems I am now not of a mood to give my confession to a devious tart-mouthed siren such as yourself," he said for her ears only.

Branwenn chuckled, thinking him only a bit vexed by her delay in forgiving him. "*Siren?* Me?" she said, just as quietly.

His eyes narrowed slightly.

Recognizing now that his anger at her ran deeper than she'd first believed and that laughing was not the best way to soothe him, Branwenn sobered and began, "Callum—"

"Tell me," he said harshly, "do you enjoy dallying with all the men, my love? Stirring their desire for you to such a degree that they'd give their fighting arm to have you beneath them, sweating and straining in the age-old rhythm?"

Branwenn's entire face flushed hot with both mortification and anger as her gaze darted about the chamber to make sure no one had heard him. Her molten amethyst eyes narrowed as well when she settled them upon him once more. "No, I do not," she whispered.

Callum's smile was cold when he said, not as loudly as before, "Oh, I believe you do, sweet." He tipped his head in Robert's direction. "See you how avidly the man awaits your return to his side. His eyes have not left you since you came into the hall this morn. And he told me this night past that he was set to give you his troth last *Hogmanay* after you danced so prettily with him 'round the fire." He studied Robert more closely. "Oh, aye, he wants you. Badly." Turning back to Branwenn, his eyes shot daggers at her. "Just, I'm sure, as was your intent."

"I do not want to wed, nor do I have a desire for, Robert MacVie! And,"—her eyes followed the same path as her angry betrothed's—"he looks not at me, he's talking to my brother, Bao, for heaven's sake." She turned her gaze upon Callum once more. "Truly, Callum, what has got into you this morn?"

"And all your seductive smiles," he continued his diatribe as if he hadn't heard her, "your whispered words, your sweetly trilling laughter, the glide of your tongue over that lush lower lip of yours, *your gentle touch to his arm*, were not meant to entice him? Ha! I think you play me for a fool." He grabbed hold of her hand and squeezed it tightly in his fist.

"Ouch! You hurt me, loose your grip!"

He ignored her dictate. "I've played the cuckold before, and I won't do it again. Do you ken me?" He tossed her hand down onto her lap.

Branwenn rubbed her abused digits, though, in truth, the pain in her heart was much harsher. She gritted her teeth against them, but tears still formed in her eyes. "I did not do this thing you accuse me of," she said, her voice trembling. "'Tis not my nature—I thought you knew that, for I"—she swallowed down a whimper that threatened to rise up—"was a v-virgin that first t-time we..." She turned on the bench and put her back to him as she lightly touched her pinky to her lower lids, hoping that none of the others in the chamber would notice her breakdown.

He took hold of her upper arm and forced her to turn back to face him. "Aye, the barrier was there, but how many others, I wonder, have felt the sultry cavern of your mouth about their cock? Have felt you spasm against their tongue? Will Robert—or, mayhap, he already has? Last night?" He shook her arm slightly. "Do you give to him what you hold back from *me*? Have you lit the tapers for him so that he might see what you have yet to allow me sight of?"

Her brows slammed together. "NAY!" she hissed. "If this is what you believe of me, then we should not be wed!" She'd said the words without thinking, acting purely on her hurt and anger. Turning her back on him once more, she prayed he'd settle and beg her forgiveness now that that horrible volley had been thrown. For, no matter what, she knew he wanted to wed her—hadn't he nearly begged her for such? But, when, after several very long, doom-filled seconds, she'd not got the response she'd been hoping for, her heart began to pound in her chest. This was followed swiftly by a mad whirring in her ears, until, finally, she was overtaken by dizziness as she at last gave a nod of understanding. 'Twas the thing he'd been set on from the moment she'd sat down next to him a moment ago. "I believe we must tell the others forthwith of our broken betrothal," she said thickly, "as 'tis not too late to keep Maryn and Jesslyn from beginning their journey here."

Dead silence met her words and then: "Aye."

Did her heart actually crack in two in that moment? She felt the weight of his eyes on the back of her neck as he stood up and paused briefly. Then he was gone, his footsteps pounding against the stone floor as he stormed from the chamber.

Branwenn leapt to her feet and fled to the first place she could find for a bit of privacy: the buttery. She broke down in truth then. Her heart wrenching so harshly inside her chest, she couldn't take a breath. She pressed both hands over her gaping mouth as silent sobs formed, moving her vocal cords up and down in her aching throat as a flood of tears splashed over her cheeks, her lips, her chin, finally forming into wet rivulets that streamed down her neck and dampened the front of her chemise and gown. Her entire body quaked and her knees grew so weak she crumpled to the ground and lay on her side with her hands covering her face. *Callum, Callum, Callum, Callum.* How was she to live without him now that he'd taken her very soul into his possession?

* * *

Callum leaned against the wall just outside the doorway of the great hall, his breathing harsh, his head thrown back, and his eyes clamped tightly shut. Had he just made the worst mistake of his life, or the best decision? Had she given him falsehood or truth? His heart was screaming that he'd been wrong, wrong, wrong and should go back in there right this minute, delay not another second, go down on his knees and beg Branwenn to forgive him for his lackwitted words. But, his mind would not listen. For, what if he wed her and she turned out to be just as Lara had been? Could he bear it? And what was more, was that the sort of woman he wanted raising his daughter—having more bairns with?

Nay, 'twas not.

* * *

"*Branwenn!*" Maggie cried, falling to her knees next to her soon-to-be daughter-in-law. "Whatever did that scoundrel of a son of mine say to you to get you in such a state as this? Tell me, and he will be made to fix it, I swear this to you, lass." Her own eyes misted in sympathetic tears as she watched Branwenn's body wracked with sorrowful sobs.

"H-he...w-we-ee-ee...are no longer betrothed! He *hates* me!"

"Branwenn!" Maggie said, shocked. "'Tis the very

last thing he feels for you, child. How can you even think such a thing?" An angry gleam came into her eye. "Tell me he did not actually *say* such to you! I will string him up by his toes, the rascal!"

Branwenn, still lying on the floor, turned her face away from Maggie's view and hid her eyes in the crook of her elbow. Her only answer was a shake of her head.

Maggie patted Branwenn's back. "All will be well, you shall see."

* * *

Callum sat on a stool in the solar an hour later looking from one to the other of the seven people—his grandmother, mother, stepfather, two massive cousins, and Branwenn's brother-germane, as well as Robert—standing over him and feeling like the defenseless prey to a sloth of hungry bears, with first one batting at him, then the other, and all leaving with yet another piece of his pride laid to waste. And, he admitted, his suspicions as well.

"Callum, dear, 'twas not as you believe at all. Your mother and I inveigled that poor guard to pretend an interest in Branwenn as a means of prodding you into doing what you should have done the first time the two of you were together—told her you loved her!" Lady Maclean chided.

"And I have no recollection of the lady ever touching me," Robert interjected before Callum had time to form a retort. His eyes widened as the light of understanding dawned. "Ah! Mean you when the page spilled a bit of the contents of my trencher on my sleeve? When Branwenn did the ladylike thing and wiped it off for her guest with a cloth?"

Callum gave him a sheepish look.

Robert howled. "Are you insane? Truly. Are you? Because 'twas clear to me from the moment I began speaking with the lady this morn that her thoughts are never far from you. Why, she must have asked me fifty questions about you, just while we ate." He began to count on his fingers as he gave examples. "*How long have you known Callum?*', '*What was he like back then?*', '*Was he always so good with a sword?*', '*...With a lance?*', '*Did he always hate to dance as he does now?*'" He looked up with a huge grin on his face, and added, "And, my favorite: '*How many lasses has he bedded?*'"

Everyone laughed but Callum. He only squirmed.

"This one, I confess, I gave a bit of a lie to her on— I said only your *wife*"—the whole company roared at that one and Robert had to raise his voice to be heard above the laughter—"since I was trying to aid your cause with the lady, not ruin it, as you evidently believe." He waited for the raucus sounds of mirth to subside before continuing, "I have no interest in your betrothed, Callum, and she certainly has none in me."

"And," Reys interjected, his arms crossed over his chest, "forget not, I can easily take her home with me— an idea I'm growing more fond of with each passing second of hearing your driveling, I assure you—and have done with this contract that I'm sure to be made to regret signing in any case when my princely cousin learns of it."

Callum leapt to his feet. "Nay, no need!" he said as he plowed through his cousins and hurried to the door.

"She's mine. I'm hers. No problem." Now, to gain her forgiveness and, if need be, convince her all over again of just that.

* * *

CHAPTER 11

*C*ALLUM FOUND BRANWENN seated in the north bailey garden not many minutes after Robert's and Reys's last words to him in the solar. He'd not taken the time to fetch his cloak from his chamber, but, it seemed the need for it was not so great, as the day had turned unseasonably warm for this close to *Samhainn*.

He saw she was seated slightly sideways on the stone bench with her head bowed a bit as she gazed at the frost covered, now almost completely winter-brown garden to her left, her hands loosely clasped, palms up, in her lap. Her dark brown cloak was thrown back on either side, its edges draped over her shoulders and the gown she wore was one of the old ones that his mother had given her upon her arrival here. She'd changed since earlier. Why she tended toward the looser garments, he had never quite figured out, for 'twas God's truth, she could stop his heart with her loveliness when she wore one of the form-fitting ones his grandmother had had made for her. But, after his horrid behavior in the face of another man giving her attention this morn, 'twas no doubt better that she not wear such enticements when there were male guests about.

As if feeling his presence, she turned her head and their eyes met across the last small distance between them. In three strides, Callum was by her side. He dropped down to his knees before her and took her hands in his. She resisted, but then, as if deciding it mattered little one way or the other, she relaxed and allowed the contact. Her eyes were like frozen violets suspended in a crimson-rimmed flower bowl. Cold now, but proof that once there had been fiery tears stinging them.

"I'm an idiot."

She shrugged.

"You are perfect, pure, and I truly do not deserve you."

He watched her eyes shift from one to the other of his own as if trying to see into his soul. Then she nodded.

"I adore you. I want to be your husband. 'Tis truly my fondest desire, and has been since, I believe, the moment I first met you outside the stables at the Maclean keep that day so many moons ago now."

With a cry, she threw herself into his arms, her own wrapped tightly about his neck, and he fell backwards onto the ground, taking her with him. He laughed and held her tight as the vise around his heart snapped free, allowing the tormented organ to once again beat with joy.

"I adore you, too," she whispered happily between kisses to his neck, his cheek, his ear.

He rolled her onto her back, her fur-lined cloak cushioning her from the cold, hard ground, and settled between her thighs, rucking the hem of her gown up on one side as he did so before beginning a long, slow caress of her outer thigh and hip. "Mmm...soft, just as I remembered." He bent his head down and kissed her, using his tongue and teeth to tease that lower lip of hers that daily drove him mad for a taste and had only a few hours past been the source of his jealous wrath.

After a moment, he left her mouth to enjoy the sweet taste of her velvet-smooth neck. As he did so, he inched his hand around to grasp her sweet, rounded bottom and press her more snugly against his now painfully swollen arousal.

"Oh, Callum, it's been so long since we"—she drew in a sharp breath when his finger entered her feminine sheath from behind as he rotated his hips to tease her clitoris—"oh, Gaawd," she groaned, arching her back.

Callum clamped his mouth over the turgid nipple of her breast that showed through the material of her clothing. He sucked hard a second before saying, "I want to strip you naked right here, right now. I want to see the winter sun's rays light every inch of this luscious figure you hide from view. I want to see you, Branwenn. Please, let me see this lovely body of yours at last."

Branwenn, her eyes clamped tightly shut as she

trembled on the verge of release at her lover's skilled hand, shook her head. "Nay, Callum, please. Not yet, I'm not ready."

Callum's hand was drenched with the proof of that falsehood. "Oh, you are ready, my love, very ready." He kissed her sweet lips again before opening them wider by thrusting his tongue deep several times, repeating the motion with the finger he had inside her slick passage as he arched above her. In seconds, she went rigid, her muffled cries vibrating against his teeth and gums, and the walls of her canal clasping and unclasping his love-dewed digit.

It shocked him a second later when his own body jerked uncontrollably in sudden climax. "Branwenn!" Dazed and still seeing black spots, he collapsed upon her now-limp form.

After another second, he rolled to his back with his eyes shut against the sunlight, still reeling in a release-induced haze. It took several minutes more for his breathing to return to a more natural meter, but when it did, he turned on his side and propped himself up on his elbow, resting his cheek on his fist. He smiled as a wave of the most intense tenderness he'd ever felt washed through him. Branwenn had dozed off, her face now a serene mask of innocence and youth.

Why would she not allow him to see her naked? It made no sense. She was so open in her sexual curiosity, actually rather pleasingly adventurous for one with only the experience he'd thus far given her. Hell, if it had not been for that one time, their first time, when he'd lit a taper afterward, he would never have even seen the one—lush, succulent, full, tip-turned (like her eyes), rosy peaked, *with a freckle*—breast that had been accidently revealed when the sheet drooped a bit before she covered it.

Her eyes opened as he gazed upon her and they were once again the color of crushed violets—as they were whenever her emotions were high, he'd discovered. Touching his fingers lightly to her brow, he moved the dampened dark locks to the side before leaning down and placing a soft kiss on her mouth and then repeated the action on her cheek. "Now, who is embarrassed, I wonder? I look like a wee lad just out of swaddlings with this stain on the front of my tunic."

Her eyes wandered down to the offending wet spot. "I could get you a new one?"

He grinned and quickly released the strings of his damp braies—thankfully, he'd worn his long tunic this day—saying, "Actually, that would be rather helpful,"—he scooted both that undergarment and the hose attached off of his torso and legs, flicking his shoes off at the same time—"as I have no desire for either of your brothers to learn of this lover's tryst we've just enjoyed." He wadded the material and tossed it over his shoulder, then put his feet back inside his shoes, before rolling to his side once more and propping his cheek on his raised fist again.

Branwenn groaned and threw her hands over her face. "Oh, Callum! We were going to wait until our wedding night!" She turned her wrath-filled eyes upon him once more. "'Tis all your fault! Why can we not spend five minutes together without doing"—she waved her hand in the air—"this?!"

Callum came closer to her and dropped his arm over her waist. "Aye. 'Tis my fault. For, you see, you are much too enticing a creature, my sweet *fey Mai*, for one such as I, a mere mortal, to resist your siren's call."

"Pardon? Did you just say 'twas *my* fault?"

"Nay, I said 'twas *my* fault."

"How is that exactly? For, according to you, I am enticing you, calling you, and you are only a mortal unable to resist it. Somehow, tho' 'tis certainly a pretty speech, if you hear it logically, it's really your way of blaming me."

Callum growled in frustration. "All right! 'Tis all my fault because I'm a lecherous male and all I think about when I'm with you is seeing you naked and fucking you—does that satisfy your sense of justice now?"

Branwenn giggled behind her hand. "Aye." After another moment, she sobered and said, "Callum, you hurt me so deeply with those horrible accusations you made. Why did you think I would do anything like that—ever?"

He studied her for a long moment, his gaze tracing the shape of her face and form before returning once more to look into her eyes. "'Tis a thing I didn't expect to ever feel again. Not with you, for this is a love match we have. But when you spurned me so coldly this morn, and in a manner much like my wife, Lara, had done when she was displeased with me—as often she was—and then you gave your whole attention to Robert instead—also a thing that Lara had done—I became angry and sure that I was setting myself up to be a cuckold once more. A thing I never want to be again." He paused. "You do know what happened between Lara and Robert last *Hogmanay*, do you not?"

"Nay, though I know what she tried to do with Bao. He almost lost Jesslyn over it."

Branwenn's hand was resting just below her breast and Callum picked it up and softly stroked the top of her fingers with his thumb. "Bao and I found the two of them together."

"But Robert's your friend!" She whipped over onto her side and lifted up on her elbow. "Why ever would he have done such a thing to you! I shall never speak to the man again!" She dropped her gaze, shaking her head.

"When I came upon them, 'twas clear they'd done the deed, so Lara accused him of raping her."

Branwenn's gaze flashed back to his. "What! Did he?"

Callum shook his head. "Nay. And he'd only bedded her because..." Now here was the tricky part.

"Because...?" Branwenn prompted.

He cleared his throat. "Because I'd bedded his sister,"—Branwenn sat up, her eyes glued to his countenance—"a thing he thought of as traitorous."

"You..." Her voice was small but grew louder as she continued, "bedded *Isobail!* You *are* a traitor! To me! You said there was naught between you. You...you...aargh!" She crossed her arms over her chest and turned her back on him.

"Branwenn," Callum began soothingly. Rising up himself into a sitting position and placing his hand on her shoulder, he slowly caressed her. "I was thirteen summers at the time—that was over eight years ago now—and she was a lass of fifteen. She was my first, but I was not hers. She'd had quite a few lovers by the time she set her sights on me—and then, I found out later, 'twas only in order to make the lad she'd decided she must wed—Laird Grant's nephew—jealous enough to give her his troth."

Branwenn relaxed back against him with her head bowed as she spoke. "So the two of you never...after that?"

"Nay. Never."

She lifted her head and shook it. "The Isobail I knew did not seem at all like the lass you just described."

Callum sighed and rested his forehead on her shoulder a second before lifting his head and saying, "Aye, the lady you knew was the true Isobail. At the time of our youthful affair, however, she'd had a bit of a heartbreak and was punishing, I believe, her father for his role in her pain. Tho', again, I learned of this much later."

Branwenn raised up and twisted around so that she was facing him once more. "I only wanted to be kind when I spoke with Robert this morn, since he just lost his dear sister. I wasn't dallying with his affections, I swear this to you."

Callum nodded gravely. "Aye, I know that now." He scrubbed his fingers roughly over his brow. "Isobail's death is a sad loss to both him and David." He lifted Branwenn's hand to his mouth and kissed each finger, one by one. "My thanks for spending the eve with the lad. When I spoke to him before breaking our fast, he seemed much better settled than he had been after I spoke to him before his mother's passing this day past."

"Grandmother Maclean and your mother aided in that as well. They always seem to know just the right thing to say." She took her hand from his and placed it on his cheek as she gazed directly into his eyes. "I understand much better now what happened this morn. I was wrong to treat you so coldly; I should have spoken to you about my misgivings instead. And, knowing what I now know about Lara and how you were treated by her, I can see why you reacted as you did when I spent my time with Robert. But, I beg you, do not ever think that I will cuckold you, for you are my body's and my heart's one desire."

Callum took her hand in his once more and, bringing it down to rest on the ground between them, he leaned forward and kissed her. After several rather heated moments of this, he at last lifted his head and said, "Robert told me what you spoke of this morn. *Me!*"

Branwenn slowly opened her eyes and looked at him. He had the most grotesquely happy, self-satisfied grin on his face she'd ever encountered.

She watched him lean back with his arms out behind him to rest on his palms before saying, "Aye, he told me you'd bedded every young maid, daughter, and widow in the shire by the time you were fifteen summers."

Callum sat bolt upright. "He did?! That cur dog spawn of the devil! He said he'd told you I'd only slept with Lara!"

Branwenn howled. "Ohmygod! 'Tis true! I only said such to tease you, for I knew Robert's answer to be false." Her eyes wide with shocked mirth, she waited for his reply.

Callum's cheeks burned, so he knew he was blushing. "Well, 'twasn't *every* daughter."

Laughing, Branwenn threw her arms around his neck. "Oh, Callum, I love you!"

He chuckled and shook his head. "I love you, too."

* * *

The next morn, Robert left with a small wagon containing his sister's body inside, wrapped in burial shrouds and covered over with several layers of furs. The pall that hung about the place that morn was heavy and grim. No one seemed inclined to speak, so they quietly trudged back inside the keep after saying their farewells to the man, and one final farewell to the lady whose body lay so quiet and still beneath the covering of blankets.

"Aye, she was a dear, lovely lass, that one was," Chalmers broke the silence once they were all settled around the hearthfire and drinking a bit of mulled ale. "And the poor lad, how it breaks my heart that he's lost both his parents in the same twelvemonth!"

Branwenn's eyes misted. Callum, seeing her distress, reached over and took hold of her hand and rested both of them on his knee, stroking the top of hers with his thumb. He cleared the sudden thickness in his own throat before saying, "He seems a bit less fretful since the ladies—and Bao and Daniel—spent time with him the day of his mother's death."

Branwenn looked over at her brothers. Bao and Daniel stood a bit away, both silent, both in the same wide stance with their hands behind their backs, both keeping their eyes from meeting anyone's as they listened to the conversation going on around them. The half-brothers had each lost a mother they loved dearly when they were young. Bao, when he was a bit younger than David, and Daniel when he was a bit older. She could only imagine how hard it must be on them right now, as they were reminded once more of the tragedy of their youths.

And, even though she'd never known her own mother, she'd certainly felt the loss of that gentle lady her whole life. But how much deeper the pain must go when you actually know your mother and lose her!

She thought of Reys then. He'd been a lad of only five summers when their mother, hers and his, had been yanked from her life in Cambria and forced into servitude to Bao and Daniel's evil father. How sad Reys must have been—how lost. 'Twas strange but, in all these moons since learning of her history and meeting him, she'd never once thought of how those long-ago events must have affected his life as well. She'd, rather selfishly, she now admitted, only thought of how it had affected her—and how it might affect her foster family. Never Reys. Never once. Until now. An urge to see him overcame her. Where was he? Oh, yes, he was with Alyson bow hunting again. But later. Later, she would speak with him and learn a bit about his life, as she'd grown to care for him, almost as much as she did her other brothers.

* * *

A sennight later, the wives arrived. First Maryn, Daniel's wife, and then a bit later in the morn, Jesslyn, Bao's wife. Neither one of them had brought their babes, as the weather was becoming harsh, and they worried they'd catch a chill. Since Jesslyn's young son, Alleck, had begun his page training a couple of moons past at Maryn's father's holding, he was not in attendance either. Jesslyn and Bao had decided to keep the lad close while he paged and then allow him to do his squire's training, as Alleck's father had desired, with Daniel at the MacLaurin keep.

There was a time, not many sennights prior, when Branwenn would have wondered why 'twas taking the two couples so long to come down to the great hall for the nooning meal. Now, it only made her envious.

Only two days more!

And this eve would be the bonfire and feast, for 'twas the eve of *Samhainn*.

Callum came into the hall, with David at his heels. "Will you allow me to lead your warhorse onto the lists?" The joust was set for a fortnight after his wedding day, and Callum had yet to officially appoint the young lad to that position.

"Aye, I said I would, did I not?" Callum replied. The lad had been sullen since his mother's body had been taken away, and this was the first show of spirit he'd had. They'd just come from the training field, and it had clearly reminded David of his avid desire to participate in some way at the joust.

David sighed in frustration. "Aye, but you haven't told Daniel or Bao, so they will not let me practice." He cocked his head to the side, a question in his look. "Who will be your Kipper?

"Why not ask Bao to do it?" Branwenn chimed in, thrilled to see David's spirited interest. "For, 'tis truth, he is the biggest warrior I've ever seen—he should have little trouble at all getting your prize from the other man's frame." She said the last, a bit tongue in cheek, for 'twas truth—she found the whole process frightening and not just a bit, well, barbaric. Lads! Warriors!

Callum chuckled. "Aye, I believe I will ask your brother that very favor." He turned his head slightly, looking down at his page. "What say you, David? Should Bao be my Kipper?

David threw both hands over his mouth and laughed.

Branwenn and Callum looked at each other and shared a smile of relief before turning their eyes back to their young ward.

Lifting one fist in the air, David jumped and shouted, "Aye!" He looked at Branwenn. "Will that not be ever so merry to watch? Surely, every warrior will give him his armor freely, else their brains will be rung out from the clamor of Bao's club against their helms!"

Evil glee. Those were the exact words that flitted through Branwenn's mind as she watched, amused, the lad's evident thrill at the prospect. She only prayed he could continue to find a bit of joy each day in the next moons as he daily grieved the loss of his young mother.

Callum ruffled the lad's hair. Then, sidling up to Branwenn, he said, "David, will you go to the solar and ask my mother what she has planned to feed us for the feast this eve?"

There was a definite glint of...something...in Callum's eyes as he watched her, and Branwenn had an idea what that 'something' just might be. She turned to David and said, a bit too loudly, "Nay! No need. For I can give Callum the list, as I've been working on it these past minutes."

David, who'd already turned toward the door, began turning back toward the two adults and then sighed heavily when Callum said, "Nay, David, I'd like you to go in any case, as my mother has told me she has a special errand she needs done, and she will only trust you to see it through." Callum's smile was smug when he turned it on his, now clearly flustered, betrothed.

Branwenn bit her lip to keep from grinning like a loon. He'd won the mental joust, but, truth be told, she wasn't the best opponent in these moments. For, ever since their horrid fight and that wonderful time in the garden when they'd shared their thoughts, their feelings, to a degree they'd never done before, she had been craving another bit of time with him—alone.

But, there was also that stubborn, romantic part of her that craved for their wedding night—only one more day and one more night and one more day away!—to be special. And that night, she would, she had determined, no matter how embarrassed she was, allow him to see her without a stitch of clothing on.

Her heart did a little flip in her chest and her palms

began to sweat. What if he thought her ugly? That disgusting patch of red on her inner thigh.... Her heart tripped, then hammered inside her chest. What if he was angry with her for not allowing him to see it before they wed? What if he.... Nay, she would not think such thoughts. He loved her. He daily told her how lovely he found her. Surely, that one, vile and disgusting spot wouldn't turn him against her for evermore, as the old drunken nurse always told her—would it? Nay, it wouldn't. After all—he'd not turned from her after seeing the mar on her breast, had he?

David rushed out and the two were left alone in the hall. The meal would be served in only a quarter-hour's time, so Branwenn hoped they'd not be long alone in the chamber. She glanced nervously at the entrance. Where on earth were her grandmother and Aunt Maggie?

"I've a present for you, love," Callum said seductively, much too close to her ear for her to keep her resolve for very long.

She turned and looked at him. "Y...You have?" she asked breathlessly.

"Aaaye," he drawled into it and then lightly ran his tongue over the outer edge. "'Tis in the pouch attached to my belt." He took her earlobe between his teeth and nibbled it a bit before softly sucking it into his mouth.

Branwenn's knees turned to jelly as a rush of hot and cold shivers ran up the side of her neck to her ear. She felt her nipples harden and abrade the material over her breast, and tingles of pure ecstasy traveled from the center of her womb out over her skin to the tips of her fingers and toes. "Mmm?"

Callum grinned against her lobe. "Why do you not check inside? I'm sure you'll like what you find." He took her hand and placed it on the pouch.

Branwenn's fingers trembled as she opened the drawstring and slid them inside the opening. As her fingers traveled downward she felt the hard ridge of his manhood hidden behind the material of his tunic and shirt. Oh, God! How she wanted that. Deep inside her. Now. Not two nights hence, but *now*. Here. On the table behind them. Her heart pounded in her breast and her breathing grew harsh.

Callum placed his hands on her shoulders and pressed his cheek against hers. "Branwenn," he rasped, his voice had a bit of a tremble to it now. "Godamercy, how long 'til we are wed? I swear, I cannot wait much longer to be inside you again." With a jerk, dropped his hands to his sides and took a step back. "Pray, pardon me, my love. I played a bit too close to the fire, it seems. I thought I had more discipline than that." He quickly brought out the thing he'd meant to give her from his pouch and thrust it toward her.

'Twas a ring. A lovely amethyst and emerald ring. Two pea-sized oval stones mounted next to each other in a gold filigree setting. "Here. Take it."

Branwenn's eyes grew wide with pleasure as she gazed upon the gift. "Callum! 'Tis lovely." She glanced up at him and then quickly down at the ring once more as she reached out and took it. She brought it close to her face and looked at it from every angle. "My thanks."

Callum stepped forward. "Here, let me put it on you," he said. Taking the piece of jewelry, he slid it over the middle finger of her left hand. Afterward, because he could resist it no longer, he settled his lips against her forehead and wrapped his arms around her shoulders. "'Twas my grandmother's—my father's mother's. I'm glad you like it."

* * *

Branwenn found Reys on the lists and waived at him. He dipped his head at her before cantering over to her on his steed. After lifting the helm off, he smiled and gave her another brief nod of greeting, saying, "Good day to you. Do you search for Callum?" Pointing with his thumb, he twisted slightly on his saddle in the direction of the southern end of the lists. "I think he's further down, practicing with Daniel."

"Nay, I came to speak with you, actually. Have you a few moments to spend with me in the garden, mayhap?"

His brows lifted. "Yes. Just give me a moment to wash up a bit. Shall I meet you there, in say, a half hour's time?"

Branwenn smiled and nodded. "All right." She turned and walked toward her destination. She was a bit nervous at the prospect of speaking with Reys about his youth, as she had no idea whether it had been pleasing or horrid. And if it had been horrid, he'd no doubt not want to tell her about it in any case. But, ever since this sennight past when she'd realized how little she knew about the brother that shared her blood, she'd been anxious to speak with him, to let him know that she cared about him a great deal and hoped he'd not suffered too greatly when his mother—*their* mother—had been taken from him. Unfortunately, she'd been thwarted in her previous attempts to gain a privy word with him, either by one or both of her brothers demanding his presence on the lists or by Grandmother Maclean and Aunt Maggie insisting on her presence in the solar to go over last minute details for her coming nuptials. It finally became clear to her this morn that she must *force* the meeting, so had determinedly set out to insist upon, if need be, a meeting forthwith.

She'd barely gotten settled on the bench, when Reys came through the arched entry to the garden. "You look awfully clean for one who only took—what?—five minutes to bathe?" she jested.

Reys gave her a sheepish grin. "I decided it best to only pour a bit of well water over my head and wash my face, as you seemed troubled and avid to speak to me. And, as you see, I'm still in all my mail."

"Come," she said, patting the space next to her on the stone bench, "sit with me awhile."

When Reys was settled next to her, she placed her hand atop the one he had lightly gripped around the edge of the bench between them and turned slightly toward him. "I want to give you my confession of sorrow that I have never once asked you about your life in Cambria after our mother was taken away from you and your father."

"*Our* father," he corrected gently. "And you were taken from us as well."

Branwenn looked away. "Aye, but I was not yet

born, so 'twas not as great a loss, I trow."

Reys turned his hand up and twined his fingers through hers. "Yes, Branwenn, it was. For both my father and for me. And my search was not the first one—'twas only the first one that was successful."

She tucked that admission away, to be studied later, when she was by herself once more. "But, how hard it must have been for you to retrace Jamison Maclean's steps, to find the kirk where our mother was buried!"

Reys stared down at their intertwined hands. With a sigh, he nodded slowly. "Yes, 'twas a very painful mission our cousin sent me on; one which took me away from my wife, who was still carrying my twin girls in her belly." He looked at her then, his eyes full of purpose, "But, I tell you truly, 'twas a mission I wanted. Wanted more than I wanted my next breath."

Branwenn's eyes widened a bit and she sat forward, "Why, Reys? Why would you have wanted such so badly?"

"Because I owed it to my mother—our mother—and you."

He got up abruptly and took a few paces away and then stopped cold, running his hand through his hair, before rubbing the back of his neck with his palm. She'd asked, so he would now tell her. As he'd sworn to himself he would do in any case...someday soon. 'Twould be the final act of contrition for the horrible sin he'd committed. "You see, I held a shame in my very soul all those years after her abduction. There was a debt to her and you I had to pay."

Branwenn watched him, fascinated. He was like

some black wolf, in the sights of a band of hunters' bows, tensely awaiting the killing volleys.

His hand fisted at his side, then opened, the long, masculinely tapered fingers flaring out like a cockscomb. "You see, I told her I *hated* her the day I last saw her,"—Branwenn sucked in her breath—"told her that I wished she was dead," his voice, as hollow as a fallen oak, cracked on the last word.

"Reys!" she whispered harshly.

He turned back to face her, a look of tortured despair on his darkly handsome face. "Yes, I know, 'tis the most horrid, awful, *vile* thing to say to anyone. And I said it to my own mother."

"But you were so young—only five summers, is that not right?"

He nodded. "Yes."

Branwenn stood up and walked over to him. She placed her hand on his arm, a show of comfort and understanding. "She knew you meant it not, I'm sure."

He shrugged, taking in a deep breath and releasing it with a huff. He cleared his throat and said, "I was so angry with her, I remember." He chuckled but there was torment in the sound. "I wanted to stay at the keep; my friend, Owain, and I had a wager on the number of times we could toss a stone in the air and catch it without it dropping to the ground. If I won the wager, I'd win his new pair of stilts, a thing I avidly desired after having used them earlier. I was on my twenty-seventh toss, with ten more to go to beat his number when my mother came up to us and said 'twas time for us to depart on our journey to her sister's holding." He looked away. "I pleaded with her, as I continued my tosses, to allow me to stay to finish the game, but she refused—and then she caught the stone and gave it to Owain. I was so furious with her." His voice turned bitter. "I thought: Why could she not allow me to stay a few more moments to complete my game?" A wayward tear fell from the outer corner of his eye and he quickly scrubbed it away with the base of his palm. "Of course, I learned later that she'd given Owain's mother an oath that she would not allow me to make wagers with my friend anymore." He crossed his arms over his chest and bowed his head. "And when she took hold of my hand to lead me away I...God's Bones!" Pressing the base of his palm into his eye, he said brokenly, "I *hit* her—in the stomach!"

"Reys!" Branwenn's mind reeled. 'Twas truly an awful thing he'd done, yet he had been so young at the time. "Was she...did she..."

He cleared his throat. "She was not harmed, God be praised." He looked over at her then. "And, neither were you."

A chill ran down her spine and she shivered in reaction. A faint memory niggled at the corner of Branwenn's mind, and, all at once, she knew. "Godamercy! You were with her when Jamison Maclean abducted her!" She tugged on his sleeve without realizing it. "How ever did you manage to not be captured—how did you survive—and how did I not know of this before?"

Reys returned her gaze, placing his hand over the one she had fisted in the sleeve of his tunic. "While my mother's guards were fighting the brigands, she told me that no matter what happened, I was to remain still and silent. I agreed, but not without several long seconds of fearful debate, for I was crying and shaking by this time. And, oh, God! Branwenn"—he threw his head back, his eyes squeezed shut. Finally, he opened them and settled his gaze on her once more—"even then, I didn't give her my confession of sorrow for what I'd said to her earlier." The hand that covered hers clenched slightly. "A thing that haunts me to this day. Why did I not say the words? I thought them, I assure you, but I didn't say them to her. All I said, over and over again, was 'I'm afraid, Mama.'

"Reys," Branwenn whispered sadly, not knowing what else to say to him.

He continued, as if he'd not heard her, "Then, she rolled me in her cloak and tossed the contents of her spew bucket over it—gambling that the fiends would leave it be once they saw that the garment was ruined."

"Spew bucket?" She looked up from her dazed and blind stare at the gold and red badge on the left breast of his dark blue tunic.

His lips pressed together a moment before he nodded, saying, "Yes. You recall, she was carrying you at the time?"

"Oh. Aye. Spew bucket."

"Anyway, the ploy worked, for when the men threw the door open to the caravan and yanked my mother out, taking whatever small items she had with her in the thing, they left alone the cloak she'd arranged, as if wadded up, on the opposite seat."

"But, Reys, how on earth did you survive until your father and his men arrived? Were you still there or had you left the place?"

"I'd left. I was so frightened, so terrified, actually, that the men would come back. But, I, being such a young boy, had no idea what to do—so I just moved, walked forward, in the opposite direction of where we had been headed. I just wanted to get home. And find someone who would chase the men down who'd stolen my mother from me." He moved away from her and sat down on the bench with his hands braced on its edge and his arms straight, his whole body rigid. "One of my father's men found me on the side of the road a couple of days later. I was ill from lack of food and drink. He lifted me up and took me back to our keep." Turning his head, he gazed, unseeing, at the brown and grays of the winter garden. "I was not well for quite a time afterward, from exposure to the elements and hunger and thirst, but also from the trauma of losing my mother and knowing that I'd told her I wanted her dead. God had punished me for those words, I knew."

"Reys! Surely 'tis not true!"

He shrugged. "For many years afterward—many years—until I found you, in fact,"—he turned to look at her once more—"I wore a hairshirt as penance for my sin."

* * *

Two hours later, as Branwenn was dressing for the feast, her mind turned once more to the tale she'd gotten from her brother that afternoon. Her heart ached for him. Lord, the wide swath of damage and destruction that had been caused by Jamison Maclean. It amazed her still that such a vile, horrid devil could produce two such generous, honorable men as Bao and Daniel. God be praised that the evilness had not been handed down in the blood. She sighed as she washed her face over the basin. But, she supposed, 'twas clearly not aberrant blood, but evilness of mind and spirit, as Jamison Maclean's mother, Lady Maclean—and by all of that lady's accounts, his father also—was a generous, honorable person as well.

What anguish Reys had suffered! And—this still amazed her, even now—to such an extent that he'd actually worn a *hairshirt* for *years*! She shuddered.

Drying her face with the cloth, she turned toward her bed, where a new emerald green gown was laid out. Yet another of her grandmother's generous gifts. But the lady, no matter how much Branwenn whined, refused to have them made any larger. Branwenn lightly ran her fingertips over the soft silk of the bodice. 'Twas much too form-fitting for her liking. It made her feel...exposed...too much in the light, and not far enough in the shadows, as was her liking. For, when she was not noticed, she could make graceless mistakes with no one being the wiser. And if her hair was not quite the right style or length—then, who would notice such?

With a sigh of resignation, she shrugged and began dressing and allowed her thoughts to wander back to her brother, Reys, and what he'd told her that day.

She shook her head in wonder. Her Cambrian relatives had actually been searching for her—all those years! What would her life have been like, she wondered, had they found her? Had they taken her back with them when she was but a bairn? She supposed her life would have been much as any other young lady of means. She would, no doubt, have been taught the rudiments of taking care of an estate and a husband, as Grandmother Maclean had set out to do near to fifteen moons past when Bao had left her with the lady for that purpose. But, that was before Reys had found her and scuttled her back to Cambria to wed Gaiallard, the Norman.

Aye, she would no doubt have had a much more prosperous style of life, and even might have—nay, *would* have—had the love of her family-germane, but she'd not have had Bao. And knowing all he'd sacrificed for her—that his love for her ran that deep, she worried what would have become of him had she been taken from him then. For, a lonely, desperate lad—a lad who'd been forced into the trade he'd been forced into—might never have risen above it had he not had a purpose for doing so. Her.

Nay, she was glad, desperately glad, that she'd not been found by her Cambrian family early on.

Looking down at the gown, she grumbled under her breath, but then smiled and shook her head before lifting the garment and wriggling into it.

* * *

CHAPTER 12

THE BONFIRE CRACKLED and popped in the cold night air, sending orange sparks and larger embers shooting into the sky, before quickly turning the lit wood coals to pale gray ghosts that flitted in the smoky hot breeze atop the fire's mad dance.

And this night, Callum would dance as well, with her, Branwenn thought happily as she trudged across the bailey toward the section of the fortress where the bonfire had been erected. The pipers and other minstrels were already playing a lively tune and several of the young lads and lasses were twirling about together near them.

In her right hand, she held a basket filled with hazelnuts, and in her left, a cloth sack of apples. Grandmother Maclean had given her the nuts to toss into the blaze a bit later in the evening. They were marked with the names of the unwed lads and lasses of the clan and would, she'd said, when placed in the fire and popped, divine which lass went with which lad.

But the apples were for her. And Callum. Mostly for them to share together, as they had that day in the bailey. She sighed. Their first kiss. And what a kiss it had been! Even now, her knees wobbled with the fervency of the memory. But one of the apples would also provide a merry game. For, she would peel it, as was the tradition, in one long strand and then toss the peel over her shoulder. The shape it took upon landing would be the initial of his name, proving that they were meant to be wed. And there was no doubt in her mind that 'twould be in the shape of a 'C'—for 'twas the most common shape, no doubt, that type of apple peeling would make. But, just to be certain, she'd slyly force it more to that shape as she tossed.

The stone of the curtain wall rose up behind the fire, she noticed as she approached, making eerie light and dark shapes on the stones. 'Twas clear the fire was doing what it should: keeping the spirits of the evil dead at bay. She shuddered. Like Jamison Maclean, Bao and Daniel's vicious sire—and the man who'd caused such torment in Reys's life as well. Aye, keep him far away from her brothers, she thought, for he'd done enough to them while he lived.

Her eye scanned first one direction and then the other, landing at last on David. But 'twas also the night when the veil between the world of the living and the world of the dead was thinnest, and she knew that the lad, along with Maggie and Grandmother Maclean, had set a trencher of food and a cup of wine out for Isobail, should she decide to visit her son this eve.

"Good eve, my love," she heard just as someone placed a hand at her waist.

"*Eek!*" She whipped her head around. "Oh, 'tis you! Good eve."

"And, who else would be calling you 'my love'," Callum asked a bit peevishly, but there was a warm smile attached, so she knew he wasn't truly angry.

She smiled as well. "'Twas the thoughts I was having that made me jump when you touched me."

A heated look came into his eye. "What, pray, were you thinking—something carnal involving me, I hope?"

With a chuckle, she shook her head. "Nay, 'twas of the thin veil between us and the Otherworld, and the dead that may be in residence this very eve, that my mind had been turned to."

Callum's smile became a grin. "Truly? Are you frightened of ghosts and goblins, then?"

Branwenn swung around and faced him full on. "Are you not frightened? Even a wee bit?"

Callum shrugged and looked toward the bonfire. "Mayhap, when I was much younger, I was. But now?" He shook his head. "Nay, I'm not." He turned an indulgent smile on her. "Should I put on my armor and fight the beasts back with my broadax and sword for you?"

She laughed and shook her head. "Nay, no need. For I have it on good authority that they're more interested in food than flesh this night."

Callum's eyelids drooped and his eyes turned a smokey green as he studied her mouth. "Aye, and I am much more interested in flesh. Yours."

She gave him a cheeky grin. "First, you must dance with me." She twirled around and headed toward Maryn and Jesslyn, whom she'd spied just before Callum arrived.

"Dance?!" he croaked.

"At least ten times!" she called out over her shoulder and began to jog as he took off after her.

* * *

Much later, after they'd danced *three* times, which was as many dances as she could inveigle him into, Branwenn and Callum settled on a blanket a bit away from the bonfire, and the others. She took out a couple of the apples and gave one to him, before taking a big *chomp* out of her own.

Callum took a bite as well and lay back, resting on his elbows and forearms as he crossed one leg over the other. Looking up at the night sky, he said, "Lord, but there are thousands of them up there tonight, are there not?"

Branwenn craned her head back and looked up. "Aye, 'tis lovely."

"See that one?" He pointed up and to his right a bit. "That one is you, for you are the brightest, most dazzling star in the Highland heavens. No one can compete with your loveliness."

"*Callum!*" Branwenn cried softly, and then she threw herself into his arms and kissed him, right on the mouth. She only prayed he still felt that way two nights from now when he saw *it*.

Callum chuckled behind his *smushed* lips and then wrapped his arms around her and strategically placed his hand over her sweet, round bottom before opening his mouth and taking a real taste of what she'd so freely offered him.

They stayed that way for several hot, sultry heartbeats, but finally Callum grasped the sides of her face in his palms and lifted her head from his. He was out of breath, but managed to say, "Enough! Else I'll have you right here, right now, in front of the entire clan." He lifted his head and gave her lips one last, quick kiss, before continuing, "I'd say we could go to your chamber for a while to finish what we started, with no one the wiser, but I know you'll only say me nay—am I right?"

Branwenn dropped her forehead down on his chest and nodded. On a loud sigh, she said, "Aye." After another moment, she sat up and grabbed another of the apples out of the sack. "Hand me your dirk."

Callum's brows lifted. "Pardon? Did you just ask me for my dirk?"

Branwenn grinned. "Worry not, I shan't cut you for plying me once more with your pleas to bed me before we are wedded."

"Ha! What a wit you are," he said, but he handed her the knife.

She slowly began to peel the apple, beginning at the very top, where a portion of the stem still hung.

"What do you?" he asked, sitting up in a cross-legged position to watch her more closely.

"Why, I'm peeling the apple in one strand—know you not the custom?" She dared not take her hand, or her eye, off of her work, else all might be lost.

Callum's brows drew together and his eyes narrowed as he tried to recall what custom she could possibly be meaning. After a moment, he shrugged and shook his head. "Nay, I suppose I know it not. What is it?"

"I'll tell you in a minute, I must attend what I'm doing."

Callum shrugged again, but remained silent.

"There!" she cried as she lifted the long, curly, sticky, strand of peel up high in the air to show him. "I did it!"

Callum laughed. "Aye, that you did, for I was a witness. So?"

Branwenn huffed and then said, "You shall see." She settled the peel in as much of a circle as she could in the palm of her other hand and then tossed it over her shoulder. Twisting around, she looked into the darkness for the apple skin she'd just thrown. "Ah! There it is!" She hiked up her skirts and walked on her hands and knees toward the divining peel. "Hmm...how odd," she murmured, her head cocked sideways.

"What? Let me see," Callum said and crawled over to look at the thing as well. "What's odd about it? Ah! Do you mean that it looks like a 'G'?"

She cleared her throat. "Nay, not a 'G', 'tis a 'C'—'C' for Callum." She looked up at him then.

Callum lifted his eye to her as well. "'C' for Callum? I ken you not." He looked down at the apple skin again. "And 'tis definitely a 'G' I see, not a 'C'—look there"—he traced the design with the tip of his finger—"at the way the bottom end curves inward." He nodded. "Aye, a 'G', not a 'C'." At last, her meaning dawned on him and he sat back on his heels. "Mean you that this was meant to divine whom you will wed?"

"Ummm...well..." She sighed and then nodded. "Aye."

Callum laughed and grabbed hold of her hand, twining his fingers through hers. "You're wedding me, two days hence, I care not what that apple skin says." He looked down at the design once more and his eyes narrowed. "What is the name of the guard who liked you so well? I struck his name from my memory."

"Callum! For heaven's sake, you know Grandmother Maclean and your mother asked him to talk to me!"

He looked at her, his right brow lifted.

"Oh, all right. His name is Kerk."

He nodded. "Good."

Another thought struck. Looking down once more at the peel, he said, "And do not think that 'tis Gaiallard de Montfort's name that design signifies—"

Branwenn took in a sharp breath. It caught in her throat. 'G'! *Gaiallard!*

Returning his gaze to her, Callum tugged her closer to him. "He will never have you. Never," he vowed. "I'll skewer him through if he even attempts such."

Branwenn's heart beat hard inside her chest as she studied her betrothed's determined expression. After a moment, she nodded shakily and said, "I pray you'll never have a need to prove that vow."

Callum relaxed a bit and brought his other hand up to her cheek, stroking the soft rise of it with his thumb. "Aye, and I as well, but I am prepared to do what I must in any case."

***

The next morn Branwenn woke up early, before the chimes of prime, and flew to the washstand. In seconds, she was heaving and gagging, sweating and coughing. "Dear God, I feel awful!" she moaned, swaying a bit on her feet as she washed her face with a damp rag. Had she eaten some meat that was off? Lord, she wondered if anyone else had the same illness. 'Twould not be good if Grandmother Maclean got sick as well.

Oh, Lord! This was the night they were to have a small feast in anticipation of the wedding and larger celebration on the morrow, as well as to celebrate *Samhainn*. What if she was too ill to attend? Or, worse, what if she was too ill to wed Callum on the morrow? She vehemently shook her head. Nay, naught on this earth would keep her from saying her vows to him. Naught. Even if she had to be carried down on a litter, she'd be wed to her man by tomorrow night.

All at once, Reys's words about his mother and the bucket came back to her.

She stumbled over to the bed and sat down with her hands gripping its edges. Nay. Surely not. For Callum had been very careful not to spill his seed inside her. But, how long had it been since her last flowering?

Let's see...*Godamercy!* She leapt from the bed. She hadn't flowered since...since...oh, God! A fortnight before that first night!

She began to pace, gnawing on the knuckles of her right hand. Would Callum be dismayed? She settled a splayed hand low on her belly. A babe! *Their* babe! A thrill of utter delight shot through her and she grinned. Nay, Callum would be glad, very glad. For, hadn't he said he wanted *five* bairns?

And, after all, they'd be well wed by the time the babe arrived. So, 'twould arrive a bit early—'twas not such an unusual thing. Was it?

But, when to tell him? Her wedding night of course! For what could be a better gift than that?

Another thought struck on the heel of the last and Branwenn laughed out loud, though with just a bit of guilt as well as she'd never want the lass to know she'd ever found even one shred of humor in that mortifying situation. But she had actually spoken to Alyson, at length, about the monthly cycle just days past—and not once had it occurred to her that she, herself, had missed two of them!

* * *

Gaiallard de Montfort stood at the base of the incline that led up to the gate of the fortress. For a good bit of coin, he'd left his steed, armor, and other supplies with the old hag that lived in the wood that edged the sea. What he wore now was the clothing he'd purchased off a silver merchant in the town of Duglyn just after he'd arrived on the mainland.

Today, he'd do a bit of spying inside the fortress. He was well enough disguised that, as long as he remained outside the sights of Branwenn, Reys and Alyson, he'd be able to get the information he sought with little effort.

And, on the morrow, he'd arrive as himself—as planned.

* * *

"Give a promise to me," Callum said sultrily into Branwenn's ear from behind the screen she had just positioned herself in front of. 'Twas late and the hall was filled with happy revelers enjoying the minstrels' show.

A thrill of excitement traveled like a lightning bolt down her spine. She made a brief nod, but kept her eyes strictly focused on the players several yards in front of her.

She felt his grin of satisfaction against her ear. "Stay perfectly still, completely silent, while I recite to you all of the wicked things I shall be doing to that delectable body of yours in just eighteen hours' time." He didn't wait for a response, but continued in a deeper tone, "First, I shall remove that ridiculous veil that covers your lovely raven locks and toss it in the hearthfire. Beshrew my grandmother for making you wear it this eve!"

Branwenn chuckled despite herself, but quickly sobered when the person in front of her turned to regard her.

"For shame, my sweet," Callum said, tho' there was laughter in his tone. "For that transgression, you must now make forfeit to me your timidity and give yourself the ultimate pleasure this eve."

Branwenn began to turn toward him, curious to know his meaning, but Callum quickly checked the movement by placing his hand at her waist.

"Nay love," he said with a grin in his tone, "you must not give anyone understanding that I am here with you now, else they'll surely separate us." Giving her waist a slight squeeze, he demanded gently, "Stay still."

When she gave him an abbreviated nod of assent, he explained, "Just as the midnight bells begin to chime—in only one hour's time—I shall expect you to be bare-skinned upon your bed, and thinking of all the sensitive, oh-so-sweet, places on your body that you would like to feel my hands, my mouth. And as you do so, I want you to slowly run your fingertips over your plump, pink lips and then suck them inside, wetting them with your tongue."

Branwenn's shivered.

"Afterward, you must trail them from the small shell of your ear, down your neck to that lovely, succulently sweet, freckled breast"—Branwenn's cheeks flamed—"and spend a moment imagining the feast I shall be having tomorrow eve upon it. And then do the same to the other one."

"Callum!" she whispered, shocked to the core, but tingling with awareness just the same.

He ignored her outburst. "When you have readied them for my mouth, I want you to run your fingers down over the soft skin of your midriff—for my tongue and teeth will take delight in that adorable place as well, know you this well. But do not tarry there for long, my sweet. Nay, those fingers of yours will be my tongue's proxy, and they must move ever further south, to that feminine delta where I will finally be allowed to quench my thirst and at long last drive my barge."

Branwenn's limbs quivered. Her heart pounded

with excitement—and not a little dread. He was asking—demanding, actually—that she *touch* herself—*there!*

Callum paused, his breath coming more rapidly now as a soft sheen of sweat cooled his overheated skin. And his betrothed was not so unmoved by his words, either, he noticed with satisfaction. For her breathing was ragged, as well.

"You must move your fingers over those lovely, scalloped inner lips, imagining that 'tis my tongue there instead. Find that hidden jewel at their peak and tease it, tickle it, softly rub it until your delta trembles and quakes, sending waves of love tide gushing forth. And when that happens—oh, sweet heaven—when that happens, I want you to put two fingers inside yourself and feel what I feel when you come around me."

Branwenn shook her head slightly. Absolutely not. Was he jesting? She certainly hoped so.

"Aye, you must, my love," Callum urged. "And know you why? Because at that same moment, I shall be in a like condition upon my own lonely bed, finding my own release in the same way, imagining my hand is your perfect, snug little canal sending me to the stars.

He allowed his tone to turn pleading. "'Tis the only way we can make love together until we are wed, and I cannot wait another night for you." 'Twas true. And tho' it had not been his intent when he'd first come upon her, now that he'd gone through the entirety of the fantasy, he wanted badly for it to take place. He'd kept his hand upon her waist as he'd given her his erotic request. Now, he slowly stroked it up and down as he said, "Do you agree, my love?"

Branwenn nodded. What else could she do? She wanted to make love to him just as badly. And the knowledge that he would be thinking of her in that way at the same time thrilled her body and warmed her heart enough to give her the courage to do his bidding.

"Til midnight, then," he said, his words a promise, and then he was gone before she had time to turn around.

* * *

CHAPTER 13

"YOU LOOK SO lovely, lass!" Grandmother Maclean exclaimed as she walked through the doorway of Branwenn's bedchamber the next morn. "The pale lavender silk was a good choice, I trow."

"Aye, tho' the purple violets and pink roses that trim the neckline and sleeve were nearly the death of me!" Maggie chimed in. "But, seeing how lovely you are in the gown, makes the work well worth it."

"The seamstress who made the gown did not do the needlework?" Jesslyn asked.

"Nay," Branwenn answered for her soon-to-be mother-in-law. "I asked Aunt Maggie—pardon—*Maggie* to do the stitching, for her skill is unmatched, I trow." She turned to Callum's mother. "Beg pardon, I'm certain to someday learn to simply call you by your name."

Maggie smiled at her and gave her hand a little squeeze.

"This filet will be lovely with the gown as well," Maryn said. Turning the hair ornament in her hand, she stroked her fingertips over the filigreed design. "'Tis truly exquisite. May I try it on?"

Branwenn shrugged and nodded. "Aye." She tipped her head toward the corner table. "There is a looking glass over there, if you wish."

Maryn walked over to the table and, taking off her own filet—she hated veils and rarely wore them— placed Branwenn's on top of her auburn-haired head and studied the outcome. "'Tis a bit small for me, but 'tis beautiful!"

Maggie lifted Branwenn's left hand. "And just look at the ring Callum's given her. 'Twas his father and Chalmer's mother's ring."

"But, what ring will he give her later, then?" Maryn turned and asked.

"There's another portion, just a small band, that will settle next to this one quite well. 'Twas a set, I believe. Her betrothal and wedding ring, as I recall. His grandmother wanted Callum to have them to give to his bride."

Branwenn yanked her hand back and looked more closely at the ring. This was something Callum had not told her. "Had he given this to Lara as well then?"

"Nay, lass!" Maggie said. "That union, as you should know by now, was just barely a marriage. Why, 'twas more a bitter alliance than anything else. And her, carrying another man's bairn the entire time!"

This reminded Branwenn of her own childing state and she nearly revealed the secret without meaning to when she lifted her hand to place it on her belly, but quickly caught the action and lifted her hand instead to her cheek and brushed her hair away from it. She'd awakened with the sickness again this morn, but was relieved that, after her initial purging, her stomach settled. God be praised, she seemed to only feel horrid upon waking.

Maggie shrugged. "Tho' 'tis thrilled I am to have Laire for granddaughter." Sighing and patting Branwenn's hand, she said, "Aye, it all turned out very well. Very well indeed." She looked first at her mother and then at Branwenn. "Tho' I would *never* have wished Lara the end she came to, ken me well on that."

"Aye," Lady Maclean agreed, "the lady was troubled, and she did cause a great deal of mischief during her time at our own holding." She gave Jesslyn a pointed look, and a moment of understanding passed between them. For, Lara had tried hard to come between Jesslyn and Bao—had even lied to Jesslyn to make her believe that Bao had been unfaithful to her. Turning her eye once more to Branwenn, Lady Maclean walked over to her and began fussing with her gown, tugging the long, tight sleeves further down and rearranging the hem to settle more attractively about the bride-to-be's feet. "There," she said at last. "Now, we must hustle you down to the chapel to meet your anxious betrothed."

* * *

"Did you do as I requested last night, love?" Callum said into Branwenn's ear as they waited, facing each other, for the priest to come from behind the screen of the chancel and begin his oration. They were on their knees at the altar, her hand held lightly in his.

She felt the fire of her blush rush over her skin and settle like two hotly glowing coals on her cheeks. She nodded shyly. "Aye," she whispered, barely audibly.

Callum grinned. He felt a bit of heat on his own cheeks, also. "I, as well." He softly stroked his thumb over the top of her dainty fingers. "You look lovely in that gown. Beautiful. Tho' I confess, I cannot wait to take it off you."

"Of what are you two speaking?" Bao said, walking up beside them. He wanted a quick word with the priest once he came from behind the screen and before he gave his blessings to the couple, so he'd decided to wait near the altar.

"We were just speaking of your taste for rudely thrusting yourself into conversations that do not concern you. 'Twas quite edifying," Callum said.

Bao grinned and ruffled Callum's hair. "That's a good lad. Mayhap, after the priest gives his blessing, we'll spend the rest of the day on the lists?"

Callum swallowed a roar of indignation and combed his hair back down with his fingers. He would not punch his new brother-in-law in the nose. Not today at least. "You have an extremely rich fantasy life—do you not?"

Branwenn giggled. "Bao, what are you doing up here with us, for heaven's sake? Go sit with your wife."

Bao shrugged and cleared his throat. "I just wanted to speak to the priest a moment."

The priest came from behind the screen just as the door to the chapel banged open.

All eyes turned toward it.

"Bishop Richard!" the Priest said.

"Halt the wedding! I've a letter that may prove it not to be a legal alliance!" The Bishop said, huffing and puffing his heavy, ornately covered weight toward them. There was a scroll in his right hand that he waved in front of him as he moved.

Chalmers rose from his seat on the bench and held his hand out toward the holy man, indicating that he should hand the letter over to him.

The priest stepped down from the altar and moved toward his superior.

In the next instant, Gaiallard de Montfort stepped through the door.

"*Gaiallard!*" Branwenn whispered on a harsh release of breath. A buzzing began in her ears and black spots swam before her eyes as she swayed slightly on her knees before falling into a never-ending well of darkness.

Reys leapt to his feet and turned, his hand settling protectively upon his young wife's shoulder.

"Branwenn!" Callum hurtled to her prone side. He stroked his thumb over the rise of her pale cheek. "Branwenn," he said again, more softly.

Bao rushed to Branwenn's side and fell to his knees as well. "We must get her out of here. I'll take her up to her chamber—you stay and find out what this outrage is all about."

Callum nodded and rose to his feet at the same time Bao did, him holding his sister in his arms. When her brother began to walk away, Callum realized that he'd never released her hand and he forced himself to let go of it.

Bao barreled down the aisle toward the door and Daniel got in step behind him.

Reys leaned down and whispered in Alyson's ear and in the next instant she was scurrying in Daniel's wake.

Maryn nudged David, who sat beside her, telling him to go with Alyson.

When David began walking beside her, Alyson took the boy's hand and continued her hurried exit.

The blond Norman, who stood in a wide stance with his arms crossed over his chest, stepped out of Bao's way as he strode past him. Time to deal with that annoyance later, Bao thought.

Daniel stepped in front of his brother and held the door open for him. "Make haste, for 'tis plain we may be about to hear the terms of siege," he said in a low voice.

Bao gave him a short nod of understanding and continued on through the doorway.

When Daniel realized Alyson and David were directly behind him, he took Alyson by the elbow and escorted her and the lad out of the chapel as far as the steps then hurried back inside.

"This letter advises that Gaiallard de Montfort is legally betrothed to one Branwenn verch Gryffyd, otherwise known as Branwenn Maclean, daughter to Gryffyd Duy ap Kenneric and Gwenllian wreic Gryffyd of Penhros," the Bishop explained to Chalmers.

Chalmers unrolled the scroll and studied it for long minutes. Reys came up behind his shoulder and

Chalmers lifted the document up a bit so that Reys could better peruse the thing. "What think you? Could it be forgery?" Chalmers asked softly.

Reys shook his head and lifted one shoulder in a quick shrug. "I know not. It could be—or, it could be genuine."

Chalmers turned back to the Bishop. "How did you get this?"

"I was given it by the Norman knight standing at the door. He came to my bishopric in Dunkeld late last night and asked that I do all that I could to stop this illegal wedding from taking place."

Gaiallard, having heard his name spoken, as well as all the questions attached, strode forward. When he was several paces from Chalmers, he said, "I assure you, that is no forgery. King John has overridden my uncle's decree that all has been settled with Reys ap Gryffyd's marriage to my sister, and has assured me that I will receive all that was promised me when I bring Branwenn home as my wife."

"But, the two have already had the civil ceremony, not an hour past, on the steps of the chapel," Daniel said. "They've given their consent in front of the clan, the bride's ring has been placed on her hand, and the land and monies to be exchanged have been openly promised before witnesses. 'Tis only the blessing of the priest that has yet to be performed." He turned his eye on Gaiallard. "My sister and Callum are wed, mayhap not in the eyes of the church, but certainly in the eyes of the law."

"Yes, and I shall dispute that in the Scottish king's

court, should you force me to take the matter that far."

"Aye, and the church will not bless the match until we hear the verdict of the king in the matter," the Bishop warned.

Pointing to the scroll, Reys asked Gaiallard, "And, what has my cousin to say about this?"

"I assure you, he is in full agreement of any alliance he can make to further his power in Cambria. And with King John behind this match, he has no argument."

Callum stepped forward. "But, you see, I do."

Gaiallard turned to face him. "Ah, the thwarted bridegroom. And, what, pray, do you intend to *do* about it?"

"Fight you to the death, of course. Here. Now." For 'twas not just his heart's survival for which he'd be fighting, but also the deep-seated need to rid this world of at least one of the deviants that would dare force himself upon a bairn—and this one had touched his own sister! An image of Lara flashed in his mind. Aye, Lara, he was convinced more than ever, had been ruined by such a one as this.

Gaiallard crossed his arms over his chest and scanned his eyes from Callum's head to his feet. He snorted, clearly finding a lack in what he saw. "'Tis a good plan, as I'm in need of a bit of exercise before my wedding night."

Callum roared. "To the lists!" he commanded and took a step forward.

"Callum!" his grandmother exclaimed. She rose from her seat and hurried to stand in front of him. "Do not act in haste now," she warned. "'Tis passion talking, not reason. You've a daughter, have you forgotten?"

Callum looked at her for a long moment his shoulders rising and falling rapidly with the heavy breaths he took. "Aye, and she's about to lose her mother to a Norman *swine*." He took hold of his grandmother's hand and squeezed it. "Branwenn cannot be allowed to go back with him, no matter what that missive states."

Lady Maclean nodded. "Aye, you are right." She turned and walked over to where her daughter was standing and took hold of her hand. Jesslyn and Maryn stood up as well and moved to stand with the other two women.

"Are we to meet on the field, or has the lady convinced you otherwise?" Gaiallard said to Callum.

Callum's eyes narrowed. Daniel and Reys moved to stand behind him, their arms crossed over their chests and their expressions set in a determined mien. "Aye, we will meet. Let God decide."

"But two days hence," the Bishop rushed to say. "For the two of you must have a day of fasting and prayer—and you must give your confessions as well—before meeting in mortal combat. Now, the terms must be written and signed."

* * *

Branwenn woke to the feel of a cool, damp cloth stroking lightly across her brow and cheek. She opened her eyes and looked directly into those of her betrothed—or was it husband? They'd said their vows, just not had the Priest's blessing, nor repeated them in the chapel.

"How are you feeling?" Callum asked gently.

"Well, I think." Her eyes widened and she tried to sit up, saying, "Where is Gaiallard?!"

Callum pressed her back onto the pillow. "Sshhh. Fret not, for he is no threat to us. I swear this to you, my love. He is at the Gordon's holding. Laird Gordon has agreed to house the bastard until two days hence when we meet on the lists and decide this thing for good."

"What mean you, 'meet on the lists?'" Branwenn sucked in her breath and sat up once more. "Callum!" She thrust his hands away when he tried to settle her again. "Has he challenged you to a trial by combat? Do not do it, I beg you!"

Callum lifted her tensed hand and brought it to his mouth. Softly, he kissed each fingertip before finally answering her. "'Twas I who challenged him, my love. 'Tis the only way to be rid of him, I trow, else he's set to challenge our union at our King William's court with a letter he holds signed by King John of England."

"Let him challenge it! At least you will not risk your life."

"Branwenn," Callum chided gently, "you, who lived in Perth, so close to the court for many years, must know this could bode very ill for us, if our king should be of a mood to yield to him in order to better the alliance between us and England."

She shrugged, keeping her gaze on their clasped hands.

"Do you not see? This is a noble challenge, one that neither king will dispute—for, in the end, 'twill be God who decides the day."

She threw her arms around his neck and held tight. "Do not die, I beg you."

"I shall not, this I swear. God will not forsake me."

After a moment, he pulled back and brushed away the damp tears from her cheeks with his thumbs. "Meet me in the cave tonight, after the chimes of midnight have rung."

She nodded.

He took one of the keys from around his neck and gave it to her. Holding her face in his hands once more, he leaned down and kissed her mouth. "I love you. You are mine, never forget that," he said after a moment, resting his forehead against her own.

"Aye. I'm yours. Oh, Callum! I love you, too!"

* * *

Alyson slipped the folded piece of parchment from its hiding place inside the sleeve of her gown. A servant had given it to her as she was leaving the great hall. She'd thought it a note from Reys, but when she saw her name, written in the familiar hand of her brother, scratched across the front, she'd tucked it into her sleeve and made haste to her bedchamber. With trembling fingers, she opened first one end and then the other before turning it so that the lettering was right-side up.

"My dearest sister," it began.

"Do not believe that you have escaped from our little games so easily, for there's much I've yet to teach and much you've yet to learn.

"As I told you so often in my previous letters, I do not take

kindly to those who thwart me. But you are lucky, little one. For I've a taste for you that has yet to be quenched and so, you see, I cannot yet destroy you as had been my first inclination."

Alyson's hands began to shake so uncontrollably that the writing became blurred. "Oh, God. Oh, God," she whispered. 'Twas a prayer. She numbly turned and laid the letter down on top of the bed and leaned over it, continuing to read.

"Did you know that I saw you and Reys that morn at the edge of the wood? I thought I'd stumbled upon a lovers' tryst, but 'twas only some dull maneuvering of clothing—you must enlighten me on that tidbit the next we meet.

"Has the troubadour not had" you yet, then, my little dove? Not heard your cries and whimpers as he fucks you noisily in the dark of the night?

"Do you miss me, then?"

She shuddered. "No! Never!"

"Earlier, when I saw you in the chapel, so frightened to look me in the eye, my blood raged to have you beneath me, as we used to do. Oh how I enjoyed those battles we had before you at last surrendered to me."

Her eyes pooled with tears and she bit her trembling lip until she tasted blood. A visceral memory of the pain he'd caused her each time he'd taken her by force made her womb burn in reaction. *I hate you,* she thought.

"And, once I've gotten this nuisance of a wedding out of the way with the black-haired whelp, then 'twill not be long before we can begin again where we last were. Will you not like that, dear one?

"Did you know that there is also a demand in King John's

letter that you bear your husband an heir within a year of your wedding, else the contract shall be annulled," "Godamercy!" she said, lifting her eyes to stare blankly a moment at the wall in front of her. Then, compelled to read further, she lowered her eyes once more to the letter and continued reading: *"and you will be given back to me, your guardian brother?"* "NO! Reys will never let that happen," she cried. *"I'm sure 'twas this, more than the matter regarding his sister, that sent your husband to his cousin in such haste, for you came with quite an estate attached, did you not? And, lest you are of an inclination to believe the letter a forgery, I assure you, 'tis not.*

"Let us speak of this face-to-face. Meet me at midnight tonight at the boulder you hid behind that day near the wood."

And 'twas signed, *"Your 'loving' brother, Gaiallard"*

* * *

"Aye, 'tis a sad day indeed." Lady Maclean said softly on a sigh. She and her daughter, as well as Maryn, Jesslyn and Alyson, were seated in the solar. Their tapestries and other sewing were settled on their laps, but none of them had put a stitch in any of their projects in many long minutes.

"Callum will win," Maryn said. "He's been training with Daniel and Bao for two moons now—and he was already so skilled."

"Yes," Alyson said softly, "he will win." For she had a plan, a plan that had been brewing in her mind since she'd first read the letter from her detestable, wicked brother earlier. No matter what, Gaiallard would not win that trial.

"Aye, I pray you are right," Maggie said thickly. Her

eyes were red and puffy from the tears she'd been shedding since Callum gave Gaiallard the challenge. "But, the bairns...."

"Bao and I want to take them with us to raise, Maggie. If...," Jesslyn said softly, unable to finish the thought. "Bao is going to speak to Callum about it later."

Maggie smiled sadly. "You are a dear lass, Jesslyn."

"Hardly a lass, m'lady," Jesslyn said, "as I've two bairns, buried one husband and wed another."

Maggie patted her hand. "Aye, but you are still so young—I cannot think of any of you young ones as anything but lasses and lads!"

"'Tis glad I am that Bao will ease Callum's mind about the future of his bairns, should he not survive the trial," Lady Maclean said. "For, 'tis not uncommon for a warrior to have the burden of worry so heavy upon him that he makes mistakes in his judgments on the battlefield—and loses his life."

"Oh, Lord, I had not thought of that, Grandmother Maclean!" Maryn said. "But, you are right. Daniel has told me stories of men he's trained or gone into battle with who have been given news of home—whether good or bad—just before a battle begins, and they are so distracted by it, that they make mistakes they normally would not have made and are either maimed or killed because of it."

Branwenn leaned against the wall, just outside the door of the solar and gnawed on her knuckles. She'd heard the entire exchange and now there was more for her to ponder and worry over. After a moment, she whirled and fled back up the stairs to her chamber.

* * *

Branwenn chewed on her bottom lip as she paced back and forth in her bedchamber a quarter-hour later. Then, as if that nibbling could not stem the crushing dread in her soul, she began gnawing at the fingernail on her right thumb.

What was she to do? Should she tell Callum of their babe this eve, as had been her plan since discovering the blessed state two morns past? Or, would that worry his mind to such a degree that he might lose the battle against Gaiallard? Oh, God! What if it did—what if he died because she'd given him yet another worry to think on when he needed to concentrate on winning against Gaiallard?

And, if Callum was killed—how could she allow that Norman swine to raise his bairn?

If only she could get some advice from Grandmother Maclean! That lady always knew the answer to any trouble Branwenn had ever brought to her. But, what if she insisted on telling her brothers? What would they do? Would they risk their own lives then to keep her and her babe here with them, if Callum did not win the day? *I beg you, Lord, let him win the day!* she prayed for what must have been the thousandth time.

Nay, she must keep silent, she decided. No one could know of this babe until after the joust two days hence, not even Callum. For, she'd rather live with the guilt of having not told him—allowing him to go to his grave not knowing his seed had taken root in her—than live with the towering guilt of knowing she might have caused his death by telling him such before the trial.

With that decision made, she set about planning the midnight tryst she'd be having with Callum in the cave that night. Understanding that this might be the last time they were ever together, she'd decided to bring quite a few tapers, for she would do this thing for him this night—as she'd sworn to both him and herself that she would do on their wedding night. This would be the night that she allowed him to see her at last; allowed him to see the ugly mark on her thigh. She only prayed she would not lose her courage.

Nay, she would not, *could* not do so. For she'd given him a vow and she would not break it. Not tonight, when all could be lost for evermore in two days' time.

* * *

"Are you prepared for this Callum?" Bao asked him as they stood just inside the arched entry to the training field. "There is a chance, tho' I'll admit, I believe it to be very slim, that Gaiallard will win the day."

Callum nodded grimly. "Aye." Looking toward the lists, he said, "Let us practice the maneuver you showed me one more time. I want to be sure I can perform it well."

"I have another one I learned during a tournament two years past. I believe, if it's done properly, and with just the right thrust, you can topple your opponent from his horse rather easily."

Callum narrowed his eyes at Bao. "Why did you not show me this before, cousin?"

Bao gave him a sheepish grin. "I thought to save

some surprises for the day I met Daniel on the lists!"

"You were going to challenge Daniel?"

"Aye. Why not? It seemed like a good exercise for both of us. And it would be rather comical, I thought, to hold ransom his armor, do you not agree?"

"But, you were to be my Kipper...."

"Aye, but did that mean I could not joust as well?"

Callum shrugged. "I suppose not." Turning the subject, he asked, "Where was Reys going in such haste earlier?"

"Off to Cambria he flies, to see his cousin. He's sure the letter Gaiallard carries is a forgery, but needs to see the contract his cousin holds with the English king's signature and seal on it before he can be sure. He's to bring it back here to compare the two side-by-side." Bao placed his hand on Callum's shoulder. "No matter what happens, cousin, Branwenn will not wed that Norman, Reys is set on that. We may not be able to keep her here with us if all does not end as planned, but she will not be tied to that deviant. Reys gave Daniel and me his oath while you were with Branwenn earlier."

"Good, that eases my mind."

Bao cleared his throat. "About Laire and David...Jesslyn and I want to take them, raise them, if..." He shrugged.

Callum gave him a relieved smile. "My thanks, cousin. I'd hoped to ask you, as you are Laire's godparents, to do just that, but it pleases me more that the offer to take both of them came before I had to request it." He paused, rubbing the base of his palm over his cheek. "'Tis important to me that Laire never be allowed to live with her Gordon kin, but I fear Laird Gordon may insist upon it. Do all that you must to keep it from happening."

Bao's eyebrows lifted in question. "All right," he agreed. "Why?"

Callum sighed and placed his arms akimbo. "I believe—tho' I've no proof—that Lara was meddled with in much the same way as Alyson when she was a bairn. I know not if 'twas a member of her family, or someone else, but I think 'twas what caused much of her selfishness and brazen behavior toward men."

Bao nodded. "I confess, I'd never thought of such before, but, hearing this from you now, I see how you could be right. For there were several such women I knew during the time I was at the Procuress's house."

"So you see why it would ease my mind to know that Laire will not ever reside there," Callum said. "Of course, I will need to send word to Robert, but I think that he will not fight me on this decision for you and Jesslyn to take his nephew to raise."

"It's agreed, then," Bao said. Shoving Callum ahead of him, he said, "Go, soldier. To the lists!"

* * *

CHAPTER 14

SHE WORE HER sea faery clothing to the cave that night. For some reason, she thought it appropriate to do so—after all, they'd never met in the cave as Callum and Branwenn; always it had been Callum and Mai, or *fey Mai*, as he liked to call her.

And Branwenn wanted what might be their last night together to be filled with magic. Tho' just the thought of once again feeling Callum's mouth on her bare skin, of having him deep inside her, of knowing that she gave him pleasure, was magical in itself.

And tonight, he'd see the thing she'd been hiding from him since their first time together. *Please, Callum,* she thought, *love me in spite of it!*

She was surprised to find that Callum must have already been here earlier, for there were several layers of furs laid out against one wall of the cavern, near where he'd lain when he'd dropped from the ceiling that fateful day last summer. On top of the furs, he'd spread a sheet of linen and placed a folded woolen blanket on top of that.

She walked closer to it and stared down at the lush bed he'd prepared for them. There were four pillows and—she leaned down, her lit taper out before her—rose petals! She smiled happily, a warm thrill of joy spreading out from her heart's center into her whole being. *Oh, Callum! I do love you!*

For that, he truly did deserve as many lit tapers as she could find places for about the bed.

* * *

"You are here," Callum said as he walked the last few steps into the cave from the passage. When Branwenn turned toward him, he opened his arms to her.

She ran to him and propelled herself into him, holding tight. "I thought you'd never get here!" she said against his chest.

Callum smiled down at her, stroking his hand over the silky-soft hair on her head and letting it trail down the back, finally coming to rest between her shoulder blades. "Are you Mai, then?" he asked, at last noticing what she was wearing. "Will you be taking me back to your faery kingdom, as you once threatened?"

She shook her head, her cheek rubbing against the rough material of his woolen tunic. "Nay, tho' I wish with all my heart I could—we could—just fly away from here and live out our lives together as we'd planned."

He leaned back a bit and cupped her cheeks in his hands, bringing her chin up, forcing her to look him in the eye. "We *will* live out our lives together as we planned. I swear this to you. We must. For God will surely give me the strength, the cunning I need, to beat that devil and get him from our lives for good."

"I pray—have been praying—that you are not wrong."

Callum looked around the cavern chamber. "Branwenn! There must be o'er a hundred tapers in here—tell me you did not take them from the chapel?" he teased.

She shrugged and dipped her head. "Nay," she said softly, "they were given me by your mother this day past for our"—her voice cracked—"wedding night."

Callum curled his fingers under her chin and rested his thumb on top of it. With a nudge, he brought it up so that he could see her countenance once more. "'Tis perfect, then, do you not see? For this *is* our wedding night."

"Aye, tho' 'twas never blessed by the priest, I feel the same. We are wed, and this is our wedding night."

"Come, my love, let us settle upon our wedding bed where we can be more comfortable, for I've much to say to you before we join our bodies at last—and once again—to consummate this union."

Branwenn nodded and allowed him to lead her by the hand to the bed of furs. After he'd positioned himself upon it with his back against the cave wall and two pillows behind him as a cushion, he settled her between his legs, her back resting on his chest, his arms wrapped around her and tucked under her breasts. "Lord, you feel so good," he rumbled against her ear.

She nodded. "Aye," she agreed. "You, as well."

They sat in silence for several moments, each lost in their own thoughts and enjoying the close contact they now shared.

"Did Jesslyn tell you that she and Bao want to take Laire and David to raise, if I am killed two days hence?" Callum asked softly.

Branwenn tensed. "You swore you will not die!"

"Aye, and I surely plan to do all I can to live. But, Branwenn, there is always the chance, no matter how small we believe it to be, that all will not go as we believe. Therefore, we must think of our bairns." He gave her a light squeeze. "Do you object to your brother and Jesslyn taking them?"

"Nay." She tipped her head up and to the side, looking up at him. "But what of our vow to Isobail? We swore that we would raise David and now we are forced to foster him to Bao and Jesslyn. Do you think Isobail would not approve, be angered?"

Callum rested his head back against the wall and thought on that a moment before answering at last. "Nay," he said with a shake of his head, "she would not. Not knowing all that we know and seeing that we are acting in good honor and to ensure justice."

Branwenn's brows furrowed. "Reys came to see me in my bedchamber before he left. He's sworn that, no matter what happens, my cousin and he will never allow a union between me and that depraved Norman to whom I was once betrothed."

"Aye, and neither will Daniel or Bao, that is certain. They will each challenge the man to the same trial as I have done, should I lose this battle and my life, and aught happens which undermines Reys's promise."

Branwenn sat up straight. "Nay! They must not! I will go with the Norman before I let that happen."

"Sshhh, love, no need to fret now, for I do not intend to lose this trial."

Branwenn settled back against him, but her mind churned with yet a new worry. No matter what Callum said, she would not allow her brothers to risk their lives—again—for her. For, Bao had already come near to death last spring due to her, with the injury he received during her cousin's siege of the Maclean holding, and that alone had given her such a guilt. So much so, in fact, that she had yet to completely feel relieved of it.

Callum leaned down and pressed a kiss first to her cheek and then moved up to her ear, nibbling and stroking the outer perimeter with his tongue and teeth. "I'm remembering that day in this cave—do you recall?" he said, his voice a rumble and his breath hot and moist against the inside of her hearing canal.

Branwenn had no idea why she did so, but she blushed. 'Twas hot and it stung her cheeks. Why, after all they'd shared, the memory of the first time they'd been together, of what she'd demanded, of what he'd offered, should suddenly make her shy, she could not fathom. But it did.

"Aye," she whispered with a nod.

"I've often wondered—what made you request such a thing of me?" He tightened his hold around her, bringing her buttocks more snugly against him. This is when she realized the extent of his arousal. Her own body readied in response and some of her timidity fell away.

She felt a tickle on the side of her cheek and she rubbed it against her shoulder. "Umm," she began. "Well..."

"Aye—what? Tell me," he urged.

Her heart pounded. But, she wanted to tell him, be honest with him. For, this might be their very last time together alone and she wanted him to know her, *really* know her, as if they'd been wed for fifty years and there was naught else to learn, and all was comfortable, as some of the old couples she'd known in the Maclean village had been. Aye, 'twas what she wanted. To be the wife she would have been to him fifty years from now. No secrets.

Except one, her heart whispered, but she ignored it. For, she would not risk Callum's life this close to the trial. For the other thing—the patch—would be secret from him no more by night's end.

Before she could talk herself out of it, she said hurriedly, "I saw my brother and Jesslyn—together—at the waterfall in the wood."

"Together?"

"*Together*. I watched them."

"*What!*" Callum exclaimed, and then, in a voice as smooth as warmed *uisge beatha*, "Branwenn."

She felt his manhood throb against the base of her spine and he pressed her closer still. "Christ's Bones! I know not whether to be appalled or amused! But, in either case, I admit, the thought of you watching anyone making love causes my blood to rush."

She lowered her head and looked at her hands, clasped in her lap. She shrugged. "I was curious. They seemed to like what they were doing very much, and I wanted to know what it felt like, so...I asked you."

Callum nuzzled her neck. "And now you know from experience," he whispered. "Tell me, is it as good as you hoped? As it seemed to them?"

A gush of moisture flooded the junction of her thighs. "Aaaye," she sighed, her head lolling to the side to give Callum better access to her neck. Her nipples tightened and abraded the material of her chemise and tunic.

"I think its time, love. We've waited long enough."

"Aye," she agreed.

The two of them stood and Branwenn watched shyly as Callum hauled first his tunic and then his shirt over his head—him with a knowing grin on his face the entire time!

"Now, 'tis your turn," he told her.

"Bu—but you still have on your braies and hose!" She glanced even further down. "And your boots as well!"

"Aye. Those will come off last—after you've removed your tunic and shirt." He came closer and lightly ran his finger over the hem of her shirt's neckline. "Let me see those sweet breasts, love. I crave another sight of that delightful freckle I found that night."

She dipped her head and, with numb fingers, released the clasp of her girdle and let it fall to the floor.

Next, she began pulling up the hem of her tunic. With a jolt, she felt Callum's hands move her own aside and he quickly swung the article of clothing over her head and onto the ground at their feet. "Callum!" she squeaked. But, before she had time to recover from that surprise, he did the same with her shirt.

The cool air of the cave had not been lessened to much of a degree by the fire she'd made earlier and her skin pebbled. Her nipples constricted so tightly they stung. She tried to lift her arms to cross herself, but Callum took hold of her wrists and forced them to remain at her side. The sound of his rough breathing amplified and she forced herself to look up at him. The heat in his eyes as he gazed upon her sent rivulets of heat coursing through her, over her. Like warm honey, it traveled across her skin, making her tremble.

"God, has there ever been a lady fairer than you?" Callum said. He was in such a thrall to his bride that he was not even aware he'd spoken the words aloud, until he heard her answer, "Aye, many are much more fair. You should visit the court at Pembroke, if you believe me not."

"Branwenn," Callum chided, "have you forgot? I've seen my share of lasses and ladies in my time. Question me not on this—you put the stars in the heavens to shame, your beauty burns so bright."

"Well, you have yet to see the rest of me—you should hold your judgement until then, I trow."

Callum chuckled. Stroking a stray lock of silky black hair away from her cheek, he said, "Branwenn—I may not have seen you with my eyes these past moons, but

I've certainly 'seen' you with my hands, my mouth, my tongue, my body. I believe I know your loveliness quite well."

Wait until you see the horrid blot on my thigh! This made her even more nervous. He'd found her attractive thus far—but, God! How she hated that ugly thing. It made her cringe just to look upon it. Which she rarely ever did. How could she expect Callum to feel any differently about the thing? The old nurse was right. He'd surely find it as disgusting as she and the nurse did. Could she bare to see him turn from her in horror? Or worse, to try valiantly to hide his revulsion? Nay, she could not.

Her heart began to pound and she grew dizzy as she tried to catch her breath.

"Branwenn!" Callum stepped closer still. Placing his hands on her shoulders, he bent his knees and tipped his head to the side a bit so that he could see her face more clearly. "What has you so afraid? How can a lass so bold as to secretly watch two lovers coupling be so fearful of allowing her lover—her husband—to see her in the bare?" He pressed his lips to her temple and said softly, "Help me understand, I beg you."

She began to tremble in his arms, and he knew 'twas not from desire, but fear.

He wrapped his arms around her and held her tightly to him, cradling the back of her head in his hand and pressing his lips to her brow. The feel of their naked upper torsos pressed so tightly together after so many sennights of waiting for this very contact nearly made him go insane with the need to make love to her once more. But he tamped down tight on that urge, understanding that there was something vital regarding her continued shyness with him that needed to be explained and finally, finally, put to rest. "Tell me."

Branwenn squeezed her eyes tightly shut. "I—I've a...patch, a mark on me." Her hand flew to her mouth. "Oh, God! I know you'll find it as hideous as I do when you see it!"

Tho' the last had been muffled, he still understood the words. He lifted her chin and kissed her. Deeply, passionately. She fought him at first, but in moments she was returning the kiss with just as much feeling. When he felt her body relax into him, felt the tension leave her limbs at last, he broke away slightly and murmured, "Take these faery threads from your delectable frame, my love. Let me see this thing that has you so afraid—will you?"

After a brief pause, she nodded and stepped out of his embrace. "Turn around and close your eyes."

He knew better than to argue with her on that score, for 'twas plain how skittish she was and he had every intention of doing all in his power to first lessen and then finally rid her of that fear. He did as she bade. In moments, he heard the familiar rustling of ties being loosened, of fabric being slid from bare skin, followed by the light plop when it fell onto the ground. Finally, an even more arousing sound came to his ears: That of her sliding beneath the top sheet on the makeshift bed of furs and the flapping sound of the woolen blanket as she opened it and tossed it atop her as well.

In another moment, she said softly, "All right, you

may open your eyes now."

Callum turned around and gazed upon her for long minutes before he at last reached down and took his boots off. He kept his braies and hose on, however, wanting to take things slow this time. He got in bed beside her. Remaining on top of the blanket, he unhurriedly rolled to position himself snugly over her. Dipping his head, he kissed her. Softly at first, but then ever more passionately, until, at last, he was exploring the recesses of her mouth with his tongue.

Branwenn's bones soon felt as if they were consistency of warm honey, but somehow she managed to wrap her arms around his waist. As the kiss progressed, her hands began to move over him, exploring first the ridge of muscles along his back and then going lower to rest over the hard, muscular mounds of his linen-covered buttocks. He began to move. Lightly rocking against her as she continued her long caress of his backside. Even through the layers of clothing and bed covering, she could feel the urgency of his arousal pressing against her mons, unerringly searching for that tenderest of places just below its rise that would send her reeling with little effort.

She wanted desperately to open for him, but her lower limbs would not heed her demand. Instead, they remained tightly clamped shut, tho' all other parts of her body were as fluid as mulled wine warmed o'er a winter hearth.

As Callum kissed his nervous bride, he planned the course of his conquest. Who would have guessed, he thought with amusement, that the tactics of warfare he'd been taught by Bao and Daniel, might easily and successfully be employed when seducing a shy bride?

First, learn your conquest's weaknesses by thorough exploration and then besiege them using every piece of equipment in your arsenal.

Callum slowly broke away from her mouth and lightly trailed kisses across her cheek; over to her ear, where he spent considerable time teasing her earlobe with his teeth; and then down her neck. At the base, where her neck met her shoulder, he opened his mouth wide, suckling and lightly biting the skin for long minutes. Branwenn whimpered, trembling beneath him and his blood rushed, nearly out of control. But this time he forced his mind to counting bottles of *uisge beatha*. For he would not hurry this thing. Not this night, and not as had been their habit these past moons. He would take control of his passion for her and he would at last see this mark on her body that she was so afraid for him to see.

Second, employ stealth, where necessary.

He released her at last from his mouth's grasp and soothed the teeth marks he'd left on her tender skin by circling the design with the tip of his tongue.

"Oh!" Branwenn cried out, arching her back as a shudder of sheer delight swept through her. When he blew on the spot, her canal clenched tight and then widened. She was having trouble catching her breath.

With light, damp kisses, Callum moved further down, ever so slowly tugging the edge of the blanket and sheet away to reveal her naked breasts as he went. He felt her tense beneath him when she realized her upper torso was fully exposed to him, but when he took the peak of her left breast into his mouth and softly tickled it's rosy bud with his tongue as he began a gentle suction on it, she relaxed for a mere second before furiously arching into him. Her hand came up to the back of his head and she pressed him further against her. "Ohhh God!" she ground out.

Callum scooted his hand under the sheet and blanket that was still pulled up to just below her waist and splayed his fingers through the silken, curly hair covering her mons. He rested it there a moment, gently caressing the soft, cushion-like flesh beneath the hair as he released her left breast and licked, nibbled and kissed his way over the rose-scented, warm flesh valley to her right one and began the same onslaught on that succulent mound.

When her pelvis began rocking against his hand, he crept lower still. Finding her thighs still tightly clamped shut, he wriggled his middle finger down between them and, first taking a bit of her dew onto it from her drenched canal, he brought it up and rotated it over the tender hooded nubbin that crowned her lush sex.

In seconds, her thighs were spread and her hips were churning in rhythm to his finger's ministration. She was growing so slick now, he was having a hard time staying on target.

Branwenn thrashed her head back and forth and threw her arms high over her head. "Ohgodohgodohgodohgod," she moaned. She felt her body begin to tremor and quake as Callum brought her ever closer to release.

Knowing she was nearing orgasm, Callum suckled harder on her taut nipple and redoubled his teasing caresses of her sensitive core until she at last climaxed.

"Ah-ah-ah-ah-ah!" Her body went rigid with the shattering pleasure of release. When it was over, she collapsed back, breathing hard. Too weak to even open her eyes, she lay there with her head turned to the side, enjoying the slight dizzying effect such an experience always gave her.

Third, wait until your conquest's guard is down.

Callum swept the covering off her, and off the makeshift bed as well, and for the first time saw the gorgeous, red center of her, ornamented by lovely black curls. "Godamercy!"

Fourth, attack.

Callum swooped.

Branwenn's eyes flew open and her legs clenched firmly shut. "Oh, God! You hate it! I *knew* you would! It's horrid!" She covered her eyes with the base of her palms, her face crumpling.

Fifth, when all else fails, know when to make an organized retreat.

Callum raised up on his knees and looked down at her, mentally kicking himself. "I didn't see the patch, Branwenn. 'Twas merely an utterance of desire I gave." She slid her hands from her eyes and looked at him. He saw hope reflected there, but also dread. "Enough, love. I'm putting out the tapers, for 'tis not my wish for any portion of our night together to be unpleasant for you."

He began to rise to his feet, but Branwenn stayed his

movement by taking hold of his wrist. "Nay, you mustn't. For, I promised you that I would reveal all to you this night, and I want you to know all. I beg pardon. Please, give me another chance to do this thing."

Callum studied her for long seconds. Her dew-misted, crushed violet eyes held regret and earnestness in their depths. "You are sure?" he said at last.

"Aye, I am sure," she replied.

She surprised him then. She bent her knees and spread her legs wide, revealing even more of herself to him than he'd seen earlier.

His heart tripped and began a hard thudding beat against the inside of his rib cage. Again, his eyes focused only on that lovely feminine berth he longed to explore and, ultimately, find dock in.

Branwenn gritted her teeth and forced her eyes to remain on Callum's countenance. His eyes were hot emerald coals, his nostrils flared with harsh breath. Curiously, his gaze had yet to settle on the grotesque mark on her left thigh.

"I want to taste you," he ground out.

Her heart began to pound, both with the familiar anticipation those words always built in her, but also the dread that came with it. She couldn't explain it, tho' she'd tried often enough, both to him and to herself, but she feared that he'd be revolted by her flavor. It just didn't seem clean for some reason. After all, 'twas the place her flowering came from. Tasting Callum just wasn't the same thing. Not at all.

"What if you find me...ill-flavored?"

Callum hastily settled on his side beside her, leaning up on his forearm and elbow. "How can you say such? For you are a succulent morsel, my sweet. Sometimes, in fact, I think you are too succulent." He settled his hand over her abdomen. "Let me taste you finally, the way you've tasted me so oft."

She nodded. "Al...All right"

Callum didn't give her time to change her mind. With determination and perfect aim, he positioned himself between her thighs and dipped his head to feast upon the feminine banquet laid out before him.

He nearly grew intoxicated on the scent of her alone. 'Twas the headiest mix of sex dew he'd ever encountered. A perfume of rose-tinged musk and that elusive, incomparable scent that belonged only to Branwenn.

First he teased her labia lips with his tongue, now tasting the moist residue of her earlier release.

Branwenn jolted, her hips rising slightly off the bed.

Callum rested his hands over the sharp blades of her pelvic bones and gently pressed down, in a silent demand to stay still.

He brought his hands down between her thighs and, using his fingers and thumbs, opened her outer lips before continuing his tongue's exploration of the lovely red scalloped shell of her inner lips. With light, quick strokes, he avidly tasted—every once in a while dipping his tongue into that deliciously moist and cushiony canal that so perfectly cradled and worked his own sex.

Finally, unable to keep himself from it another moment, he plunged his tongue deep inside her, craving to feel those same muscles tug his tongue. Her sheath clenched in reaction and he almost came right then and there. He made a swift retreat, rumbling into her womb, "You taste so, so good."

"Oh, God! What are you doing to me?" Branwenn cried out, her entire being aflame with the need for release once more. Whatever it was, was keeping her just on the edge of orgasm, making her so desperate for it, she was going mad. She was trying to keep still, as he wanted, but she needed to move, needed to feel his mouth on her where his finger had been earlier. "Please!"

Callum understood. With slow, light strokes he began his journey up to the apex of her sex. When her hips began to move beneath him, he pressed down on her thighs with his forearms, his fingers still spreading her labia lips wide for his onslaught.

When he at last made it to the peak, he stroked and rubbed the tight, turgid little nubbin until her whole body was atremble and her arms and head were thrashing against the bed. Suddenly, sex dew gushed from her canal. Needing to feel her convulse, he sent two fingers into her and began a quick in-and-out motion with them as his tongue continued its rapid lapping.

"Callum!" Branwenn arched her back, her hips rising high off the bed as she tumbled into the intensely gratifying abyss of sexual release.

When Branwenn was just past the crest, Callum suckled the nubbin into his mouth. He continued to send his fingers inside of her as he did so, and in the next second, his efforts were rewarded when Branwenn groaned and splintered once again.

Callum hurriedly pulled off his braies and, just as she was settling back, positioned himself on his knees between her thighs and plunged. High and deep. "Aarrgh!" he yelled, throwing his head back. With his hands on her hips, and her knees crooked over his forearms, he lifted her even higher.

She was so slick now, he had little trouble slipping further inside her. Before he knew it, the head of his sex was pounding against her womb and she was coming again, her strong inner muscles tugging him and taking him so close to heaven he began to see stars behind his lids.

He was sweating and straining now, straining not to come inside her, but desperate for this pleasure not to end so soon.

Finally, leaning forward, he placed his hands near her head and rested his weight on his palms, forcing her legs to splay over his shoulders.

This caused her to climax again, bringing him to completion as well. "God's Bones!" he yelled in a strangled voice, jerking out of her at the last minute, his seed spewing instead on her dewy, quivering belly.

He released her legs and collapsed down onto his forearms, his breathing ragged, the sweat from his brow running down over his temple and into his eye. He pressed it absently into his bicep until the sting went away. When he'd recovered enough to speak, he said against Branwenn's ear, "Worry not, I brought cloths this time—and there is an urn of water I left here earlier for us to wash with."

Branwenn was so completely dazed from the number of climaxes he'd given her that it took her a very long minute to comprehend his words. When she did, at last, ken them, she replied lazily, "Good."

Callum chuckled and rolled off of her. Tho' he was still a bit weak from the pleasurable exercise and release he'd just experienced, he knew she must be far, far weaker than he. So, he set about obtaining the cloth and the urn so that he might give her the bath she deserved after the delightful experience he'd just had between her thighs. Lord, he could taste her still, and 'twas a flavor he'd never grow tired of. What a treasure he had in her. He did not take it for granted.

Tho' Branwenn could hear the rustling sounds of Callum's movements around the cavern chamber, she had not the strength, nor the will, to open her eyes to see what he was about. 'Twas not until she felt the cool, damp cloth on her belly that her eyes flew open and her head jerked up. "'Tis cold!" she scolded.

But Callum's hand had stilled and his eyes, she saw, were at last settled upon that horrible, horrid, disgusting, revolting, *thing* on her thigh. "Oh, God!" she said as her hand flew to cover the offending mark.

Callum stopped her movement by taking hold of her wrist and bringing her hand back down to her side. "Nay, love, hide it not from me, for 'tis lovely." He reached out and traced the rather large patch with his finger. Some of it was a bit obscured by the black curls of her labia lips as the design came up into the soft flesh where her inner thigh joined her torso. "'Tis the shape and color of a raspberry. Which reminds me"—he looked at her and grinned—"quite pleasantly, of that day in the stairwell. Remember?"

Branwenn felt her cheeks flush with heat. "Aye."

"You tasted of them and, I must say, 'twas quite arousing. I wonder..." He leaned down and pressed a kiss to the mark before tasting it with his tongue. "Mmm. Rosy." He turned his head and looked at her. "Just as are you."

"Do you not find it ugly? Even a bit?"

Callum smiled and shook his head. "Nay, not even a wee bit. Not even by one tittle, in fact." He sat up and absently tossed the damp rag to the floor next to them before resettling on his side facing her. He lightly slung his arm over her waist and moved her closer into him. "What a shame that all that kept me from seeing this beautiful body of yours all these sennights was that sweet, wee raspberry mark on your pale, white thigh. In truth, it only makes me want you more." He leaned down and gave her a quick, gentle kiss on her lips before saying, "Why ever did you think it so unsightly that I would not want you after gazing upon it?"

Branwenn turned her head away. Shrugging, she said, "My old nurse—she said 'twas the mark of the devil. 'Twas hideous and foul and I'd best not let my husband e'er see it, else he'd n'er put a babe in my belly."

Callum growled. "What a..." he bit his tongue to keep from saying aloud the base epithet he had for such a one as she. He took hold of Branwenn's chin and gently tugged until she at last turned her countenance to him. Looking into her eyes he said, "'Tis no devil's mark you hold, Branwenn. If anything, 'tis the mark of a heavenly cherub, deeming you one of their own. But they cannot have you, for you are mine."

"Caa-lum." Her eyes misted a bit at his sweet words.

He leaned down and nuzzled her ear, lightly kissing its fleshy lobe before continuing, "And I swear this to you: I will put as many babes in your belly as you will allow, after this trial is done. For I'll have no other as the mother of my bairns, whether they be of my loins or otherwise. Who else, besides the nurse, knows of the mark?"

Branwenn shrugged. "Only Bao. He raised me, as you recall. And I want no others to ever know of it!"

Callum raised up and touched his finger to the corner of her eye, moistening the tip of the digit with a stray tear that hung suspended on one of her lower lashes. "Nay, love, 'tis beautiful. In fact, I pray that *all* our future bairns carry that same mark upon them."

Branwenn brought her arms around his neck and hauled him down on top of her as she attacked his mouth with her own in the most joyous, ravenous kiss she'd ever bestowed upon him. She ignored the twinge of guilt and the voice in her head which chided her to tell him now that he'd already put a babe in her. For she was still set on not risking his life even further by giving him such tidings that could muddle his thoughts during the joust.

Long minutes later, both out of breath, but grinning like two madmen, they collapsed onto their backs and stared up at the ceiling of the cave.

A vagrant thought flashed into Branwenn's mind and caught, circling and whirling about until finally she sat up. "Callum! The apple skin. Godamercy!" She looked down at him. "'Twas a 'G'!"

Callum chuckled and rolled slightly onto his side. He lifted his hand and lightly touched her chin with his fingertips. "Nay, 'twas a 'C'—you were quite adamant on that score, as I recall."

"And you were just as set that 'twas a 'G' the peel had made."

"Well, even if 'twas, you cannot truly believe that such a thing could foretell whom you will wed. Have you forgot? You wedded me just this afternoon on the steps of the chapel."

Branwenn worried her bottom lip with her teeth. "Aye, but if he kills you...."

"Then Bao, Daniel, and Reys will fight the man. No matter what happens, you will not be Gaiallard de Montfort's bride." He sighed loudly. "What is it in you that will not believe me when I tell you this? Have I not said similar words to you before? And yet, the doubts keep rising in your mind." He squeezed her chin between his fingers and thumb and jiggled her head slightly, "Will you let those doubts fly? For, I vow, you worry needlessly."

She rolled to her side, turning her back to him, and bringing her knees up close to her chest. "This is what I feared—one of the reasons I would not agree to wed you. All of you will risk your lives for me—for ME! I cannot abide it; I truly cannot. Not again." But what could she do? She carried Callum's babe, and she would never, *never* allow that vile Norman within miles of the young one. Should she flee? Nay, for the challenge had already been given, the trial set. But after. After. If Callum was killed. Then she would flee. Flee so far, so quickly, and with much greater stealth than she'd used prior, that none would ever find her. Mayhap, she should go north, to *Northvegia*. 'Twas not as far in miles as she wanted to go, but 'twas far in custom, and as far from what Gaiallard would consider civilized as she could get. He'd never look for her there.

Callum curled on his side behind her and, wrapping his arm tightly around her, he rested his chin in the curve of her shoulder, then brought his knees up behind her own. "Branwenn, I pray you, do not fret so. For there are none among your champions who would think twice about doing what is necessary to keep you safe."

"Aye, but what of their wives? Their bairns?"

Callum was silent for long seconds. "Even they, I believe, would do all they could to see you safe from the Norman's clutches."

* * *

CHAPTER 15

THEY'D MADE LOVE twice more between intervals of dozing sleep, but when they'd stood together just outside the entrance of the cave and seen the sun's pink and orange rays barely visibly emerging from below the horizon, they'd known 'twas time for them to part. And when they'd said what might be their final farewell—tho' neither had dared utter such aloud—they'd held tight to one another, neither wanting to be the first to break the embrace.

And to Branwenn, 'twas an added blessing that the illness that had been overtaking her these past morns had not occurred on this one.

Callum had urged her to exit first, and when she had, 'twas as if a vital part of her being were being ripped from her body. She'd cried her heart out the entire journey back to her chamber.

And now she stood at the window in the solar, nibbling at her thumbnail, blindly looking out toward the garden in the north bailey. 'Twas naught she could do about Callum's challenge on the morrow, but there was much that could be done to keep her brothers from issuing the same challenge to Gaiallard, should Callum not survive. *Please, Lord, let him live!* she prayed once more—'twas now an habitual incantation.

Since thinking of the idea of escaping to *Northvegia* last night, she'd been ruminating and scheming in her mind to devise an unfailing plan to do just that. After her experience traveling by sea vessel, as well as the ease with which she'd journeyed along the coast, she was sure 'twould not be such a trial to find another ship to purchase passage upon. After all, there were merchant ships traveling north through the isles of the Hebrides nearly each sennight.

With a nervous flip of her hand, she tugged at the ends of her hair. She took in a deep breath and let it out on a sigh. 'Twould mean cutting it. *Again.* Lord, but would she ever be able to let it grow out? When she thought of how long it had been, only a bit over sixteen moons prior, her throat clogged with unshed tears. For the loss of it just seemed to underscore the twisting, turning route her life had been forced down.

But this would be the last time she cut it, she vowed. The *very* last time.

And, she'd need to obtain a few more items of clothing as well. She still had a cap, one tunic, one pair of braies, and hose. But she'd need another cloak and a pair of boots; preferably fur-lined, for she feared that this place she intended to live would be colder even than the Highlands. At least she still had a pouch full of the coins Reys had given her. 'Twould, if used wisely, last her until well past the babe's birth. She had only to find a very modest cottage. 'Twould also be of benefit to find work as well, she supposed.

The door swept open behind her and she turned. "Good morn, Grandmother Maclean."

"Good morn to you, lass. How fare you?"

Branwenn shrugged. And then, before she realized she was going to do it, she burst into tears.

Grandmother Maclean hustled over to her foster granddaughter as quickly as her aged legs would allow and swept her into her embrace, cradling her face against her bosom. "There, there. 'Tis not as dire as that, I trow. Callum is a strong warrior; a skilled combatant." She brushed the hair that clung to Branwenn's damp cheek away. "Did you know that I've seen the lad on the lists several times now?"

Branwenn shook her head.

"Aye, I have. Why, when he was just fifteen moons, he was already competing in tournaments. Oh, 'tis true, he lost quite a few in the beginning, but with each new joust he entered, he brought with him all he'd learned from the previous. He honed his skills quite effectively that way. And with the additional training he's received from his cousins, why, 'tis truth, I doubt there's a single thing that Gaiallard de Montfort, that miscreant Norman, could try on the morrow that would surprise my grandson." Lady Maclean had been repeating similar words to herself these past hours since the challenge had been given, and sometimes it helped to settle her fears, but sometimes—like now—it did not. But she'd never allow Branwenn to see her uncertainty.

In fact, Callum had spoken at length with her this very morn to tell her just that. He, himself, had been battling his own demon of doubt, but was determined that Branwenn would not know of it, for 'twould only serve to heighten her already deep dread for him and, he'd told her, he simply could not bear to see his bride in such a state before this match.

And neither could she. Nor could any of the others of the family. 'Twas why they'd all decided 'twas best to say only words of confidence when Branwenn was within hearing. She was such a sensitive lass.

* * *

Callum walked into his daughter's nursery just minutes after her feeding, it seemed. For the nurse was fussing softly in dulcet, cooing tones as she fought valiantly to wipe the remains of Laire's meal from her rosy cherub-cheeks. He chuckled. "It looks as if my daughter would prefer to keep the mess on her face."

Laire's big blue eyes turned toward him. "*Da! Da! Da! Da!*" she squealed, her chubby fists flailing as she bounced. She rose up a bit from her sitting position in the crib and the nurse quickly settled her back down before turning and giving him a weary smile. "Aye, that it does. I trow, the babe's wee fists are as powerful as a warrior's when she's set on not having a bath. And 'tis time to trim those sharp nails of hers as well." She turned back to Laire. "Is it not, my beauty?"

"*Ga!*"

The nurse handed her a hard, day-old bannock and Laire immediately began chewing on it.

Highland Magic

"She's another tooth coming through and she was a bit warm earlier, but she seems fine now."

Callum strode over to the cradle and settled on a stool. He felt his daughter's forehead with the back of his fingers and then scrubbed at a dried spot of gruel on her chin.

Laire grinned at him and offered him the slobbery bannock.

Callum grinned back at her and took hold of it on the bottom end, where she'd not yet begun to gum on it, and brought it up to his mouth. He pretended to taste it. "Mmm. Delicious." And then he handed it back to his daughter. When Laire gleefully took the gooey treat, he leaned down and placed a kiss on her soft pate.

She *gurgled* and handed the bannock back to him.

Callum played this game of 'pass the bannock' with her for several more minutes, his heart a twisted knot of pain in his chest.

He cleared his throat. "Know you that Laire and David will be taken to raise by my cousin Bao and his wife, should I not survive this trial on the morrow?" he asked the nurse.

"Aye, your mother told me as much this day past, sir."

"I worry that Laire will be distraught if she has no one familiar caring for her. Will you consider moving to the Maclean holding with her—at least until she is older and has had time to know her new guardians?"

"Aye, sir. As I've no other ken to keep me here, I would not think of leaving the wee one's side at such a time."

Callum sighed. "That eases my mind. My thanks to you."

Laire settled down onto her side and began to doze.

Callum watched her sleep. Needing to keep some physical contact with his daughter, he lightly ran his finger over her closed fist. In seconds, it opened and grasped hold of the calloused digit and held tight. Unable to bear leaving her just yet, he remained in that position for two hours more. Every once in awhile, he leaned down and gave her a kiss on her warm, baby-soft cheek.

He'd never have thought it possible, but saying what might be his last farewell to his daughter was even more difficult than had been his last farewell to Branwenn earlier that morn. 'Twas only the knowledge that Laire would be given over to a man he respected so highly, a man he knew would do anything to keep his daughter safe—as Bao had proved by the incredible sacrifices he'd made when raising Branwenn—that made knowing he might be leaving his daughter for good somewhat bearable. And, he prayed, somewhat forgivable to her.

* * *

"That's the game then," Callum said to David two hours later. He had gone directly from his daughter's nursery to find the lad, with the intent of spending some time with him and answering any questions David might have regarding the trial on the morrow. He and the lad had now played four games of knucklebones, and David had beaten him every time, but there had yet to be one word from the young one about what might happen after the trial.

'Twas clear, Callum decided, he would need to be the one to broach the subject. He hoped he would be able to ease David's worry; he knew that Bao was intending to have a talk with him later that day as well, and that would aid the lad also.

"Grandmother Maclean told me that you found the basket of tarts empty the morn of *Samhainn* which you'd left out for your mother the night before. Did Isobail visit us then, do you think?"

David's face, which was still flushed with the glory of victory, sagged a bit at the question. His chin dropped to his chest and he looked at his hands. Shrugging, he shook his head. "Nay, 'twas only old *Anail Iasg*; he lapped up all of them and my mama didn't get even one."

"How know you that the old hound got into the fare?"

"'Cuz I found him layin' on his back near the hearth and there was purple berry juice all over his tongue and chops."

Callum nodded. "Ah, I see." He cleared his throat. "Are you still set to lead my horse out onto the lists on the morrow?"

"Aye," David answered in a small voice.

"'Tis very brave of you, lad, to insist upon doing this thing when you know not what the outcome will be for you—nor me, for that matter—on the morrow. Your mother would be very proud of you, I trow."

David shrugged. He couldn't seem to force his eyes back to his guardian's face, so he just kept looking at the rough, new callous on his palm formed after many blisters from the warhorse's reins as he'd practiced leading the animal around the horseyard.

Callum tried another tack. "I've sent for Jasper, your hunting hound, to be brought here. Does that please you?"

David's head popped up and his eyes glowed with pleasure as a huge grin spread across his countenance. "Aye, sir, it surely does."

"If all does not go as we plan on the morrow, the hound will go with you to your new home on the Maclean holding. 'Twill be a balm to your worries, I'm sure, to have an old friend by your side as you get settled there."

David nodded, scrubbing his chin on his shoulder. "Aye."

Callum cleared his throat again. After a slight pause, he said, "'Twould be a great boon to me if you would give me your vow to care for Laire—your new wee foster sister—to protect her with your life, if need be."

His page's spine straightened and his chin lifted. 'Twas clear no one had ever given the lad such a responsibility before, due to his young age, and now he relished the duty. "Aye, you have my vow," he said, his voice holding a shadow of the future authority it would bear as an adult.

"Let us clasp hands on it then to seal the vow." Callum thrust his arm out toward the lad and David did the same, each taking hold of the other's hand in a tight grip.

* * *

Highland Magic

Hours later, near midnight, Callum looked into the flame of one of the twelve 6-inch lit tapers he'd placed around the statue of Saint Quiricus in the chapel, measuring to that hallowed saint. As was the custom in battles such as these, he'd be here the remainder of the night, praying and readying his mind for the coming battle. 'Twas the custom as well to fast the night before, and he'd done that as well, not joining his family at the evening meal, but instead spending his time in his chamber going over his mail to make sure there were no chinks in the armor he'd missed that needed fixing before the battle, and cleaning and sharpening his sword and dirk as well.

David, tho' still a page, had wanted to shine his armor for him, but he'd not allowed it, wanting—needing—instead to be the one to tend his old, faithful friend this night.

He'd spent a bit of time with his destrier as well, brushing it down and looking him over one last time to make sure he was in readiness. The stallion had been given a treat of apples before he was led back to his stall.

By this time tomorrow, with God's will, he'd be once again in the arms of his love. And that Norman usurper, blonde meddler of bairns, would be wrapped tight in his death shroud and away from this place.

* * *

"I saw your lady, sir, with the Norman this day past," David told Callum just a bit past dawn the next morn as he walked beside him toward the stables. Callum had bathed, eaten, and been aided by Daniel and Bao in putting his armor on these two hours past, and now 'twas time for David to lead the warhorse onto the lists.

Callum's head swivelled around so quickly, he got a sharp twinge in his neck. "Where? Where did you see the Norman?"

"In the forest. I was with two of the MacGregor hunters." He cocked his head to the side as he looked up at him "Why did she meet him? Is he not our enemy?"

"'Twas not my lady you saw, I trow. 'Twas some other lass of similar height and build, no doubt."

"Aye, 'twas the lady Branwenn we saw. The wind blew the hood from her cloak and we saw clearly 'twas her that met the Norman."

Callum's brows slammed together and his eyes narrowed. "For how long did they meet?"

David shrugged. "I know not for how long they'd been there by the time we espied them, but they left soon after."

Callum's jaw relaxed. "Hmmm. 'Tis most likely that Branwenn was caught unawares by the bast—*ahem*—fiend." He lifted a brow at David. "So, she was not, umm, bothered by the man in any way? She made it safely back to the keep?"

"Well...he..."—he shrugged again—"he grabbed hold of her hand and *kissed* it."

Callum gritted his teeth. "And that was all?"

"Aye. Then she turned and fled. But the other hunters said she'd no doubt cuckolded you, just as Lara had done." He tipped his head to the side. "Who is

Lara? What does 'cuckold' mean?"

Callum ground his teeth and halted, facing the lad. Ignoring the first part of his question, he answered the second. "She did *not* cuckold me—and you'll find out when you are older." He resumed his pace. After a moment he asked, "So she was unharmed? You saw her after, at the keep?"

David nodded. "Aye, she was at supper last eve."

The vise around his lungs fell free. "Well, then." He ruffled the lad's hair lightly with his gloved hand. "No real harm was done, I trow." Tho', when this trial was over, and if he'd won the day, he'd ask her about the matter.

* * *

CHAPTER 16

THE DAY WAS crisp and clear that bright November morn, the air thick with the hush of the crowd in the stands, the scent of stirred-up sand and horse flesh filling Callum's nostrils.

He was already sweating. So much so, that he could feel his undergarments clinging to his frame under the padding and heavy mail.

He stood next to his restless steed at the far end of the lists looking directly ahead into the closed visor of the helmeted Norman devil, who, two days past, had become his worst enemy. Today, there would be no quarter given; no rules of conduct on which to adhere. Nay, 'twas no sport they were about this day, but a trial with a deadly purpose, from which one—or both—of them would not walk away. His destrier redistributed its weight, causing its own body armor to make a *chinking* sound in the deadly silence.

Bao and Daniel stood a bit away, acting as his

attendants.

The Norman had attendants as well; strangers, no doubt acquired with Norman coin for this trial.

The marshal moved to the center of the field, taking the place of the herald, who'd called out *"Do your duty"* three times a few moments ago to solicit the two combatants out onto the field from their pavilions. Facing the bishop, the marshal lifted his arm, his hand fisted about a white glove. With a swift downward arc, he threw the glove through the air, shouting the first of the triumvirate command, *"Let them go!"*

Before the glove had settled lightly upon the remaining hoarfrost, Callum and his nemesis were on their steeds; their attendants shoving their lances and shields into their hands.

Once the lances rested upright in their feuters, the two combatants' attendants leapt back, and then each man spurred his horse forward.

Callum directed his gaze only on his opponent; all sound from the spectators became some vague part of the background as his mind focused solely on the man ahead of him and the task before him.

He spurred his destrier and charged forward, advancing down the field toward the Norman.

Gaiallard lowered his lance and did the same, running directly at him.

With no tilt-fence running down the center to guide the horses, Callum propelled himself forward in as straight a line as he was able so that his steed would not collide into his opponents; for, 'twas paramount that he retain his seat as long as possible.

The distance between them was closed in mere seconds, their lances glancing off the other's wooden shield.

Thrice more they charged at each other with fresh lances given them by their attendants, and thrice more their wooden shafts met some portion of the other man's armor with a tremendous clangor.

* * *

Branwenn sat perfectly still, every muscle in her being, tensed. Her mien blank of all emotion, she watched the horror before her. She sat inside the family's spectator's box, at one end of the same bench occupied by the other ladies and Chalmers.

Alyson had declined watching the trial, so was not present.

Chalmers sat at the other end of the bench with his wife, her hand clasped in his and resting on his thigh.

With every crashing blow of the lances against helmet or shield, Branwenn fought her body's reaction to cringe or jump, her throat's desire to gasp or cry out, as she worried that she somehow might distract Callum with any overt reaction on her part.

She'd remained awake praying all night, much as her love had done, and her eyes were gritty and red-rimmed from lack of sleep. But the loss of sleep was naught compared to the loss she might have later, if all did not go in their favor. *Please, Lord, let it go in our favor. Do not forsake us, Lord!*

She'd had no contact with Callum since the dawn prior, knowing that he needed some time with Laire and David, as well as time to mentally prepare for this

Highland Magic

trial.

When she'd first seen him this morn as he'd come out on the field, her heart had skipped a beat. For never in her life had she seen a man look so purposeful, so set on his path, as Callum was at that moment.

And 'twas all for *her*. He was risking his life for her. And there was still a place inside her that felt undeserving of such devotion from such a one as he.

But mostly, she just felt fortunate. Fortunate to have been his love, even if it turned out that their lives together would be cut short. For, 'twas a blessing, she continued to remind herself, that she'd known that kind of love at all.

With numb fingers she stroked the smooth stones in the filet on her head. She'd worn it for him—and her lavender wedding gown as well. Just a small token—a loving message—of support.

Callum had only scanned the spectator's box once upon arriving on the field, but she knew he'd seen, and understood, her message, for he'd given a brief nod in her direction before turning to face his opponent.

* * *

Both Callum and Gaiallard took a moment to rest at his own end of the field.

Then, bracing their shields, they spurred their mounts, and once again advanced on their opponent.

After two more tries, one in which they each struck the other's helmet so hard that sparks flew off the shiny metal, Callum at last succeeded in giving Gaiallard an almost killing blow.

The sharp end of his lance broke through the other

man's shield and tore into Gaiallard's left shoulder, rending both flesh and cartilage.

The sound of the clash echoed off the stone walls surrounding the lists and the force of the blow unseated both combatants.

"You whoreson, I'll kill you for that!" Gaiallard bellowed.

"You shall try!" Callum replied with as much force.

Then, both rising to their feet, they faced off before the bishop's box, circling each other, their swords raised.

"Worry not, *boy*," Gaiallard said, "for I shall take good care of your land after I wed your widow. And I shall use the coin from your bride price to build a fortress upon it, as there shall be no need to give it to the Welsh prince now."

"Norman dog!" Callum growled and propelled himself forward, swinging his sword in a wide arc towards his opponent's neck. "You shall never wed her, nor have any portion of my property!"

Gaiallard brought his shield up to block the blow, swinging his own sword at the same time. It hit and glanced off of Callum's shield.

For the next tense moments, the two men swung, thrust, and parried.

The winter sun glinted off one of the amethysts in Branwenn's filet, making a purple-hued spectrum trip and glide over Callum's visor.

He glanced up.

Gaiallard lunged forward. "Ha-ha!" he cried, driving his sword into Callum's thigh. Blood shot from the wound and ran down his leg.

"Aargh!" Callum struggled to remain standing, and conscious, as his mind fogged from the dizzying effect of the instant massive loss of blood.

"'Tis my coup de grâce, this," Gaiallard told him, "my leaving a mark just here—a reminder before you die of the patch that the lovely Branwenn sports so prettily in much the same place."

Knowing he'd given his opponent a killing blow—that he'd lose blood too quickly now to fight for long, to live for long, Gaiallard withdrew his sword and stood, swaying to and fro as he faced his nemesis, with the intent to taunt him a bit more before thrusting his sword through his heart.

Callum struggled to focus. With every heartbeat, a font of blood spurted from the wound in a scarlet arc into the air. The Norman was telling him something, but he could not concentrate on the words. His only thought was to overcome this lethargy as quickly as he could and pounce once more on his nemesis.

"Did you know she met me in the wood this day past? That she sucked my cock dry? That I gave her such a tongue lashing her cunt actually spurted?" Gaiallard's upper torso tilted forward a bit as a high-pitched ringing began in his ears. He shook free the dizzying effect and laughed. "And then I fucked her. Twice. What a tight little cunt she has—and that freckle!" He spread his feet wider apart in an attempt to gain his balance. "She did it for you, she swore. She wanted me to leave the two of you be; to release her from her betrothal contract." He laughed again. "I, being no fool, took what she offered before reversing my promise."

Callum's vision began to blur as a black mist rose along the periphery of his sight, and tho' he saw the Norman's lips moving, the roaring in his ears and his determination to finish this thing, prevented his comprehension of the words. But he'd needed the reprieve his opponent had given him to rest and regain some strength. He blinked away the black mist and took a step forward, but his leg wouldn't hold him. "Christ's Bones!" He fell to his knees.

Gaiallard staggered forward and stood swaying above him as, with both hands on the hilt, he lifted his sword high in the air.

* * *

"*Godamercy.*" Chalmer's shoulders slumped. "That's it then," he said, his voice bleak. "The battle is all but won by the Norman fiend."

Maggie gripped tight to her husband's hand, leaning forward to see her son more clearly. "Nay, it cannot be! He will rally!"

With a trembling hand, Lady Maclean swiped at her tear-streaked face using the small square of linen she kept tucked in her sleeve. "Aye, he shall—"

Branwenn jumped to her feet and fled.

"Branwenn!"

She ignored the older woman's exclamation of her name, blind to all as she flew down the steps of the box. She could not watch him die. She could not. In a matter of seconds she was outside the walls surrounding the field.

The sound of a collective gasp from the spectators filled the air and she bit back a groan of despair as she hiked up her skirts and dashed toward the keep.

He was dead, or as good as. Her love was dead. And her brothers would battle the Norman knight in the same manner if she didn't leave forthwith. 'Twas time to follow through with her plan.

It didn't take long for her to reach her chamber. Closing the door behind her, she leaned against it. "*Callum*," she whispered at last, her pain deeper than tears.

Dry-eyed and determined, she pushed herself away from the door and walked over to stand before her clothing chest. Slowly, she opened the lid and began to pack. She'd take only the few garments she came with; she couldn't bear to be reminded of any of her time here. The filet and rings—both hers and her mother's—she'd wrap up and take with her, however, for the babe she now carried beneath her broken heart. His babe. The one he'd tried so hard not to place inside her. Her head flew up. *The babe!* He knew naught of the babe. She must tell him now, before he takes his last breath.

She turned and flew out the door and down the passageway. With tripping tread, she rushed down the stairs. At the second landing, she stopped short.

Nay, she shouldn't tell him. For she could not give him the last painful blow that he left a babe behind as well.

But, aye, she should. She started her flight once more. Then Callum's last thoughts would be of the sweet consequence of their undying love for one another. Their beautiful, wonderful babe.

She would do this thing, tell him of his babe, be with him as his soul left this world. She was his wife. 'Twas her duty. She could do this.

Then, then she would leave. Afterward. Somehow.

* * *

Some inner reserve of strength and resolve revived Callum in time to parry the blow the Norman would have given him. Gaiallard stumbled backward, giving him time to rise to his feet once more.

Callum forced his leg to hold him, staggering forward, toward his opponent. And then, with every ounce of might he still retained, he swung his sword with so much force at Gaiallard's head that it broke the lock and hinge on his helmet. The thing went flying.

Callum lunged and Gaiallard fell backward, bringing Callum with him to the ground. The iron-ore stench of blood filled Callum's nostrils, so strong he tasted it, reviving him even further. This was a fight to the death, and neither he, nor his opponent, was dead. Yet.

They began to wrestle, rolling about on the hard, cold ground, each looking for an opportunity to skewer or slice the other through.

* * *

Alyson watched the action from the parapet of the stone wall that she hid behind. It overlooked the lists. Dressed in the drab brown woolen boy's clothing she'd been wearing to hunt in these past sennights, with her hair tucked under a cap, and her face smudged with the ash from the hearthfire, she brought the bow up, nocked her arrow, and set her sights on her enemy. She only prayed she'd not waited too long to send him to the fiery eternity he deserved; that Callum would survive the injury her brother had given him before she'd been able to sneak into position here.

* * *

Gaiallard rolled on top of his opponent and arced his sword arm back. With a driving force, he brought the weapon down onto Callum's helmeted head.

The clash of steel on steel resounded inside Callum's helmet, and all around them. His strength waning, 'twas only his desire to save his bride from this fiend that drove him forward. His fingers numb, but his resolve firm, he wrested his dirk from its sheath as the other man continued his pummeling blows to his head. As Gaiallard swung his arm back for the last time, Callum pressed his advantage, swinging his arm forward, the blade in precise line to his opponent's jugular.

In the same instant that Callum's dagger slid into Gaiallard's throat, an arrow went with perfect accuracy, directly into the man's right eye.

The Norman died instantly, his heavy weight falling forward onto Callum. He only had time to roll the Norman off of him before darkness descended.

* * *

'Twas as if he was rising up through the fluid, silent depths of a deep, Cimmerian abyss. Words echoed eerily inside his mind, but he knew not whose voices the words belonged to.

"Will he live?" was repeated more than once. And, *"Aye, if our Lord wills it,"* as well.

Callum tried to open his eyes, but his lids would not cooperate. After a time, his energy exhausted, he drifted once more into the benighted void of dreamless sleep.

* * *

Callum awoke to the feel of a cool hand on his brow. His eyelids seemed as heavy as portcullis gates. 'Twas a struggle, but he at last was able to lift them far enough to see who was tending him.

Branwenn twisted slightly on her stool, turning her head in the direction of the doorway. "Grandmother! He awakes!" she called out, hoping to catch the older woman before she was too far down the passage to hear her. She turned back to her husband. "Callum, can you hear me? How do you feel? Does your leg pain you?"

"Drink," he rasped.

Branwenn nodded and poured a bit of water from the ewer that sat on the table next to her into a silver cup. "Can you lift your head a bit—or would you like me to give you aid to do so?" she asked, bringing the cup forward, toward his lips.

Callum tried, but was too weak to lift his head. "Need...hh...hhhelp."

Branwenn sat the cup back down and rose to sit beside him on the bed. Gently, she nudged first her hand, and then her arm, under his neck and lifted his head slightly. With her free hand, she took hold of the cup once more and brought the rim up to his parched lips. "Drink."

Daniel and Lady Maclean hurried through the opened doorway. "Do not give him more than a few swallows at a time," Daniel instructed, "as his stomach will not hold down more than that right now."

He strode up to stand on the other side of the bed from Branwenn and lifted the blanket that was draped over Callum's torso, revealing the bandaged and elevated leg beneath. "The wound dressing is still clean. A good sign."

Branwenn helped Callum settle his head back on the pillow. His eyelids fluttered slightly before closing. In seconds, he was asleep again.

She turned to her brother. "He's so weak, Daniel! What if he does not recover?"

"He'll recover, fear not," Lady Maclean said as she walked up to stand next to Branwenn. She took hold of her granddaughter's hand. "Now that he's at last come out of his sleep, he's sure to. For he's a strong lad."

"Aye," Daniel replied, "'tis true. He was in his senseless slumber for only a few hours, not days, as we all feared." He settled his gaze on hers. "And now 'twill be much easier to get him the water he requires. Wake him every hour and give him more, in the same way that you did just now. All right?"

Branwenn dropped her gaze back onto her husband and worried her bottom lip with her teeth. Nodding, she said, "Aye."

"I think that you should allow one of us to relieve your vigil, my dear, for you need your rest," Lady Maclean said to her.

"Nay, I cannot—will not—leave his side in any case, so 'tis best that I do this duty." And she must tell him of the babe. The moment, the very moment, that he became aware enough of his surroundings, she must do it.

Which meant she must be here day and night, if need be, else she might surely miss the opportunity. For what if Daniel and Lady Maclean were wrong? What if he did not recover? She could not bear to know that he'd gone to his final peace without knowing of this wondrous gift he'd given her.

Lady Maclean patted her hand. "I must go tell my daughter that her son's revived."

"I'll escort you down, Grandmother," Daniel said. Then to Branwenn: "I'll have some meat broth brought up. He needs his strength rebuilt."

After the two had left the chamber, Branwenn settled once more on her stool. She felt under the blanket until she at last found Callum's hand. Wrapping her own around his much rougher, larger one, she pleaded in a whisper, "Do not leave me."

* * *

Sometime around the chimes of compline, Callum awoke on his own again. And this time, he felt much less dazed, less weak. The room was dim, the only light, that from the hearthfire and a single candle that flickered on the table beside his bed.

His eyes ached as they slowly panned the chamber, then halted and fixed onto the shadowed figure seated in the window's alcove. *Branwenn.* His heart leapt, then settled into a rapid, joyous beat against his ribs.

He'd survived. Praise be to God. A vague glimmer of a remembered speech flitted through his mind, something he tried to hold onto, something about

Branwenn, but was gone in a flash before he could grasp its meaning.

"My love?" he said, his voice raspier than he'd expected. When she didn't respond, he cleared his throat and tried again. "My love? Might I have a bit of water?"

Branwenn swung around. "Callum!" And in seconds she was beside him, running her hand over his brow. "How do you feel?"

"I—"

"Your eyes are much clearer than they were before. And your cheeks have more color. Are you well?"

Callum chuckled. How was he ever to give her his answer if she'd not still that tongue? "I'm much recovered, I trow. And hungry. Is there naught to fill my stomach but that broth?" He indicated with a scan of his eye the vessel containing the liquid meal that sat next to the water ewer on the table beside him.

"I'll have something brought up from the kitchens for you. But first, I'd best get Daniel, for he knows better what you should be eating now." She started to turn but Callum grabbed hold of her wrist and halted her flight.

"Nay, stay here with me awhile. My stomach can wait to be filled. For now, 'tis my eyes that need the filling. With the sight of you."

"Oh, Callum. You *are* better!" Branwenn leaned down and gave him a quick kiss on the mouth. Callum lifted his arms to deepen the kiss, but Branwenn scooted out of his reach. "Nay, you must eat and gain more strength, for I've something to tell you when you have. Something wonderful."

And then she was off. Out the door and down the hall before Callum could say "aye" or "nay" to her words. With a sigh, he smiled and rested his head back onto the pillow.

He lived.

And Gaiallard, the Norman fiend, was dead.

He closed his eyes. Instantly, an image of his opponent standing before him with his sword thrust deep into his thigh swam behind his lids.

"...patch...Branwenn...freckle...sucked dry...tongue lashing."

Callum's eyes flew open and he tried to sit up, but he was stymied by his wound. He gritted his teeth and bellowed as a sharp, eviscerating pain shot into his groin and down his leg, all the way to his toes. "Blood of Christ!" he ground out through clenched teeth as beads of sweat instantly formed on his brow and upper lip.

His lungs blowing hard from his struggle against the pain, he gingerly settled back onto his pillow and stared, unseeing, up into the darkness of the bed's canopy above him.

Gaiallard had known about the mark on Branwenn's thigh. And the freckle as well. How could he have known of them if he had not done as he'd said he'd done?

How?

He could not. For the position of the mark was in a place that only someone who had been granted intimate access to her naked, delectable body would be able to see it.

Highland Magic

Only a lover....

Callum growled. She'd lied to him.

More of Gaiallard's words floated up from the depths of his memory. *"And then I fucked her. Twice. What a tight little cunt she has!*

His skin crawled. She *was* tight. How could he know? Unless...Oh, God! She'd lain with that bastard!

"She did it for you, she swore. She wanted me to leave the two of you be; to release her from her betrothal contract."

Had she? Had that truly been her reason? And even if it were, he'd never forgive her for it. Never. For, if she'd give her body to another when she was already wed, then she was not the woman she'd convinced him she was, not the woman he wanted as wife.

Another memory came to the surface. This time of a feast night a few sennights after his marriage to Lara. Of overhearing some of the soldiers, deep in their cups, wagering on him. On when he would discover that his wife offered herself each night to a new man; that she complained of her husband's inability to please her.

Callum felt the hot flush of remembered shame sweep o'er his cheeks.

Had Branwenn played him for a fool these past moons, pretending timorousness in regard to unveiling her body when, clearly, she had no such compunction with her Norman lover? Callum's fists clenched at his sides. And what of her flirtation with that guard? Even if his mother had brought the guard to Branwenn only as a means to force Callum's hand, the way Branwenn had reacted to him still rankled. Now, more than ever, he was sure that she was weaving her spell on Robert as well, even if the man was too dull witted to know it. Aye, she was a siren, a *Boabhan Sith*, irresistibly drawing him—and all men—to her.

He growled low in his throat, more certain with each passing moment that he'd been duped. That he'd once more entangled himself with a faithless woman.

Her duplicity twisted his gut and ripped at his heart like a blunt, rusted dagger.

She'd lied.

Just as Lara had done.

And that lie had made him the fool, the cuckold.

Again. As he'd sworn he'd never be. Ever again.

And—Blood of Christ!! The clan *knew* it. The hunters had seen the proof and now Callum would once more feel the brunt of his clansmen's disparaging wit.

A great tide of humiliation crashed through him. He'd sworn, after Lara, after the ousting by the Maclean clan, that he'd be a man, not a lad. Be responsible. Do his duty. Wed a lady of high character, worthy of mothering his children. Be the man his family expected him to be.

And, once more he'd thoroughly blundered.

But 'twas not too late to make things right. And he knew just what he must do.

* * *

CHAPTER 17

BRANWENN MET BISHOP Richard outside the great hall. "My husband has revived, sir. Will you give us your blessing now, for I've something of great import to tell him, and I'd like it to be *after* the marriage is blessed." Branwenn's cheeks heated, but she kept her eye steady on the man of the cloth.

The Bishop smiled and gave her a wink. "Ahh. I ken you well, my dear. And 'twould give me great pleasure to give you the blessing. Allow me to retrieve my holy book and I shall meet you in his chamber in a quarter-hour's time."

"Oh! Bishop. Will you not give me an hour? For he must have a meal first. And I must tell the others, as well, so that they may be there also."

Bishop Richard nodded. "Aye. An hour then."

Branwenn sighed and grinned. "My thanks to you," she said and scooted past him through the doorway of the great hall.

* * *

All the family were settled around the hearth. Daniel, who faced the door, saw her first and stood up. "Is he awake, then?"

Branwenn smiled. "Aye, and hungry for heartier fare than what he's had these past hours."

"We must get the lad something to eat." Chalmers indicated with a nod of his head to one of the servants to have a tray of food prepared for his stepson.

"I must check on his wound dressing," Daniel said, and strode toward the door.

"Wait!" Branwenn called out to him. "First, I must tell you that the Bishop has agreed to bless our marriage in an hour's time. I want all of you to be there." She scanned her eye around the gathering. "Where is Alyson?"

"She's not emerged from her chamber since the sheriff questioned her regarding the arrow that went into her brother's eye," Maryn said.

Branwenn walked over to the stool that Daniel had recently vacated and slowly sat down. "*Was* she the one to do the deed?"

"Aye, I believe so," Lady Maclean answered. "Tho' no one outside the family will ever learn the truth of it."

"We told the sheriff that 'twas a stray shot from one of the young squires we have training on guard duty," Chalmers said, "that he no doubt was practicing where he should not have been and the arrow misfired."

"Truth be told," Bao said, releasing Jesslyn's hand for a moment to scrub the back of his neck with the rough pads of his fingertips, "'twas Callum's dirk that killed the man, so even tho' the sheriff was suspicious of our tale, he wrote the incident down in his book as an accident and let the matter rest."

"It aided our cause, I trow, that his wife is a MacGregor," Maggie said.

"Aye, no doubt," Chalmers agreed.

"When will Reys be back?" Branwenn said.

Chalmers sighed and shook his head. "I hope 'tis not more than another moon, for 'tis plain his wife needs him."

* * *

A quarter-hour later, Branwenn and Daniel walked back inside Callum's chamber, the servant bearing the food tray directly behind them.

Callum, his head making a deep well in the pillow beneath it, turned his face away from Branwenn. "Get out, Branwenn."

"What? Why? Are you fevered?" Branwenn rushed to the side of the bed and tried to place her hand on her husband's brow, but he thrust it away.

"Get. Out." Callum sat up a bit and winced, a harsh groan bursting past his tightly clenched lips and teeth. "NOW!"

Daniel took the tray from the servant and set it on a table by the hearth then quietly indicated that the servant should leave.

"But...Callum...please. We are to at last have our vows blessed by the bishop—in only a few minutes' time."

Daniel walked over to stand with his arms akimbo a bit away from the scene, his eyes narrowed in speculation as he studied his young cousin.

"We shan't wed. The offer of my troth is rescinded." He turned back to face her. "Get OUT!" he shouted, rising up again, tho' it pulled his leg injury. His face crinkled from the pain it evidently caused.

"But...you love me," she said, tho' there was doubt in her voice now, "and I love you!" she continued with more surety.

"Nay, I love you not. I could never love a *whore*. Allow a whore to raise my bairns! And you are that—you slept with that Norman—and God knows who else, besides!"

Branwenn sucked in a sharp breath. "Nay! Never! How ever could you believe such?"

"You lie! For he told me so, on the field this day. And I—and half the MacGregor hunters—know you met the man this day past in the wood." He gave a derisive snort. "I thought 'twas only some chance encounter, even worried that the man had threatened you in some way, when David told me of it this morn. But then the Norman proved it to be a much more intimate meeting when he relayed a bit of knowledge of your body that only a lover could know. Ken you of what I am speaking, Branwenn, or do I spell it out in front of your brother?"

Branwenn shook her head in numb disbelief. "How? How could he know of such? *How?*"

Callum's eyes narrowed. "*Precisely*," he said through gritted teeth.

"And now I wonder if you shone that purple specter from that filet directly into my eyes apurpose. To distract me. Did you decide after bedding the man that he was the better lover?"

"Nay!—" Branwenn said.

"*Callum—*" Daniel said at the same time. 'Twas a warning.

Callum ignored both of them, too caught up now in his own misery. "That you'd rather have him 'tween your thighs than me?" He pointed towards the door. "Leave. I cannot bear the sight of you another moment."

Branwenn's heart twisted so violently in her chest, she couldn't take in a breath.

"Branwenn, leave us," Daniel said in a dangerously quiet voice.

Knowing she was in real peril of breaking down in earnest, Branwenn did as her brother bade. Whirling around, she fled the chamber.

Daniel, his shoulder resting against the jamb of another door, raised his hands and pounded his palms together slowly. "Well done. I do believe we've seen at last the underside of that silver tongue of yours."

Callum glared at him through bloodshot eyes. "Go to the devil, you son of a whoredog," he said hoarsely.

Daniel ignored him. Instead, he slowly straightened before sauntering over to the stool at Callum's bedside and sitting down. "So we are back to this again. Another accusation of inconstancy thrown at my poor sister's head, with little or no proof to support it. Truly, you do not deserve to be her husband. Mayhap 'tis for the best that the blessing has not been given, for 'twill be of no matter to void the other."

Callum's brows slammed together and his face grew even more red. "Good! Do it forthwith, for I shan't spend another sennight wed to such a one as she. And take her back with you. I'll not have her kind sullying my bairns." He dropped his head back onto the pillow and turned his face away. "And I do have proof. Undeniable proof, in fact."

"Well, I see you've recovered some blood. But your sense has clearly been addled. What proof could you possibly have? My sister, if you recall, *ran* from the Norman—was nearly drowned in the process. Why would she give herself to him?"

Callum was silent for a long moment before saying at last, "He said she did it as a bargain so that he would not meet me on the lists this day."

This gave Daniel pause. He could see his sister doing such if she were desperate enough. But *had* she? It bore investigating. "And you call her 'whore' for doing what she could to save your life?"

"'Tis not the first time she's enticed men. Remember Kerk and Robert? And all those lads she danced with 'round the bonfire? And what's to stop her from doing such again? Nay, she's just like Lara, and I'll not be wed to another of her ilk. *Ever.*"

"Branwenn is naught like Lara. Get that thought out of your head forthwith."

Callum turned to look at Daniel once more, determination glinting like diamonds in his eyes. "I won't take the chance. Not again. I won't be a cuckold, the pity and laughingstock of my clan—*ever again*! I owe it to my bairns, to my family."

Daniel sighed. 'Twas clear Callum was in no mind to speak rationally about this now. And who could blame him? He'd come near to dying only a few hours past. Mayhap 'twas best to allow the man some more rest before broaching the subject again.

All at once Daniel recalled the ploy that his father-in-law had used with him and Maryn. He decided to try it on his cousin. "Well, there's naught for it then, I suppose. I'll do what I must to get the contracts voided."

The look of a cornered deer in direct line of a hunter's arrow came into Callum's eyes. "Good."

"But 'twill take some time. Mayhap even a moon."

Callum's heart ached and a lump formed in his throat, but he'd be damned to a fiery hell before he let that stop him. "Fine."

This was what he wanted, what needed to happen. He'd get over her after a time and he'd go on about his life as he had been doing before...before he...God's Bones! Before he met *fey Mai* in the cave that day. He would. He had to. 'Twas for the best.

* * *

Daniel found Branwenn in the solar with Bao, wringing her hands and pacing. But she was dry-eyed, praise be. He hadn't made it two paces into the chamber before she said, "Is he fevered?"

"He's not in his right mind, this is certain. But nay, he's not fevered."

"Does he truly hate me? Believe me faithless?"

Daniel sighed and crossed his arms over his chest. "Aye, he does."

"But *why?* Why does he believe so easily I'd betray him?"

"Because.... Did you allow the Norman to bed you as a bargain to keep Gaiallard from meeting Callum in the trial?"

"*Nay!* Is that what Gaiallard told him?"

Daniel nodded. "Aye. And truth be told, it crossed my mind that you might have done such to save Callum's life."

Branwenn bit her lip then nodded. "Aye, I suppose I might have, if I truly thought Gaiallard would follow through with such a bargain. But I knew him too well. He'd not, and in the end, I would have only compromised my marriage by doing so. Besides, Gaiallard had no desire for me in that way. None at all."

Bao stepped forward and placed his arm around his sister's shoulder. "I find that hard to believe."

Branwenn snorted. "Believe it, for 'tis truth. You may ask Alyson if you do not believe me. He spent most of his time at Pembroke wooing a Norman lady by the name of Caroline de Montrochet.

"Callum said you met the Norman in the woods—that others saw you with him," Daniel asked. "Is that true?"

Branwenn sighed. "Aye. That part is true. But...I didn't meet him there on purpose. I..." She sighed. "I followed Alyson. She'd been very quiet since her brother's arrival, so when I saw her leaving out of the gate to the keep with such, I know not, furtiveness? I decided to see what she was about." Branwenn crossed her arms over her chest. "It didn't take long for me to find out: Gaiallard was waiting for her in the wood. He grabbed hold of her arm and yanked her toward him, then he began shaking her."

"That bastard!" Bao growled, and then: "Tell me you didn't do what I think you did."

Branwenn shrugged and gave him a sheepish look. "Aye, I suppose I did. But, Bao! I could not allow the man to harm her—and there was no time to get aid!"

"What happened then?" Daniel asked, his voice low with suppressed anger and fear.

Branwenn turned and looked at him. "I ran up to them and yelled for him to release her." She shrugged again. "Gaiallard let her go and then he rounded on me." She shivered. "He grinned and said, 'Ah, my soon-to-be-wife. Do you disapprove of my visiting Alyson? She is my sister after all.' I told Alyson to flee and she did." Branwenn paced toward the window and stared out at the blackness of night that enveloped the courtyard below. "We only traded a few barbed words before I, too, fled."

The two brothers exchanged glances filled with both relief and irritation and then Daniel said, "I've told Callum that the contracts will be voided; that he may have that for which he asks."

Branwenn whirled around. "*Daniel!*" She rushed up to him and grabbed his hand in both of her own. "Nay!"

Daniel brought his other hand up to cup her cheek. "List me well, wee one. 'Tis not as you believe. I told him 'twill take at least a moon to do the deed. This will surely give him the time he needs to recover and see the error in his judgement. But, for now, I thought it best for his recovery to allow him to believe we'd do his bidding."

Branwenn squeezed his callous-roughened hand. "My thanks, brother."

"Now, tell me what this 'proof' is that he says is undeniable."

Branwenn began to tremble. "Nay."

The look of terror in her eyes broke his heart. Not knowing what else to do to ease her, Daniel wrapped her in his arms. "'Tis something regarding your frame, Callum said. Something of which only a lover could know." He gave Bao a questioning look.

Bao's brows slammed together as he tried to think to what Callum would be referring. All at once, he knew. His eyes widened. "I believe 'tis—"

Branwenn jerked out of Daniel's embrace. "NAY! Say *naught* more."

Bao crossed his arms over his chest and gave her a short nod. "All right."

Daniel's brow lifted as he drilled his brother with a steady gaze.

Bao shrugged. "'Tis for Branwenn to tell, and it appears she has no desire to do so."

Daniel rested his palms on her shoulders and gently turned her to face him. "Is it so awful then? Something you will not tell me of, your own brother?"

Branwenn gave him a pleading look. "I beg you, try to understand. 'Tis simply too privy a thing, too horrid."

Daniel glanced at Bao, who shook his head in

disagreement, and then brought his gaze back to Branwenn. "*Horrid?*"

Branwenn's face crumpled and she lifted her hands to cover it. "Aye! Horrid! Please, do not press me more to tell you."

Daniel sighed and kissed the crown of her head. "As you wish. I'll leave the matter be."

Daniel felt her shoulders relax beneath his palms. She dropped her arms to her sides. "My thanks." Looking first at Daniel and then at Bao, she said, "Whatever am I to do about Callum?"

"Give the man a bit of time to heal. Then we shall see how set he truly is against remaining wed to you," Daniel said.

"Aye," Bao agreed, "'tis certain that once he's had a few more days of recovery he'll not be of the same mind. He's sure to see the error in his reasoning then."

"I pray you are not wrong," Branwenn said.

* * *

An hour later, their worried sister at last appeased and gone off to attempt a word with Alyson, the two brothers settled by the hearthfire in the great hall. Their ale tankards filled almost to overflowing, they each took a long pull before resting the base of the vessels on their knees.

"This proof that Callum has worries me," Bao said, breaking the companionable silence.

"Aye?"

Bao sighed and pressed his thumb and forefinger against the lids of his tired eyes. "There is no way—and believe me, I've been trying to work one out this past hour—that the Norman could have known of this thing unless he'd...well, he'd had *very* close, intimate contact with the lass. It's on the portion of her body where only a lover would have access, do you ken?"

Daniel's eyes narrowed. "Then, pray brother, how ever do *you* know of such?"

"Get your mind out of the gong pile," Bao said. "I raised her from the day she was born, remember you that? 'Tis common practice to see a babe in the bare when one bathes her or changes her swaddlings, you old lecher."

Daniel settled back in his chair. He ignored his brother's insult. "So, 'tis some birthmark of which he speaks, then?"

Bao scrubbed the back of his neck with his palm and shook his head. "Nay, I've told you more than I should have already. Branwenn will be hurt if I say more."

Daniel took that as a 'yes'. "So, you think our sister did allow the Norman to bed her?"

Bao growled low in his throat. "I know not! I want to believe her, but, as I said, I cannot see how the man would have known of it otherwise. For, as you saw yourself, the lass will not speak of it—to anyone. In fact, as far as I know, 'tis only I and the old nurse I hired to live with us as she grew that knew of this"—he shrugged—"thing."

Daniel sighed and rested his head on the chair's back. He gazed up at the raftered ceiling, his mind in chaos. "So, Callum's accusation is valid." He lifted his head, a light of determination in his gaze as he looked at his brother. "But even the Norman admitted she only did so in an attempt to save Callum's life. Tho' 'twas folly on her part, her motive was pure. Surely, in time, Callum will see that."

Bao nodded. "Aye, let us pray so."

They were both silent a moment, lost in their own musings. Finally, Bao shook his head, saying, "Nay. Nay, I simply do not believe she did this thing—at least not after she wed Callum—priest's blessing or no. Nay, I think she must have had some contact with the man while she was in Cambria. Mayhap while they were betrothed and together at Pembroke. What say you?"

Daniel studied his brother a moment as he worked this out in his mind. He nodded. "Aye, that makes much more sense." He leaned forward. "Is it possible that naught more went on than, *ahem*, preamble? Would he have seen this thing in that case? For, Callum has been quite sure these past moons that he...well...that Branwenn had been an innocent, prior...."

Bao chuckled in spite of the dire subject of their conversation. "You truly cannot bear to think on our wee sister as a woman grown, with desires, can you?"

Daniel couldn't help it. He cringed. "Nay. So let us keep to the general and not the specific, all right?"

With a nod, Bao said, "Aye. And, aye to the other, as well. 'Tis more than possible that the Norman might have acquired this knowledge during the"—he choked back a laugh but it came out as a snort—"*preamble*, did you call it?"

Daniel drilled him with a steady glare. "'Tis glad I am that I can offer such amusement to you, but would you mind concentrating a bit more on the subject at hand? It *is* our sister's shattered hopes of which we are speaking, after all."

Bao immediately sobered. "Aye, you are right." He cocked his head to the side. "Have you noticed how quick Callum is to compare our wee sister to that viper to whom he was wed, Lara?"

Daniel took in a deep breath and slowly released it. "Aye, I have. And I know not how to reason him out of it, for he has a demon riding his back. 'Tis something he alone has the power to overcome within himself. Naught we say will make him see with different eyes. Not this time; not without proof that the Norman lied."

Bao nodded. "Hmmm." After a moment, his spine straightened. "God's Bones! I cannot believe you would think I'd bedded my own sister!"

Daniel rolled his eyes. "I was jesting!" He shrugged. "A wee bit."

"Arse."

"'Tis better to be the arse than the hole."

Bao shot to his feet. "Mayhap 'tis been too long since we met on the field. What say you to a bit of a wrestle, brother?"

"'Tis black as pitch outside!"

"Naught that a few torches will not amend."

Daniel stood. "Let us to it, then. I admit, giving you a good trouncing will be a pleasant way to end this horrid day."

Bao strode towards the door. "Worry not, old man," he called over his shoulder, "you'll no doubt be aided to your bed in only a few moments time, for it shan't take more than a move or two for me to knock you on your *arse.*"

Chalmers, Maggie and Lady Maclean entered just as Bao said the last.

"Oh, my, are you two at it again?" Maggie said.

Chalmers chuckled. "Leave them be, my dear. 'Tis good practice and they'll not do *too* much damage to themselves, I trow."

"Aye, and after the events of the day, I'm sure they need a bit of exercise to calm them," Lady Maclean said. She touched her fingers to her daughter's wrist. "Besides, you know well how warriors do enjoy testing their skills."

Maggie stepped away from her husband, making a clear path to the door for Bao to go through. "Aye, I suppose you are right, Mama."

Bao dipped his head to her and strode out, with Daniel not three paces behind him.

* * *

Later that night, near the chimes at midnight, Branwenn silently stepped across the threshold of Callum's bedchamber. After quietly closing the door behind her, she rested back against the hard, rough wood and gazed toward the closed canopy of the bed.

She'd sworn to leave Callum be. To allow him to recover before speaking to him again, but she found she just couldn't do it. Not knowing that he still had no knowledge of the babe he'd put in her womb.

And, surely, once he knew, he'd stop this talk of voiding the contracts; he'd realize how wrong he'd been in his belief that she'd been with any other but him. And then they could begin building their lives together as they'd planned.

She tiptoed over to the side of the bed and spread the drape back with her hand enough to see the dark outline of Callum's large form.

"Get out, whore."

Branwenn sucked in a breath, both in surprise and anguish at the epithet he continued to use for her. She began to tremble, but she resolutely held her ground. He'd change his mind soon enough, when he knew.

"And on the morrow, hie yourself to one of your brothers' holdings, for I will not have you sullying my home another moment. You disgust me. You *and* that vile patch you sport."

Branwenn's heart twisted. Her eyes misted, but she blinked the moisture away. Not this night. She'd not give in to her weakness this night. "You said you liked it—that you wanted all our bairns to have it, and now there just may be—"

"'Twas a lie, my dear. Just as you lied to me about your lack of experience. What a fool I was to believe you innocent when you inveigled me to speak of the act of coupling in detail that day. 'Twas more likely some cunning ploy used to entice me that you use on all your men."

"Callum! How could you think such! 'Tis not true, I swear it."

"You *swear* it? Truly? And what good are vows from you when you so easily break them—only one day after you gave them!"

Mayhap she *had* been in Bao's trade in Perth, Callum suddenly thought. Bao had vehemently denied it when he'd asked him that very question last year, but now Callum was no longer convinced. She was much too bold for a true innocent. Why, she'd nearly devoured him that day in the cave. *Sucked* him *dry*. The Norman's vile words still haunted him, made him ill. Aye, that was no act of a true novice.

And she'd seduced him as well. In this very bed he lay upon now. How bold she had been, teasing his cock with that hot mouth of hers and then straddling him and taking him inside her. Like a veritable proficient. Had she truly been a virgin? Mayhap that had been an act as well.

"I love you, Callum. And you said you loved me, many times. Do not do this to us, I beg you."

Callum closed his eyes against the enticement of her standing so close to him that he could smell the sweet rose scent of her, feel the seductive heat of her lovely body, ripe and ready for the taking, if only he'd reach out his hands and accept what she offered. But not again. He'd not be made the fool again by another deceitful wife. Not now, not ever.

'Twas a struggle, but he managed to say in a bored tone, "As it turned out, 'twas a rather fleeting desire I bore for you, not love. Now, you only vex me with your simpering and mewling. Leave me to my rest."

Branwenn choked back the cry that rose from deep inside her. She turned and fled, all thoughts of telling him of their babe driven away by his cruel words and stubborn disbelief.

* * *

CHAPTER 18

*M*Y DEAR, YOU'VE not had more than a few bites of meat this whole eve! Are you not well?" Lady Maclean asked Branwenn.

'Twas a fortnight since the joust; a fortnight since Callum's horrid accusation and her subsequent flight from his chamber. "Aye, I feel well, Grandmother. I'm just a bit tired. This feast started so early this day and now 'tis surely nearing the chimes of compline."

Lady Maclean patted her hand. "Well, the players are about to perform; that will surely wake you a bit. I know how you enjoy their antics."

Branwenn gave her a tired smile. "Aye, I'm sure you are right." After that terrible night when Callum had denied his love for her, Branwenn had followed Daniel's advice and allowed him to convalesce with no further contact from her.

"Ahh! Here they are," Lady Maclean said. "This should be quite entertaining, for it looks as though they've got one of the younger players dressed as a lass. 'Twill be a story of two lovers no doubt. I do so enjoy that type of play." She leaned close to Branwenn and said, "'Tis such a shame that the others could not be here to see this. But Maryn and Jesslyn would not be swayed. They wanted to return to their babes—and who could blame them?" She chuckled and gave a bit of a shrug. "And 'tis a good thing, I trow, that Bao left as well, for even I was beginning to worry over his and Daniel's desire to compete with each other over the slightest thing."

Daniel had evidently heard his grandmother's last comment, because he laughed good-naturedly and said, "Not the *slightest* thing, Grandmother, I assure you. I'm sure I'd give him the last turnip, if he wanted it, for example."

Lady Maclean chucked him on the chin. "Aye, but only because you have no real liking for them! You cannot fool me, my lad."

He gave her a sheepish grin and shrugged. "Mayhap."

While Daniel and Lady Maclean continued their lively banter, Branwenn squirmed on her stool. Some mad compulsion that she had yet to overcome made her look in Callum's direction for the thousandth time that eve. Her heart shot into her throat when her eyes were instantly swept up in the green fire of his own. He smirked and dipped his head to her in snide greeting before turning back to the other young clansmen—his friends—whom he sat with at one of the soldiers' trestle tables below the dais where the family's table was located. Branwenn quickly turned her eye back to the performers.

The play started with a song. Two of the players, one male and one dressed as a female, danced toward each other. Then, as the two stood facing each other, the music stopped and the man said:

"Why if it isn't the beautiful Mai. What's brought you to this cave, oh fey one?"

A feeling of foreboding filled Branwenn. *Mai? Cave? Fey one?* She shook her head. Nay, 'twas a strange stroke of chance. Surely. But she straightened on her stool and watched closely the rest of the scene in any case.

By the end of it, she was atremble. She remained stoic, however, her mein sedate and her eye never wandering from the place where the players staged their entertainment.

But inside, she was appalled—and growing more so by the second. For this was some malicious re-enactment of her and Callum's wedding night. And only one other person could have given the tale to the players: Callum. Was he that set against her then? To humiliate her in front of everyone?

'Mei' spoke then:

"I—I've a...patch, a mark on me."

Branwenn's heart stopped, then started again in a mad, pounding race against her rib cage. She watched with near panic as the player repeated her words, her actions of that night. Then he covered his mouth with his hand and said:

"Oh, God! I know you'll find it as hideous as I do when you

see it!"

She began to quake in earnest. Her palms and underarms grew moist with sweat. Without conscious thought, she turned her eye on Callum.

He wasn't watching the performance either; he was looking directly at her. His countenance no longer held the snide humor of a few moments past. In its place was something else. Something indefinable, unsettling. No longer did his eyes hold fire in their depths. Nay, now there was only ice—as cold as the winter winds on the highest peak of *Sìdh Chailleann*. Brutal in its lack of warmth. As the two green glacial shards pierced her through, she suddenly knew. Knew what that look was. 'Twas hatred she saw there. Unmitigated and unyielding.

'Mei's' lover spoke then:

"'Tis the mark of the devil!"

Branwenn's head whipped around in horrified anguish. In the next instant, she was on her feet and off the dais.

"Branwenn! Are you ill?"

She heard her grandmother, but was too distraught to stop her flight. She felt the hot flush of her humiliation spreading up from her chest, to her neck, and finally covering her entire visage. She must get out of here before everyone realized that the play was about *her!*

She hurried across the great hall with as much dignity as she could muster. Her head held high, she kept her eyes focused directly ahead of her. When she passed Callum's table, she fought the urge to allow her eyes to turn in his direction.

Finally, finally, she was outside the hall and in the dimly lighted antechamber that held the stairs leading up to the family's quarters. She'd only gone a couple of steps when someone grabbed hold of her arm. Before she knew what was happening, she was crowded up against the stone wall and being voraciously kissed.

At first, she thought 'twas Callum. And even though he'd hurt her deeply these past days—and just now with the humiliating play he'd arranged—her heart still loved him, held hope, forgave. So, she kissed him back, with all the feeling she'd been holding inside her.

Realization was just beginning to dawn when the man—'twas one of Callum's friends!—lifted his head and said, "Callum was right, you *are* a sweet berry, ripe for the ff—*plucking*."

She pushed with all her might against his chest. "Get off me, you dull-witted beast!" she said between clenched teeth. But he was much too big, much too strong for her.

He ground his pelvis against her mons and twisted his hand in her hair, forcing her head back. He bit the rise of her breast.

Branwenn let out a scream. "Release me!" she yelled.

"But I paid good coin for you. And your husband will not be pleased when he discovers you denied me my due."

"Callum *sold* my favors to you?" Branwenn asked, stunned.

"Aye, as is his right."

"Godamercy," she whispered.

"God had naught to do with it, I assure you," the warrior said. Then he put his big, beefy hand on her breast and squeezed.

Branwenn renewed her struggle to get out of his embrace, but with little success. The more she struggled, the more impassioned his hands and lips became.

"Callum should have warned me what a wee cockfighter you are," the man said. "And worry not, I'll not be repelled by the mark on you—not as your husband is."

Branwenn's stomach twisted and she felt bile rise into her throat. "Oh, God," she moaned.

* * *

At first, Daniel had thought to allow Branwenn some time alone before following her to make sure she was all right. He'd had his suspicions about the piece they were being presented when he'd heard the players speak of a mark on the skin. But when, as he watched her, Branwenn first lost all complexion, then her skin flamed, and then she'd departed in such haste, he'd known 'twas as he'd suspected: Callum had set the players to perform the piece purely as a means to humiliate the lass.

But after only a few minutes, Daniel found he was too anxious to see how his sister fared to leave her be for long. He excused himself and made his way to the doorway of the hall. He was just walking through it when he heard a man say:

"I like a lady with a bit of a deformity. It heats my blood."

* * *

Branwenn twisted and turned, but couldn't get free from the iron embrace. "I won't let you bed me, no matter how much coin you paid Callum! I'm not his to sell!"

She'd begun to feel faint, begun to see pinpricks of light dance in her sights, when all at once she heard a mighty growl. The man was hauled back and off of her, and thrown onto the stone stairs. He landed with a harsh cry, a muffled moan, and a tremendous crash and clatter.

"Daniel!" Branwenn cried and flew into his arms.

The man lifted his head and groaned, but in the next second, his eyes rolled back in his head and he fell back once more, silent.

"I'm going to kill him," Daniel said. "Leg wound or no leg wound, Callum's a dead man on the morrow."

Branwenn struggled out of his embrace. "Nay! Do not touch one hair on his head!"

"Branwenn! How can you defend him? What he's done is indefensible."

Even now, she couldn't get the words past her lips. The words that would help Daniel understand. The words that would tell him that this horrid beast Callum had become these past sennights was not truly Callum, not at all. And...that Callum was the father of her babe. So, instead, she simply shook her head and said, "I beg you, leave him be." She paused and then said what she should have said a fortnight ago, when Callum had first reviled her. "Take me home. Take me to the Maclean holding. I'll not tarry here another day, waiting for something that I see now will never be. Callum does not love me, does not want to be wed to me any longer. And 'tis time for me to let him go, to give him what he wants."

Daniel kissed her brow. "All right. We'll leave at first light." He leaned back and, placing both hands on her cheeks, lifted her chin so that he could see her face. "After I escort you to your chamber, I want you to throw the bar across the door. You aren't to leave that room again until I come for you, is that clear?"

"Aye."

"Are you sure you do not wish for me to kill him?"

She smiled, tho' she knew he was only half-jesting. "Aye. Do not kill him." She sighed. "He'll not be a bother to me any longer after the morrow, in any case."

"All right. But, if you change your mind, let me know."

"Daniel! I shan't change my mind, so get the notion out of your head!"

* * *

Callum took a long pull on his ale and then slammed the tankard down on the table next to him. The result of the play hadn't managed to rid him of his heartache, eviscerate his desire for Branwenn from his being, as he'd thought it would when he'd first conceived of the idea a few days past.

"Ho! Callum," Ramsay, one of his drinking partners said as he stumbled up behind him. "I just saw Kenrick knocked out cold on the stair."

Callum turned his head and looked up. His sight was growing a bit bleary, now that he'd finished his tenth tankard and swallowed down a good portion of *uisge beatha* as well, but he did manage to focus well enough to see who was speaking to him.

"D'ya think 'twas yer feisty wee wife's brother who did the deed then? I tol' you 'twas no' a good idea, what ye did." He shook his head. "Not a good idea a-tall."

Callum shrugged. It made him weave a bit, but he balanced himself with his forearm on the table. "I need—*hick*—ed the coin. Besides, if she's goin'ta shleep wi' e'ry man a'tha keep, why shouldn't I make a bit of profit fro' it?"

All at once, the room began to spin and Callum's stomach churned. In the next second he fell forward, his cheek hitting the table with a loud '*thunk*' and his arms sprawled across the top of it.

"Hey!" Ramsay called out to one of his other cronies. "Another one's down, and I think he's spewed his supper!"

* * *

It had taken two full days of travel to arrive at the Maclean holding, and Branwenn had been hard-pressed on the journey to keep her condition from her brother and Grandmother Maclean—who'd insisted upon traveling back with them—as she was still fighting her morning ills each day. But, somehow, she had managed to keep her secret, and now, a sennight later, she was seated at her hearthfire in her chamber, busily sewing a few shirts for her babe.

She'd yet to sew one swaddling cloth, however. She just couldn't seem to find it within herself to do so. Did babe's *truly* need to be bound so tightly? She shrugged and bit her lip. If only she could speak to Grandmother Maclean about it!

But, nay, she simply was not yet ready to reveal the wondrous (and oh, so frightening!) news. Not yet. Mayhap in another moon? Surely, by that time, she'd have found the words to explain why she'd not told the babe's father before she'd left.

She needed more time. For, what if they insisted upon sending word to Callum? With a groan, she dropped the linen into her lap and lifted her head, staring straight ahead. Assuming he believed 'twas he that had sired the babe—which, after what he'd done to her the night of the feast, she doubted he would—he might demand to renew the marriage vows. For the babe's sake, of course. And her heart could truly not bear being wed to a man she loved so much, but who hated her to the same degree. If not more.

She sighed and shook her head. Nay, she must wait as long as she was able to reveal her condition to her family. And, surely, 'twouldn't be *so* difficult to hide her condition until then, would it? For she'd begun to wear only the looser fitting gowns that Maggie had given her, as the ones that Grandmother Maclean had had made for her were now growing tight in the waist. Fortunately, none of the family questioned the move, as she'd been prone to wear the larger gowns often in any case.

She placed her hand over the small mound that her growing babe had formed under her belly. A wash of pure bliss filled her as she thought of the wee one she'd hold in her arms next spring. With that happy thought, her gloom from the moment before receded and she went back to her sewing, a cheerful tune tripping from her tongue.

* * *

In that same moment at the MacGregor holding, Callum turned the corner of the chapel and stopped short. His eyes narrowed as he watched in disgust the scene before him. There was the guard, *Kerk*, with his arms around the alewife's rather buxom daughter, his face buried in her neck.

The lass giggled, but allowed the intimacy. Kerk must have whispered something to her, because she squirmed away and cheerily cried, "Nay, I'll not! Not 'til later, at least." She shoved at his chest and said, "Now, off with you before the lieutenant sees that you've not resumed your post."

Kerk grumbled something, but he nodded his head and began walking in the direction of the guard tower. The lass turned back to the well and dipped a bit of water out of the bucket into a pitcher.

Callum jogged to catch up to the guard. "Ho, there! Kerk?"

Kerk turned around and stopped. When he saw who'd called him, his eyebrow lifted and a smirk formed on his lips. "Aye?" he said, crossing his arms over his chest.

Callum bristled. He knew he had the authority to slap the man's impudence down, but it wouldn't serve his purpose. For he wanted answers, honest answers, and the best way to get them was with a bit of diplomacy, not force.

"The alewife's daughter's certainly a comely lass."

Kerk's eyes narrowed. "Aye, that she is."

"Tho' not the type that usually appeals to you, I'd wager."

"Oh, really now? And how would you be knowing that, I'm wondering?"

Callum cleared his throat. With a shrug, he said, "She hasn't the small, slender frame you've desired before."

Kerk threw his head back and laughed.

'Twas a struggle, but Callum managed to hold onto his temper and not take a swing at the man's jaw.

Kerk's laughter trailed off, but his grin was in full prominence when he said, "I care not that you are the nephew of the laird, I'm going to say this anyway: You are truly a lack-wit. And an arse as well. I cannot ken what the lass saw in you." He turned and continued his trek across the courtyard. "Now, I've my duties to attend," he said loudly enough for Callum to hear, "so why don't you go find your irksome friends and harry them instead?"

Callum felt the heat of his blush spread up his neck and over his cheeks. He ground his teeth together. That had not gone as he'd hoped. Just as the guard had done that other time, when Callum had confronted him about his attentions to Branwenn, Kerk had had another good belly laugh, clearly, but curiously, at Callum's expense.

Ever since the night of the feast, and Branwenn's subsequent departure, he'd been a virtual outcast amongst his family and most of the clan.

He shouldn't have sold Branwenn's favors; he knew that. It had been *the* most childish, stupid thing he'd ever done in his life—and he'd racked up quite a list of them these past years. Even Kenrick, once he'd sobered, had castigated not only himself, but Callum as well for inciting him to act in such a manner.

Callum growled low in his throat. It should have been he who bore the bruised ribs and lump on his head for the crime. He pressed the base of his palms against his eyelids. "Aargh!" he bellowed. Yet, once again, 'twas someone else who endured the brunt of his own ridiculous behavior.

Tho', in truth, he had suffered greatly from the barbs delivered by his own conscience, as well as the cool reception from his family these past days.

But by the night of the feast, his resolve had slipped and he'd known that if he didn't get Branwenn from this keep forthwith, he'd give in to the violet-eyed siren's charms once more. And then, all would be lost.

So he'd conceived of the plan to humiliate her, to tell the world her closely-held secret. That, he'd been certain, would be enough to send her speeding from this keep, and purge her from his soul as well.

But then the drink and his sore heart had brought his anger at her betrayal to the fore once more and the next thing he knew, he was offering her up to Kenrick for only a few coins.

Truly, truly, Daniel should have run him through for that one. And the fact that he still lived, he had an uneasy feeling, was due in great portion to *Branwenn*.

Branwenn. Who, Kenrick had revealed to Callum later, had rejected his attentions—quite vociferously, in fact. A thing that Lara would never have done. A thing that even now wore at Callum's belief in her duplicity.

* * *

"The alewife's daughter seems to be enjoying that guard's attention," Callum said to Chalmers two nights later. He was still curious at the man's change of taste. For, tho' the lass had a pleasing enough countenance, she was in no way as perfectly lovely, perfectly formed, as Branwenn.

Chalmers followed the line of Callum's gaze. "Oh. Aye, as well she should for she's not been his bride for more than three moons I trow. Hardly time for them to grow weary with the other, I'd say."

Callum straightened in his chair, his gaze sharper now as he more closely studied the couple, his mind doing a quick calculation. "They're *wed*? For three moons?" But that was the same time that Branwenn and the guard were so clearly enjoying each other's company.

Chalmers cocked a brow at Callum. "Aye." He shook his head. "Why do you care so?"

Callum shrugged. "I do not. 'Twas just a passing curiosity, is all."

A half-hour later, Callum walked up to Kerk and tapped him on the shoulder. When the man turned his head, Callum said, "'Twas quite a jest you played on me the other day, I trow."

Kerk nodded and gave him his usual smirk. "Aye, I thought so."

"I have to say—and ken me well, your wife is quite lovely—I'm a bit confused as to why you would choose the lass over Branwenn, when 'tis clear you held her favor."

Kerk turned and faced him full-on. Crossing his arms over his chest he said, "'Tis clear is it?" Kerk snorted and shook his head. "I see that you have not the wit to work this out on your own, so I must give you a bit of assistance." He took a step closer and bent at the waist slightly. "The Lady Branwenn and I never spoke more than a handful of times, and most of those conversations dealt with things so dull that I cannot even recall them now. And—list me well, for this is the only time I'll say it—the lass, to my eye, is not even half as lovely as you believe her to be. In fact, 'tis clear to me that you've gone a bit daft and lost most of your sight as well." He straightened and then continued in a gentler voice, "Do not mishear me, for the lass is pleasant enough to look upon, and is kindhearted as well, with a keen wit that some would like, but she's not near so toothsome as you crow on about."

Callum fought the twin demons of offended pride and anger. His fists clenched at his sides, he trembled with the need to take the man down. "Meet me on the field at dawn." He turned and strode out of the hall, up the stairs, and into his bedchamber. His lungs blowing hard now, he slammed the door behind him and stood stock-still in the middle of the room, his mind spinning as he struggled to keep the doubts regarding his beliefs about Branwenn at bay.

After a moment, his resolve once more in place, he

took his sword from its place on the wall and began the soothing process of cleaning it.

* * *

Dawn came early the next morn, or at least it seemed so to Callum. Tho' he'd been on the field for at least a half-hour prior to the time he would meet his opponent, he already regretted the challenge he'd given the guard the night before.

Yet, again, he'd reacted like a bairn. With a low growl, he lifted his sword and swung it in a harsh, downward arc. *Swoosh! Swoosh!* Twice more he swung the weapon, twice more he felt the futility of the endeavor in the *ping!* of humiliation he got with each forceful stroke.

After another hour had passed with no sight of Kerk, Callum at last allowed himself to fully embrace the growing realization that he'd made a total arse of himself last eve—and these past days as well. 'Twas a realization long in coming, but with an impact that reverberated through him as if the fine-honed edge of a battle axe had hewn through his body armor, directly into his soul, laying bare and open the man inside.

As he walked back to the keep, he made a plan. His yearly obligation to his uncle had been fulfilled. So, on the morrow, he would begin his long-delayed building of the manor house on the property he'd been ceded.

But first, he must find Kerk and apologize. Hell, 'twas time and past for him to apologize to his family as well.

* * *

The next day, Callum took a ride to his land with

two craftsmen in tow. He needed a project. He needed to focus. He needed something that would keep the demons at bay; that would keep his thoughts off of Branwenn; that would bury the ache in his heart; that would soothe his bruised pride. And, most of all, that would stop reminding him of his own humiliating behavior of late.

The short, hastily rehearsed speech he'd given Kerk—once he'd found him—had been one of the lowest moments in his life, but one of the best as well. For, even tho' Kerk had given him his usual smirk as Callum had spoken to him, he'd also said something afterward that had resounded in Callum's mind for hours afterward. He'd said, "'Tis good to at last see a man before me." Aye, Callum thought, 'twas time and past for *everyone*, including himself, to see such.

And the talk he'd had with his family later had been painful. But at least he'd made some amends and, thankfully, he'd regained at least a bit of his family's regard in the process. But not all. Nay, not by a mile. And 'twas clear that he wouldn't until he'd made some amends to Branwenn as well for the vicious way he'd treated her before her departure.

But he couldn't do that—not yet at least. For, tho' 'twas quite clear to him now that he'd been wrong for believing her capable of behaving like Lara, there was still the matter of her bargain with Gaiallard. A thing he still could not forgive.

And so, 'twas best that he move forward with his plan to build his manor. And then, when 'twas completed, he and his daughter would move into it and start life afresh. David would remain at the MacGregor holding to finish out his page training, but Callum would see him often during that time, as the manor was not far from there.

"Just there," Callum said, pointing to a snow-patched rise several yards away. "This, I thought, would be the best place to position the manor." He and the two craftsmen—the master stonemason and the ingeniator—reined in their horses and silently studied the landscape before them.

"Aye, 'tis large enough for what you have in mind, I believe" the ingeniator said. "But a measurement will tell us for sure."

"Barring a snow storm, we can begin on the morrow, if that pleases you," the master mason said.

Callum gave the man a quick nod. "Aye, good."

"What of the stone?"

A sharp feeling of desolation pierced Callum's heart. He'd ordered the stone the day after he and Branwenn had first made love, so set had he been upon wedding her and giving her a home. "It's set to arrive two days hence," he said, crossing his arms over his chest. Unfortunately, it didn't relieve the weight of the sadness there.

He spent the remainder of the day in further consultation with the two craftsmen. The men assured him that the main living quarters and kitchens could be finished, barring any long bouts of rain or snow, by *Bealltainn*. The garden walls, gates, and outer buildings would be completed much later.

Within a fortnight, the foundation and several layers

of stone for the outer walls of the manor were in place. In the meantime, Callum had found a master stone carver to carve the designs for the corbels, doors and window dressings.

He stood a bit away watching the disparate lot of well over 400 apprentices and journeymen under the guidance of the master mason working diligently to get the third tier of the outer wall placed. He'd approved the hire of as many men as the Ingeniator needed in order to assure a hasty, but well built, completion. And thus far, the work was going well. Mayhap, if the warmer winds continued to blow and melt the frost each day as it had these past days, he and his daughter could move in earlier than had been expected.

And that would be a welcome thing, indeed. For, the longer he remained at the MacGregor holding, the harder it became for him to hide his heartache from his family.

The stone carver walked up to him and held out a sheet of vellum with a lovely scrolling script dancing across its front. "Is this what you had in mind for the stone above the entry?"

Callum studied the document for a moment. *Tryamour Manor* the lettering said. The 'T' had a sea faery with a filet of seashells crowning her hair curled into its curving base, the 'M' had two more of the fey creatures settled under its arches. "Aye. 'Tis a good job you've done." He handed the sheet of vellum back to the craftsman. "When will you have it completed?"

The man rubbed his bristled chin with his fingers and thumb. "Well...it shouldn't take longer than a sennight, I'm thinking, after the slab of rose marble arrives on the morrow."

Callum nodded. "Fine then. My thanks."

The man dipped his head in farewell and walked back to his makeshift workshop near the stacks of stone.

* * *

CHAPTER 19

ALYSON WALKED OVER the rise, David and his hound Jasper following just behind her, and quickly nocked her arrow and let it fly.

"That's twelve!" David said, grinning. He hurried over to the downed rabbit, with Jasper grinning and slobbering as he bounded alongside him, and picked it up by its hind legs. After taking the arrow from its neck, he tied it with the other ones he carried. "'Tis all Cook asked us for then. We should return to the keep now, else he'll surely be vexed."

"Yes, let us make haste."

They hadn't taken more than five steps in the direction of the keep before Alyson heard their names being called. She darted a look at David, but 'twas clear the lad had heard naught.

Alyson, her brow furrowed in worry, looked in the direction of the voice, but stepped up her pace a bit as well. "Hurry David!" she said, taking the boy's hand in her own.

"Alyson! David!" Callum called again a bit louder, waving this time to try to get their attention. He wasn't on horseback, as he'd felt the need for a bit of exercise after standing for so long watching and supervising the building of his manor, so he led his steed by the reins instead.

When Alyson saw that it was Callum, she relaxed and halted, tugging David to a halt as well. "'Tis your foster father, David," she said. She should have known 'twould not have been anyone who'd do harm to them—that man was cold in the ground now, God be praised.

David grinned and waved. "Ho!" Lifting the string of rabbits, he said, "See you what a good hunter is the lady Alyson? Cook's sure to make a fine stew this eve!"

Callum glanced at the largesse and chuckled. As he now stood only a pace or two from the pair, he leaned forward and took the rabbits from David and held them up for his own inspection. "Aye, 'tis a good number." He turned and tied them to his saddle. Swiveling back around, and with a courtly bow, he said, "Lady Alyson, may I offer you a ride on my steed?"

Alyson giggled behind her hand, for she looked more like a lad in her feathered cap, tunic and hose than the lady he so gallantly called her. "Yes, sir knight, 'twould be a great pleasure, I'm sure," she answered with as courtly an air as she was able as she offered him her hand.

Callum grinned and took the proffered appendage before quickly settling her on his bay.

Jasper bounded across the glen, kicking up earth and snow as he traveled. "Hey!" David yelled and took off after the hound.

"Have you heard from your husband?" Callum asked after a moment.

"Nay," Alyson said on a sigh. She worried her bottom lip with her teeth. "I worry that something terrible has happened to him—Do you think he could have come to some harm?"

"Nay. Fear not, for 'tis more likely that his meeting with his cousin took longer than he expected. No doubt, he's on his way back even now."

Alyson was quiet for another moment, then, as if she could barely get the words past her lips, she said, "You...you know that 'twas *I* that sent the arrow into my brother, do you not?"

Callum shot her a quick glance to gauge her expression. "Aye," he answered a bit hesitantly, "but your secret is safe with us, Alyson. And, besides, 'twas my dirk that killed him, not your arrow. 'Twas not murder, 'twas an honorable death on the tournament field. With witnesses."

"Yes, but, 'tis truth, I *would* have murdered him, if you'd not gotten him first."

Callum sighed and patted her knee. "But you didn't. And that is all you must know, must think on. Understand?"

Alyson started chewing on her lip again. After a moment, she nodded. "All right." And then: "Will you tell him? My husband?"

Callum gave her a gentle smile, but there was pity in

it as well. "My lady. Do you not think that your husband will ken exactly who let fly that arrow the minute he learns the details of the joust?"

Alyson bowed her head and fiddled with one of the metal rings in the chained girdle around her middle—a small vanity, even if she was wearing lad's attire. She shrugged.

"Reys will feel exactly as we do, I'm sure, after his heart returns to a normal meter. He'll only be glad that no one who might want to exact punishment knows of the incident. And no one ever will. My stepfather made sure of that."

Callum searched the glen and relaxed when he saw David and Jasper further ahead, but still within earshot.

"Your lady and my brother...."

Callum's head whipped around. "Aye?"

Alyson sat forward. Leaning down a bit, she said earnestly, "They did not...*she* would not have."

Callum pressed his lips together into a grim line.

"She loves you too well. And the fr—"

"Aye, and 'tis for that reason that I believe she did."

"But—the ff—"

"Nay, I won't speak more. I've said too much as is. Leave the subject be, my lady, for, 'tis truth, you know naught of it."

Alyson shook her head, but remained silent. What a pity. 'Twas so clear that he grieved for his lady love as if she'd died instead of merely traveled to her brother's keep. If only he would forgive her, or believe her. With a sigh, she resettled on her mount. Mayhap, when Reys returned, *he* could make Callum listen.

* * *

Branwenn decided to take the long route to reach the cave chamber she and Bao had dwelled in for that short time nearly two years prior, the one which led her from another entrance to the cave and then through several long passages into the chamber. The access they'd used two summers before had involved climbing a pine tree, and she thought it not prudent to do such in her current condition.

She'd now been at the Maclean holding for nearly a moon and yet she'd still not broken the news of her childing state to her family. And 'twas time. For even her larger gowns were no longer hiding her rounding middle the way they had only a couple of sennights before. Her babe was growing faster than she'd expected. She'd been careful to rid the bucket of her stomach's purging each morn before the chamberlain saw it, and thankfully, those bouts had ended recently. But last eve, Grandmother Maclean had settled her hawk's-eye gaze directly on Branwenn's belly for what seemed an eternity as Branwenn scurried across the great hall to find her seat at the table. Thankfully, the older lady had given her naught more than a greeting and then proceeded to speak to her of things more mundane. However, she had also pressed her to drink a bit of milk and eat more of the kale that had been prepared, which only heightened Branwenn's unease that the lady was growing suspicious.

So, upon rising this morn, Branwenn had determined that she would tell her family this very day. But first, she wanted to spend a bit of time alone with her babe—far from curious eyes—to rehearse the words she'd say to them this eve. And the only place she could think of that would afford her that type of privacy was the cave chamber.

Besides, this place held such warm memories for her that she knew she'd also gain a bit of comfort as well from revisiting their old dwelling.

Once inside it, she quickly kindled a fire and settled next to its glowing warmth.

She was deep in her thoughts, preparing her speech, when she was startled from her reverie by the harsh sound of someone clearing his throat. She swung her head around and looked in the direction of the noise. "Bao! What do you here?"

Bao ambled toward her. "I followed you, wee one. What, pray, is this about?" He looked around the chamber, an expression of confused amusement on his countenance. "Why the affinity for this place? 'Tis cold, 'tis dank, 'tis stark. Hardly the cozy situation I expect my sister to enjoy."

As Bao settled down next to her, Branwenn shrugged and took a look around the place herself. "It holds fond memories for me, is all." She looked at him then. "When we dwelled here those few moons, 'twas just you and I, no one else, with no King's campaign to hie you off to who knew where, or for how long." She shrugged again. "I enjoyed that."

The look in Bao's eye became gentle as he reached out and took hold of her hand. "Aye, 'twas a special time." Straightening, he said again, "Now, tell me what is this about?"

***

First, Callum strode over to the place on the wall where his sword hung and gazed up at it for a moment, then, still restless but deciding against cleaning the thing again, as he'd done every morn and night these past sennights, he turned and strode over to sprawl in the chair next to his bedchamber's hearthfire. He was only down a second or two before he was up once more and marching toward one of his clothing trunks. The pain in his chest was almost too much to bear, so tight was the invisible band, that each breath he took was harsh and labored. His hands, loose at his sides, fisted and opened, fisted and opened, as he looked down at the lid to the wooden container.

After forcing air into his lungs twice more, he finally reached out and lifted the lid. The smell of wood and dust met him. His heart thudding against his ribs, he crouched down in front of the container and simply stared. After a moment, and with slightly sweating hands, he moved aside the filet and set of marriage rings he'd given Branwenn, which she'd left when she'd departed nearly a moon prior, and then rubbed his fingers over the now brown-red stains on the soft linen sheet beneath. *Branwenn.* His lips formed the name, but not a sound was uttered. He savored the feel of it on his tongue. Gloried in it.

But then his jaw hardened and, with a decisive movement, he slammed the trunk shut once more and pushed to his feet. He turned, strode to the door and left the chamber. 'Twas barely light out yet, but by the time he arrived at his property, the men would be at work. What he needed was exercise—and what better means could there be than to maneuver heavy stone?

***

"I think it best that we inform Callum of Branwenn's condition," Lady Maclean said that evening. She, Bao and Jesslyn were all seated in the solar, drinking mulled wine. It had begun to snow rather heavily earlier in the day and the air in the chamber was quite chilled and dank.

Jesslyn, who a bit over a year past had gone through a similar quandary, was possibly the only one among them that understood why Branwenn might want, and deserve, to keep those tidings from the father of her babe. "Can we not wait a bit longer? Surely, in a moon or two, Branwenn, herself, will want Callum to be informed." She gave her husband a pleading look. "Is it *such* a travesty to keep Callum in the dark a bit longer? After all, the marriage contracts are voided, and have been for nearly a moon."

Bao, who'd borne the unpleasant effects of Jesslyn's subterfuge, was fully standing behind Callum's rights as a father. "I'm sending a missive to him in a quarter hour's time."

"But, after what he did to her—"

"Aye," Lady Maclean said with a sigh, "I do worry a bit that the foolish lad will question the paternity"—she gave her grandson a steady look—"and I wouldn't put that poor lass through more heartache for any amount of relief to my conscience our telling Callum of the babe might render."

Bao was resolute. "I'm sending the missive. If he's

fool enough to reject his own bairn, so be it. At least he'll have no excuse other than himself for such an action."

* * *

Callum limped toward his hearth chair and nearly fell into the seat as he sat down. Every muscle in his body ached, and he now had so many cuts and scrapes on his hands and arms, he looked as if he had been in a wrestling match with a mother bear. But he also was filled with a sense of accomplishment, a thing he'd not felt to this degree since those first years of squire training when he'd entered all those tournaments and become ever more skilled at the craft. He'd soaked in a hot bath in the kitchens for nearly an hour, but his body was still giving him much protest. And he was expected to return to the great hall in a half hour's time to have the evening meal with his mother and Chalmers. He only hoped taking the stairs down would be easier than the climb up them had been.

The construction of the manor was going very well. In fact, the ingeniator was quite impressed by the design changes Callum had asked for. But, they'd had to stop work a bit earlier than usual due to a late afternoon snow storm, so some of those modifications would not be started until the morrow. Even still, the master mason and ingeniator were sure that they would be able to have the main quarters habitable by *Bealltainn*, as originally promised.

With that in mind, and his sore conscience no longer a thing he wanted to live with, Callum had come to a decision. At the morrow's dawn, he would leave for the Maclean holding.

'Twas time to speak to Branwenn.

***

Callum had taken the faster, but more treacherous route, which got him to the Maclean loch near the old Roman outpost close to the chimes of Nones a day and a half after his departure. Fortune had smiled on him, for warmer winds had begun to blow once more and most of the snow from the storm of two days past was now melted, making the traveling easier. But the ground was still damp, and his bay's hooves kicked up heather, turned winter-brown from the cold, and dark earth as well, as he steadily picked his way ever closer to his destination.

Perhaps 'twas some primitive need to heap additional punishment on his already bruised and battered soul, but he found himself nearing the ruin before he realized he'd turned in that direction. He hadn't seen the outpost since finding Robert there with Lara nearly a year ago.

The outpost was positioned on the edge of a crop of pine and juniper and as it came more fully into view, Callum pulled up short. Someone, no doubt Bao, had restored the thing. Where before, a portion of the limestone and mortar wall had been tumbled, now all four walls were set to rights. And a heather-thatched roof had been added. Curious.

Callum prodded his bay and headed toward the front door. There was now a stone post on which a horse's reins could be tied just outside it.

After tying his horse to the post, he headed to the

arched oak door and swept it open.

"*Eeeek!*" Branwenn whirled toward the noise, nearly jumping out of her skin at the same time. Her brows slammed together and she crossed her arms over her middle. "What are you doing here? Hie thee back to hell, devil."

Callum's eyes drank in the sight of her. Even if he'd wanted to, he couldn't find his voice to say a word in response to her. He took another step inside and closed the door behind him before resting his back against its hard surface and crossing his arms over his chest. He couldn't help it. He smiled.

Lord, but she was beautiful, and those crushed violet eyes he hadn't seen in much too long sent brilliant, warm ripples of joy through his being. Her hair had grown a bit since the last time he'd seen her, the ends were now several inches below her chin, and her cheeks were rose-blushed, her skin almost shimmery, like pearl dust. And, Godamercy, that pink, full mouth was already sending carnal missives through his bloodstream and into his groin. He couldn't catch his breath.

His eyes dropped lower still. She was covered up in a thick midnight-blue miniver-lined cloak. Suddenly an image of her standing in the sea cave, partially naked and nervous as hell, settled in his mind. What wouldn't he give to have her in that state once again, all his for the taking?

Branwenn's eyes darted left and right. The ruin was much too small, she thought, frantic now. Callum was only two paces away from her; so close she could feel the wind buffet of each heavy breath he took. She knew that look, and her body was already reacting to it. She had to get out of here. But how? He blocked the only exit. Why was he here? Had the messenger somehow made it to the MacGregor holding the same day as the missive was sent? Impossible. Why would he not speak? His silence was making her even more nervous. She would not do what her body was begging her to do. Not this time. Not ever again. He hated her. And she would never, ever, ever trust him again. Not ever.

But she needed more space between them. Now. She took a step back, but her foot twisted in the blanket she'd only just begun to lay out before Callum's entry. She stumbled and began to fall backwards. "Aaahhh!"

"Take care!" Callum leapt forward and grabbed her around the waist and shoulders, bringing her up against his chest and pelvis. "Oh, God. Branwenn." She was in his arms now, just where he wanted her and he didn't hesitate. He brought his palm up to cradle the back of her head and dipped his own, taking full possession of her lips before she could possibly know his intention. The rose scent of her, the sweet, fiery taste of her was all Callum could fix his mind upon. He deepened the kiss, running his tongue over her lower lip and then sucking it into his mouth before taking it between his teeth and nibbling. 'Twas not enough—not nearly enough. He fisted the hair at the back of her head in his hand and tugged, forcing her head back, and her mouth to open wider still. She mewled in reaction and it heated his blood even more. He was out of control. Out of his mind with need for her. He lifted her off the ground slightly and plunged into the dark, delicious recesses of her gorgeous mouth, showing her with his tongue what he wanted to do with his sex inside hers.

Branwenn felt as if her entire body was a raging, seething inferno of scorching flames. All reason was lost to the burning ache of need he could engender in her within mere seconds. He was dangerous. Dangerous to her heart. Dangerous to her senses. But she couldn't break free of the spell his body had over hers. Without realizing it, she lifted her arms and wrapped them tightly around his neck and shoulders, pressing her frame even closer into his own.

In the next second, they were on the ground, him with his tunic hiked up over his hips and his braies untied, revealing the extent of his need for her, and her with her own clothing rucked up at her hips and her legs wrapped high around his waist.

Callum didn't falter. He entered her quickly and deeply, afraid she'd change her mind and not allow him access. He swallowed her shocked moan as it reverberated against the back of his throat. He couldn't bear for her to say him nay. He needed it too badly. Needed her. Needed the ultimate pleasure, the absolute delight, the loving solace only her delicate, sweet body could bestow.

When he was sure that she would not push him away, he began to rock against her, with only the shallowest of movements at first, letting his slight rotating motion against her prepare her further. After another moment, he lifted his lips from hers and began trailing open-mouthed, nibbling kisses across her cheek and down her neck.

Branwenn felt her thighs begin to tremble. What was he doing to her? "Oh God! Oh God! *Callum!*" She held tight to his buttocks as he lifted himself up onto his palms and strained against her, each new thrust, deeper still. A wave of violent pleasure crashed through her and she splintered. His name burst from her lips once more on a long moan.

As the last eddy undulated through her, she opened her eyes at last. Callum was drenched in sweat, his face flushed a deep red, and his eyes and jaw tightly shut. He was close to completion. He would leave her soon. Still dizzy from her own release, it took her a moment to hear the words he was mumbling feverishly through his teeth with each hard plunge he made into her. "*I'm sorry, I'm sorry, I'm sorry,*" he said over and over again and then he suddenly reared back, lifted her calves over his forearms, held her hips steady, and yelled out "*I love you, Branwenn!*" as he ejaculated inside her with fast, forceful thrusts. For the first time.

Callum collapsed forward and then rolled onto his back next to Branwenn. Did he still live? If he'd known how acutely pleasurable would be the climax inside her, he'd never have been able to wait this long to do it. He opened one eye a crack and looked at his love. She was no doubt in shock that he'd done the deed when they were no longer legally wed. But that could be easily rectified. In fact, he saw no reason why they couldn't get their vows blessed this very afternoon. The contracts could be signed and sealed later, surely. Everyone already knew what the terms would be, as they'd gone through that before.

And besides, he really didn't care any longer what his clan thought about their union; whether his family approved or disapproved of what he did. In fact, he didn't care about anything except building a life with Branwenn and their bairns, as they'd planned. "We can have the priest bless our vows this eve and then we can go back home on the morrow—or, would you prefer to stay here awhile longer? It matters not to me, as the living quarters in our manor won't be completed until the time of *Bealltainn*." She wasn't looking at him. Her eyes were focused on the rafters above their heads.

"We're not getting wed, Callum." She looked at him. "This was a mistake, which I won't ever let happen again." She sighed and sat up, pushing her cloak and gown down over her legs as she brought her knees up and wrapped her arms around them. She turned her head and looked back down at him. "Go home. It's over between us."

His brows slammed together and he rolled to his side, then raised up on his elbow. "Impossible. You could even now have my babe growing in your belly. We *must* wed."

Branwenn turned her face away. 'Twas so quiet inside the ruin in those moments before she spoke that they could hear each other breathe. "You have no worries on that score for, you see, I've a babe there already."

Callum's heart did a somersault before plunging into his stomach. He bolted upright and reached around, taking her shoulders in his hands and twisting her about to face him. "Whose? The Norman's?"

He looked deeply into her eyes, watching as the black centers expanded and filled most of the space where, just a moment prior, the dark, bruised purple had been, before they swiftly contracted to a mere black pinprick in a sea of purple velvet. There was sadness there as well. "'Tis mine," she said at last with a nod.

He took that as an affirmative. "I care not, Branwenn, truly, that it be the Norman's. I understand that 'twas your love for me that made you waver in your vows to me, and 'tis all right." He took a deep breath and let it out slowly. "Come home with me. We'll wed. I'll be father to the babe, just as I've done Lara's—*my*—daughter Laire." Callum released his grip on her shoulders, but settled his palm over the top of the hand that she had splayed on the ground for support at her side.

Branwenn shook her head. "It cannot—it *will* not—be, Callum. 'Tis time for you to go forward with the life you've chosen, and allow me to do the same." Her voice cracked but she managed to finish, though her throat ached and the words nearly choked her. "We...*us*..." Her eyes misted and she gritted her teeth to keep the tears at bay, to keep her jaw from trembling, her face from crumpling with grief. She took in a shaky breath. "We were not meant to be. Let go, as I have. 'Tis for the best." She gave him a watery smile. "And, after all, we are still friends—and family as well!"

'Twas too much for Callum. He wouldn't give up on her, on them, but this new twist—she was with child!—was something he needed a bit of time to come to terms with himself. So, he decided not to press her further; to instead allow her to believe that they would part this day and that would be the end of it for them. But he knew it would not, it could not, be so.

He curled his fingers around her hand and lifted it to his lips. After brushing a brief, warm kiss upon its back, he said, "May I offer you a ride to your brother's holding at least?"

She was awash in relief. And despair. But her smile never wavered as she shook her head and answered, "Nay. I think it best if they do not see us together."

He looked around, suddenly realizing that they were sitting on a blanket. "What were you about in here, anyway, *fey Mai?*"

Branwenn's heart twisted in her chest at the term of endearment he'd adopted for her so many moons ago now. She shrugged. "Bao told me that he'd had this ruin renovated, and I was curious to see it, so I thought to use it as a private place for me to rest awhile and enjoy sewing my babe's clothes."

Callum's eyebrows lifted. He nodded his head as he continued to gaze about, studying the small enclosed room, and finally noticing the satchel in the corner with a bit of white linen emerging from the opening. "Hmm. I see." He settled his gaze upon her once more. "Does my grandmother know of your condition—does Bao?"

"Aye. I told them of it a few days past."

"And what say they? Do they believe 'tis mine?"

She couldn't meet his eyes. She dipped her head and studied a bunch in the woolen blanket beneath her. "Aye. I believe they do. They...sent a missive to you a couple of days ago. I suppose you and the messenger passed each other without realizing."

"I took a shorter route; we no doubt were never even near each other as we traveled." Callum could see that Branwenn wanted him to leave. Winning her back was going to take some planning, and, if he were honest with himself, he needed a bit of time by himself to consider the role he would play in her babe's life.

There had been, at first, a glimmer of hope within him that the babe was his, but with Branwenn's confirmation that 'twas the Norman's, he let go of that desirable notion. After all, he and Branwenn had not lain together for quite some time—excepting the night of their wedding—and even so, he'd always been careful to do what he must in order that she wouldn't conceive. But the Norman had said that he'd taken her more than once that day. And there was no doubt in Callum's mind that the man had not had the decency to withdraw before he spilled his seed inside her.

Aye, he needed time to think and to scheme. "I should leave. There's an inn about an hour and half ride from here that I can stay at for the night, but if I wait too long, 'twill be full." He rose to his feet and walked toward the door. Just as he was about to leave, he turned back and said, "Take care, Branwenn." And then he turned and walked out, closing the door behind him and not looking back until he was once more on his bay's back and a good distance away. It wouldn't be easy, but he was determined to win her. And this time—aye, he'd learned his lesson well—this time, he'd *never* let her go.

* * *

CHAPTER 20

BRANWENN SMILED AS she trod through the brightly blooming flowers of purple, yellow and white toward the Roman outpost she'd made her private sanctuary these past moons. The sun was high in the sky and the heat from its rays made each color seem even more vivid, warming her skin as well. There was a sweetness in the air that she hadn't smelled in far too long, it seemed. But the scent of winter snow was long gone now, and in its place, the smell of summer sunshine now reigned.

As she watched, a small brown butterfly with yellow spots on its wings flitted about in front of her, from one blossom to the next, in search of a meal. Mayhap, 'twas a wee faery sprite keeping company with her, Branwenn thought, and then giggled at the notion.

She wondered what the 'wee folk' had left her since her last visit. It had been five moons and five days since she'd met Callum in the ruin, but not since she'd seen him last. Tho' he surely did not ken that she knew he spied upon her while she was there, 'twas plain who was leaving her gifts.

The first time had been some three sennights from that day last winter. The weather had been harsh, she remembered. So harsh, in fact, that she had almost turned back halfway to the outpost. But some inner need to find a bit of solace from her aching heart had driven her onward. And when she'd arrived, she'd found a lamp, lit for warmth and light, and in the corner, a beautifully carved pine chest. Resting upon its rounded top lay a vellum scroll with a red silken ribbon twining its middle. When she'd unfurled it, another red silken ribbon had fallen out that tied two keys together which she instantly recognized: They were the keys to the heart locks that closed off the keep from the sea cave. Then, as she'd gazed upon the beautifully illuminated lettering on the vellum, she'd been charmed. For faeries idly sprawled upon the letters there. "Tryamour Manor" it said.

Then, when she'd opened the lid to the cask, she'd found it full of the best quality linen, wool, and velvet, with some thirty spools each of brightly colored silk and cotton thread as well. And resting on top, an unusual, finely made silver needle, a lovely pair of sharply-honed scissors, and three perfectly sized copper thimbles.

She'd looked for him then, but to no avail. But each fortnight after, on the same day, she found another gift. Once, there had been a small cask of seashells and a string of pearls. Another time there had been a baby's rattle and a small cradle with a thin down mattress tucked inside. Then, there had been the banquet, a bounty of her favorite foods. That had been her favorite, after the cradle and rattle.

The same dull ache that had been plaguing her since early this morn started again, like a band around her middle and lower back. She stopped and rested for a moment, trying to stretch a bit to relieve the pressure. Grandmother Maclean was sure 'twas a sign that the babe was coming, and she'd told her not to wander far from the keep, but Branwenn had needed the exercise. And besides, it had taken hours and hours for Maryn to have her babe, so she surely had time to see what Callum had brought for her this time. She had to admit, he was wearing down her defenses against him with his devotion and his steady wooing of her. And, he'd seemed different the last time they'd been together, swearing that he didn't care that she carried Gaiallard's babe. He'd even told her that he would *raise* the babe as his own!

Branwenn sighed and bit her lip as she resumed her trek to the ruin. And though it angered her still that he thought she'd allowed the horrid man to bed her, it had, after she'd had time to think upon it, soothed her that he no longer hated her, thought her a whore. 'Twas in those times of quiet remembrance, that she would contemplate wedding him again, as he wanted.

But then she'd recall how quickly he could change, could rip her heart out and trample it under his feet, could coldly take away all he'd freely given. So, once again, she'd walk away, back to her brother's keep. Her heart safe, but her soul desolated.

As she came through a stand of pines into the small clearing around the outpost, she stopped and gazed at the scene before her. A large wild rose bush was now planted by the entry and full of pink, fragrant blooms. And at its feet, violets swayed and dipped their purple-velvet crowns. 'Twas the gift he'd given her a fortnight ago. As she resumed her step, she began to hum a familiar tune, one she'd heard Callum sing to Laire a few times, as she pushed wide the door to the ruin and stepped inside. "Oh, Callum!" she cried, hurrying, as best she could with her awkward gate, over to stand by the birth chair, intricately carved and painted with wee sea faeries, shells, and roses intertwined with violets.

All of a sudden, a great wave of fluid flushed from inside her womb, down her legs and onto her feet. "*Godamercy!*" Branwenn lifted her now drenched skirts with trembling, nerveless hands and waddled to the door. She was having her babe! She could feel a very strong contraction begin as she flung the door open and stumbled outside the cottage. "*Callum! Ohmygod! Callum, the babe!*" she yelled as loudly as she could. Then, unable to keep herself upright any longer by herself, she held tight to the doorframe and doubled over.

* * *

Callum's heart leapt into his throat. In the next second, he was on his bay and kneeing it into a hard gallop, forcing it to leap over logs and debris. The animal nearly lost its balance when it slid in some muddy, soft soil by the side of the loch, but with some quick maneuvering, Callum and the horse were once again headed in the direction of the ruin.

The babe was early. By at least two moons. This wasn't good. And surprisingly, the thought of losing the babe broke his heart. He'd grown accustomed over the past sennights of thinking of it as his own; watching Branwenn's body grow and gently harbor the wee one under her heart had softened his own.

At the door of the building, he quickly tied the reins to the post. "I'm here," he said, lifting Branwenn into his arms and then taking two steps inside so he could settle her upon the blanket as best he could.

Branwenn still hadn't opened her eyes. Her brows were furrowed, her face, flushed, and her skin was drenched. She was panting and whimpering as she held her belly. "The babe's coming, I can feel it!" she said suddenly. She opened her eyes and lifted up a bit, straining forward. "Oh God, Oh God! It hurts!"

Callum hadn't been allowed in the childbed chamber when Lara had delivered their daughter, so he was frantic now. He had no knowledge of what must be done, what he could do to help her. A thought struck, and 'twas not a good one: What if he lost her as well? Nay. Remain calm. 'Twas the only way. He took a deep breath and looked around. The birth chair! Praise be to heaven! "Branwenn, I must try and get you out of these soaked clothes, I think, for they surely will only get in the way in a moment."

Branwenn's eyes were tightly clamped shut once more, as were her teeth. She gave him a short nod.

Callum quickly unlaced the gown she wore. Thankfully, the laces ran down the side and not the back. 'Twas a struggle, but he was at last able to lift it from under her prone body and up over her head. Luckily, the chemise lifted off with the gown, leaving Branwenn completely bare. He was stunned momentarily by the beauty of her fertile form, but when she threw her head back and cried out, he put his arm behind her back, saying, "I think we should get you in that birth chair. I believe it aids the mother to deliver her babe, somehow. At least, 'twas what the craftsman told me when I gave him coin to carve it."

She opened her eyes and looked at him. "Will you look first to see if my babe is coming out of my womb? It feels like she is."

Callum nodded and she settled back on her elbows, opening her legs. "Do you see her?"

For the first time, Callum noticed the small amount of blood and nearly swooned from the dread it caused him. Was it natural, common? *Oh, Holy Father*, he prayed, *I beg you, let it be common!* Then he realized he was looking at the crown of a very dark-haired head. "Aye! The babe's starting to push out. I've got to get you to the chair, love, now!"

He put one arm behind her back and the other under her knees and shot to his feet. In a matter of only a minute, she was settled on the stool and bearing down once more. "Oh, God! My womb's tightening up again! Here she comes, Callum, take hold of her!"

Callum thrust his arms under the opening and his daughter dropped into them. Just as quickly, and as beautifully, as that. As he reverently brought her up toward his face so he could see her more clearly,

Branwenn said, "Grandmother Maclean said something about clearing the babe's mouth and nose and then holding her and rubbing her back until she cries. Make haste!"

Callum placed his sticky daughter, still attached to her mother, up to his chest. The breadth of her back was half the size of his hand span. He began to rub her back, as Branwenn had told him to do. *Oh, God. Please don't die.*

She let out a lusty cry, and continued to do so as Callum and Branwenn looked at each other in joyful amazement.

"I think you have to cut the cord now. But Grandmother Maclean said she always douses her scissors with spirits before she uses them, for luck. 'Tis a Maclean tradition."

Callum thought quickly. "I have some *uisge beatha* in my satchel. Here, take her," he said, leaning forward and handing her the babe. Then he was out the door. Before Branwenn had time to say more than a few words to her daughter, who was now quiet again, he was back inside and rustling through the sewing cask for her scissors. He strode over to them and efficiently cut the cord and tied it off—that much he knew to do, as he'd seen the result of such after Laire's birth.

Branwenn felt her womb tighten. "Oh, Lord! I forgot. Grandmother Maclean said to expect the sack attached to the cord to flush from my womb once the babe arrived." She handed her daughter to Callum and sat forward to relieve the pressure. In a moment, the deed was done and Branwenn was beginning to feel a deep lethargy overtake her.

Callum helped her to rise and settled her on the blanket. "I need to clean the two of you up a bit. Do you mind if I use the *uisge beatha*? 'Tis all that I have."

Branwenn would have laughed if she'd had the energy. Instead, she smiled and said, "You're sure to make the lass thirst for the stuff for all her days, but, aye, 'twill be fine to do so."

He strode over to the sewing cask once more and lifted out a fine piece of linen. After dousing it in the liquor, he quickly wiped the babe clean and then settled her back on Branwenn's bosom. The babe found her nipple as quickly, and ravenously, as he did. Callum laughed, but thought better of saying his thoughts aloud.

Branwenn felt dozy. But excited as well. Her babe was so beautiful. She had all her fingers, and all her toes. Did she have the mark? She opened her wee legs and looked. Aye, there it was. And 'twas beautiful. Gorgeous. Not ugly at all.

Branwenn grinned down at her hungry bairn. 'Twas such a strange and glorious feeling, nursing her babe. And she looked so much like Callum when he was at the same pursuit. She could feel the milk being drawn from her breast, but she wanted to make sure. 'Twas a bit of a struggle, for the lass had a powerful hold on it, but she at last freed the nipple from her daughter's mouth long enough to test that enough was coming out before offering it up to her babe once more.

As Branwenn nursed their daughter, Callum washed clean her thighs and, as lightly as he could, dabbed the remnants of the childbed from the outer flesh of her womb. "Praise be, there's no tearing." He lifted his gaze to her countenance. "Are you well? Do you hurt?"

Branwenn met his gaze and smiled. "Aye...and Nay, I feel wonderful, in fact. Glorious." Her babe made a loud sucking noise and they both laughed. Branwenn turned her attention back on her babe once more.

After a few minutes, she felt Callum settle next to her on the blanket and looked up. He wasn't looking at her. Nay, he was looking at their daughter—and he had the same expression now that he had had that day so many moons before when he'd held Laire in his arms, and she'd realized she loved him. Lord, but he was beautiful. Lovely and strong, gentle and generous, was he.

"All right. I'll wed you."

Callum's eyes shot up to her own and he grinned like an idiot. "Praise be. I'm a lucky man." He leaned forward and kissed her. Not with passion—although, she certainly could feel the heat hidden deep in the embrace—but with awe. And love.

* * *

CHAPTER 21

THE MACGREGOR CHAPEL was a silent, reverent place that July morn as Callum and Branwenn once again rested on bended knee at the altar awaiting the priest. Their daughter—Mai, they'd named her—would be baptized afterward as well, as they'd waited until Branwenn was allowed back inside the church after childbed in order that she, too, could be part of the baptismal services. Maryn sat holding their daughter on the front bench behind them, and all their other family, save one—Reys—were there as well.

Alyson had only had one missive from him all these moons, for he was caught up in a bloody campaign with his liege lord, Prince Llywelyn, and did not know when he might return to retrieve his young bride.

He had confirmed to them, however, that the contract Gaiallard had extolled as genuine was a forgery, which eased everyone's mind that there might be further problems coming to bear from King John regarding Branwenn.

The priest shuffled from behind the screen just then and had only taken two steps toward the couple when the door swung open behind them.

"Blood of Chr—"

"Callum!" Branwenn elbowed him in the ribs, but still turned to see who was interrupting the ceremony.

"My pardon," Callum said irritably as he turned toward the opened door as well. "But, truly, NOT AGAIN!"

Alyson jumped to her feet. "Reys, at last!" She scurried up the aisle and stopped short just in front of him. She smiled and dipped a quick courtesy. "Husband," she said.

Reys smiled and took hold of her hand and gave it a light squeeze before lifting it to his lips and brushing a soft kiss over the top. "Wife."

Alyson blushed. "Come, you must settle next to me on the bench, for the priest is just about to bless Callum and Branwenn's vows. Make haste."

After Reys and Alyson had taken their places on the bench, the priest began the ceremony, first asking Callum and then Branwenn to swear to the affirmative regarding each one's legal age to wed, that each had the consent of their family, that they were not within the forbidden degree of consanguinity, and finally, that each of them freely consented to the marriage.

Then, after the priest gave a short lecture regarding mutual faithfulness, the importance of keeping the peace in the home, and the need to educate their bairns in the ways of the Church, he asked Callum for the ring and blessed it. After which, Callum took the double ring set passed down to him from his grandmother and slipped the set in turn on each of three fingers of Branwenn's left hand, saying, "In the Name of the Father, and of the Son, and of the Holy Ghost." At last, he fitted them on her third finger, saying, "With these rings I thee wed."

"You may both rise now," the priest said. He bestowed the Kiss of Peace on Callum, and Callum in turn settled it on Branwenn's lips, tho' his held much more heat than had the priest's.

The couple turned, grinning merrily, and, even though 'twas strictly forbidden, every single member of the family stood up and cheered.

Thankfully, the priest only shook his head and smiled. He, after all, was well aware of just how much these two had endured to at last get to this moment.

* * *

"Lady Maclean, she's such a tiny thing!" Alyson said as she gently, tho' a bit awkwardly, held Mai in her arms the next dawn. The newlyweds had traveled to their new manor for the night and had left their young ones in the care of their family until later in the day. Alyson looked up at the older woman. "Is it common for babe's to be so small?"

Lady Maclean came up to stand behind Alyson's shoulder and gaze down at her newest great-grandchild. As she reached around and softly stroked her finger over the rise of the babe's cherub cheek, she replied, "Aye, 'tis quite common for lasses as wee as our Branwenn to have daughters as small as they. But worry not, Alyson, the babe is hearty and hale." She looked up at Alyson and grinned. "As her lusty cries and bobbing legs and fists have shown us."

Reys, standing a bit away from the ladies and leaning against the wall near the window, studied his young wife as she held his niece in her arms. 'Twas a sight he hadn't known he craved seeing until this moment and it stunned him. He wasn't ready—she wasn't ready—for such intimacy yet. It had only been a bit over a year since his first wife and daughters had perished in that terrible fire and, even now, his heart ached for them.

And Alyson. The poor girl still couldn't bear to be touched by him in any way that could possibly be construed as visceral.

'Twas good, he supposed, that his liege was calling him to duty so soon again. 'Twould give both of them time to heal, to prepare themselves for that part of their marriage. And Alyson, tho' disappointed that he would leave her again so soon, was not completely displeased with the notion of staying for a time with the nuns at the convent near her family's home in Normandy. They were to hie there, in fact, directly from here on the morrow.

* * *

It was not until Reys and Alyson were ready to depart from their short visit to Tryamour Manor the next day to continue on their journey that the mystery of Gaiallard's knowledge of the birthmark and freckle was at last revealed to Branwenn—with her husband standing directly beside her.

In the past days, Reys had heard the tale of

Gaiallard's final coup against the couple and was determined to set all to rights with the truth. "Your daughter is beautiful, Branwenn," he said as he tucked a woven sack full of cheese and a portion of mutton into his satchel for their meal later. "Does she sport the mark of the wizard, as most of our father's family has done since the time of Arthur?"

Branwenn flashed a look at Callum before settling her astonished gaze back on her brother. "Aye, she does. As do I, but—Are you saying that *you* sport the mark as well?"

Reys chuckled. "Yes. And if you'd stayed in Cambria, you would have realized 'tis quite a famous tale in the land. Most of the natives believe us to have magic, in fact. But, that, I can promise you, is not truth. There is no magic in our line." A thing he had dearly desired to have that long ago day on the road when his mother had been taken from him forever.

Alyson blinked at the pair. "Magic? Mark?"

Reys turned to his wife and explained: "'Tis an ancient tale, but most in our family sport a birthmark on our thigh. 'Tis rumored to be a wizard's mark." He held his hand out and waited, curious, but patient, to see if she would place hers inside it. She did—tho' hesitantly—and he continued, "Both my daughters had the mark and, I should warn you, there is every chance that ours—yours and mine—will show the same."

Callum silently took hold of his wife's hand and placed it over his heart. He looked at her and she turned to look at him as well. No words were spoken, but in the look, much understanding passed between them. His was of grieved remorse and hers was filled with gentle forgiveness.

"I wonder," Branwenn said at last, turning her gaze once more on Reys. "Gaiallard..." She cleared her throat. "Does the tale also include a freckle, mayhap?"

"If 'tis a certain freckle upon yourself of which you speak," Alyson interjected, "Gaiallard was told of it by the lady's maid who helped us dress each eve. He came into my chamber while she was adorning my hair and they spoke of it. He was not pleased to find out that you had such a blemish."

Callum growled low in his throat.

Alyson looked at Callum. "I did try to tell you about it that day in the glen—remember? But you would not allow me to do so." She dropped her hand from Reys's and stepped toward Branwenn. "Gaiallard and the maid were lovers, I believe," she whispered.

Callum put his arm around Branwenn's shoulder. "I was such a fool to listen to that bastard Norm—pardon, Alyson—cur dog."

Reys grasped Callum's shoulder and gave it a shake. "It all ended well. Finally," he reminded.

Callum's mouth tightened in a grim line, but he nodded. "Aye. Finally. Praise be."

Reys turned and helped Alyson mount her palfrey. "We must make haste, if we are going to arrive at the inn by sunset." He turned back to Branwenn and opened his arms to her.

She stepped into his embrace and held tight. "When ever are we to see you again?"

"I know not, for our princely cousin is fighting his

kin and the marcher lords for dominion in Cambria. 'Tis no secret that he wants to be king of all Pura Wallia."

"Take care and send us word of how you fare." She looked up at Alyson. "And you as well."

Alyson smiled and gave a brief nod of consent.

Reys mounted his steed and the two of them turned and left through the courtyard gate.

Callum and Branwenn stood silently watching their departure. When the two travelers were out of earshot, Callum turned his wife toward the rose garden. "Come, I've something to show you." They hadn't gone more than three paces forward when Callum suddenly halted and stood stock-still, his eyes wide with wonder. He turned and placed his hands on top of her shoulders. "Mai is *mine*! Yours and mine!"

Branwenn grinned. "I was wondering when you were going to figure that out." She poked him in the ribs. "It took you long enough!"

"Why didn't you tell me? That day in the ruin? All this time, I've worried the babe was born too soon."

Branwenn shrugged a bit sheepishly and dipped her head. Her gaze settled on the center of his chest. "I suppose 'twas just a wee bit of vengeance on my part." She forced her eyes up to his. "The things you said to me in those hours after the joust—what you did! You broke my heart, Callum." She turned and continued walking toward the garden. "Besides, I had every intention of telling you on the lass's first birthday."

Callum jogged to catch up. "Her first *birthday*! You would have left me in the dark that long?"

Highland Magic

She grinned at him, just to let him know she was jesting. "Aye, for I know how you mighty warriors do love to impress your ladies with your sharp wit—I simply wanted to give you enough time to figure out the puzzle on your own."

"For that, my dear, I should have the mason take back the gift I had him make for you."

Branwenn's eyes widened and there was a definite spark of glee in them now. "What gift do you give me this time?" She didn't wait for his response. Instead, she hiked up her skirts and jogged through the arched doorway of the garden—the only portion of the wall that had been finished thus far. She skidded to a halt just inside the entry. "*Callum!* 'Tis the most beautiful thing I've ever seen!"

'Twas a fountain. Set on a large circular base, a mermaid and two young ones, each having the look of Branwenn, Mai or Laire, were basking on a rock with waves crashing all about them. The one that looked like Branwenn held up a large sea shell, and from it bubbled forth frothy, burbling water.

She looked at him, grinning. "The mason can't have it back. 'Tis mine." She threw herself into his arms and wrapped herself around him like a vise, attacking his mouth with her own, and not giving him even a second to reply. A few long, hot, steamy moments later, she lifted her head. "Standing up or lying down?" she asked, her voice husky with need.

Callum's breathing was harsh. "Both."

She nodded and kissed him again. After a moment, she lifted her head once more and said anxiously, "I'm sorry I didn't tell you sooner, but I still had some doubt that you'd believe me."

"How can I blame you for feeling such? And I'm sorry, too. For everything. I love you."

"Good. Me too."

Callum moved his palm to the back of her head and pressed down, groaning low in his throat as he took possession of her lips, ripping at the ties to his braies at the same time.

They stayed in the garden the remainder of the morning. Fortunately, no one disturbed them.

* * *

EPILOGUE
The Maclean Fortress
Hogmanay, 1206

"ANOTHER YEAR GONE! Alas, where does the time go?" Lady Maclean said, shaking her head as she stood with Maryn's father, Laird Lachlan Donald and his new bride, Marguerite de Bussey watching the flames lick higher and higher up the dried wood of the bonfire.

Laird Donald took hold of his lady's hand and brought it up to his lips. "Aye, but this year's been a wondrous one," he said, gazing lovingly into his bride's eyes.

Laird Donald, always a rather portly, agreeable sort, had noticeably added a pound or two since last Lady Maclean had seen him. And no wonder! For 'twas rumored the lady he wed had been chef to a Frankish duke at one time. And all who knew the laird were fondly aware of his healthy appetite. Aye, 'twas a good match.

Branwenn ran up to them laughing, her cheeks hectic with color, with Callum close behind and in much the same state. When she stopped short in an effort not to plow into Marguerite, Callum grabbed her up and twirled her around. "Now I've got you, my wee faery sprite!"

Branwenn shrieked. "Put me down! I'm growing dizzy."

The older folk chuckled at the young couple's antics.

Bao and Jesslyn strolled up. Jesslyn settled her hand over the small bump that was a new babe growing in her belly. "Just seeing the two of them twirling about in such a way unsettles my stomach." She covered her eyes with her hand. "Nay, I cannot watch!"

Callum released his prize, setting her down on her feet. But grabbed her again when she stumbled into his arms. Then he kissed her.

Daniel and Maryn came from around the other side of the bonfire and when he saw Callum mauling his wee sister, he cleared his throat, loudly.

Callum cocked an eye open and grinned, but continued kissing Branwenn another second, just to irritate his cousin.

Just as he broke the kiss at last, a young guard, with the devil in his eyes, by the name of Angus, and one that Callum knew to be a knave with the lasses, trotted up to Branwenn and took her hand. "Pray, dance with me again, as you have done these past two annals." He glanced at Callum. "I'm sure your husband will bear the separation well enough."

Branwenn tugged her hand from Angus's and swung her gaze to Callum's, dread clear in her eyes. "Nay, my thanks Angus, but I shall stay by my husband's side, I think."

Callum's heart ached at the look. Still she feared his swift reprisal, his unreasoned jealousy. After this long. He lifted his fingers to her cheek and brushed a quick kiss over her lips before saying, "Nay, go, my love. You enjoy the dance so well, and you know 'tis not my favorite pastime. I shall be here upon your return." He raised his gaze to Angus. "Dance at least three with her, will you old friend?" He couldn't help sending him a wee glare of warning, however, even still, which Angus acknowledged with a small nod and an up-tip of one side of his mouth.

Daniel heard the exchange and stepped up beside Callum, following his cousin's line of vision as he watched Branwenn and the young guard become part of the dancing throng. "'Tis pleased I am to see you've learned to trust our Branwenn's heart is true."

Callum nodded. "Aye, she's no Lara."

Daniel clapped him on the back and walked the couple of steps back to where his wife was standing with Jesslyn and Bao.

"Are you not feeling well?" Maryn asked Jesslyn. She, herself, was nearing her delivery day. 'Twould be by *Uphalieday* she was sure.

"Aye," Jesslyn answered. "Tho' my stomach is churning a bit."

Maryn lifted her gaze to her husband. "Daniel, do you have a bit of ginger in your healer's box that Jesslyn might take to ease her belly?"

Daniel glanced at Jesslyn and nodded. "I'll just go up to our chamber and get it for you." He turned and strode in that direction.

Callum was surprised—and pleased more than he was willing to admit—when Branwenn rushed back to his side after only one round with Angus. Her eyes, bright with merriment, her face flushed with the heat of the dance, and her smile glowing, she flew into his arms and hugged him tight. "My thanks, husband, but 'tis truth, I prefer to dance with *you!*"

Callum took hold of Branwenn's hand and pulled her further into the darkness of the bailey. When they'd gone far enough away from the others so that they could no longer hear their conversation, he pulled her into his arms once more and kissed her. After a long moment, he lifted his lips a fraction and said, "Let's make another babe soon, all right?"

"All right."

"Mayhap by the time of Laire's second birthday?" They'd been using the seed wool and paste these past two moons since Branwenn's flowering began again that the old woman in the cot gave them. They had been assured it would work better than the previous method Callum had employed to prevent conception. 'Twas against the Church's teaching, but he was pragmatic. 'Twas not safe for his wife to conceive so soon after childbed, and he was damned if he'd give up their right to enjoy each other in the meantime. And from the looks of things, his cousins must be of the same mind.

"Aye."

"Good. And this time I shall enjoy watching you grow round with my child. I missed so much of that with Mai."

"Aye, but you helped birth her! Surely, that was enough of a recompense for whatever lack you felt prior."

Callum grinned. "Aye, and now that I know how easily you shoot them out, I shall be part of that process from now on."

Branwenn snuggled closer into Callum's embrace. "Have you thought more of reconsidering the MacGregor chieftainship? Chalmers seems set on you taking it after him. Why ever did you decline it?"

Callum sighed. "Aye, I've thought on it." He tipped her chin up and studied her face a moment before saying, "Last year, after I'd spurned you, I spurned the lairdship as well. I thought, if I start afresh, I could rid myself of the ache of losing you. 'Twas when I started building the manor. But I soon found that even in that, you were there. Always in my thoughts, never far away." He cradled her face in his palm and stroked the rise of her cheek with the pad of his thumb. "'Twas not until I at last let go of all my old beliefs, my old feelings, that I finally could see with clearer sight. And now that our manor is finished, and the grounds and outer buildings are well underway—now that I have you, my love, and our bairns as well—I am able to contemplate once more doing this thing; leading these men as my stepfather believes I am able to do. Am the best man to do so, in fact."

"Hey! Branwenn, Callum!" Alleck called.

The couple turned in the direction of the lad's voice. He'd grown by a good two or more inches since the last time Callum had seen him, and he'd gained a bit of weight as well. Clearly, he was enjoying paging at the Donald holding. He and David—with Jasper at his heels—each had hold of one of their cousin's hands. David had hold of Nora's, Maryn and Daniel's firstborn, and Alleck had hold of Bao Junior's. Coming up behind, the MacGregor nurse held Mai in her arms and had Laire's hand clasped in her own.

"Is it that time already?" Branwenn asked the nurse.

"Aye, m'lady. 'Tis nearing the chimes of midnight."

"I wonder who shall be our first footer this year." Branwenn sighed, reminded of two years past when 'twas her brother-germane, Reys, who'd stepped across their threshold and changed Branwenn's life for evermore. There was little chance it would be him again this year, however, for he was truly entrenched now in a campaign with their cousin. It could be years before she saw him again.

Laire toddled over to Callum and lifted her pudgy arms, in a bid to be picked up. Callum gladly complied, giving her a loud *smack*ing kiss on the cheek as well. Laire giggled and kissed him back the same way, before resting her head on his shoulder and snuggling against his chest.

The nurse came up to stand next to her mistress and Branwenn held out her arms in order to take Mai for awhile. Her daughter was clearly groggy. "She's been fed then?"

"Aye, and ready she is for sleep. But I knew you wanted her out here with you for the end of the festivities."

Just then the chimes began to ring and everyone walked toward the bonfire. The minstrels were playing a lively tune and some of the young folk still twirled about, dancing and enjoying the music.

Branwenn was filled with such joy, such peace, as she looked about her and saw every member of her foster family—her heart's true family—standing close by.

She looked over at Bao and Daniel, who stood next to each other, and caught their eye. 'Twas clear, from their expressions, they were in much the same state of mind as she. For their journey to this place, this here and now, had not been an easy one. Each one of them had fought hard to get here, had struggled, like the intrepid, vigorous roots of some ancient oak to find purchase in what at first had seemed fallow, fruitless soil. But now, aye, now they knew that they were here to stay, that the family, the love, they'd found would keep them nourished, would make them grow, would keep them in one place. In the bosom of the family whose one evil member had been the catalyst which had ultimately brought them all home.

Callum leaned down and whispered in her ear, "Look you, who's come."

She turned her damp eyes in the direction Callum indicated. "Reys! Alyson! Praise be, praise be."

"Uncle Robert!" David shouted with glee.

Branwenn saw him then, his satchel slung over his

shoulder and his face a bit drawn, but he'd made it, as they'd pleaded with him to do. For David needed some time with the only remaining member of his family-germane.

Callum put his free arm around her waist and moved towards the new arrivals.

Aye, Branwenn thought with a grin and a sigh of utter contentment as she looked at the two dark-haired first footers, 'twas sure to be a very good year indeed.

THE END

Thank you for reading
Highland Magic : Book Three : Highlands Trilogy

If you enjoyed Highland Magic, I would appreciate it if you would help others enjoy this book, too.

Lend it. Please share it with a friend.

Recommend it. Please help other readers find this book by recommending it to friends, readers' groups and discussion boards.

Review it. Please tell other readers why you liked this book by reviewing it.

Author updates can be found at
http://www.kesaxon.com

Connect with K.E. at:
http://www.facebook.com/kesaxonauthorpage

ABOUT THE AUTHOR

K.E. Saxon is a third-generation Texan and has been a lover of romance fiction since her first (sneaked) read of her older sister's copy of *The Flame and the Flower* by Kathleen E. Woodiwiss. She has two cats, a 26-year-old cockatiel, and a funny, supportive husband. When she isn't in her writer's cave writing, you can find her puttering in her organic vegetable garden or in her kitchen trying out a new recipe. An animal (and bug) lover since before she could speak, she made pets of all kinds of critters when she was a kid growing up. Her mother even swears that she made a pet of a cockroach one time (but K.E. doesn't believe her). She likes to write humorous, sexy romances.

* * * *

OTHER BOOKS IN THE MEDIEVAL HIGHLANDERS SERIES:

THE HIGHLANDS TRILOGY: The Macleans

Highland Vengeance
Book One

A Family Saga / Adventure Romance

DANIEL AND MARYN'S STORY

* * *

Highland Grace
Book Two

A Family Saga / Adventure Romance

BAO AND JESSLYN'S STORY

* * *

The Cambels

Song of the Highlands
Book Four

A Family Saga / Adventure Romance

ROBERT AND MORGANA'S STORY

Now the rascal Highlands warrior knight from Highland Grace and Highland Magic has his own romance adventure!

IF YOU ENJOYED THIS MEDIEVAL 'HIGHLAND MAGIC', YOU MIGHT ALSO ENJOY READING ABOUT A MODERN-DAY CELTIC FAERY AND THE MAGIC SHE WEAVES ON TWO UNSUSPECTING COSMOPOLITAN SISTERS

DIAMONDS AND TOADS: A MODERN FAIRY TALE
(Erotic Comedy FairyTale Romance)

What readers are saying about it:

~ *"...just plain old fun reading...A cross between Bewitched and Cinderella."* ~

~ *"HOT! HOT! HOT! What a great story! I love the characters! What a Hot and Sizzling Fairy Tale! I thought my Kindle would start smoking, it was so steamy!"* ~

Read an excerpt on the following pages.

****

Diamonds and Toads
a modern fairy tale

K.E. Saxon

Sugar and spice and everything nice...and, oh yes, naughty—times twice.

Together, sweet Delilah and wicked Isadora make the perfect woman. But the Perrault family fairy is a troublemaker and imbues diamonds upon one sister and toads upon the other. Now up is down and down is up in a world where no good deed goes unpunished. Leather, blindfolds, and handcuffs purge sweet of all reserve. A few misspoken words of lust gives wicked a whole new meaning.

Once upon a time, there were two sisters, one cursed and one blessed by fairy magic...

Bibbidee-bobbidi-boo, They're naughty. How about you?

Excerpt from Diamonds and Toads: A Modern Fairy Tale

PROLOGUE

Delilah Perrault fanned the perspiration from her cheeks with the folded *Houston Press* she'd snagged out of the dispenser and took a bite from her chocolate bar. She was supposed to meet Chas Regan here in front of the main branch of the Houston Public Library for lunch, but she was so nervous about it, she'd run down to its basement and bought the candy from the machine.

No, she wasn't really hungry, and *yes*, she knew she shouldn't be eating sugar and fat if she wanted to get that last six pounds off before the gala at the Crystal Ballroom eight days from now, but her compulsive need to fill her mouth with food wouldn't let her be.

An old beggar woman in a faded-to-purple pea coat with a stained and frayed scarf around her neck pushed her shopping cart filled with—Delilah was sure—the woman's life possessions across the cobbled pavement a few feet from where Delilah sat.

The poor thing looked as shop-worn as Delilah felt.

She glanced toward Delilah then dropped a hungry gaze to the candy bar.

Delilah lifted the cold Coke from the short marble wall she was sitting on and walked over to the woman.

"Here. You're welcome to both of these, if you

would like? I haven't eaten much of the candy yet—Or—would you like me to buy you something else?" She scanned the area. "I'll bet there's a deli or something in that building over there. I could get you a sandwich?"

"What a kind girl you are. But no, these will do just fine." The old woman captured the fare, captured Delilah's gaze. Her eyes, silver blue and bright, were more youthful than Delilah expected. Odd. Shivery goose bumps formed on Delilah's arms. "I have a sweet tooth, don't you know," the woman continued.

"Oh—" Delilah jerked a nod. "Okay." She turned away from her and walked back toward the two-foot-high granite wall she'd been seated on earlier.

"Bless you, Lila, dear," the woman said.

Delilah stopped short.

A loud *crack!* split the air and Delilah whirled around. A sudden scent of patchouli filled her nostrils. All around her, a rosy watercolor haze washed over the landscape. A giddy bubble of fear tripped up Delilah's spine as a spray of glitter dust drifted in the space where the woman had been. And in her place, a yellow parrot perched on the handle of the cart, staring at her from one beady black eye.

Delilah hawked a reflexive cough and something small, hard, and cold fell from her mouth into her palm. "Sweet Jesus, Mary, and Joseph." *A diamond.*

* * *

Excerpt from Diamonds and Toads: A Modern Fairy Tale

CHAPTER ONE

Chas Regan slammed the phone down. *Fuck!* What the hell was he supposed to do now? He leaned back in his executive chair, allowing the front rollers to lift off the floor, and dug the base of his palms into his eyelids. His heart still raced so fast that it caused a shot of stomach bile to blast into his throat.

The company was lost. Gone. No more. His entire family's empire, a glimmering speck of its former glory lost in the vast abyss of others that had gone before it.

He could have saved it, too, he knew, if only he'd been able to come up with that measly five million in time. But he hadn't been able to liquidate enough capital before tonight's deadline. If only that blasted prospective buyer would loosen her grip on her cash, he'd have had his two-year-old thoroughbred sold a month ago and his problems would be solved.

He needed more time. More money and time.

The intercom on his phone buzzed, followed by his assistant's voice saying, *"Chas, Delilah Perrault is here to see you. Should I show her in?"*

His churning stomach sank to his toes, but he couldn't see a way out of meeting with her right now. He sprang into an upright position and did a quick finger-comb through his hair. "Yes. That's fine,

Excerpt from Diamonds and Toads: A Modern Fairy Tale

Sharon."

* * *

Delilah walked into the office with a big grin on her face. She couldn't wait to tell Chas all that had happened this morning. He'd been a sage advisor these past few months since they'd begun working on the charity together and she hoped he wouldn't mind giving her a little more now.

After the strange encounter with the beggar woman two days ago—and the 'found' diamond—Delilah had called Chas and canceled their lunch. To tell the truth, if it weren't for the diamond that rested in the bottom of her coin purse, she'd have tossed the whole thing off as a lucid dream.

She hadn't told a soul about the encounter, either, and she was pretty sure she wasn't going to.

"Hi," she said, noticing immediately the sexy contrast between his slightly rumpled blond hair and his crisp, tailor-made suit. Her already jangled nerves started to tap dance across their endings the closer she came to him. *Breathe in, breathe out.* Thankfully, she'd managed to keep her deeper feelings for him to herself, thus far. She could just imagine how awkward their friendship would become if he ever realized what she felt. He probably wouldn't want to work with her anymore.

It wasn't until she'd taken a seat on his leather couch that she picked up on the tension lines around his eyes and mouth. "Is this a bad time? Am I interrupting something?" She shot to her feet. "I'll just leave now. I- I shouldn't have come without calling first. But I *have* got some exciting news to tell you, so maybe—could we meet for dinner?" She took a step toward the door.

Chas jumped up and waved her back to her seat. "No, no, no. Sit. Tell me the good news."

She hesitated and then shrugged. "Well, if you're sure?" She sat down and beamed at him. "Guess what?" She was so excited and proud of herself, she wanted to do a jig. Instead, she clasped her hands in her lap and said, "I'm a multi-millionairess as of ten-thirty-two this morning."

"No shit?"

"No shit."

"How many? Two? Three?"

"More." She sat forward. "It's like all my years of training as a gemologist have finally paid off." She bit her lip to keep from grinning like a buffoon and glanced down. Lifting her gaze to his, she said, "A couple of days ago, I got it in my head to put some of my savings in diamond stocks—not a lot—just enough to get my feet wet."

Chas's brows shot into his hairline. "A couple of *days* ago?"

"I know. Amazing. Anyway, today I made—I made a hundred million! Dollars."

Chas jackknifed forward in his chair. "A *hundred* million? That's—that's near to impossible."

She laughed. "Exactly! I feel like crowing! You were the first person I thought to tell because you're so—so good with money. Will you help me to invest it?"

A strange look flashed in his baby blues as he studied her for a moment. It unnerved her. Maybe she'd overstepped their friendship with the request? She was about to apologize to him and tell him she'd find someone else to help her when he laughed and the look changed. Brightened. Became recognizable. Comfortable. Compelling. For the first time since she'd entered his office, his face relaxed into the boyish grin that had become so familiar to her since they'd started working together on the charity event months ago. "Well, I guess I can't propose to you now. You'll think I'm only doing it for your money."

Her heart tripped, then hammered against her ribcage. It took every ounce of her willpower not to let on with her eyes, her hands, or any other part of her body that he'd just spoken her deepest wish, made it a joke. She hoped the grin she gave him was less hungry than friendly. "Hey, women do it all the time—why not a guy?" She linked the fingers of her hands together and did a little stretch. Did her voice sound as out of breath, wobbly, to him as it did to her? "Besides, I could use a financial wizard for a husband, now that I'm worth loads of dough."

Chas's expression grew serious. He swiveled around and pulled something from his desk drawer then rose to his feet and came toward her. Instead of sitting next to her, as she expected, he knelt down in front of her.

"What's this?" A nervous chuckle escaped her throat. "What are you doing?" Against her will, his close proximity brought on a fiery blush.

He lifted both of her hands. When her fingers twitched over the velvet box in his palm, her breath caught in her lungs. "I know you think I wasn't serious," he said. "But I was. I'd been planning to ask you to be my wife on Valentine's Day, but if I wait any longer, you'll be suspicious of my motives."

He released her hands and opened the box. Resting inside was a brilliant cut solitaire in a platinum setting. "Will you marry me, Delilah?"

A rush of euphoria made her head spin, but somehow she managed to say, "YES!"

* * *

Delilah was so high with happiness, she felt as if she floated across the parking garage toward her car. She sighed. They'd finally kissed. She lifted her fingers to her lips. They still tingled from the warm contact. It had been as wonderful as she'd dreamed it would be. He'd tasted so masculine, felt so strong. It'd made her feel feminine, sexy even.

She shook her head and grinned. She was going to marry Chas Regan. Amazing. All this time she'd been pining away for the guy and—who knew?—he'd been doing the same thing for her!

Since he'd returned to the family business a year ago, moved back to Houston from Boston, they had formed a companionable friendship. Based mostly on their shared interest in charity work. He was very much involved in funding for cancer research—his mother had died of a rare form of it a little less than two years ago—and that was one of Delilah's pet charities as well.

Once they'd met up again at a charity benefit, become reacquainted, they'd started sharing meals together several times a week, sometimes twice in the same day. He'd even begun confiding in her about his

Excerpt from Diamonds and Toads: A Modern Fairy Tale

devastation at his mother's sudden illness and death, a thing, she was sure, he didn't speak of with others. And the more she learned about him, the man he'd grown up to be, the more she'd fallen in love with him.

Of course, she, being the fat one in her family, never thought for a second that he could ever think of her in any romantic way.

She stopped walking and thrust her hand out in front of her. The ring sparkled, even in the dim light, and the fit was perfect. He must have done some sleuthing to get it just right. The thought of him planning for weeks such a romantic proposal gave her a giddy feeling in her chest. He loved her! Oh, he hadn't said the words—he wasn't the sort, she knew. So many men weren't. At least that's what she'd read in loads of women's magazines. But she hoped that one day, somehow, she'd finally get him to say them aloud.

She started to walk again, and then it became a jog, and then a full-out run, which wasn't easy in her floral print slim lined dress. She couldn't *wait* to tell her stepmother and half-sister! Wouldn't their jaws drop to the floor! Not only had she managed to pull their family back into the financial realm they'd been in before her father's imprisonment, but, *she*, Delilah Perrault, had snagged the one perfect prospect her stepmother had pegged to be her skinny, beautiful half-sister's future husband.

* * *

Chas hung up the phone. Relief washed over him. The creditors were going to give him until a week from this coming Monday to wire them the money now that

Excerpt from Diamonds and Toads: A Modern Fairy Tale

he had access to some funds.

He sat back and gnawed on a piece of dead skin next to his fingernail. Okay, asking Delilah to marry him hadn't been the noblest way to deal with his dilemma. But he'd been desperate. He'd briefly thought of simply asking her for the money, but he'd quickly nixed it. He needed this all kept under wraps, and keeping her in the dark about it while he 'borrowed' some of her money—just long enough to swing things back in his favor—seemed the best plan of action.

His already burning stomach twisted into a knot and he popped several antacids into his mouth. Okay. He admitted it. He'd taken advantage of a sweet girl who had a crush on him so that he could keep the hounds at bay a little longer—and get hold of those funds he needed.

He'd pay her back. With interest. And heck, he just might go through with the marriage, too. If she really wanted him. He liked her a lot. She was a good friend. And easy to talk to. Most times, made him feel calm and settled inside. His stomach hardly ever gave him grief when he was with her. That was something, wasn't it?

She was pretty, too. Electric blue eyes, dark silky hair, long limbs, but soft and curvy. At five-eight, she was just right for his own six-three height.

And, dear God, that kiss they'd shared! It had sent shock waves all the way through him. No, it wouldn't be such a bad match. Not such a bad match at all.

Except, he needed her to be on his arm over the next few months while he proved to his creditors that

Excerpt from Diamonds and Toads: A Modern Fairy Tale

he was a responsible sort—they could trust him with their money. So, he'd best spend a little less time at the office and spend some real time with her. Not in bed, of course. He wouldn't be that much of a bastard. Once he'd paid back the money, then yes. After that kiss—hell yes. But not until then.

His gaze dropped to the ring box on his desk. Good thing his last fiancée—the fourth to be exact—had over-nighted that ring to his office eight months ago. It had come in handy.

* * *

~End of Excerpt~

Made in the USA
Lexington, KY
22 July 2015